AFTER
ANNA

Alex Lake is a British novelist who was born in the North West of England. *After Anna* is the first book to be written under the author's pseudonym, and it has been a No.1 bestselling ebook sensation, receiving over 100 5* reviews online. The author now lives in the North East of the US.

AFTER ANNA

ALEX LAKE

HARPER

Harper

An imprint of HarperCollins*Publishers*

1 London Bridge Street

London SE1 9GF

www.harpercollins.co.uk

This paperback edition 2015

17 18 19 20 LSCC 10 9 8 7 6 5 4 3 2 1

First published in Great Britain by

HarperCollins*Publishers* 2015

A catalogue record for this book is available from the British Library

ISBN: 978-0-00-825643-2

Set in Sabon by Born Group using Atomik ePublisher from Easypress

Find out more about HarperCollins and the environment at
www.harpercollins.co.uk/green

To my three musketeers: O, F and A

Prologue

It was easier than you had expected. The girl came without complaint. You spotted her as she left the school, alone, looking around, clearly bereft of a parent to pick her up. Who would do that? Who would be so negligent as to leave a five-year-old in such a vulnerable position? It was appalling, it really was.

But it was good for you.

Not so good for her, and definitely not so good for her poor, soon-to-be grief-stricken, self-hating parents, but good for you.

No one saw you. You were sure of that. You'd been watching them closely. Watching them mill around the school gates, waiting for their spoiled progeny to emerge so they could pepper them with inane questions.

How was your day? What did you learn? Were you a good girl, my princess? Were you a brave boy?

1

They were raising a generation of precious, weak children, who thought the world revolved around them, that it would adapt itself to their whims, would always allow them to win and never force them to struggle. It was a silent disaster, and it was creeping into every corner of society and no one was doing anything about it.

Except you. You are going to do your part to stop it, however small that part is.

And it starts with the girl.

She is yours now. Now, and forever. You like things to be yours. You have never been good at sharing. You would rather destroy something than share it. You know it is not your most attractive trait, but you don't fight it. There is no point. It has always been that way.

And you will not share her. She is yours. Vanished into your car; traceless.

It has gone very, very well. As well as could have been expected.

You have to admit to being a little bit pleased.

You have to admit that you allowed yourself a pat on the back.

Have you been lucky, even? Maybe. You need luck. Everyone does. You are no different, at least not in that regard. In some others, yes. In some other ways, you are very different. Better. More clear-sighted. More decisive.

So maybe it wasn't luck, after all. No, you don't think it was. It was down to good planning. Yes, you prefer that. It was down to good planning. And ability, of course. Nerve and skill. It was you who'd done it, you who'd made it happen. Luck was not part of it.

Not that you are becoming complacent. That would not do. That way, disaster lies. Complacency is the path to failure. And you did not take the girl, did not get this far, to fail at the last.

So now she sleeps, the girl, dark-haired and beautiful and young, she sleeps in the back seat of your car. She is drugged, hidden away from prying eyes until the time comes for you to use her for the purpose for which you took her. For the purpose that meant you *had* to take her. It is a shame she has to be involved in this; a shame that she will pay the price for what others have done. It isn't fair, you know that, but then the world isn't fair. Life isn't fair. You know *that*, too. Fair doesn't come into it. Does the wolf slaying the lamb worry about fairness? About wounded innocence? No, it cares only about its hunger. There is no fair or unfair for the wolf. The wolf takes what it needs, and its need is the only justification necessary. Right, wrong; fair, unfair: they play no part in its world.

And they play no part in yours either. There is only strong or weak, winner or loser. The cry of *it's not fair* is just a tool the weak use to constrain the strong. You cannot let it influence your actions.

And you don't. You didn't. You won't.

Fair does not come into this.

Fair is for the weak.

For the losers.

As you drive away you allow yourself a smile. Apart from anything else, this is going to be *fun*.

PART ONE: BEFORE

1

Life is Complicated

i.

She was going to be late. Again.

Julia Crowne looked up at the clock on the wall of the boardroom. It was one of those Swiss railway clocks, with the blocky minute and hour hands. She happened to know that it was not an imitation; it was the real thing. It went with the polished wood of the oval conference table and the comfortable leather chairs. Nothing but the best for the boardroom. The clients they met in here were reassured by that kind of thing.

Two forty p.m. The meeting about the custody of a child was supposed to be over by now, but it had not gone well, mainly because her client, town councillor Carol Prowse, was being unreasonable. It was understandable, since she had come home to find her husband, Jordi, a poet and part-time English teacher,

7

in bed with one of his former students, but it was not making things easy.

Under the table Julia's foot tapped nervously. She had to pick up her five-year-old daughter, Anna, from school at three p.m., and she couldn't be late. They had an appointment at three thirty to collect a cocker spaniel puppy from a woman who had been surprised when she woke one morning to plaintive cries and came downstairs to find that her dog – who had been suffering from a mysterious listlessness for the last week – was producing puppies at an astonishing rate.

The woman was a nurse and she worked the late shift; she had agreed to wait until three thirty, but that was as long as she could hold on. Julia and Anna had spent hours getting ready for the puppy: buying the bed, choosing where to put it, selecting the name (Anna had settled on Bella, which Julia thought was a fine name for a puppy), stocking up on dog treats, planning where they would take her for walks, and Julia did not want to have to deal with the disappointment that would follow if she had to tell Anna that the puppy would not be coming home that evening after all.

Even more than that, Julia needed the puppy to be a source of nothing but joy and affection, because she was going to be facing her own custody battle soon enough and, if it was anything like Carol Prowses's, Anna would need all the distractions she could get.

Julia hadn't found Brian in bed with one of his students – thankfully, since he taught in a junior school

– or with anyone else, for that matter. If she had she probably wouldn't have cared, which was exactly the problem. She liked Brian. She thought he was a good man and a good dad and a good husband – well, an OK man and an OK dad and an OK husband – but she just wasn't inspired by him; no, it was worse, she wasn't *interested* in him. He was like a work acquaintance that she knew in passing but didn't really care about. The kind of acquaintance whose troubles you might hear about – *did you hear Brian's getting a divorce?* – and think it was a shame but it wasn't really any of your business. That was how she felt about Brian. He just didn't belong in her life anymore.

It hadn't always been like that. For a while she had kept a photo of her and Brian on the first day of their honeymoon on her desk at work. They were on a white sandy beach on the Greek island of Milos. They had just finished eating a meal of grilled fish and the sun was setting behind them. She'd asked the waiter – a Greek fisherman who doubled up as a beachfront restaurant owner in the evening – to take it.

Afterwards, they stood, arm in arm, facing the sea.

This is heaven, she said. *It's amazing. The world is such a magical place.*

Brian laughed. *You sound like you've been smoking too much dope. Like when we used to get stoned and stare up at the stars.*

But this is real, Julia said. *It really is heaven. Our feet in the water, nothing to worry about for the next two weeks. And nothing to do right now but go back to our room ...*' she kissed Brian's cheek, taking note of his muscular arms and flat stomach, then ran her hand through his salt-stiff hair, *'where we can see if we can find a way to spend a few hours of our honeymoon.'*

They were so at ease with each other then, so tight, so intertwined. But that was all gone now. Somewhere along the way they had taken different paths, started seeking different things in life. They hadn't noticed at the time, hadn't seen that they were slowly diverging, until it was too late. Looking back, Julia thought it had started around the time Anna was born. She was their only child, and the only one they were likely to have given how hard it had been to get her, and she deserved a dad who invented wild stories and made treasure hunts and drew and painted and created with her. A dad who injected energy and wonder and awe into her world.

Brian loved her, of course her did. He *doted* on her. But he never suggested that they try anything new, that they go camping on an island in a lake or to the seaside or to see a play. He didn't build an obstacle course in the garden or put on plays in an Anna-sized theatre or assemble a trampoline and hold the Crowne Mini Olympics. Instead, he bought her the same pink Lego sets and Disney-branded dolls that every other girl her age owned. He was content for Anna to live her life in the narrow suburban confines he had allowed himself to become enmeshed in. It was too *normal* for Anna, and,

10

for that matter, for Julia. She wanted more, and Brian could not provide it.

He was, truth be told, a bit boring, although Julia would never have put it that way to him.

Or at least, she hadn't intended to, but when she'd told him a month back that she was considering their future together – specifically, whether they had one – he'd not taken it well, and they'd spiralled into a vicious argument. She'd ended up saying things she now regretted, but once things are said they have a habit of staying that way, and all you can do is live with the consequences.

You're a bit, you know, a bit – she'd been thinking boring, but she managed to find a euphemism just in time – *a bit mainstream.*

Her attempt to soften the blow didn't work. Brian clenched his jaw.

Mainstream? he'd replied. *You mean boring, don't you?*

Stupidly, with two glasses of white wine lubricating her anger, she'd nodded.

She said a few more things she hadn't been planning to share, like the fact that she didn't want her life to drift by, empty of inspiration and wonder. Or the fact that she was sick of doing the same things every weekend, going to the same places every holiday, eating at the same restaurants. She wanted more, she wanted adventure and romance and colour.

You're just having a bloody midlife crisis, Brian said. *I thought it was me that was supposed to get scared about life leaking away and spend our savings on a sports car and have an affair with a bimbo.*

And then she said the thing she really regretted.

I wish you would, she'd said. *At least I could find something interesting in a man who had some fight in him. You're ready for the pipe and slippers phase already.*

What, he said, suddenly red-faced. *What did you say?*

She repeated herself. *That you're ready for your pipe and slippers.* Julia found it odd that this, of all she'd said, was the thing that he was particularly exercised by, but his reply enlightened her.

Not that, he said. *Not the bloody pipe and slippers. You said you could find something interesting in a man with some fight in him. So I'm not even interesting to you?*

Julia realized that she hadn't been making that state-ment – it had just kind of slipped out – but now it was said it was exactly what she meant. So she nodded.

You can think I'm boring, Brian replied, *and lacking inspiration, or whatever it is you've read on Facebook that you should be looking for, I can accept that. What I can't accept is you saying that there's nothing about me that deserves your interest. Not your respect, and not, heaven forbid, your* love, *but your interest. If that's the case it really is over.*

And she had agreed. She told him he had put it well. That he really understood the situation.

Since then they had barely spoken. Brian slept in the guest room; she stayed in their room. On the few occa-sions they had been unable to avoid sharing words they had not discussed their future, until about ten days ago, when she had told him she'd made up her mind. She wanted a divorce.

Which was what Carol Prowse wanted, and would get. The problem was that she also wanted her husband only to have custody of their nine-year-old son when supervised. Her demand was ridiculous and vindictive, and it would never be granted.

Jordi Prowse had shaken his head when Julia said it, and now he was laughing.

'Forget it,' he said. His hair was greying at the temples and he had a relaxed, easy manner. 'That's simply unthinkable. There's no grounds for that.'

There was a long pause. Carol Prowse looked at Julia. 'That's not what my lawyer thinks.'

That *was* what her lawyer thought, but it was not what Councillor Prowse wanted her to say. Julia glanced again at the time. Two fifty. She needed to wrap this up.

'Given the age of the girls you were having an affair with I think that there are grounds to argue that you are not fit to be left in charge of a child,' she said. 'Moral grounds.'

His lawyer, an old friend of Julia's called Marcie Lyon, shook her head. 'There's no way that'll fly,' she said. 'You know that.'

Jordi grinned. 'You're just feeling humiliated,' he said. 'So you're making empty threats.'

Carol Prowse stiffened in her chair. Julia had been here before, this could get ugly. It was the way that custody battles went. Both parties went in with the best intentions to reach an amicable settlement; both parties ended up locked in a battle for their kids, which ripped whatever was left of their relationship to pieces. But she couldn't wait around to see this one. She looked at the clock again. 'I think,' she said, 'that we might have achieved all we are going to achieve today. I would suggest that Ms Lyon and I meet later in the week to discuss the case.'

Jordi West shrugged. 'Sure,' he said. 'You can meet and discuss how stupid her—', he nodded at his wife 'proposal is.'

Julia smiled. 'We'll discuss many things, I'm sure,' she said. 'Can we consider this meeting over?'

She had to get out of the room. She had accepted that she was not going to make it in time to pick up the puppy – it was a twenty-five-minute drive to the school, then another half hour to the lady's house – but now she had a more pressing concern. She needed to call the school and tell them she was running late so they could hold Anna back. She got to her feet, aware that she was rushing the three other people in the room. Marcie gave her an odd look as she left; Jordi didn't look at either Julia or her client.

Carol Prowse shook her head. 'Can you believe that?' she said. 'He's so damn arrogant.'

Julia could see that her client was in the mood to debrief, and normally she would have provided the sympathetic support she wanted, but right now that was simply not an option. She nodded agreement. 'I'm sorry,' she said. 'I have to go. It's my day to pick up my daughter from school.'

God, it sounded lame. This was the problem. She was expected to be a model professional, focused on her career, which meant she was at the beck and call of her clients, as well as being a model parent, which meant she was at the beck and call of her daughter. It was impossible to be both, but that didn't lessen the expectation any.

In the corridor she took her phone from her bag and pressed the button.

The screen was black. It was out of battery.

She swore quietly. She fished around in her bag for a charger. Not there; of course not. It was in the car. She could run up to her office and call from there, but it was on the other side of the building. No – the quickest way was to get to the car and charge it there.

She hurried down the corridor. She didn't doubt everything would be fine, but she still didn't like the feeling of being late to pick up her daughter.

ii.

As she drove away from the office, Julia tapped her finger on the logo at the centre of the screen of her phone, even though she knew it would not shorten whatever process it went through when it switched on. She did the same thing when waiting for a lift; if it was slower to arrive than expected she would press the call button again. And sometimes again.

Won't come any faster, some wag might say, and she'd reply, with a thin smile, *well, you never know.*

Come on, she thought. *Come on.*

This had happened before, resulting in an uncomfortable encounter with Mrs Jameson, the retired teacher who stayed after school with the children whose parents had neglected to turn up on time. It was going to happen again today. There'd be the stern, disappointed look, then the gentle reminder of school policy.

Mrs Crowne, I realize you are busy but could I remind you that the school cannot provide after-hours childcare without prior arrangements being made. If you need such assistance then we can provide it, but you must *inform us ahead of time so that we can make the necessary arrangements.*

I'm sorry, she'd mumble, feeling like she was back at school herself, hauled in front of the head teacher for smoking or wearing her skirt an inch too short, *but my case ran over and I would have called but my phone ran out of juice and thank you Mrs Jameson for being so flexible. I appreciate it, I really do.*

And then she'd leave, feeling like a terrible parent but wondering why, since Anna would be perfectly fine, babbling away in the back seat, telling Julia about her day and asking what was for dinner and could they read *The Twits* again that night, and Julia would be shaking her head and thinking *I'm not a bad mother, just a busy one.*

And she was about to get busier. When she and Brian separated she would have to pick up almost every day, and God knew how she was going to do that. At least now she had Edna, Brian's mum, to help: she took Anna on Mondays and Wednesdays, and Brian normally got out of school early enough to get her on Fridays, which left Julia with two days on which she had to cram her meetings into the morning and spend the evenings catching up on emails. From time to time, if she was going to be late, she could give Edna a call; in fact she had tried that morning, but Edna was out so she had left a message, a message that Edna had ignored. And then, damn it, in the dash from one meeting to another she had stupidly let her phone run out of battery. Mental note: always keep the phone charged on Tuesdays and Thursdays.

And maybe other days as well. She doubted she would be able to rely on Edna after the divorce; behind her sweetness, Edna was a traditional matriarch, and Julia had never felt that she liked her son's wife all that much.

Anyway, it would be what it would be. Whatever happened, Julia could take it. That was the price she would have to pay for the life she wanted.

Finally, her phone beeped as it booted up. She found the school's number and pressed send. It rang through to the answering service pick up.

'This is Julia Crowne,' she said. 'I'm running a little late, but I should be there—', she glanced at the clock on the dashboard 'around three twenty. Anyway, just to let you know, I'm coming.'

Ten minutes later she arrived at the school. As she pulled up outside the school gates, her phone rang. She unplugged it from the car and opened the door.

'Hello,' she said. 'This is Julia.'

'Mrs Crowne,' a voice said. 'This is Karen, from Westwood School.'

'Oh,' Julia said. 'Don't worry. I'm here. I just arrived.'

'Mrs Crowne,' Karen said, her voice uncertain, 'do you have Anna with you?'

'No,' she said. 'I'm coming to pick her up. I left a message.'

'I thought that was what you said,' Karen murmured. 'Mrs Crowne, I think there's been a mix-up.'

A mix-up. Not words you wanted to hear in connection with your five-year-old daughter.

Julia stopped. She stared at the cast iron school gates. Both were adorned with the school crest: an owl clutching a scroll above the letters 'WS'.

'What do you mean?' she said, her voice tightening with the beginnings of worry. 'What kind of mix-up?'

'Anna's not here,' Karen said, her tone retreating into something official, something protected. 'We thought she'd left with you.'

iii.

Julia broke the connection. She ran through the gates to the school entrance and pushed open the worn green door, then ran along the corridor in the direction of the administrative offices. Karen, the school secretary, tall

18

and thin, with a head of tight black curls, was standing outside the office door, her face drained of colour.

'Mrs Crowne,' she said. 'I'm sure everything's ok. Perhaps your husband picked her up.'

The twitchy, alert look in her eyes belied the calm reassurance of her tone. Julia's stomach fluttered, then contracted. She had a sudden, violent urge to vomit.

'I'll check,' she said. She dialled Brian's number.

'Hello.' His voice was hard; his dislike of her deliberate and obvious. 'What do you want?'

Julia licked her lips. They were very dry. 'Brian,' she said. 'Is Anna with you?'

'Of course not. I'm at school. It's your day to pick her up.'

'I know,' Julia paused, 'but she's not here.'

There was a long silence.

'What do you mean she's not there?' The hardness in his voice had softened into concern. 'Where is she?'

'I don't know,' Julia said, wanting, even in this situation, to add a sarcastic *obviously*. 'Maybe your mum picked her up?' She almost smiled with relief. This was the answer, after all, of course it was. Edna, her grandmother, had come on the wrong day. The relaxation was almost palpable, like the glow from a stiff drink.

'It wasn't mum,' Brian said. 'She's at home. She called an hour or so ago to ask about something. She wanted to know where the stopcock for the mains was. Apparently, there was some kind of leak in the kitchen.'

The hopeful glow faded. Julia swallowed; her mouth powder dry. 'Then I don't know where she is.'

They were words you never wanted or expected to say to your husband or wife or anybody at all about your five-year-old daughter. Five-year-old children were supposed to have known whereabouts at all times: with one or the other parent, at school, at a friend's house, with a select few relatives, who, in Anna's case, were Brian's mum Edna, or, occasionally, when they were back from Portland, Oregon, Brian's brother Simon and his wife Laura, these being the extent of their relatively small family circle.

'You don't know where she is?' Brian asked, his voice caught between anger and panic. 'You'd better find her!'

'I know.'

'And it's nearly half past three! How come you're just calling now?'

'I was a bit late,' Julia said. 'I just got here. I thought the school would be – I thought she'd be here.'

'Did you let them know you'd be late?'

'No, I ... my phone was dead. I just assumed ... ', her voice tailed off.

'Jesus,' Brian said. 'She could be anywhere. In thirty minutes, she could be anywhere. She could have wandered ... ' he paused. 'I'll be there as soon as I can. Start looking for her. Search the grounds and the streets nearby.'

'OK.' She felt frozen, unable to think. 'We'll search for her.' She looked again at Karen, who nodded.

'I'll tell the cleaning staff to help,' Karen said. 'And Julia – don't worry. She'll turn up, I'm sure. She's probably in someone's garden, or the newsagent, or somewhere like that.'

Julia nodded, but the words were not at all reassuring. They were little more than meaningless sounds.

'Brian,' she said. 'I have to go. I have to get started.'

'One more thing,' Brian said. 'Call the police.' He hesitated. 'In fact, I'll call them. You start looking for her. Start looking for Anna.'

The line went dead. Julia's hand dropped to her side. Her phone, loosely gripped between her thumb and forefinger, dropped to the floor.

Oh, God,' she said. 'Oh, God.'

2

The First Hours

i.

These were the crucial hours.

If you *had* been seen then the police would learn about that soon enough. First, they would check the immediate area, then they would drive the route to the girl's house to see if she had set off for home alone. When they didn't find her they would contact all the parents and staff who had been there at three p.m. and ask them what they had seen. Then they would interview the family. They always looked close to home first, not that they would find anything.

And, of course, they would check the school's CCTV. You knew you weren't on that. All they would see was the girl walking out of shot and into oblivion.

Of course, there was always the possibility that there was a camera in the area you hadn't spotted. You'd checked carefully, but it was possible.

And if there was, or if they had seen you, and realized who you were, then the police would be here soon enough, knocking on your door.

But that was OK. You had a plan for that. For these first hours the girl was elsewhere, stashed in your neighbour's garage; your neighbour who was in Alicante for the fortnight, and who had left you their house keys *because you're our only neighbour so you can keep an eye on the place in case anything happens.*

Something had happened, but not something they could have imagined.

You'd backed into their garage and unloaded her, then put your car away. No one would have seen. There was no one *to* see. No prying eyes. No spying eyes. It gave you comfort that you were invisible to the world, allowed you to get on with your life unobserved. Not just now, with the girl, but the other times as well.

And now the girl lay there, sleeping on the floor of a large doll's house that the father had built for his kids, his braying, noisy kids, who had outgrown it. It was just big enough for her to lie full length in, her feet by a small table, her head on a bag of sand, which was destined to re-fill the sand pit that the two spoilt kids who loved to disturb your afternoon peace played in.

She could stay there until midnight. That was when you would bring her inside and introduce her to her new home.

Her temporary new home.

She wouldn't be here for too long.

ii.

Julia ran out of the green front door of the school. Ahead of her were the gates, still open from when she had come in. They were supposed to be kept locked at all times. Supposed to be. The problem was that things that were *supposed to be* often weren't. She was *supposed* to have been there to pick up her daughter, but that didn't help much now.

She pictured the school at the end of the day. Kids in uniforms pouring out of the school doors, the younger ones heading straight for the parents outside the gates, the older ones running into the playground for a last few minutes of fun before home and dinner and bedtime, the teachers hanging back, making sure that everything went as it should, which it would, because it always did. Every child would be accounted for, either picked up by whoever was supposed to be there for them or held back inside the sanctuary of the school because their adult was late. No one slipped through the cracks, not at this small, fee-paying private school. The parents here could be relied on to make sure that their children were properly looked after, that they were not left waiting and vulnerable. The chance of a mistake was vanishingly small.

But it was not impossible.

Julia pictured a small, dark-haired girl with a pink Dora the Explorer backpack and new black leather shoes walking out of the gate with the other pupils and looking around for her mother, frowning when she didn't see her. And then maybe walking a little further down the street, perhaps thinking that she could find the familiar black Volkswagen Golf her mum drove. And then, a hand tapping her on the shoulder, a large, man's hand, with thick fingers and black hair sprouting from the point where the hand met the wrist – Julia blinked the vision away. She had to stay calm, or at least calm enough to look for her daughter.

'She's fine', she said, talking to herself. 'She's fine. She's just waiting somewhere.'

The words didn't make her feel any better. There was a ball of fear and panic knotted somewhere between her stomach and her sternum so big and real and hard that it was making it difficult to draw breath and to keep her head from dizzying.

But she had to act. She had to do something. And the quicker the better. She ran towards the iron gates. She would start outside the school. If Anna was in the building or the school grounds then she was probably OK. She could wait to be found. If she was outside – well, she needed to be found as soon as possible. Outside were cars and dogs and buses and people who might have an interest in an unaccompanied five-year-old girl that they shouldn't have.

'Anna!' she shouted. 'Anna! Where are you?'

She heard a similar call from inside the school, as Karen started her search.

'Anna!' Julia shouted. 'It's Mummy! Where are you, darling?'

She exited the gate and faced her first decision. Left or right? Left, towards the village centre, or right, towards a small development of overpriced cookie-cutter commuter boxes surrounded by scrubby fields? Boxes with closed doors and sheds and hiding places, boxes that were unoccupied and unobserved during the day when the inhabitants were at work or at school, boxes into which a girl could be smuggled. So, left or right? It was normally such a small decision. If you got it wrong you could backtrack and try again. But this time it felt bigger, more important. This time it was not just left or right: it was towards Anna or away from her.

But do something, Julia thought. *Standing still is the worst option.*

She went left, towards the village. It was more likely Anna had wandered that way, gone towards people and the newsagents and the recently opened old-fashioned sweet shop that sold sweets in quarter pounds and half pounds from jars behind the counter. The Village Sweete Shoppe, it was called, and Anna loved it.

The narrow, tree-lined road to the village curved left then descended a small gradient. The houses along the road were old and large and concealed behind high sandstone walls and thick foliage, which was both a good and a bad thing: it was unlikely that Anna would have been able to get into the gardens, but if, for some reason she was in there, she would be impossible to see.

26

These were the thoughts Julia had now. She saw once innocent gardens as threats to her daughter. The whole world was twisted into a sick new configuration. It made her head spin.

'Anna!' Julia was surprised at how loud her voice could go. She hadn't used it like that for years. Even when she and Brian were in full flow she didn't turn it up this much. 'Anna! It's Mummy! If you can hear me, just say something. I'll come and get you!'

There was no reply. Just the distant barking of a dog (*is it barking at Anna?* Julia wondered) and the noise of a car engine (*where's that car going?* she thought. *Who's in it?*) and somewhere, incongruously, a pop song being played at loud volume.

She ran down the hill, her heels clicking on the pavement. 'Anna!' she shouted. 'Anna!'

There was a rustle in a thick rhododendron bush to her left. Julia stopped and pulled back the branches. The inside was cool and smelled of wet earth.

'Anna?' she said. 'Is that you?'

There was another rustle, deeper in the bush. Julia pushed her way in; her heart thudding.

'Anna' she called. 'Anna!'

The rustle came again, then a blackbird emerged from the other side of the bush. It looked at Julia, then took flight and vanished into the branches of a sycamore tree.

Julia stood up. To her left was a driveway leading to a covered porch. A man in his sixties, with grey hair and walking cane, was standing in the doorway, looking at her.

27

'Everything OK?' he asked. 'I heard you shouting.'

'It's my daughter,' Julia said. 'I can't find her.'

The man frowned. 'Oh dear,' he said. 'What does she look like?'

'She's five. Dark hair. She has a pink rucksack and she's in uniform.'

'Is she at the school? Westwood?'

Julia nodded. 'Have you seen her?'

'No. But I could help you look?' He lifted his walking stick. 'I'm not very mobile, but I could drive around and look for her.'

Julia looked as him, suspicion clouding her mind. Did he have Anna? Was this some double bluff? She caught herself; he was just someone trying to help, and she needed all the help she could get at the moment. Probably, anyway. She'd mention him to the police later, if it came to that.

'That would be wonderful,' Julia said. 'Maybe I should drive, too.'

'You can probably look more closely on foot. I'll take my car, though. And my wife is home. She'll take the other car. What's her name, if we do see her?'

'Anna. Just stay with her and call the police.'

'OK,' the man said. 'Good luck.'

'Thank you,' Julia said. She pulled herself out from the bush, wincing, as a twig or thorn or branch scratched her bare calf, then carried on towards the village.

As she ran, she examined everything – every hedge, every fence, every parked car – but felt she was seeing nothing. She didn't trust her eyes, didn't trust that Anna might not appear where she had just looked, and so she found herself checking the same places two, three times before allowing herself to move on. Part of her knew it was unnecessary and irrational, but she couldn't help it; the stakes were just too high, the consequences of missing her daughter – who must be somewhere nearby – were too awful for her to allow herself to make a mistake and miss what was – what might be – in front of her nose.

She'd heard that when the police searched for evidence, when they got one of those lines of people to sweep a field or moor or wasteland, they never let the people who were involved – that is, the people who were looking for their loved ones – join in. Apparently, if you were too close to whoever was lost your searching abilities were compromised in some important way. Perhaps it was that you wanted to find whatever it was too much to maintain the calm, patient detachment required.

Whether that was true or not, she certainly did not feel calm or patient. What she felt was panic, a panic that threatened to overwhelm her and leave her in a heap on the pavement. It took a monumental effort for her not to put her face in her hands, sink to her knees, and start to pray.

'Oh my God,' she muttered. 'Oh my God, oh my God, oh my God.' Then, for a moment, the panic rose and did take over and she stopped, her head craned forward, her gaze sweeping from left to right.

'Anna!' she screamed. 'ANNA!'

She began to sprint. She had an image of Anna in The Village Sweete Shoppe, sitting on a stool by the window with a black liquorice stick staining her hand, her lips blackened with its juice. That was where her daughter was, she was sure of it. That was where Anna would have gone. There was nowhere else: Anna didn't know anywhere else, really. At five, her world was the house and garden, school, the houses of some friends, and a few places that she visited with her parents. One of those was the sweet shop.

They went there sometimes after school. Julia didn't give her daughter too many chocolates or crisps or ice cream or other junk food, but for some reason the stuff in The Village Sweete Shoppe felt different, more wholesome. It was the experience as much as anything: talking to the proprietor, weighing the various choices – pear drops, Everton mints, cola cubes – and counting out the price. It was old-fashioned, the way it had been when Julia was a child, when she had taken her pocket money on a Saturday morning and gone with her dad to the local newsagent and chosen the sweets she wanted, and she liked the thought that her childhood and her daughter's shared something.

They went there, once or twice every month. They left the car parked outside the school gates, walked down the hill, and went to buy sweets. It was about the only thing they ever did straight after school, the only thing that Anna knew. And she loved it.

So she was there, Julia knew it and as she sprinted she knew she was going to get there and find her daughter and sweep her up into a protective embrace from which she thought she might not ever let her go.

The bell above the door jangled. Julia took a couple of quick steps into the shop, looking wildly from corner to corner.

'Hello,' the owner, a retired postal worker called Celia, said. 'Can I help?'

'Has my daughter been in?' Julia asked.

The owner thought for a second, trying to place Julia. 'Your daughter's Anna, isn't she? A dark-haired little girl? Likes chocolate mice?'

'That's her. Has she been in?'

The owner shook her head. 'No,' she said. 'She's a bit young to come in on her own.'

'Are you sure?'

'I've been here all afternoon. Hardly anyone has been in, and I'd remember her, especially if she was alone.' Celia leaned forwards. 'Is everything OK?'

Julia looked past the foot-long lollipops and chocolate rabbits to the street outside the shop window. Anna wasn't here. She was somewhere out there.

Somewhere. Out. There.

Now the panic did take hold. She turned back to the Celia, her legs weakening.

'I've lost her,' she said. 'I've lost my daughter.'

iii.

It happens to every parent, one time or another. Perhaps in a supermarket, perhaps in the library, perhaps in the back garden.

31

You look around and your child is not there.

'Billy!' you shout, then, a little louder. 'Billy!'

And Billy replies, and comes toddling into view, holding a bag of flour, or a book, or with a worm in the grip of his pudgy hands. Or maybe he doesn't, and you have that sudden lurch of fear, that tightness in the back, and loose feeling in your stomach, and you look around a little wildly, before running to the end of the aisle or to the kids' books section or to the back gate, and there he is. Little Billy; safe and sound.

And you swear you're going to make sure you don't let them out of your sight again, not for a second, because a second is all it takes.

And a second *is* all it takes. In one second, a kid can step out from behind a parked car or be shoved into a van or even just walk round a corner and get lost enough that it takes you ten agonizing minutes to find them, which, although agonizing, is the best possible outcome. You find them sitting on a bench chatting to a kindly stranger or playing with some kids they met or just wandering about absorbed in all the things they are seeing on their own for the first time.

And then you really swear that you aren't going to let them out of your sight again, because, in that ten minutes your mind races to the worst possible conclusions: they've fallen in the canal, they've been hit by a car, they've been abducted.

And that's the one that bothers you the most. They've been taken. Picked off the street in a neglectful moment and taken. Gone forever. Alive or dead, it doesn't matter. You won't ever see them again, but you won't ever be able to stop looking. And you won't ever forgive yourself.

But, of course, even when you're contemplating that horrific, tortured possibility, a still, calm voice at the back of your mind is telling you not to worry, that everything is ok, that it'll all work out because it always does.

Except it doesn't. Not always.

And you know that. Which is the most frightening thing of all.

Julia ran out of The Village Sweete Shoppe. She glanced left and right: the same choice again. Left into the village or right, back to the school. She turned left and jogged down the hill. If there was news at the school someone would phone her. At least this time her phone was charged.

A woman of her age, with short hair and an expensive-looking bag, was walking towards her. Without thinking, Julia caught her eye.

Julia, like many English women of her age and social class, had an aversion to both making a scene and bothering people that bordered on the pathological. She would no more have asked a stranger for help – to lend her money, perhaps, or let her use their mobile phone, or get assistance changing a car wheel – than she would have walked unannounced into their kitchen, opened their fridge, and made herself a salad.

This, though, was different. It was not a time to worry about social proprieties.

'Excuse me,' Julia said. 'I'm looking for my daughter. She's five, she has dark hair and a pink rucksack, and she's in school uniform. Have you seen her?'

'No,' the woman replied. Her face took on an odd expression, a mixture of concern and sympathy that Julia found discomfiting. 'Has she been missing long?'

'Not that long. Twenty minutes. Maybe more.'

The expression deepened into a frown. 'Gosh. That's a long time.'

'I know,' Julia said. 'Would you keep an eye out for her?'

'Of course. I'll help you.' She gestured to the village car park. 'I'll look around the car park and check the library. There's a playground round the back. She might be there.'

'Thank you,' Julia said. 'Her name is Anna,' she added. She set off down the slope. On the right was a pub; on the left a post office, although neither seemed the same as it had the last time she had seen them. Then they had been simple buildings, parts of the infrastructure of the village, communal places that offered warmth and light. Now they were threatening; places where Anna might be kept hidden.

She put her head around the post office door. There was a queue of four waiting for the one open booth.

'Excuse me,' she said, aware of her breathlessness. 'I'm looking for someone. My daughter. Anna. Maybe you've seen her in the village?'

'What's she look like?' a man in paint-splattered over-alls asked.

Julia gave the description. It was already horribly familiar: *dark hair, rucksack, school uniform.* It fitted many five-year-old girls, but that didn't matter, because there was one element that marked Anna out from all the others.

'She'd have been alone,' Julia said.

After a sympathetic pause – Julia was already starting to hate sympathetic pauses – followed shaking heads, murmured negatives: she hadn't been in, and they hadn't seen her.

Julia ran across the road to the Black Bear pub. It was dark inside, the windows grimy, the smell of smoke still lingering despite the ban on inside smoking. There were only three customers: an underage couple skulking in the corner and a man at the bar.

There was a woman tending the pumps. Julia walked over to her.

'Excuse me,' she said. 'I'm looking for my daughter. She's five.'

'A bit young to be in here, love,' the woman said. She was in her early fifties, Julia guessed, but looked older. She had heavily tattooed forearms and a lined face and was wearing a push-up bra.

'I thought, maybe, she wandered in,' Julia said. 'I've lost her.'

The man at the bar looked up from his newspaper, his nose and cheeks red with broken capillaries.

'Not seen her,' he said. He patted the stool next to him. 'I'll buy you a drink, though, darling.'

The woman behind the bar – probably the landlady – shook her head in disapproval, but she didn't say anything. She probably didn't want to upset a regular. Couldn't afford to. The pub was shabby; it didn't look as if it was doing so well.

'Can't help you, love,' she said. 'Not seen her.'

Julia nodded thanks and left. She was glad to emerge into the sunshine. Next door was a bakery specializing in local dairy products and artisan breads. On the other side, a café.

'Excuse me,' she said. 'I'm looking for a little girl. My daughter.'

The man behind the counter raised an eyebrow. He had dark, curly hair and dark eyes, and huge, flour-dusted hands.

'What does she look like?' he asked, in a Scottish accent.

Julia told him. He shook his head, then leaned over the counter, addressing the café side of the building.

''Scuse me,' he said. 'This lady's looking for a wee lass. Her bairn. Anyone seen a girl on her own?'

No one had, but one lady got to her feet.

'I'll help you look,' she said.

Others joined her, and the patrons of the café spilled onto the main street of the village. They organized themselves and headed in different directions.

Julia looked around for somewhere else to search. A river ran through the bottom part of the village, and, where it disappeared into a copse, there was a small depression where the council had once put a few benches. It wasn't obvious why; it was damp and dark and only occasionally occupied, at least during the daytime. The beer cans and cigarette butts that littered it suggested that it saw more action in the evening. It was just the kind of place teenagers would have been drawn to: a bit off to the side, away from the action, the fast-flowing river beside it conferring a hint of danger and exoticism.

Julia crossed the road and walked towards the railings at the edge. She didn't think Anna would be there, and she wasn't, but she leaned over the railings and looked down at the water anyway. The river had been artificially narrowed and the water sped up before disappearing into a tunnel under the main road. There was a damp crisp packet by her right foot. She kicked it and it fluttered down into the water, then was swept away.

If that had been Anna, she thought, then stopped herself. *She wouldn't have come down here. She just wouldn't. She wouldn't have got this far, not on her own. She wouldn't have dared. She must be closer to the school.*

She headed back to the main road. As she reached the pavement, her phone rang. It was Brian.

'Where are you?' he asked. 'Have you found her?'

'I'm in the village. And no. Where are you?'

'I'm just arriving at the school. The police are already here, it looks like.'

'Do you see Anna? Is she with them?'

'No,' he said. 'She isn't.'

'What should I do, Brian? Should I keep looking down here?'

There was a long pause. 'I don't know. We need to talk. I'll come down to the village and pick you up.'

She stood on the pavement. It was cobbled, and she could feel the hard curves of the stones through the thin soles of her shoes. It was the only thing that felt solid; the shops and cars and people that surrounded her seemed slippery, ungraspable, unreal.

'Anna,' she shouted. 'Anna!' It was as much a wail of loss as a call that she expected an answer to; she realized when she tasted the tears on her lips that she was crying.

Her phone rang. She didn't recognize the number.

'Mrs Crowne?' a voice said. 'This is Jo Scott. I was wondering whether you were still coming?'

For a moment, Julia could not work out who the woman was, then she remembered. The dog woman. The woman with Bella, Anna's puppy.

'Oh,' she said. 'I'm sorry. Something came up. Can I call you back?'

There was a pause. An irritated pause, Julia thought.

'Ok,' the woman said. 'Call me back. But I have to leave for work now, so it'll have to be another day for the puppy.'

As Julia hung up a car pulled up next to her. It was Brian.

'Hi,' he said. 'Get in. The police are at the school and they want to talk to you.'

iv.

They pulled up at the school and got out of the car. As they walked towards the door, Julia reached out for Brian's hand. It was a while since they'd touched in any but the most perfunctory way and she was surprised how much reassurance it gave her, how much she needed to feel another human being.

She squeezed his fingers.

He looked at her, eyes narrowed, and pulled his hand away.

'Brian,' she said. 'Please.'

'Now's not the time,' he said. 'You need to talk to the cops.'

Mrs Jacobsen, the headmistress, approached them. She was accompanied by a uniformed officer. He nodded at Julia. He had a bustling, efficient presence. At the far end of the corridor another office was talking to a woman in jeans and a sweatshirt.

'Mrs Crowne,' he said. 'I'm PC Davis. We received a report that your daughter is missing?'

'Yes,' Julia said. The presence of the police officer was as disturbing as it was reassuring. If the police were here, then this was real. She felt her legs weaken. 'I don't know where she is. Help me find her. Please.'

PC Davis nodded. 'We will, Mrs Crowne. I'm sure that she's close by. That's normally the case in these situations. There are quite a few members of the school staff out looking for her,' he said. 'Now, you were in the village?'

'Yes,' she replied. 'Anna – there's a sweet shop she likes, that we sometimes go to after school. I thought she might be there.'

'Is there any reason you thought she might have gone there?' PC Davis asked. 'Has she done this before? Walked away from the house, or the school?'

'No,' Julia said. 'Never. She knows not to.'

PC Davis nodded again. 'Have you traced the route back to your house?' he said. 'Often when a child is missing from school they have simply gone home alone.'

'She wouldn't have done that,' Julia said. 'We live three miles away. I doubt she even knows the way.'

'Maybe not,' PC Davis said. 'But children sometimes decide that they are ready for something when we don't expect it. We need to check the route to your house.'

'No,' Julia said. She knew Anna, and she did not think for a second that she was merrily strolling home on her own. 'I don't want to waste time.'

'Mrs Crowne,' PC Davis said. 'We need to check whether Anna left on her own. I understand your concern, but we have to be systematic in our approach. Could you give me your address?'

'Of course,' Brian said. He gave the address.

'Thank you,' PC Davis said. 'We'll send a car to drive the route.'

'What else are you going to do?' Julia asked. 'Anna could be hurt, or in danger.'

'We're going to do everything we can, Mrs Crowne,' PC Davis said. 'But we have to take this one step at a time.'

Julia stared at him. She didn't like him, this burly officer who thought of this as a process, as a problem that could be solved with a step by step approach, when it was her daughter, her only child, who was five-years-old and missing, now for almost forty minutes.

Forty minutes. Yes, she might be on the route home, or playing in a local park, but what if she wasn't? What if someone had taken her? She could be forty miles away by now.

'What can we do?' Julia said. 'How can we help?'

'Call around,' PC Davis replied. 'Anyone you can think of. Anna's friends' mothers, relatives. Anyone who might have picked her up. Think if there's anywhere else she might be? Does anyone else ever pick her up? A relative maybe?'

'Her grandma, on Mondays and Wednesdays,' Julia said.

'Is there any possibility she came today, by mistake?'

'No,' Brian said. 'I spoke to my mother about two p.m.. She was at home. The kitchen was flooded.'

'Anyone else?' PC Davis asked.

'No,' Julia said. 'Only myself or Brian or Edna pick her up, and she knows not to go with strangers.'

'Could another parent have seen her alone and taken her home? Maybe tried to call you?'

'I don't think so.' Julia looked at her phone. 'There are no missed calls.'

'It *is* possible, though,' PC Davis said. 'Who would be the most likely to do something like that?'

Julia looked down. Her shoes were scuffed from the search in the village. 'Perhaps Dawn Swift's mum, Gemma. Or maybe Sheila Parks.'

'Could you call and ask them?'

Julia nodded and found Gemma Swift's number on her phone. Gemma picked up on the second ring.

'Hi Julia,' Gemma said. 'How's it going?'

She hesitated for a moment, hoping that Gemma would fill the gap with a declaration that Anna was with her and she hoped Julia didn't mind but she'd brought her home when she saw she was alone at the school and she'd meant to call but the girls wanted a snack and then the dog had to be fed, and you know how things can get away from you.

'Are you there, Julia?' Gemma said.

'Yes. Gemma, did you happen to see Anna at school today?'

'No. Why?'

'I was late. And when I got here she was gone.'

'What do you mean, gone?'

'She wasn't at the school. I can't find her.'

'Oh my God.' The horror in Gemma's voice was like a sudden blow to the stomach. It crystallized everything that was bad about this situation into one moment, and it left Julia short of breath.

This is real now, she thought. *This is the real thing.*

'Jules,' Gemma said. 'Can I help?'

'I don't think so. The police are here.'

'I'll call round some people,' she said. 'The more people looking the better.'

Julia was suddenly sick of this conversation, sick of everything it meant.

'I have to go,' she said. 'Thanks Gemma.'

'Could you call the other person you mentioned?' PC Davis said. 'And anyone else that springs to mind. In the meantime, I'm going to radio in for some more officers.'

Julia nodded. Mrs Jacobsen gestured towards her office.

'You can go in there,' she said. 'Have some privacy.'

Fifteen minutes later the door to Mrs Jacobsen's office opened. PC Davis came in. He had the false smile of someone who had bad news but wanted to be reassuring.

'We did not find Anna on the way to your house,' he said. He paused, 'so we have to consider the possibility that she's a little further afield.'

Julia reached for Brian's hand again. This time he took it.

'What does that mean?' Julia asked. 'Where's Anna? Where's my daughter?'

PC Davis shuffled uncomfortably from foot to foot.

'My colleague will be here shortly,' he said. 'She'll have more information.'

v.

Twenty minutes later a woman in a dark suit came into the headmistress's office. She was in her late thirties and had a confident bearing, the kind that comes with many years of taking control of situations. *Don't worry,* everything about her was saying. *I can fix whatever's wrong here.*

'Mrs Crowne?' she said. 'I'm Detective Inspector Wynne.'

Detective Inspector Wynne had short blonde hair, blue eyes, and an unsmiling expression. Her eyes were steady and intense, but she looked tired; there was a puffiness to the dark circles around her eyes that suggested lack of sleep or too much booze, or both.

Her demeanour was calm and professional, but to Julia it looked as though DI Wynne took her job too personally for her own good. Not that Julia cared: she wanted DI Wynne to feel like finding Anna was the most important thing in her life.

The detective looked at Julia, then at Brian, then back at Julia. Her expression softened. 'Mr and Mrs Crowne, I understand that you are worried – more than worried, I'm a mother myself – but try not to be. The vast majority of the time we find the child and everything is ok. And trust me, we will do everything we can to find her.'

'Thank you,' Julia said, feeling no calmer at all. 'So what's next?'

'Perhaps you can take me through what happened. Step by step, if you could. As much detail as you can remember.'

'There's not much I can tell you,' Julia said. 'I arrived here around three thirty—'

'Late,' Brian said. 'School finishes at three.'

'I was late,' Julia admitted. 'But I thought she'd be here!'

'That's ok, Mrs Crowne. Just the facts for now, please. Did the school know you would be late?'

'No! I was stuck in a meeting and my phone was dead and I couldn't call them.'

'In a meeting?' DI Wynne said.

'I'm a solicitor. Custody cases, mainly.'

'I see. Well, it's a busy job. So when you got here, there was no sign of Anna?'

Julia explained what she had done, how she had guessed that Anna would be in The Village Sweete Shoppe and gone down there, how she had asked some people for help, how she had searched the village until Brian called. When she was finished, DI Wynne nodded and chewed her lip thoughtfully.

She turned to the headmistress. 'Mrs Jacobsen, I'll need a list of all the parents and children who were at the school today, as well as all the employees of the school, whether they were here or not.'

Mrs Jacobsen nodded. 'It's not only parents who pick up the pupils,' she said. 'But we have a register of all those who are permitted to do so. I can let you have it.'

'Do you have CCTV inside the school?'

Mrs Jacobsen's mouth tightened into a slight moue. 'Yes,' she said. 'We do. Much as I prefer the promotion of civil liberties – we aim to produce responsible citizens who do the right thing because it is the right thing to do, and not because they think they are being observed – we have bent to the general panic about these matters and have installed CCTV.'

'You must be glad you did, now,' DI Wynne said. 'And there might be something else in the area we can use. Could you make sure that the officers get access to the CCTV?'

'Of course,' Mrs Jacobsen said. 'Right away.'

'I have a question,' Brian said, turning to the headmistress, his face a dark red. 'How the hell did this happen? I thought the teachers did not let children out of the grounds unless they knew there was a parent there?'

That was right, Julia thought. The school had a pick-up policy and it was strictly adhered to. Only parents or designated carers could pick up children, although they were not allowed on the school grounds; the pupils were accompanied to the school gates and handed over to their responsible adults. In the case of an adult being late, they were to notify the school, and that pupil stayed inside. If, as Julia had done, the adult failed to notify the school, then the child would be ok: they would be left at the gates with a teacher, and brought inside to wait.

But it hadn't worked this time.

'I've spoken to the teachers,' Mrs Jacobsen said. 'They said that they thought you were there, Mrs Crowne. They expected you to be there since you had not called to say you would not be.'

'She wasn't there, though, was she!' Brian said. 'And you were supposed to take care of my daughter! That's what we pay your obscene school fees for!'

'Mr Crowne,' the headmistress said. 'The school adhered to its policies. I am sure the CCTV will show that. We do everything we can to ensure the safety—'

'But not enough!' Brian shouted.

'We have policies in place that have been independently reviewed and which are in accordance with all necessary legislation,' Mrs Jacobsen said. 'And I am, of course, open to any questions you and Julia might have, but I'm not sure that now is the best time to discuss them.'

'Fine,' Julia said. 'We can discuss it later.' She glanced at DI Wynne. 'For now we need to concentrate on finding Anna.'

'Precisely,' DI Wynne said. 'If you could get me the CCTV and the personnel list, that would be a start.' She turned to Julia and Brian. 'I'd like a recent photo of Anna, as well. So that we can alert other constabularies and the border control folks.'

'You think that's necessary?' Brian asked. 'You think she might be being taken out of the country?'

'I wouldn't jump to conclusions,' DI Wynne said. 'But it's a precaution worth taking.'

'God,' Brian said. He covered his eyes with his hand. 'This can't be happening. It just can't. Not again. I can't believe it's happening again.'

vi.

Detective Inspector Wynne stared at Brian.

'Again?' she said. Her calm expression was suddenly more urgent. 'You've had a child disappear before?'

47

Brian shook his head. 'No,' he said. 'Not a child. My father. He left home when I was in my early twenties. He vanished. Didn't leave a note; nothing. Just went.'

'Have you heard from him since?' DI Wynne asked.

'No.' Brian looked at his hands. He picked at the cuticle of his left index finger. 'Not a word. Not even a Christmas card.'

'And you don't know where he is? He just disappeared?' DI Wynne pressed.

'Yep.' Brian shrugged. 'It was during the school holidays. Dad was a headmaster. He was nearing retirement. One day he was there, and the next he wasn't.'

'And you don't know why? Or where he went?'

'No. No idea.'

Julia knew that Brian was not quite telling the truth. Yes, he had no idea where his father was, but he did have some idea of why he had gone there. He had told her once – and made her swear that she would not ever tell Edna that he had discussed it with her – that he suspected his headmaster father had been having an affair with a younger member of staff and had run away with her. He wasn't sure – his mother never talked about it – but he had managed to piece that much together over the years.

Still, he had no idea where his dad had gone, nor why he had never got in touch with him.

Julia had an idea. Not of where he was, but of why he hadn't been in touch. She suspected it was the price he paid for his freedom: Jim had an affair and Edna gave him an ultimatum: get out of her life and start again with his girlfriend somewhere far from her, and she'd let him go quietly. Let him avoid the disgrace. The catch was that he had to stay away, from both her and Brian.

Or he could stick around and she'd make his life a misery. And Edna would be good at that.

So off he'd gone, probably to some beach in Spain or chalet in Switzerland, where he spent his days hiking and reading and skiing while his young bride taught in an international school and had discreet affairs of her own.

Maybe, anyway. Julia didn't know for sure. All she knew was that it had hit Brian hard, and now, from his point of view, it was happening again.

'We'll want to get in touch with him,' DI Wynne said. 'Any information you have would be most helpful.'

'I don't have any,' Brian said. 'I can ask mum.'

'Thank you,' DI Wynne said. 'I appreciate it.'

She wouldn't get much from Edna, Julia thought, but she could try.

'Right,' Brian said. 'And that's enough standing around. I'm going to look for my daughter.'

Julia watched him leave. She looked at DI Wynne.

'I'm going too,' she said.

DI Wynne nodded. 'Of course. I'll be here.' She wrote down her phone number. 'Call if you find her.'

As she picked up her car keys, her phone rang.

It was Edna. She lifted the phone to her ear. Before she could speak, she heard Edna's strident tones.

'Julia, what's going on? Brian left me a message, about Anna. I tried to call him but he didn't answer.'

Julia swallowed, hard.

'She's missing,' she said. 'She's gone missing.'

There was a pause. 'What do you mean, missing? When?'

'After school. She wasn't here when I came to pick her up.'

'How's that possible? The school has policies. They have to—'

Julia interrupted her. She was going to have to say this sooner or later, and it was better to get it out of the way.

'I was late,' she said. 'I was stuck—'

'But the school know to hold the children back, if a parent is going to be late.'

'I didn't call,' Julia said. 'My phone was—'

'You *didn't call*?' Edna said. 'Julia, what on earth got into you?'

'I was telling you, my phone—'

'Never mind,' Edna said. 'There's no time for talking. We need to act. I'm at home, but I'll be there as soon as I can. Twenty minutes, at the most.'

DI Wynne caught Julia's attention.

'Who is it?' she asked.

'My mother-in-law,' Julia said. 'She's coming to help.'

DI Wynne nodded. 'Could I talk to her?'

Julia passed her the phone.

'Mrs Crowne,' she said. 'This is Detective Inspector Wynne.'

Julia heard Edna's voice on the other end, faint, but still recognizably Edna. It sounded as though she was giving orders, taking charge.

'Thank you for the suggestions, Mrs Crowne,' DI Wynne said. 'We have everything in hand. What would help us most is if you could go to your son's house and wait there. There is a possibility Anna will find her way home and we need someone she knows to be there if she does.'

It seemed Edna agreed. DI Wynne handed the phone back to Julia.

'I'll be here,' she said. 'Good luck.'

Ninety minutes later – ninety minutes that felt like nine hundred, or nine thousand – Julia was back.

She had driven every minor road she could think of, climbed out of her car and looked under hedges and in ditches. There was no sign of Anna.

She took out her phone and dialled Brian's number. It rang through to his voicemail.

'Hi,' she said. 'I'm back at the school. Call me if … if anything happens.'

Julia ended the call and stared out of the window.

She's out there, she thought. *She's somewhere out there. I have to find her.*

Julia had never considered the limitations of time and space. Sure, she'd wished for more hours in the day or had to prioritize one party over another because, like everyone, she couldn't be in two places at once, but she had never really bothered about it. It was, at worst, an inconvenience; a fact of the universe that might have been an occasional pain, but which there was no point complaining about because there was nothing you could do about it.

For the last two hours, though, it had been the only thing that mattered. She wanted to be everywhere at once. It was the only way she could be sure she would find Anna.

But that wasn't possible. You really can't be in two places at once. You can occupy only one patch of earth, one volume of air. And the one she was in was not the same one as Anna.

And might never be.

She couldn't keep that thought away. It forced its way into her consciousness, trailing hysteria not far behind.

What if she's gone for good? Dead? Sold into slavery? Locked in a madman's basement? What if I never see her again?

In the moments after she thought this way, before she was able to grab some small measure of control over herself, she was filled with an emotion so strong that it stopped her doing whatever she was doing. If she was drinking water, the cup would fall from her lips, the contents spilling over her hand and onto the floor. If she was walking she would sink into the nearest chair or against the nearest wall; if she was talking to someone she would stop, mid-sentence and clutch her hands against her stomach.

And it was all the worse because she was to blame.

It was incontrovertible. Yes, she may have some kind of paltry excuse – her meeting ran over, her phone was dead – but if you stepped away from the details, it was clear. If she had been there at two fifty-five, waiting for Anna outside the school gate, then Anna would be with her now. They'd be at home getting ready for Anna's bedtime, maybe reading *The Twits* by now.

She definitely *wouldn't* be here, at the school, sitting in the head teacher's office with DI Wynne and a cup of coffee while, through the thick glass of the window, the sun dipped slowly over the horizon. And Anna wouldn't be – well, Anna wouldn't be wherever she was.

The door to the office opened and two police officers came in. They were both men, both in their twenties.

'Did you find her?' Julia asked, even though she knew from their expressions that they hadn't.

'No ma'am,' the one on the left said. 'Not yet.'

DI Wynne followed them in. She had her phone to her ear. 'OK,' she said. 'I'll let you know if anything changes.' She cut the connection and looked at the officers. 'Nothing?'

The one on the right shook his head. 'Nothing. We've covered everywhere she could have walked to. Every street, every park. We've interviewed a lot of people – kids, adults, anyone – but no one saw her.'

Wynne pinched her chin with her thumb and forefinger.

'And the other parents who were here to pick up their kids?'

'We've started talking to them. We'll get to most of them tonight, the ones that agree to it. Most will.'

The other officer spoke. 'We've started knocking on doors. Asking homeowners if they have any information. We're rounding up as many bodies as we can to start searching. And we'll get a general appeal on local radio.'

They've done this before, Julia thought. *Oh God, they've done this before. This really happens. And it's happening to me.*

'Can I come?' she asked, suddenly. 'Can I come with you?'

'To knock on doors?' the officer said.

'Yes. I'll know if Anna's there. I'll just know. And if I call out her name then she'll answer.'

The officer shifted his weight from foot to foot. He glanced at DI Wynne.

'I think it will be better if we leave PCs Joyce and Bell to deal with that,' Wynne said. 'It might help things to go smoothly.'

'Why?' Julia said. 'I can help.'

'Mrs Crowne, it's better if you stay here. In case Anna does show up. She could be quite distressed.'

'I'd like to go.'

'I think it's better if you don't.'

Why was this woman obstructing her? Julia thought. *Why would she not let her look for Anna?*

'I'm her mum!' she said, all of the emotion of the last few hours finding an outlet in righteous anger. 'I have a right to go! If I want to go, I can! What if she's in one of those houses? She needs me to be there!'

'Mrs Crowne, we don't think that she is in one of the houses. We're just asking for information.'

'But what if she is? You need to search them! All of them!'

'We can't just barge into someone's house without a warrant.'

'Why the hell not? If my daughter might be there, why the hell not?'

'I fully understand your frustration, Mrs Crowne, but we are not allowed to enter a member of the public's house without a warrant to do so. It's not something we have any control over. It's the law.'

'Fuck the law! If you won't do it, I will!' Julia stood up, her knee banging on the underside of the table. Her china coffee cup rattled on its saucer, bitter liquid spilling over the desk. She marched to the door, pushing between the two police officers, and turned down the corridor. She wasn't sure what she was going to do, but she was going to do *something*; she couldn't just sit here and wait, not while Anna was out there. Doing that was accepting her powerlessness, and she wasn't able to do that, not by a long chalk.

Behind her she heard DI Wynne's footsteps on the tile floor.

'Mrs Crowne!' Wynne called. 'Mrs Crowne! Where are you going?'

'Out!' Julia shouted. 'I'm going out!'

'Mrs Crowne, it's not a good idea to do anything rash. We need the goodwill of people in the vicinity.'

Julia knew that the police officer was correct, but she didn't care. She was beyond reason, in the grip of something animal and irresistible. It was the same thing that drove a mother to protect her young in the wild; that drove an eland to defend her calf from a lion, or an elk to fight a wolf to save hers, even when this came at the cost of the mothers' own lives.

When she was a few feet from the front door, it swung open. Brian stepped inside. He was pale and his eyes were red. It was clear that he had not found Anna. He looked at Julia, and then transferred his gaze to the police officer.

'What's going on?' he asked, and looked back at his wife. 'Why's she shouting at you?'

'She's trying to stop me looking for Anna,' Julia said. 'I want to go and look for Anna. I want to knock on people's doors and ask them if they've seen her. Look them in the face. She could be in one of these houses.'

'Then go,' Brian said. 'I'll come with you.'

'Mr and Mrs Crowne,' DI Wynne said. 'Could we talk for a minute, before you go?'

Julia turned round. 'Sure,' she said. 'A minute.'

'In the office?'

Julia shook her head. 'Here.'

'We have police officers going door to door,' Wynne said. 'They have experience in the right questions to ask, and if anyone has seen anything concerning your daughter then they will find it out and follow that lead wherever

56

it takes them. At this stage we need to be systematic in our search for Anna.'

'What if one of them has her?' Julia said. 'How will they know that?'

'It's unlikely.' Wynne shifted uncomfortably. 'I have to be honest with you. At this stage there are two main possibilities for your daughter's whereabouts. Either she wandered off on her own – in which case she can't have gone far and someone will almost certainly have seen her – and is now hiding in some place we haven't found or ... ', she paused and looked away for a second, before looking back at Julia and Brian, 'or someone took her.'

'Took her where?' Brian asked, his voice hoarse.

'We don't know yet, Mr Crowne,' Wynne said. 'But for now, we have to focus our efforts on the immediate vicinity, in case Anna *is* out there, cold and frightened and hurt, and that means that we have to be as methodical as possible to ensure that we miss nothing.'

'She's out there,' Brian said. 'I know she is. I can't believe anything else.'

'And we will have officers searching all night for any sign of her. Clothing, footprints, her belongings.'

'I want to be part of it,' Brian said. 'I'll help. We have friends who'll help as well.'

'Excellent,' Wynne said. 'We'll set up a base in the community centre. Call around and get as many people as you can.'

Brian's hands were clenching and unclenching on his thighs, bunching his chinos up and exposing his paisley socks. Anna had bought them – or chosen them, at any rate – for him last Christmas, Julia recalled, along with a pair of Homer Simpson socks. Brian had worn one of each, Homer on the left foot, paisley on the right. He had told Anna he loved them both so much he couldn't choose between them. Anna had made sure that he kept them on all day.

The memory of her daughter checking that her dad was wearing the mismatched socks she'd bought him overwhelmed Julia. Her hands started to shake and then she started to cry. She had not cried like that – uncontrollably, her chest heaving – since she was seventeen and she had been dumped by Vincent, the first love of her life. She had believed, as teenagers will, that he was the one, the only one, and when he had told her it was over – *it's not you*, he'd meant to say, *it's me*, except the prepared lines had come out wrong and he'd actually said, in a moment of unwitting honesty, *it's not me, it's you* – she had cried for days. It had felt like the end of the world, like nothing would ever be the same again. After a while, though, it had passed, and she'd seen that maybe life would go on without Vincent.

And now, for the first time since she was seventeen, she had that feeling again, only this time she was thirty-eight, and old enough to know that it was for real, and that it would not pass.

She pushed her chair back, suddenly weary beyond belief. 'Come on,' she said, looking at her husband's expressionless eyes. 'Let's go home and get ready.'

vii.

The search was organized quickly and efficiently. The police knew what they were doing, and they set about it calmly.

They've done this before, Julia thought. *This is the kind of thing that happens, which means this is* real.

The local community centre – a wood and glass structure built a few years previously with lottery money – was the base of operations. A large, detailed map of the area was stuck to a wall, lines made with marker pens delineating the streets that volunteers had been assigned to search.

And there were a lot of volunteers: friends of Julia and Brian, other parents, concerned locals. Julia had rung through her address book; many others had called the police asking how they could help and had been directed to the community centre, and then out to their search areas.

Alongside them, police officers pointed torches into alleys or knocked on doors or quizzed the homeless. Dog teams roamed the parks and copses and fields and woodlands. If none of these things worked, in the morning divers would search the waterways.

It was a thorough search. They were searching places that Julia knew Anna could not have got to on her own.

Which meant she had been moved by somebody, and that somebody would not want her to be found.

Brian was out with the searchers; Julia waited in the community centre with DI Wynne; waited for the triumphant smile as the detective heard that Anna was lost and cold but alive and well. But as the night wore on the volunteers came back with their news that there was no news, then went home to their beds and dreams of the poor parents who they had left behind. Julia thanked them for their effort, accepted their well wishes, their *don't worry, I'm sure she'll turn ups*.

But there was no sign of Anna, so how could she not worry? She was that woman, the mother whose child was lost, who was at the centre of a storm of sympathy and community spirit. So how could she not worry?

It was around midnight when the door opened and Brian came in. He looked at DI Wynne.

'Nothing?' he asked.

'Not yet, Mr Crowne,' she replied. 'You and Mrs Crowne should go home. Try and get some rest.'

'I'd prefer to stay,' Julia said. 'I can go out and look myself.'

'If anything changes I'll call you immediately,' Wynne said. 'The best thing you can do is to preserve your strength. Tomorrow will be a busy day.'

'If you don't find Anna tonight,' Brian said.

There was a long, uncomfortable, pause, then DI Wynne nodded. 'If we don't find her tonight,' she said. 'That's right. But go, and get some rest.'

Julia was pretty sure that rest would be an elusive quarry, but she nodded. She took her car keys from her pocket. She looked at Brian. 'I'll drive,' she said. 'Let's go.'

They climbed into the car, silent. There was nothing to say. For the first time in a long time they were both feeling exactly the same things. Fear. Worry. Dread. Panic. One after another in a horrific spin cycle.

Julia turned the key in the ignition. She almost expected the car not to start – everything else was broken, so why not that, too? – but it fired and the engine came to life. It was a short drive home – maybe a mile – but to Julia it felt like the most important journey she had ever taken; as if she was crossing an invisible border into a new land, a land in which everything had changed.

3

The First Day

i.

You slept well. In the wee hours you brought the girl inside and then went to bed, tired from the exertions of the day – the adrenaline was pumping and it took it out of you – and fell asleep in a heartbeat. Woke at six, a little bleary-eyed, and made a strong coffee.

The story is everywhere. The girl's photo in every news bulletin. Numbers for the public to call if they know where she is. The police were searching all night, helped by concerned locals. A local pub provided sandwiches and hot drinks. Dogs barked and yelped and sniffed their way across scrubland and through parks and forests.

They found nothing. There is nothing to find. You made sure of that.

Not a peep from the girl in the night. That was no surprise, though. She is young and the sleeping pills you'd crushed into a milkshake (bought from McDonald's before you took her and administered as soon as you got her in the car – kids were powerless to resist sugary drinks) were powerful. She sleeps still. She'll be groggy when she wakes, but that is no problem. You plan to keep her under sedation until the end comes – perhaps a week or so, not much more than that – after which, it won't matter anyway.

It matters now, though. You need her asleep or sedated so that she doesn't make a noise when you are not there. You can't be with her all the time. You are needed – expected – to be elsewhere, and your absence would be noted. It would cause suspicion. You know that they will be looking everywhere for the girl – pretty five-year-olds who vanish are big news – and you must do nothing that invites suspicion onto you. So you must leave her, and she must be silent when you are gone.

If she isn't? Well, even then it is unlikely anyone would hear her. She is in a safe place, hidden away in the bowels of your house, and her screams would not travel far. But maybe far enough if they happened to coincide with the arrival of the milkman or the postman. You have kept the milk deliveries up. Would the police look for people who had abruptly cancelled milk deliveries? They might, so you have maintained yours. That is the attention to detail that sets you apart from the common run.

So the girl must be silent. Just in case.

Just in case. Those are your watchwords. You examine every possibility, weigh every risk, and make your plans accordingly.

That is why you can sleep at night. Because you know you have nothing to fear. You know you have not made any errors. You know you will not get caught.

And you know you are doing the right thing. You have no crisis of conscience. Yes, you feel sorry for the girl, but her suffering is a necessary evil.

And a necessary evil is indistinguishable from something right and proper. If it is necessary, how can it be evil? If it is the only path to the right and proper outcome then it must itself be right and proper. To be deterred from doing the right thing because a little girl might undergo some temporary suffering – wouldn't that be worse than letting her suffer? If everyone made decisions like that then nothing great would ever be accomplished. How many people died in order for the great cathedrals to be built? Or bridges? Or railways? Or for the wars of the righteous to be fought? Did their deaths matter? Were they tragedies, every one of them? Yes, of course they were. But were they to be regretted? No, they were not. Without their deaths the world would be a poorer place, and that was what mattered. Their deaths were a necessary evil.

And, as you know better than anyone else, a necessary evil can be a good thing.

ii.

Julia lay in bed, staring at the ceiling. It was four a.m. and there was a chill in the room. They'd come home and relieved Edna, then Brian had disappeared with a bottle of whisky. Somehow she'd fallen asleep, for maybe an hour, which in the circumstances was the best she could hope for. Now, in the small hours of the morning, mind racing, she knew her night was over. Sleep would be impossible.

The house was still and dark; the witching hour, as her dad had called it. He was a leather tanner and he used to come home smelling of the chemicals they used to clean the leather. Whatever they were they were powerful: the run-off polluted the local rivers and polluted her dad's body. He died of brain cancer when he was in his early sixties. It happened quickly. A year from retirement he missed his first day of work from illness, then he missed another, and another, laid up in bed with a headache that left him unable to focus. He never went back. The cancer was behind his eye and worming its way into his brain.

Officially, it was just one of those things. Unofficially, Julia was convinced it was the solvents and acids he spent his days slopping around that stained his skin and fouled his lungs. Even after he had taken a bath – he took one every night, retiring to the upstairs lavatory with a cup of tea and a copy of the *Daily Mirror,* a ritual which infuriated Julia when she was teenager in a hurry to get ready on a Friday night, leading her to complain to her mum, who would frown and say *leave him, love, he works hard* – even after that long soak in the perfumed, Radoxed waters of the bath, he still gave off the hard, harsh smell of the tannery.

When she was a child, he used to lie down next to her, smelling of that smell, and tell her a story every night, a story he had made up during the long days at work. Many of them began *It was the witching hour*, and for years she had wondered what it would be like to be awake during the witching hour, what amazing events she would witness if she could just keep her eyes open ... and then she would wake up and it would be light outside and she would have missed all the fun.

As she lay there now, the house creaked and groaned. They were just the sounds that a house made, but it was easy to believe that they were the night-time perambulations of the little people. She remembered running onto the landing as a little girl when she heard the stairs creak, and shouting downstairs to her parents.

I'm scared! What are those noises?

Her dad clumped up the stairs, bringing with him a whiff of cheap beer mingled with the acid stench of the tannery.

Don't worry, petal. Houses are alive. They move around and they settle at night, same as you and me. It's just our place resting its old bones. It's saying good night to you, that's all.

Anna was one when he died, so at least she'd met him, although she had no memory of it. He'd loved her, was great with her; couldn't get enough of nappy changes and messy feedings and clip-clop horsey rides on his knees.

How she wished he was here now. She wouldn't want him to suffer through this, but it would make it so much easier to have him here. She missed him. She missed him so much.

As she did her mum, but in a different way. Her mum was still alive but had suffered her own tragedy, in some ways worse. Alzheimer's had corroded her brain, eaten her memories, dissolved who she was into a listless, confused shell. She was in a home nearby, in need of constant care. Julia visited often, but it was hard. Her mum rarely knew it was her daughter holding her hand.

They were effectively gone, her parents, as was Brian. She was going to have to do this herself.

She checked her phone. Maybe a call from DI Wynne that somehow – although she knew it was unthinkable that she would have slept through it – she had missed.

She reached out and turned on her bedside light.

There was a photo frame on the cabinet, split into uneven thirds. Anna had given it to her for Christmas, and they had spent an hour or so leafing through photos choosing which three to put in it. All of them featured Anna: as a newborn, in Edna's arms on the couch in their old house, and with Brian and Julia outside the blue door of the nursery she had attended.

God, leaving her there for the first time had been awful. Julia had felt bereft, incomplete, as though she was missing a part of herself. She had cried all morning at work, and then made some excuse at lunchtime about feeling ill, and gone to the nursery. Being reunited with her daughter, smelling her, kissing her, made her whole again, and she vowed never to leave her daughter again.

But the next day she did. And the day after that, and the day after that. Eventually, she got used to saying goodbye, but she never stopped missing Anna.

Julia stared at the photo. It was taken on that first day, Anna a mere three-months-old. Julia looked drawn and tired, still carrying the baby weight, her face tear-stained. She was holding Anna close to her chest, holding the baby that she had barely been apart from for a minute since she was born, and who she was about to hand into the care of a stranger.

Even in a photo it was obvious she and Brian were in love. They were leaning into each other, his arm around her. He was not looking at the camera, but at his wife, his expression protective, caring, concerned. Loving, most of all. It was a photo of a man who adored his wife and the daughter they had made together.

When they'd left the nursery they'd hugged for a long time. It was funny what you remembered; Julia remembered the smell of the suit Brian was wearing. It was musty; odd but not unpleasant. He was starting his new job as a primary teacher, and he was wearing a suit that he'd bought from a charity store, and in the chaos of early parenthood he'd not managed to find time to have it dry-cleaned.

He was the man she wanted to spend the rest of her life with and, back then, she couldn't have imagined any future in which she didn't.

Not any more. Now he was a brooding presence, squatting in the spare bedroom.

She pulled on her dressing gown and crossed the landing to the stairs. The top two creaked and, out of habit, she trod softly on them so as not to wake up Anna, who was a light sleeper. Julia often wondered whether it was because she and Brian had fussed over her sleeping arrangements so much: at nap time and bed time they ensured that she had a dark room at the correct temperature, and then they performed an elaborate routine to get her to sleep, rocking her in a specific pattern and then, when she was nearly asleep, laying her gently in her bed and patting her back until her breathing lengthened and she could be left without fear of her waking up. They would then tiptoe around the house, terrified of waking her up.

And now she was a light sleeper: no wonder. She had only ever had to sleep in perfect conditions. All those adults who complained of insomnia would sleep like a cat on a warm flagstone if they were rocked for half an hour before bed and then given a gentle massage. She and Brian would have done things differently with a second child, Julia knew, they would have been more relaxed, both because they would have known what they were doing and because they would not have had the time to do with another child what they had done with Anna. The second child had not come, though. A miscarriage and then an ectopic pregnancy, which had left Julia unable to have more children, had seen to that. She was barren, as Edna had once put it.

Barren. It was a horrid, vivid word that Julia hated, and it was just the kind of word that Edna would use. She could pretend that it was just what people said when she was young and she didn't know it would upset her daughter-in-law, but Julia didn't believe her. Edna knew exactly what she was doing. She always did.

For a time, Julia had grieved for the loss of her fertility, but recently, as she realized she no longer loved Brian, she had come to be relieved. For one thing, divorce would be easier with one child; for another, she had always worried that she would not love the second child as much as the first. How could she? Anna and she were mother and daughter but also best friends. She knew that they wouldn't be forever – or even much longer – but right now she loved taking her daughter to the movies or shopping or for lunch. They'd gone to see *The Nutcracker* at Christmas; Anna was open-mouthed. Spellbound. Julia understood the magic of theatre, the way it brought drama to life, in a way she had never done before. Anna asked frequently when Christmas was coming, so she could see it again.

Yes – her love for Anna was all-consuming, so maybe it was best that she have only one child.

One child who was now gone.

And, although she would not admit it to herself, part of Julia was sure Anna *was* gone. Of course, she still hoped that Anna would show up. She had to. Without that hope she would probably not have been able to carry on. But, however much she tried to ignore it, she was aware that she might never see her daughter again.

Might never meet – and disapprove of – Anna's first boyfriend. Might never watch her fall in love, graduate, marry. Might never become a grandparent. There was an entire future at stake here, both for her and for her daughter and husband.

Before she fell asleep, alone in the bedroom, her only company the sound of Brian's footsteps as he walked from the kitchen table to the booze cabinet, she'd googled 'missing children'. It was a mistake, just like it was a mistake to google your symptoms. Persistent runny nose? Not a cold – it was brain fluid leaking out of your cranium. Always tired? Not a condition of being a parent – it was a rare virus that would gradually eat away at your muscles until you wasted away to nothing. Constipation? Bowel cancer. The difference was, these were false diagnoses. In the morning, a doctor would tell you not to worry and send you on your way.

When it came to missing children the facts – or the patterns, at least – were pretty clear.

Kids, especially five-year-old kids, were either found in the first few hours, or not at all.

Yes, there were exceptions (and that was where the hope came from) but for the most part (and please let Anna be different, please) five-year-old kids either showed up pretty soon after they went missing – at a friend's house, or in the care of a concerned adult who had seen them alone – or they didn't show up at all.

She had read accounts of police investigations; read about the kinds of people who abducted young girls, and

71

the reasons they did so. She read about criminal gangs who kidnapped kids into slavery, or for rich people who couldn't have kids of their own, she read about lone wolf predators who took kids and hid them for years, until the kids grew up and lost their appeal and were murdered. She read about paedophile gangs, who took kids and passed them around their network, filmed them being raped to order, and then disposed of their broken bodies in landfill sites in the Third World.

She'd run to the bathroom sink and vomited until there was nothing left to come out other than bile and saliva. It was funny how your body reacted to extreme emotion by emptying the stomach. She didn't know why that would be the case; you'd think it would be better to retain the food so as to have some energy to deal with whatever crisis it was.

Even so, she wasn't hungry now. The thought of food held no appeal whatsoever; she wasn't sure it ever would again. As she reached the bottom of the stairs, there was a creak behind her. For a second, instinct took over and Julia thought it was Anna coming down for an early morning cuddle; her spirits rose, the gloom lifted. And then she turned to look and reality reasserted its grip.

It was Brian. His eyes were red, his face unshaven. He was one of those men who grew facial hair very quickly. If they went out in the evening he would have to shave for a second time in the day. She had found it interesting, at first. Charming. Manly. Part of the husband she loved. Now she found it off-putting, and there were plenty of other things about him that had a similar effect: all his physical imperfections, the smells and blotches and sagging muscles, now repelled her.

'Brian,' she said.

He ignored her. They had barely spoken since leaving the school. That was part of the reason she'd googled 'missing children'. She'd been alone and unable to stop herself.

He walked past her to the kitchen; shoulders slumped, and flicked the kettle on. He put a teabag in a mug. When the water boiled he poured it into the mug and added milk. The milk spilled on the countertop. His hand was shaking. He'd drunk a lot when they had got home, enough to pass out around midnight, but not enough, it seemed, to stay passed out.

'Brian,' she said. 'We need to talk.'

He looked at her over his cup of tea. 'Do we?' he said. His voice was broken and hoarse.

'Yes. Our daughter is missing.'

'Because you weren't there to pick her up. You didn't show up and now she's gone.'

Julia wanted to defend herself, out of habit. It was how things were between them: he criticized her or she criticized him and they argued. Right or wrong didn't come into it. Not giving in was what mattered. You didn't give an inch. You stood your ground. Sometimes she felt like Tom Petty singing 'I Won't Back Down'.

But not this time. What could she say? It's not my fault? It *was* her fault, at least partially, and partially was enough. Maybe she had an excuse. Maybe she'd been unlucky. Maybe she could have been late a thousand times and each time Anna would have been sitting there with Mrs Jameson, eating a biscuit, and telling the teacher about her favourite place to go on the weekend. All those things could be true, but they didn't alter the only truth that made any difference: if she had been on time, Anna would be asleep in her bed right this minute.

So Brian was right. Cruel to point it out, but right. Perhaps if they'd been happily married, perhaps, even if they'd been unhappily married but planning to stay that way, he would have been the one to support her, to make her feel less wretched, but she had told him she wanted him out of her life, and with that she had given up any right to his support.

She reached for her car keys. Her hands struggled to pick them up. She wiped her eyes clear of tears.

'I'm going out,' she said.

He didn't reply. He just leaned on the kitchen counter and looked out of the window and sipped his scalding tea.

iii.

Reminders of Anna were everywhere.

Her booster seat in the rear-view mirror. A thin summer raincoat in the footwell. Biscuit crumbs on the backseat.

Brian had told her off for letting Anna eat in the car, for making such a mess.

Who cares now? Julia thought. *Who cares about crumbs or mess or late bedtimes? We spend so much time worrying about the little things, when they don't matter. And we let the things that do matter slip.*

When she turned the ignition a CD of kids' songs came on. She sat back and listened.

Do your ears hang low?
Do they waggle to and fro?
Can you tie them in a knot?
Can you tie them in a bow?

Anna had found that song particularly amusing, and had developed a dance in which she rocked from foot to foot and mimed tying her dangly ears in knots and bows.

Julia pulled into the street. There was a light on in the house next door, and she saw the upstairs curtain twitch. Mrs Madigan: a village stalwart in her nineties, who had an opinion on everything, and who expected, by virtue of her age – as though age conferred wisdom – that people would listen to it. She was known to be both 'formidable' and 'quite a character' and widely surmised to have a heart of gold beneath her tough exterior. People often commented on how it must be 'interesting' or 'fun' or 'quite something' to have her as a neighbour. Julia didn't tell them what she really thought: it was a pain. Once you got to know her you realized that Mrs Madigan's public persona of forthright grumpiness did not, in fact, hide a beneficent and kindly old woman; it hid a sour and angry old woman. She didn't like it when Anna was noisy in the garden and she thought nothing of shouting at her over the fence, or of complaining to Julia or Brian about their hooligan child. She would ask Brian to help when something broke in her house, and then, when he finished whatever DIY task she had assigned him, she would complain that he had done it wrong, and then ostentatiously get a tradesman in to redo the work. Above all, she complained incessantly to Julia about her two children and many more grand- and great-grandchildren, and how they were selfish and lazy and ignored her.

Julia didn't blame them. She would have ignored her too, had she been able to do so.

The neighbours on the other side – a childless couple in their late-forties – were much better. They didn't have much to do with them, which Julia was becoming convinced was the key to good neighbourly relations. Good fences make good neighbours, the saying went, and it was true.

Julia wasn't sure where she was going, but she found herself heading for the local playground. It was a pretty unprepossessing place: just a set of swings, a slide, and a roundabout on a patch of grass at the end of a residential street, but Anna and she went there often when they had an hour or so to fill. The police had checked it, but it was possible that, since then, Anna had found her way there.

Possible. Not likely.

She kept her headlights on full beam and drove slowly, scanning the streets for any sign of her daughter.

At the park, she switched off the engine and the lights cut out. She was glad; she'd found that the yellow pools disturbed her. They illuminated only a portion of the world and it reminded her of the futility of this search. Anna could be anywhere, but Julia, like the beams of light, could look in only one place at a time.

She was reminded of a conversation she'd had with a friend, Prissy (short for Pricilla, a boarding school nickname used only by her intimates, and retained as the name had a certain irony: Prissy had shown herself to be anything but, a reputation sealed by an affair with a young teacher, Sarah, who lost her job over it). The conversation had taken place a year or so back, just after a teenage girl had been found in the basement of a house only a few streets away from her home in some dusty Middle-American city. She'd been there for a decade; Prissy had declared that, if her son (she had a son the same age as Anna) went missing there was no chance he could be hidden for so long so close to home, because she would search every house in the vicinity from top to bottom, whether the occupants and police liked it or not. Julia had agreed. She would do the same. It was an easy thing to say, fired by indignant parental fervour, and it carried with it an implicit criticism of the mother of the American girl. Why hadn't she done that? A good mother would have.

A good mother would have been there to pick up her daughter, as well.

It wasn't as easy as she and Prissy had imagined, however. Firstly, there were a lot of houses, and secondly, it seemed that the police and occupants had more say over who entered them than expected.

But at least she was doing something.

'Anna!' she called. 'Anna!'

She did not have a torch, so she used the one on her iPhone and swept the park. The swings were empty, the slide a silhouetted dinosaur.

'Anna!' she shouted. 'Anna!'

'Who's Anna?' a voice said, the accent strong: *ooze Annoh?*

She jumped and pointed the beam in the direction of the voice. Two teenage boys were sitting on the roundabout. What the hell were they doing out here at this time? One of them was holding a bottle. He took a swig from it and passed it to his friend, then lit a cigarette.

She smelled the smoke: make that a joint.

'My daughter,' she said.

'Is she cute?' the boy with the joint asked.

'Yes,' Julia said, then realized her error. 'I mean, no, not in the way you mean. She's five.'

'*You're* cute,' the boy said. 'You're all right, anyway. Want to suck me cock?'

'What?' Julia said. 'No!'

'Then what are you doin' here, at this time?' the boy said. 'That's why people come down here.'

As far as Julia knew people came down here to play on the swings with their children, but apparently not.

When Anna was home she doubted they would be playing here again.

The other boy, the one who had not spoken, stood up. He was older than she'd thought, maybe nineteen, tall, and thin, and had a pock-marked face, the result of bad, untreated acne at some point in his early teens. He sniffed, then hawked and spit on the roundabout.

They were *definitely* not coming down here again.

'Come on,' he said. 'Come wi' me.' He grabbed his crotch and thrust it towards her, then nodded towards the bushes. 'You can have some of this. You've been missing it, I can tell. Don't get much off your old man, right? I've met some of your type before, not so old you've give up, still need your hole busted from time to time.'

His voice was flat and toneless and he was staring at her, his face drawn in a slight sneer, as though he was looking at something faintly disgusting.

He took a step towards her. It was quick, and purposeful.

'Come on,' he urged, 'you'll like it once we get started.'

And then she imagined Anna, wandering into this park and encountering the pock-marked boy and his friends, or people like them.

If that was the world her daughter was in, she didn't stand a chance.

Julia turned and ran towards her car. Thankfully, she'd not locked the door, so she was inside in a couple of seconds. She slammed it behind her and locked it, then fumbled in her pocket for her keys.

They weren't there.

She put on the cabin light and looked around. She checked her coat pockets again, then patted her jeans. Nothing.

There was a knock on the window. The pock-marked boy had his face pressed to the glass. He waggled his tongue from side to side in a gross imitation of oral sex.

'Well, well,' he said, his voice faint through the window. 'Seems you might have a little problem, doesn't it?'

iv.

He pulled his face back an inch from the window. There was a smear where his lips had been pressed to the glass.

'Want these?' He held up Julia's car keys. 'Dropped 'em, didn't you?'

'Give them to me,' Julia said.

'Open your door. They're all yours.'

She picked up her phone. 'I'm calling the police.'

The boy shrugged. 'I've done nowt wrong,' he said.

She dialled 999, her eyes fixed on the boy's pock-marked face. She thought he would leave now that she had the phone to her ear, but whether he did or not she wanted the police there. She was not getting out of the car on her own.

The boy examined the keys. He held a Yale between his thumb and forefinger, the bunch dangling from it.

'This your house key?' He unwound it from the bunch. He threw the rest of the keys into a bush and put the Yale in his pocket. 'Maybe I'll pay you a visit.'

'Hello,' Julia said, when the operator answered. 'Police, please.'

The pock-marked face disappeared. She heard laughter as the boys went back through the gate into the park.

When the police dispatcher came on the line, Julia was shaking so violently she found it hard to keep the phone to her ear.

'I need help,' she said. 'I'm at Queen Mary's Park.'

One of the police officers found the house key by the roundabout, where the pock-marked boy must have discarded it. He handed it to Julia. She didn't like to touch it. It felt contaminated.

'Looks like they were just trying to scare you,' he said. 'A lot of them are like that. Big talkers.'

He took out his notepad. 'Can you describe them?' he asked.

Julia had a clear picture – a picture she thought she wouldn't forget in a hurry – of a sneering, acne-scarred face at her car window. She described it to the officer.

'Sounds like Bobby Myler,' he said. 'And sounds like the kind of stunt he'd pull.'

'You know him?' Julia asked.

'He's what we call "known to the police"', the other officer said. 'In other words he's a bloody yob who's been in trouble since he first drew breath.'

'Can you arrest him then?' Julia said.

The officer pursed his lips. 'What did he actually do?' he said. 'He was an offensive little turd, for sure, but he didn't touch you. And you dropped your keys.'

'So he just gets away with it?'

'I'm afraid so. I'm sorry. I wish it were different, I really do.' The officer folded his notebook open. 'Just for the record,' he said. 'What's your name?'

'Julia Crowne.'

'And what brought you to the park at this time of the morning?'

'I'm looking for my daughter.'

His hand paused mid-word and he looked at her. 'That's your daughter? The little girl who's missing?'

'Yes,' Julia said. 'I couldn't sleep.'

He nodded. 'There are a lot of people looking,' he said. 'We'll find her, Mrs Crowne.'

He did a good job of reassuring. Julia supposed he'd had plenty of practice. But she didn't believe him. In between hearing that she was Mrs Crowne, mother of Anna Crowne, and his smile of professional reassurance, there was a gap. It was a fraction of a second, but it was enough for an emotion to cross his face, and it was the worst emotion a mother in her position could witness: it was pity.

So it's you who's going through hell, his expression said. *God help you.*

And then it was gone, replaced by that studied reassurance, but she'd seen it. The same thing had happened once before so she knew what she was looking for. The first time she'd been pregnant she and Brian had gone to a gynaecologist for the first scan. A nervous first-timer, she'd pressed for it as early as possible, and they'd gone at eleven weeks.

Well, the doctor, a woman in her fifties who smelled vaguely of cigarette smoke, had said, *the baby is due on February 3rd*.

No, Julia replied, *it's mid-January. I got pregnant on April 24th. I was ovulating then.*

Foetal development is uniform in the first twelve weeks, the doctor said, *so we can tell the age from the size, give or take a few days on either side. So we can predict the due date accurately. You probably got pregnant some other day. You can get pregnant at any time in the cycle. It's less likely, but possible.*

She was wrong. Julia knew exactly what the age of the foetus was, because it had taken over a year for her to get pregnant and she had been monitoring the dates of her ovulation and ensuring that they had sex around those dates, and then she noted it all down. On this occasion, she had left on a work trip the week after she had ovulated, so she knew precisely the day she had got pregnant.

She explained this to the doctor, and for a second the mask slipped and she saw concern on the doctor's face, the kind of puzzled concern that meant something was wrong, and then the professional countenance reasserted itself.

Let's plan for Feb 3rd, she said, *and if baby comes early, then so much the better.*

From then on, she had a bad feeling about her pregnancy. Two weeks later, she miscarried.

And now she had the same bad feeling again.

v.

It was light when she pulled up outside the house. The parking space she'd left was taken by a red Toyota Matrix. Her mother-in-law, Dr Edna Crowne, eminent cardiologist (retired), St Hugh's College, Oxford alumna, self-elected family matriarch and all round pain in the backside, was visiting.

Edna would never admit it – possibly not even to herself – but Brian was a disappointment to her. Edna viewed herself as one of the great and good of the country, and, by extension (since England was self-evidently the greatest country on earth), of the human race. People like Edna were superior in intellect, class, and judgement. They knew better than other people about … well, about everything. Public policy, legal affairs, moral issues: Edna's opinion was the final word.

It was also the final word on matters such as, how to bring up a child, and, specifically, her grandchild. Edna saw no distinction in terms of decision-making authority between a mother and a grandmother. She had as much claim on Anna as Julia, and much more than Brian had. This was why Anna was at a private school in the first place: Julia hadn't ever considered it until Edna raised it at Anna's third birthday party.

We should think about what schools (Julia had noted the plural) *Anna should attend*, Edna mentioned, a slice of sticky pink birthday cake untouched on the paper plate in front of her.

The local one, Julia replied.

Edna gave a thin smile. *What about private education? It's so much more – effective.*

It would set her apart from her local friends, Julia said.

That's rather the point, Edna replied. *It puts her on a different path.*

I don't know, Julia said. *I need to think about it.*

But you do agree private education is better, don't you? There's a reason why the professions – at the higher levels, of course – are filled with people who went to good schools and universities.

Not all the good schools are private, Julia said. *I went to state school and I'm a lawyer.*

In a small town. Which is a fine achievement, but it's hardly one of the magic circle firms. You see my point?

Julia mainly wanted to punch her, but she nodded. *I suppose. But anyway, we can't afford it.*

Edna had been waiting for this. *I'll pay*, she said. *I want the best for my granddaughter.*

And so Julia had ended up going along with it. It was hard to argue against logic that ran thus: good parents give their children the best they can afford; Edna will pay for private education, which is better for the child, therefore you should send her to private school. Edna made it seem as though sending her elsewhere was wilful neglect.

Julia wanted to point out that an expensive education – a Jesuit boarding school in Lancashire and then Warwick University – hadn't put Brian on a path to a magic circle law firm. He was a junior school teacher, which, as far as most people were concerned, was a fine thing to be, but it did not fit with Edna's view of success. Edna didn't say so, but she thought her son was soft and lacking in ambition, and she didn't intend for her granddaughter to inherit the same vices.

For Anna was the only one she had left. Amelie and Colin, the children of Simon and Laura, lived in Portland, Oregon, where Laura had grown up. Simon was older than Brian, and had left the UK with his family the year after Jim Crowne had disappeared. They didn't hear much from him, apart from an occasional email to Brian.

It was another thing in the family that wasn't talked about. Julia didn't think she had ever heard Edna say Simon's name. She knew from Brian that Laura and Edna did not get on, and that Edna blamed Laura for Simon moving away; a defeat which must have hurt Edna deeply, not only – or even mainly – because her son was gone, but because she lost. And with Simon gone that left Edna with Julia, Brian, and Anna.

Not that Edna liked Julia. As far as his mother was concerned Brian had married badly. This was not speculation on Julia's part. She knew because Edna had told her in a prenuptial attempt to stop the wedding taking place.

You won't be happy. You think he's like you, but he's not.

We love each other, Edna, whatever our backgrounds. He doesn't need some horsey girl with a boarding school education and BBC English. Meaning: he doesn't need someone like you.

Oh, I'd prefer it if he married someone like that, darling, I really would. But that's not what I'm talking about now. This is not about what he needs, darling. It's what you *need. He won't be enough for you.*

At the time, Julia had thought she was saying it because she thought it might prove effective, rather than because she believed it; now, she realized that Edna was right.

And Edna knew something about unsuitable couples getting married. Julia had never understood how she and Jim had fallen for each other. He was a warm, considerate man, charming and handsome. It was easy to imagine a younger woman falling for him; Julia had entertained a few fantasies about him herself, in the early days of her and Brian's relationship. Edna, however, was stern and upright and cold. They did not fit together. No wonder he left.

Warm as he was, he was nonetheless a distant father. He was dedicated to his grammar school and he gave himself to his work, at which he was very good. He was loved by the pupils, alumni and, for the most part, the staff; known for his careful and even-handed treatment of all those under his professional responsibility, and for his brisk dedication to their welfare. Jim Crowne never turned away from a prospective and deserving pupil in need – whatever their situation – and would use all the resources at his disposal to help them: arguing with the education authorities for more funding if he felt that more pupils deserved a place at the school, or leaning on alumni for donations to ensure that no child missed out on the school trips to Marrakech and Kiev and Hanoi that he made a central part of the school's wider curriculum. As he was fond of saying, he was in the business of education, which meant he prepared kids for the world and not to pass exams. Jim Crowne was not fond of buzzwords, but he ensured that his school lived out the full meaning of the modern passion for 'equality of opportunity'. And all he asked in return was that the pupils grasped those opportunities. He had no time for those that didn't.

It was a shame that, like so many people who devote themselves to public service, he did not find time to devote the same attention to his own offspring, and Brian had often claimed that he only ever knew his father the head teacher, and not his father the man.

Anyway, all that belonged to the past. She had plenty to deal with in the here and now.

She opened her car door. Her feet were cold and she was hungry. She had a craving for a cup of sweet tea.

Edna was in the kitchen with Brian. She looked up as Julia entered. 'Here you are,' she said. 'We were starting to worry. Thank God.'

'Here I am,' Julia said.

'I'm not going to beat around the bush,' Edna said. She was proud of the lack of beating around the bush in her life, was Edna. 'I know things haven't always been perfect between us, but now is the time for us to pull together as a family. We can resolve any differences when Anna is back among us.'

She stood up and took Julia's hands between hers. Her fingers were cold and white, bloodless. 'Julia,' she said. 'We can get through this.' She placed a palm on Julia's cheek, then pulled her into a loose, but still awkward, embrace. Julia was glad when it was over. 'We can.'

Whatever she'd expected from Edna, it wasn't this. Her mother-in-law had not hugged her – if hug was the word – since the wedding day, and that hug was for the guests as much as it was for Julia, if it was for Julia at all. Still, Julia was glad. The last thing she needed right now was Edna telling her she was a foul and irresponsible parent.

'Thanks, Edna' she said. 'I appreciate it.'

'The police called,' Brian said. 'There's a press conference at noon.'

'So soon?' Julia said. 'She's only been gone one night.'

The news is out there, The cops said it might help get more people looking. Someone might have seen something.'

'And we have to be there?' Julia asked.

Brian nodded, his face drawn, his eyes on her, his expression unguarded. For a moment she was looking at the man she had fallen in love with, the father of her child, and she leaned forward and put her hand on his.

He pulled it away.

'Yes,' he said. 'They reckon that an appeal from the parents is best. It gets people's attention.'

Gets people's attention.

This was her life now. She was a parent whose kid was missing. Who made tearful appeals on the television.

It was impossible; she couldn't believe it was happening. She couldn't believe that she was going to have to shower and dress and deal with a roomful of cameras and reporters. She didn't want to; it made it all seem so real, so incontrovertible. Some part of her still hoped it was all a mistake; that she would open Anna's bedroom door and find her daughter fast asleep in her bed, and this would all be over. That was what she wanted. Not press conferences.

She closed her eyes. She felt dizzy and sick and she pushed her tea away.

She had to do it. If it brought Anna's return any closer, she had to do it, but she could not do it alone. She picked up her mobile phone and called the only friend who could get her through this.

vi.

DI Wynne sat on the edge of the armchair. Julia was on the sofa.

'I apologize for this,' she said. 'But it *is* a necessity. In any case like this we have to speak to the parents. I'm not suggesting that you are responsible, Mrs Crowne, but we have to examine every angle.'

Julia looked at her and almost laughed. 'Am I a suspect?'

'No. But we need to interview you. Mr Crowne, too. And your mother-in-law. Anybody who is connected to Anna.'

'Fine,' Julia said. 'Go ahead.'

DI Wynne nodded. 'Take me through the events of the day,' she said. 'In as much detail as you can.'

Julia paused, then began to recount what had happened: the meeting that overran, the dead phone, the dash to the school. Wynne listened intently, occasionally making notes.

'Would you say that your marriage to Mr Crowne is healthy?' she asked.

Julia shook her head. 'No. We're having some problems.'

'What kind of problems?'

'It's more or less over,' Julia said. 'We've kind of grown apart.'

Wynne pursed her lips. 'Is it an equal decision?' she asked.

'No,' Julia said. 'It's more my decision.'

'I see.' Wynne paused. 'Is Mr Crowne taking it well, would you say?'

Julia sat back. She frowned. 'Are you suggesting Brian was behind this? He was at school.'

'No,' Wynne said. 'I'm not suggesting that. Just asking questions.' She closed her notebook. 'That's all. Thank you, Mrs Crowne.'

As Julia left the living room she passed Brian heading towards DI Wynne.

'Your turn,' she said.

vii.

Thirty minutes later Gill – a red-haired Scouser with a perpetual smile and a nervous energy that was infectious – was sitting beside her on the sofa.

91

'It'll be ok,' she said. '*You'll* be ok.'

'It just makes it so real,' Julia said. 'All of a sudden we're those parents, the ones on the TV doing the press conference. I don't know how I can pull it together. I can't even think, Gill. I'm either numb or thinking of Anna, of where she could be, who might have her—'

Her voice trailed off. There were brief moments when she managed to distract herself enough to achieve a kind of blankness, but they didn't last. Before long the panic returned. She felt as if she was standing on a stormy beach trying to beat back the waves: it was impossible, they just kept coming, wave after wave, pounding her into submission. It was all she could do to keep on breathing.

'You can do it,' Gill said. 'And you have to. I'll be there. I'll get you through it.'

If anyone could, it was Gill. She was one of those people who believe that they can do anything, and because they believe it they make it true. Julia first met her at a postnatal Yoga class; for Julia, it was a foray into exercise aimed solely at removing the baby weight. For Gill it was a gentle re-introduction to exercise aimed solely at getting her ready to return to Body Blast Boot Camp classes and marathon training.

When Gill was ready to move on from postnatal Yoga, she persuaded Julia to graduate with her. After one of the classes, her back aching, her face blotchy and red, Julia swore that she would never go back to another. After the second, she wondered if she might try one more.

After the third, she was, if not exactly hooked, at least able to muster up the enthusiasm to get out of the house and into the gym two or three times a week.

She ended up in pretty good shape, flattish stomach, toned thighs, actual biceps, but then the pressure of work and motherhood took its toll, and the gym visits became once a week then once a month then not at all.

Gill, of course, stuck with it. For her it was a way of life, one of the things that she made sure she found time for. Work (she was a buyer for a light bulb manufacturer), her twin boys, exercise, and her husband, Trevor: these were her priorities and she took care of them all. It was made easier by the fact that Trevor, a triathlete plumber, was more or less the perfect husband. He insisted that they go out as a couple for dinner once a month, a rule he had not broken even when the twins were only a month old, scooping Gill out of the door between feeds for a rapid fire meal at a sushi restaurant. Add to this his habit of bringing home flowers every Friday – so that his sons would learn good habits when it came to looking after their mum – and his refusal to let her pay for anything when they were out, which was ridiculous as Gill earned as much as him and they shared a bank account, and he was pretty much as good as it got. He was old-fashioned, and Gill teased him for it, but he was also charming and romantic and Gill adored him.

'She's out there,' Julia said. 'My little girl. Somewhere in the world. I can't tell you how it feels to know that she might be suffering.'

'I can't imagine,' Gill said. 'I don't want to. But she'll come back, Julia. You have to keep believing that.'

'And it was my fault,' Julia said. 'If I hadn't been late—'

'It's not your fault,' Gill said. 'It isn't. It was a mistake. You couldn't have known this would happen. We all make mistakes, Julia.'

'I can't stop thinking about it. I can't stop thinking *if only*. If only I'd charged my phone. If only I'd left the meeting earlier. I could have stopped this. It's hard to live with that knowledge.'

'I bet it is,' Gill said. 'But that's not the same as it being your fault. You aren't responsible for the actions of whatever sick bastard took your daughter. There are always *if onlys*, Julia, always. But just remember: this is not your fault.'

Gill believed it, Julia could see. The problem was that she found it hard to agree.

'And now,' Gill continued, 'you have a chance to do something to help fix it. Come on. Let's get ready for this press conference.'

At the police station, Julia and Brian followed DI Wynne into an office. She motioned for them to sit down.

'Let me give you an update,' she said. 'Although I'm afraid that there isn't all that much to say.' She sat forward, her arms folded, her elbows resting on her desk. It was spotless, any paperwork filed away. 'We had officers out all night, as well as the dog teams. I have to say that they are pretty effective at picking up a scent, but there was nothing.'

'What next?' Brian asked.

'We keep looking. Something might show up – some clothing, a shoe, a schoolbook. And … ' she paused, and swallowed, 'we deployed the dive teams this morning. They're searching local waterways. Canals, ponds, rivers.'

Julia felt light-headed, the edges of her vision dissolving into stars. She blinked, trying to dismiss the image of a small, muddied corpse being dragged from a silted canal. She swayed, and gripped the edge of her chair for support.

'Are you all right, Mrs Crowne?' Wynne asked.

'Yes,' Julia said, although she knew she was far from all right. 'I just need a moment.'

'Would you like a drink? A cup of tea? Coffee?'

'Yes,' she said. 'Coffee. Sweet, please.'

DI Wynne got to her feet. 'I'll get it,' she said. 'And I'm sorry, Mr and Mrs Crowne, I really am. But we're doing all we can.'

Julia didn't doubt it. She just hoped it was enough.

DI Wynne led them down a brightly lit corridor towards a heavy door, at which she paused and turned to face them.

'Are you ready?' Her expression was composed and serious, her tone professional. When neither Julia nor Brian answered, she carried on. 'Don't worry. It'll be fine.'

Then she opened the door and ushered them into the room.

It was quite a small room, but it was very full. There were four chairs behind a long table on which were four glasses of water and four microphones. The main body of the room was heaving with people. Julia felt sick at the thought that all these people were here for the same thing: news of Anna. All the plastic folding chairs were taken and people were standing at the back; the doors to the outside were open so that a few more could cram in. There was a murmur of chatter but as soon as they emerged, the room fell silent, but only for a moment: the silence was followed by an explosion of flashes and shutter clicks.

Once her nausea passed, Julia felt oddly detached, almost as though she was an actor, part of a story, and a good story at that: Julia remembered reading them herself, remembered the frisson of vicarious anguish – *Oh, how awful, I can't imagine what they are going through* – tinged with a ghoulish interest and a smugness that it would never happen to her. She would never let it.

How quickly the world turned. How quickly you could find that *you* were the story, that things happened whether you let them or not, that life was not so easily tamed.

Detective Inspector Wynne pulled out a chair and Julia sat down. Brian sat on her left, his hands fidgeting in his lap. Wynne took a seat on her right. The fourth chair remained unoccupied. Julia wondered whether someone had failed to show up, or whether the room was always set up like this.

Her detachment came to an abrupt end when DI Wynne began to speak.

'Mr and Mrs Crowne will be reading a statement,' she said. 'They will not be taking questions. Thank you for respecting that at a difficult time.' She looked at Julia. 'Ok,' she said, 'whenever you're ready.'

There was a piece of paper on the table in front of her with the statement on it. The words were printed in larger than usual type. She stared at them. The black letters did not make any sense.

'Mrs Crowne?' DI Wynne said.

Julia looked back at the piece of paper. She focused on the first word, then started to speak.

'Yesterday, our daughter, Anna, went missing. She may have strayed from the school gates or she may have been taken. Anna is five—' her voice broke, and she looked up at the ceiling, struggling to stop the tears that were forming. 'Anna is five, and is the light of our lives. If you have seen her or seen anything that might give the police a lead as to her whereabouts, then please come forwards, however small or trivial it may seem.'

She lowered the paper. The words felt impersonal, meaningless. Besides, they didn't address the one person she needed to reach.

'If you have her,' she said, 'if you're watching this, and you are the person who took her, then please bring her back. Bring her back to her home. Just bring her back and this will all be over. I won't do anything to you. You can go free. I promise you that. I won't let anyone do anything to you. I don't care about justice or anything like that. I just want my daughter back.'

'Please,' Brian said next to her, his voice barely audible. 'Please.'

There was silence in the room, then a flash went off.

'Mr and Mrs Crowne,' a woman shouted, from the back of the room. 'Is there any suggestion of negligence on the part of the school?'

Not on the part of the school, Julia thought, but certainly on the part of the mother. That would be their next question. She felt a flush spread on her neck. It always happened when she felt under pressure, or caught out, or embarrassed. She hated it. It meant that she could never hide her feelings. If she said something stupid in a meeting or didn't know the answer to a question she should have done then she could never brazen it out. Instead a hot, red bloom would cover her neck and chest and give her away.

She opened her mouth to speak – feeling as though she had to come up with some kind of answer was the other thing that she did when she was uncomfortable – but DI Wynne gestured to her to sit back, and leaned towards the microphone.

'No questions,' she said. 'Thank you for your time.' She stood up and put her hand on Julia's arm. She spoke in a low voice.

'We can go now,' she said. 'Well done.'

*

Julia, Brian, and the detective sat in an office in the police station. There were three styrofoam cups of coffee on the table in front of them. DI Wynne added some sugar and powdered milk to hers and stirred it with a plastic stirrer.

'We reviewed the CCTV footage,' she said. 'I'm afraid there isn't a lot to go on.'

'Is Anna on it?' Julia asked. 'Do you see her?'

'Yes, she is.'

'Can I see it? 'I'd like to watch it myself, if possible.'

Wynne nodded. 'Of course. Give me a minute.' She stood up and leaned into the corridor and called out to someone. They had a brief conversation, then she turned back to Julia and Brian. 'Come with me.'

viii.

The footage was good. Black and white, but high resolution. Julia had been expecting some grainy, indistinct images, but these were clear. The camera was trained on the cast iron gate. Julia guessed it was mounted above the school door. She watched the parents standing around, chatting or checking their phones.

I should be there, she thought. *If I was part of this film then none of this would be happening.*

She pictured herself appearing in the image from the left, smiling at one of the other parents, exchanging greetings and some innocuous pleasantries, then facing the school, as she had done so many times, and waiting for the door to open, for the scrum of children to appear, accompanied by their teachers, and make their way to the gates where their parents waited.

It was still a thrill, that moment. Still a joy to see her daughter's face after a day apart, and then to kiss her and walk to the car holding her warm hand, and take her home and feed her and bathe her and read to her and love her.

Julia did not appear on the screen. Instead, the door opened and the pupils spilled out, some of them running towards the gates, others walking. Right in the middle was Anna.

She was next to Amelia, her new best friend, but she wasn't talking to her. She was looking at the assembled parents. Looking, Julia realized, for her mum.

Who wasn't there. Who wasn't there to greet her as she stepped over the threshold of the school and into the outside world, into the dangerous, unsafe adult world that had swallowed her up.

The children were accompanied by two teachers, Miss Sanderson and Miss Gregory. Miss Sanderson, a tall, athletic woman in her late thirties was at the front; Miss Gregory, who was in her twenties, and was possibly Anna's favourite person in the world, was at the back.

As she walked through the gates, Miss Gregory looked up and to her right, at one of the mums, who held out a book to her, and said something, perhaps *here's that book I promised you* or *I heard you like Downton. Here's the annual* or *you'd enjoy this, it's a modern classic.*

Miss Gregory leaned over the heads of the children and took the book. She said something to Miss Sanderson, who turned and smiled. Anna was in the corner of the shot, just to the left of the gates, and she looked up at the teacher. Julia's heart lurched at the sight of her daughter's face. She looked puzzled, about to ask the teacher for something, and Julia knew what it was.

It would have saved her.

She's going to ask her where's my mummy? Julia thought. *And if she did, Miss Gregory would have kept her back.*

But Miss Gregory was busy. And a second later, Anna looked to her left, and walked out of the camera's range and out of the world.

So that was how it had happened. The teachers were distracted for a moment, and a moment was all it took.

Julia put her head in her hands. In her mind's eye all she could see was Anna, on the verge of asking where her mummy was, but not doing so. And why not? Was she too polite to interrupt? Did something attract her attention? Is that why she walked away?

'It's not a lot of help,' Wynne said. 'And unfortunately there is no CCTV covering the outside of the school.'

'So this is the school's fault?' Brian said.

'I couldn't say.' Wynne sipped her coffee. 'They could have a better security system, but then that's always true. No system is perfect. We like to think that it is, but there's always a risk. That's why we need them in the first place.'

'Yes,' Brian agreed, 'but they should have had more cameras, surely! And more teachers accompanying the kids!'

'I understand your frustration, but that's a matter for you and the school, Mr Crowne,' Wynne said. 'The problem I have is that Anna vanishes from the CCTV footage and at that point we lose track of her.'

'Why?' Julia asked. 'Why would she walk off like that?'

'I don't know,' Wynne replied. 'There are many explanations. Perhaps she thought you – or someone – might be parked up the road. Or maybe she saw a dog and went to stroke it, or maybe she just felt like it. The problem is that it only takes a few seconds, and – well, anything can happen.'

'Have you interviewed the other parents?' Julia asked. She felt unnaturally calm. Perhaps it was the exhaustion, perhaps the shock of seeing Anna on CCTV.

'Yes. A couple of them think they saw Anna leaving the school, but they can't be sure.' Wynne said.

'So she was seen?' Julia persisted. 'Who saw her?'

'Two of the mums said they thought they had seen her, standing there, but they just assumed that someone was there to meet her.'

'They didn't check on her?' Brian asked, his voice rising. 'They saw that she was alone and they didn't bother to check?'

DI Wynne sipped her coffee. 'We mentioned that to them. They said that they were focused on getting their children in the car and buckled up and, when they'd done that, Anna was gone. They didn't give it too much thought. They just assumed she'd been picked up as normal.'

Picked up as normal.

The words hung in the room like an accusation. DI Wynne shifted uncomfortably in her chair, evidently aware how it had sounded; Brian looked out of the window.

Julia pushed her coffee away. It was cold, undrunk since DI Wynne had brought it for her. Since Anna's disappearance, the smell of food and drink had made her nauseous. Even though she'd seen the CCTV, she had her own image of what had happened: Anna walking out of the gates, looking around for her mum, or dad, or grandma, some of the other parents glancing at her, then settling on their own kids, bending down to kiss them and ask them how the day had gone while Anna moved to the edge of the crowd, still searching for her parents.

And maybe someone taking notice who shouldn't have and asking her if she was ok, then taking her hand and walking away with her before anyone could notice.

And it was her fault. Never mind the school. Maybe they could have done more, but at root it was her fault. If she had been there, then it wouldn't have happened. She knew Brian would try to blame them, try and sue them, but what was the point? It wouldn't bring Anna back.

She began to cry, then looked away, embarrassed at her grief. She had no right to it because she had only herself to blame.

'Mrs Crowne,' DI Wynne said. 'We can stop if you need to, but there are a couple of other things I wanted to mention.'

'I'm fine,' Julia said. 'Keep going.'

Wynne looked at Brian. 'I was wondering whether you have any more information on your father's whereabouts? We haven't been able to trace him.'

'No,' Brian said. 'I asked Mum. She doesn't have an address for him.'

Wynne nodded slowly. 'I see. We would really like to interview your father.'

'Are you saying my father is a suspect?' Brian said. 'That's ridiculous!'

'No,' Wynne replied. 'I'm not suggesting that. But we would like to talk to him. Anything – irregular – is of interest to us. So if you do you have any information that might be of use, we would appreciate it.'

Julia looked at Brian. He stared at the floor. If he was not going to say anything she was. If it helped get Anna back she had no choice.

'He may have run away with someone,' she said. 'A teacher at the school. She went at the same time. I don't know her name.'

'That's fine,' Wynne said. 'That should give us enough to go on. We'll be able to find out who she was.'

Brian gave Julia a hard, unforgiving look, then turned to DI Wynne. 'Anything else?' he said.

'One other thing,' Wynne responded. 'We may get crank callers. People who claim to have seen Anna or even to have her in their custody. Obviously we will follow every lead, but we need something we can use to identify who might be a legitimate caller.'

'What do you mean?' asked Brian. 'You expect people to give you false information?'

The detective nodded. 'It often happens,' she said. 'People leave anonymous tip-offs claiming to have seen a missing person, or sometimes they claim to be the perpetrator.'

'Why?' Brian asked. 'Why would they do that?'

'I don't know,' Wynne said. 'Some people have nothing better to do. So we tend to hold back a piece of information.'

'Like what?' Julia said.

'Something they would only know if they were with Anna.'

Julia nodded. 'She has a birthmark,' she said. 'It's a rough circle, about the size of a ten pence piece. On her right hip.'

She could picture it clearly. When Anna was first born she had disliked it as a sign of imperfection. She'd gone so far as to ask a doctor whether it could be removed, and the doctor had said it could, but she might want to think about it before doing anything, especially, as it was in a place that was normally hidden. He told her that in some cultures birthmarks were seen as signs of divinity, as though the bearer had been touched by God and marked out for special things. Julia had gone home and thought it over and decided to leave it. Whatever it was

it was part of her daughter and she decided not to inter-
fere with it. Over the years she had grown to almost like
it; many times when Anna was in nappies she had kissed
it before covering it up. It was their secret, known only
to them.

And now the birthmark, that private thing in a place
normally hidden, was now an *identifying mark*. This one
fact represented everything that was wrong. It made
everything hard and real and irrevocable and Julia could
no longer hold herself back.

She started to cry, and she did not know how she
would ever stop.

4

The Second Day

i.

You found it a bit pathetic, as well as, frankly, stupid: *You can go free. I promise you that. I won't let anyone do anything to you. I don't care about justice or anything like that. I just want my daughter back.*

You would never have done that, never have appeared so weak. How did she think that a person who could plan and then implement what you have done – to take a child in broad daylight – would be impressed by such a display of weakness? The girl's mother should have appeared strong, threatening, powerful; that might have worried you, made you fear her. Respect her, even. But that snivelling display? Why would you care about someone like that? And the father? Even worse.

It actually had the opposite effect. It just proved that

you were right, that what you had done was for the best. Was a *necessary evil*.

Did she really think that she could sway you – *you* – with her wet-eyed entreaties? Did she think that you would see her on television and think to yourself *oh, the mother wants her daughter back, I never thought of that, better pop out and drop her off back home, then*? Did she think that you had done all this, just to hand the girl back? What kind of fool was she?

The kind that lost a daughter in the first place.

The daughter. Still there, drugged, silent. Beautiful.

Her time was coming. It would be a little while yet, but not too much longer, at least, you hoped not. It was a shame to see her like this, locked up like some kind of trophy animal, although she would know nothing of it, have no memories of it. There was not much you could give her, but that, at least, was in your gift.

As for you? You keep on waiting, waiting for the right moment to come.

And when it does, you will act. You will end this.

ii.

In an emotional press conference yesterday, the parents of missing five-year-old Anna Crowne appealed to any members of the public who might have information about the disappearance of their daughter to come forward. Mrs Julia Crowne also made a direct plea to any potential kidnappers, saying 'And if you have her, if you're watching this, then please bring her back. Bring her back to her home. Just bring her back and this will all be over. I won't do anything to you. You can go free. I don't care. I just want my daughter back.'

Speaking after the press conference, a spokesperson for the police said that there were few leads at present but that the investigation would continue to examine the evidence.

When questioned as to how a young girl could go missing in broad daylight without anyone noticing, the spokesperson said that the police had no comment to make at this stage. The spokesperson also declined to comment on speculation that the police were treating this as an abduction case, rather than a simple disappearance.

Henry Collins, a former major in the Army who now specializes in abductions, claimed that it was often the case that abductions took place in the most routine of circumstances.

'People will notice something out of the ordinary,' he said. 'Perhaps a child alone at night or leaving a school outside of normal hours. But there is nothing exceptional about a child and an adult leaving a school together at the end of the day. Provided that the child was not being taken against its will then many people would simply not notice this.' He added that this was especially true in today's world. 'A generation ago people would have known all the other mothers at the school gates and *a strange face would have stuck out. Nowadays there are all sorts of people picking up children – nannies, babysitters, friends, grandparents – and people have become accustomed to new faces at the school gates.'*

When asked about Anna's possible whereabouts, Collins was pessimistic.

'She could be anywhere by now,' he said. 'Eastern Europe is the likeliest destination, but there is no way of knowing for sure. The police will have descriptions of Anna out at every major port and airport, but European borders are porous and she could be easily—'

Julia closed the browser. The story was all over the internet. And it wasn't just in the UK. It was all over the world. It seemed that humanity shared a common interest in missing children.

The efforts of the police were also international. DI Wynne informed her that across Europe police forces were actively engaged in searching for Anna, which, the detective explained, meant that they were monitoring borders more closely, checking the internet for any relevant information and extending feelers into their intelligence networks – informers, grasses, whoever they knew – for signs of any unusual activity. There was every chance that they would find Anna, she said. Every chance.

Julia suspected the detective had thought that knowledge of the scale of the effort would bring comfort. It didn't. It brought terror. It highlighted how serious this was, how many countries Anna could be in by now. It brought home just exactly what kind of people were involved in kidnapping children, and reminded Julia of the fates that could have befallen her daughter: slavery, sexual abuse, murder.

When she had followed similar news stories in the past she had thought mainly of the parents' grief at their loss, assumed it was like the death of a child. Now she was in that position she saw that it was much worse. Not only did she have to face the sense of loss, she also had to come to terms with what Anna might be suffering, and that was worse, infinitely worse. To think of her daughter, so young, so perfect, so innocent, in the hands of a paedophile gang was a torture worse than any grief; it made her wish that Anna had been sold to a rich, childless couple who would at least love her. There was no respite. If she wasn't grieving for herself, she was torn apart with worry for Anna. Each was like an open sore, the other the salt that was rubbed in. It was pulling her apart.

Julia also understood that she was powerless. There was nothing she could do. It was not a question of knocking on doors or searching house by house in the neighbourhood. The idea that Anna's destiny was in her hands was a romantic fiction.

All she could do was wait and try not to read the news. It just made it worse.

Which didn't stop Brian. He barely looked up from his laptop, other than to replenish his whisky glass. She'd asked him about it; he said he was looking for Anna. At first Julia had not understood, so she'd pressed for details.

Chat rooms, he said. *Places in the dark recesses of the internet, places where some men go to find what they want. I might find her there.*

Julia had a feeling that he might. But that if he did, he might wish he hadn't.

iii.

Julia closed the front door behind her. She couldn't stay in the house any longer, couldn't abide the silence, broken only by the tapping of Brian's fingers on the keyboard of his laptop as he performed his pointless cyber-search.

Listening to it infuriated her. Was that all he could think of to do? But then what was she doing? What could anyone do?

She decided to go to the park. Perhaps there was a corner that had not been searched, a bush under which Anna was now sleeping, still in her school uniform, the uniform that Edna had suggested they buy a few sizes too big for her so that she would grow into it.

Julia had hated the uniform, hated the specialist private school outfitters where they bought it, hated that they were doing what Edna suggested and that her daughter would look ridiculous in an outsized blazer and skirt. Now though, all she wanted was for Anna to grow into her uniform. She would have given anything to see that happen.

112

The first day at Westwood School she and Brian had dropped Anna off together. They'd walked her to her classroom, admired her desk, kissed her goodbye. She was fine, confident and outgoing, secure in their love. She waved them a breezy farewell; they were not handling it so well. Julia had cried as she left, cried to see her little girl growing up, tears both of sadness and pride.

This time, Brian did not hug her.

She'll be fine, he said. *See you after work. You're picking her up?*

Julia nodded, and off he went. That might have been the first time she realized it was over between them, that whatever separated them was unbridgeable, that, most damning of all, she simply didn't love him.

She walked to the end of her street, and, as she turned into the main road, she passed a man, his springer spaniel wet with sweat yet still straining at the lead. He nodded and smiled, then his face froze as he realized who she was. She saw him hesitate, almost miss a step, then carry on, looking ahead. She saw the pity in his eyes.

It was no surprise that he recognized her; after all her face was all over the news. She was famous, but it was a strange kind of fame. It was not the kind that drew people to you, that caused them to approach with a pen and paper and tell you they loved your show, or well-played at the weekend, and then ask for your autograph; it was a rare kind that drew people's stares but not their company. She knew that no one would approach her. They would just watch her and pity her.

There she is, searching for her daughter, they'd be thinking. *But it's pointless. That little girl is long gone.*

Julia didn't care if people thought her search was pointless. She agreed. She didn't think she would come across Anna huddled in a bush, but that wasn't the point. She just didn't want to be at home, didn't want to be still. Motion, however pointless, was still motion.

The park sloped down to a shallow river. Some civic-minded person at one point had created a pebble beach by the bank, and she headed for it.

The river water was clear and moved quickly, swirling and eddying in random-seeming patterns. For a second she was lost in them, but then that momentary peace was shattered by a memory of Anna playing by the water when she was first walking. She had wanted to go in and had kept on waddling towards the river bank. Julia and Brian had stopped her, until Brian shrugged and took off his and her shoes.

Go on then, he said. *If you insist.*

Then he and Anna had walked into the river. Julia smiled at the memory of Anna's expression when she stepped into the cold water – shock, delight, fear and, most of all, wonder at this new sensation, at this new vista the world had to offer.

She had stripped off her shoes and socks and joined them, the three of them kicking the river water into the air.

I'll read her Tarka the Otter, Brian said. *When she's old enough. She can imagine it taking place here,* he said.

114

We'll come down and look for Tarka. I'll buy her some binoculars and we can identify the birds and plants and animals. We can have a family picnic. It'll be fantastic.

She had loved him at that moment. She could recall the feeling. At that moment she had thought he was the best dad in the world, the only man she ever could have imagined being her husband and the father of her children. She'd pictured Anna and her dad, searching for Tarka.

It wasn't going to happen now. There'd be no more family picnics. And there'd be no *Tarka the Otter* for Anna.

Julia felt the tears on her cheeks. She wanted, suddenly, to be in the water, to connect with the memory of her daughter in some physical way. She bent down and unlaced her trainers, then pulled off her socks. She didn't bother to roll up her jeans. They could dry later. Then she stepped into the river.

The water was colder than she remembered; the sensation less pleasant. The rocks were slippery and menacing beneath her feet. She waded out to the middle of the river, the water level rising to her knees. She shifted her feet, and as she did so she felt a sharp pain.

She looked down. She was standing on a broken beer bottle. Blood ballooned darkly around her foot. She watched it swirl away in the river current.

I wonder if fish will eat it, she thought.

She left her foot there, intrigued by the patterns the blood made, enjoying the sharp pain. It felt real, immediate. She was interrupted by her phone ringing. She pulled it from her back pocket.

'Hello,' she said.

It was DI Wynne. 'Mrs Crowne,' she said. 'Do you have a moment?'

I have the rest of my life, Julia thought.

'Yes,' she said. She stared at her foot. More blood was leaking from it. She hoped she wouldn't need stitches.

'We might have a lead,' the detective said. 'It seems that a former janitor at the school has gone missing.'

Julia looked up. The world sharpened into focus. 'What?' she said. 'Who is it?'

'He retired last year,' Wynne said. 'He'd only been at the school for the two years before that. He moved to the area from Dundee. And now he's gone.'

'And you think he took Anna?'

'We don't know for sure. But he's not been seen in his flat for a couple of weeks.'

'So he left before Anna was taken?'

'That's right. He didn't tell anyone where he was going. We're treating it as suspicious, at least until we locate him.'

'Why did he leave Dundee?'

'We don't know. We're looking into it.'

'Have you been in his flat?' Julia asked.

'We have. There's no trace of Anna, or of where he went.'

'It's him,' Julia said. 'I know it.'

'It's too early to say that. 'And I don't want to get your hopes up. But—'

'It has to be him,' Julia said. 'It can't just be a coincidence. It can't.'

116

'I've seen stranger coincidences, Mrs Crowne.'

Julia barely heard her. This was the man who had taken Anna. This was the moment when all this changed, when they started to get somewhere. She imagined him, an old man in a dark flat, scheming, waiting for his chance. Had he selected Anna specifically? Had he been watching her?

Whatever. They were on his trail now.

'Thank you,' she said. 'Call me if there is any news. Any at all.'

'I will,' Wynne agreed.

Julia clicked off her phone and lifted up her foot. A thin red line ran from the base of her little toe to the arch of her foot. Blood beaded along it. She was going to have to get home and put something on it.

iv.

As she turned into her street someone stepped in front of her. It took her a few seconds to realize who it was.

It was Miss Gregory, Anna's teacher. Anna's favourite teacher.

'Mrs Crowne,' she said. Her eyes were glazed with tiredness and she looked like she'd lost weight. 'I came … ' she paused, her mouth open, as though she wanted to speak but could not find the right words. 'I wanted to tell you how sorry I am. About Anna. I didn't want to call; I didn't think it was right. I thought I should come in person.'

Julia remembered the last time she'd seen the teacher. It was on the CCTV footage of the day Anna disappeared.

Miss Gregory had been escorting the children out, laughing and chatting with the parents.

Laughing and chatting when she should have been looking after Anna.

Julia stared at her. Was this woman to blame for her daughter's disappearance? Maybe, but she couldn't summon the energy to be angry at her. She just stared.

The teacher filled the silence. 'Mrs Crowne,' Miss Gregory said. 'You have to know how sorry I am. I can't think of anything other than Anna. I'd give anything to be able to go back. Anything. The school told me not to say anything, but I have to. I have to tell you how sorry I am.'

So the school did not want her to talk to Julia. The lawyer in her recognized that they were probably scared of admitting liability; probably getting ready for a court case. The mother in her didn't care, not yet. There would be time for that later. Time for Westwood School and Miss Gregory to come face to face with what they had done.

'I'm not ready for this,' Julia said. She was suddenly exhausted. 'I know how you must feel, but please just leave me alone.'

'Mrs Crowne, please,' the teacher said. 'This is tearing me apart.'

'What do you want?' Julia asked her. 'What do you want me to do? Say I forgive you? Fine, I forgive you. It doesn't change anything. Anna's still gone. If you were to blame before, you're to blame now. As am I.'

'I don't want you to forgive me,' Miss Gregory said, her voice quavering. 'I don't know what I want. I ... ' she was crying now, on the verge of breaking down, 'I just want to see Anna again.'

The last few words were lost in sobs. Julia looked at Miss Gregory, saw how much this was affecting her, saw how it would scar her for life; maybe drive her out of the profession she loved.

But she did not feel sorry for the teacher. She *could* not. There was only one emotion, one thought that had any purchase on her at all. And that was grief at the loss of her daughter.

She walked past Miss Gregory and headed for her house.

When she got home Edna and Brian were sitting at the kitchen table. Edna had made dinner. She was a good cook; she didn't do it often, but when she did she brought to it the same standards that she applied elsewhere in her life. She wasn't creative in the kitchen, but she also had no fear. She would take on complicated recipes and follow them to the letter, marinating meats overnight, clarifying consommés, baking soufflés. She also used only the best ingredients, which gave her a good start, but nonetheless there was always something a bit joyless about her meals. They were born of grim intensity, not passion, and Julia thought it came across in the final product. Her mother-in-law's food was delicious, yes, but it was also soulless, unsatisfying. There was none of the warmth and comfort of food prepared with slapdash love, just the clinical perfection of the surgeon's knife.

Julia had read once that you could tell how someone would be in the bedroom by the way they danced and the way they cooked. She'd never seen Edna on the dance floor, but her kitchen style made sense: not too often, but do a good job of it when you did.

She'd made a veal stroganoff, soft and easy to eat, and Julia put some on a plate and sat down. She couldn't eat more than a few mouthfuls. She pushed her plate away and laid her knife and fork on it.

'Try and eat,' Edna said. 'You need it to keep your strength up.'

It was the professional advice of a doctor, not the urging of a mother. Julia shook her head.

'I'm fine.'

'Some wine?' There was a bottle on the table, a strong, blood-red Italian. It was half-empty already, most of it drunk by Brian. Julia shook her head again. Her head felt clouded enough already through lack of sleep, without adding alcohol to the mix. Enough of it might help her fall asleep, but it wouldn't keep her asleep; wouldn't chase away the dreams of Anna, and when she woke up in the middle of the night, dry-mouthed and needing a piss, she'd feel even worse.

'I spoke to DI Wynne just now,' she said, as much to break the silence as to share information. 'They have a lead.'

Brian leaned forward, the glass halfway to his mouth. 'Really?'

'There was a janitor at the school. He retired last year – he'd only been there a short while – and he disappeared a couple of weeks ago. No one knows where he is.'

'That seems pretty thin,' Brian said. 'Could just be a coincidence.'

'Could be,' Julia agreed. 'But the police are treating it as suspicious. And it fits, right? Lone male, sixties, moves around the country. I hate to rely on stereotypes, but … '

Brian nodded. He was more alert now, more present. 'I guess. So what next?'

Julia shrugged. 'We wait. But I think this might be it, Brian. I really do.'

'You might be right,' Edna said. 'And I hope to God you are, and that Anna is back here soon.'

There was a long silence as the news sank in. After a few minutes, Brian put his knife and fork down beside his plate. It was still full but it was clear he had finished eating. He looked at Edna, then Anna, then back to Edna. 'I got a phone call today,' he said. 'From Simon.'

Simon. The name echoed around the room.

'Did you?' Edna said, the forced nonchalance in her tone doing little to disguise the tension that rolled off her. 'What did he want?'

'I sent him an email to let him know what happened. He's flying over. He'll be here tomorrow.'

Edna's expression did not change. 'It'll be nice for you to see him.'

Brian didn't reply; he didn't seem to know what to say. Julia broke the silence.

'Is Laura coming?' she asked him.

Brian shook his head. 'She's staying home with the kids.'

'Thank Heaven for small mercies,' Edna said. 'The last thing we need now is her showing up.'

'She's not that bad,' Julia said. She'd only met Laura twice – both early on in her relationship with Brian – and she'd quite liked her. She was funny and irreverent and bursting with self-confidence. She was also very honest, and believed in saying what she thought. She had shared with Julia that she did so on the advice of her therapist, who had told her that holding it in was *just stacking the shelves of your closet with problems for the future.*

'She's worse,' Edna said. 'She's poison.'

Despite the situation, Julia laughed. 'Oh, come on,' she said. 'She's not that bad. You and she didn't see eye to eye, that's all.'

'Julia,' Edna said. 'I suggest you refrain from commenting on things about which you know nothing.'

'So what did she do that was so bad?' Julia asked.

Edna leaned back in her chair. 'She convinced my son that he should leave me. That I was a – how did she put it? – a source of *negative energy* in his life. And, even worse, she shared this opinion with others. People outside the family.'

'She has a right to her opinion,' Julia said. *And her opinion was probably right*, she thought.

122

'Maybe,' Edna said. 'But I have a reputation to uphold, and the problem is that shit sticks.' Edna rarely swore; it was a sign of how angry she was. 'Especially to clean surfaces,' she added. 'Not that you would know too much about that.'

'What's that supposed to mean?' Julia said, her own anger rising in opposition to that of her mother-in-law.

'People think highly of me,' Edna said. 'But you hardly have a spotless reputation, do you? At least among those who know you well.'

'Are you talking about Chris?' Julia asked. 'Still? That was before Brian and I got married. Well before. We'd hardly started seeing each other. But you know that already.'

While at university Julia'd had a brief affair – if you could call it that – with an older man, an accountant called Chris. It had taken place about two months after she and Brian had met and she still wasn't sure why she had done it. He was married, with two children, so it wasn't going anywhere, and at the time she was falling in love with Brian. Perhaps that was it; she knew that she and Brian were probably in it for the long haul – at least, it had seemed so then – so she had gone looking for one last fling, maybe as a way to test the strength of her feeling for Brian. Anyway, it had all come out when a friend of Chris's wife saw her and Chris together in a pub. The friend told Chris's wife, who told everyone she knew, then left her husband a few days later. At first Chris wasn't too bothered – he thought it meant he was free to carry on his relationship with Julia, with whom he turned out to be deeply in love, much more so than Julia had ever suspected – like many British men of his age, he kept his feelings hidden beneath a carapace of cynicism and constant joking – and was heartbroken when she told him that it really was over.

Brian, after a few weeks of haughty silence, forgave her, and things went back to normal. Not for Chris, though: he hit the bottle and ended up losing his job.

'Look,' Julia said, suddenly weary. 'Why are you bringing this up now, Edna? What has it got to do with anything?'

'I'm just saying that I have a reputation to lose, and people like Laura put it in jeopardy. You might be care-less with your reputation; I am not. Your reputation is like your virginity, Julia: you only get to lose it once.'

'I think I have a perfectly good reputation,' Julia said.

'Maybe,' Edna said. 'But would anyone be surprised if it turned out that Chris was not the first married man whose family you wrecked? Or the last?'

Julia pushed her plate away from her. For a second she considered throwing the contents over her mother-in-law. She had no idea why Edna was being so deliber-ately offensive. Perhaps it was simply that now the marriage was over she was unable to restrain her true feelings from rising to the surface, however inopportune the moment.

Julia stood up. 'We're all under a lot of strain,' she said. 'But that's no reason to be rude.' She looked at Brian. 'I'm going to have a bath,' she said. 'Enjoy your meal.'

5

The Third Day

i.

The girl is awake.

The girl is *screaming*.

She should be neither of these things.

You cannot let this happen. You cannot make mistakes. But how did you? You calculated the dosage correctly. Weight, age, amount of the drug already in the system. You administered it at the right time. You are sure you got it right. You could not have made a mistake.

But you did, and now the girl is screaming.

The screaming is not a problem. No one will hear her. There is no one *to* hear her. It is what it signifies. It means she is awake. And it means she is *aware*. If she is screaming she knows she is not where she should be.

Which means more memories; memories of her captor, memories that she cannot be allowed to keep. But the drug for fixing *that* is dangerous for children, and she has had it once already, the day you took her. You don't want to give her more. You don't want to hurt her.

You *can't* hurt her. Soon her time will come and you need her perfect for that. Flawless. Unhurt. That is the only way it can be. The only way it can work.

But she cannot have memories, so the drug it will be. It *has* to be. You have no choice. You recognize that. You don't like it, but you accept it. That is one of your strengths. You are adaptable. Pragmatic. You manage. You make do. The world would be a better place if more people were like you.

So the drug it will be. There. You have made up your mind. This is your decision.

This is life, is it not? Decisions, decisions. You are good at decisions. You made the most important one after all: to take the girl. *That* was risky. *That* took courage. After that, this is nothing.

Do it. As soon as possible. Right now, in fact.

You know you have to, so you go to the hidden place – so well hidden, no one could ever find it, even if looking for it – and fill a syringe with liquid.

Then you go to another hidden place. The house is full of them; it has been hiding secrets for centuries. That is why you feel so at home here, and this, this is just one more secret in a long line of them. You like to remember that. It makes you feel better about what you have done and about what you plan to do.

You open the door and step into the darkness.

Shhh, you say, and take the girl's arm in yours. Before she can protest you clamp it between your knees and find a vein with the point of the syringe.

I'm sorry, you say, and you mean it.

But you have no choice. She can have no memories.

ii.

Midnight. Maybe one a.m. Or two a.m. … Julia had no idea. She sat on Anna's bed, hugging her knees.

Anna was gone. She had to face it. She was gone. She studied Anna's room. Her Mr Men and Little Miss books, the stuffed elephant she clung to at night, the chest of drawers full of her clothes, the top left drawer open, a pair of red dungarees hanging over the lip of the drawer.

She'd always thought that the stories about people keeping a bedroom as a shrine to a loved one were a bit morbid, but she understood them now. She couldn't imagine moving a single thing in this room. The room – the books and toys, the slight mess, the smell – was an expression of Anna's personality, of her interests, of her developing character.

The covers were kicked down to the far end, just as Anna had left them when she got out of bed and came into her parents' room those three long, long days ago. There was only one parent there that morning, only a mother for her to snuggle against; her father sleeping in the guest room.

Where's Daddy? She'd said.

I think he already went downstairs, Julia replied, an inkling of how hard it was going to be to explain the divorce working its way into her mind as she wrapped her arms around Anna. That could wait, though. For now she was going to enjoy cuddling her daughter.

That was pretty much her last memory of Anna. After a few minutes they had got out of bed and gone downstairs. Julia had an early meeting so she had got herself ready for work and left; Brian had dressed and fed Anna.

On her way out she'd kissed Anna on the top of the head.

Goodbye, darling, she said. *Have a good day.*

Bye, Mummy. I'll miss you.

I'll miss you too.

Now, as she stood in the silence, looking at the empty bed, she wondered if that would turn out to be the last time she saw her daughter; if that had been, unknown to her, goodbye for good.

It must happen all the time. All around the world, every day, in every county, people must say a cheery *goodbye* or *au revoir* or *auf wiedersehen* to a loved one, with no inkling that it was the last time they would be able to do so. It was probably a good thing; if we knew how close disaster was, if we worried that each goodbye would be the last, we would never do anything. We'd be paralyzed by fear.

She couldn't remember who'd said it – Orwell, maybe – but a famous wit had once pointed out that there is one anniversary we pass each year without celebrating, or even knowing it is there: the anniversary of our own death. There were other such unknown and unwished-for anniversaries, it turned out: she had not expected that a particular date would become the anniversary of her daughter's disappearance.

The anniversary of the day Julia ceased to be a mother. Was that what she was, a former mother? Was Anna already dead? Was motherhood over for her now? Would she no longer feel the worries and frustrations and above all the elation, the moments when she gazed at her sleeping daughter and felt the purest, most overwhelming sense of love and wonder at what she had created? It couldn't be over: it was unthinkable. She clenched her hands, dug her fingernails into her palms, tried to focus on the pain to divert her attention.

It didn't work. An Anna-less future spooled out in front of her. A bleak, colourless, joyless future.

She lay in her daughter's bed and waited for it to pass. It took a long time.

Downstairs, Julia made a coffee. There was no milk in the fridge; she grabbed her car keys and purse. The activity might take her mind off Anna, if only for a few seconds. She looked at the clock on the oven. Just gone five a.m. The petrol station up by the motorway would be open. She grabbed the car keys.

Driving did take her mind off Anna, at least partially. True, she scanned the hedges and gardens and fields on the way to the petrol station for any sign of her daughter, but some part of her mind was occupied in controlling the car, in registering red lights and other vehicles and reacting accordingly. It helped, a bit.

She pulled into the forecourt. The car was low on petrol so she decided to fill up. When the tank was full she walked into the shop. She took a carton of milk from the chiller and approached the counter.

The cigarettes behind the till caught her eye. It had been years since she smoked, but suddenly she craved the rush of nicotine, craved the occupation of smoking.

'Pump three,' she said, and hesitated. Then she added: 'And a pack of Marlboro Lights.'

The attendant was a girl in her early twenties. She looked at Julia with a blank, early morning expression, which changed, as she recognized her customer, first into curiosity and then – Julia was surprised to see – dislike.

The girl's face clouded over for a second, then she glanced at a pile of newspapers on the counter. When she looked back at Julia, she looked guilty, as though she'd been caught taking money from the till and stuffing it into her purse, and then, in an attempt to move on, grabbed the cigarettes and rang them up on the till.

'Fifty-five nineteen,' she said.

Her diversion didn't work. Julia looked at the pile of newspapers. They were all copies of a national tabloid, newly delivered and still wrapped, a narrow blue plastic tie forming cross hairs on the front page.

And in the centre of the cross hairs was her face.

The picture had been taken as she and Brian left the press conference. It was a close up of her, and he was just visible, a blurry presence in the background, which, she thought, suited his presence in her life. It wasn't that which had caused the attendant's discomfort, however.

Julia read the headline with a sense of mounting disbelief. When she reached the end, she grabbed the counter, suddenly dizzy.

She read it again.

BROKEN BRITAIN: VANISHED ANNA'S MUM ACCUSED OF NEGLECT

She grabbed the top paper and pulled. It would not come free of the plastic tie, so she tore it, taking half of the front page out, then the other half. She put them side by side on the counter.

It emerged yesterday that Julia Crowne, mother of disappeared child Anna Crowne, failed to pick up her daughter after school. She also failed to notify the school that she would be late, so no one knew to keep Anna back. Little Anna would have left the school on time and been alone, alone and vulnerable to predators.

Yesterday, Mrs Crowne was the target of some criticism from other parents. One, who asked not to be named, claimed that Anna's mother, a lawyer, had been late before.

'If you keep on not showing up then this kind of thing is bound to happen,' the parent said. 'I feel for her, I really do, but you have to ask yourself whether this could have been avoided. I mean, what's more important? A meeting or your child?'

Mrs Crowne arrived thirty minutes after the end of the school day, which was when it emerged that Anna was not there. Subsequent efforts to locate the five-year-old have proved fruitless, and it is feared she has been abducted by a criminal gang engaged in child trafficking, or by a lone-wolf child predator.

Henry Collins, a former major in the Army who specializes in abduction cases, said that in these circumstances thirty minutes is a lifetime.

'Thirty minutes is thirty miles,' he said. 'And a search area with a radius of thirty miles is big. To be honest, the people who do this kind of thing would think that five minutes is enough. Worse, once out of the immediate vicinity, a child could be transferred to another vehicle, and in a matter of another hour or two potentially be out of the country.'

'Oh God,' Julia said. 'It's not like that.' She looked at the girl. 'That's not how it happened. I swear!'

The girl didn't say anything. She stood behind the till, staring at Julia. Next to her the screen showed the price of the milk and petrol.

55.19

Julia passed her a credit card. Her hands were shaking.

The girl nodded at the torn paper.

'You can have that,' she said. 'For nothing.'

iii.

It got worse.

When Julia arrived home she was in a daze and did not notice – or did not pay attention to – the man standing a few yards up the road. It was only when she had her key in the front door that she became aware he was walking towards her.

'Mrs Crowne!' he said. 'Mrs Crowne! I'm from the *Daily World*!'

Julia stared at him, unable to believe that he was outside her house, waiting for her. He was tall, in his fifties, with a bouffant hairstyle she thought might have been a wig, and a beak-like nose. He had a London accent and looked tired, as though he'd driven all night to be there. He smiled at her, revealing yellowed teeth. The front two overlapped, giving him a beaverish look.

'Mrs Crowne,' he went on. 'Is it true you were late to collect Anna? Just a word, Mrs Crowne.'

'Go away,' Julia said. 'Get away from my house.'

'Just a couple of questions, Mrs Crowne. Were you late for Anna? Do you regret it?'

'I said go away,' she repeated. 'Leave me alone, you vile man.'

He did not appear to have heard. 'Do you feel responsible, Mrs Crowne? Like it was your fault? Do you wish you could go back and change things?'

How could he be so cruel? If she said yes, there would be an innocuous line in a story: *Anna's mum said she felt responsible for what happened, and that she wished she could go back in time and be there to pick up her daughter.* Across the country people would read it over their cornflakes and nod and say *I'll bet she does,* and then they'd forget all about it and leave the house and get on with their lives.

They would never know what was behind that line: a dishevelled, amoral man accosting a desperate mother on her doorstep and peppering her with questions that could serve no purpose other than to wound her. Was this how the press operated? Was this the cost of a story? Was there no less callous way to fill their rags?

'Do you, Mrs Crowne?' he said. 'A simple yes or no will suffice.'

'Leave me alone, you fucking piece of shit,' Julia said, her voice rising. 'Leave me alone!' She turned the key in the door and pushed it open. Once in the hallway she turned to face the reporter. 'You're disgusting!' she shouted. 'You should be ashamed of yourself!'

The man smiled. 'Maybe,' he said. 'But it wasn't me who didn't bother to show up for my daughter, was it?'

She slammed the door shut. The window above the door rattled so hard she thought it might break.

She leaned against the wall, her forehead pressed to the cold paint.

'Shit,' she said. 'Shit, shit, shit.'

And, as if the universe was playing with her, she realized she'd left the milk in the car.

'What the hell was all that?' Brian said. He was standing in the door to the kitchen and he looked, Julia realized, like hell. Ordinarily, he was handsome, with his mother's high cheekbones and dark, wide set eyes, and even though he had put on some weight – had started to collect the puddling fat that settled on the stomachs and chins and chests and backs of many of his friends, and which would require increasing levels of effort, if it were possible at all, to shift – he was still good-looking.

His looks were a large part of what had drawn her to him in the first place, which was shallow, she knew, but at Leeds Metropolitan University he had been one of the male students that the female students talked about. It whet Julia's competitiveness and so she set herself to making him hers, which she did with some ease. An approach in the student union, suggestion of a coffee, sex on the second date. She realized early that he was not a man of great ambition, but at that stage of her life Julia did not know that she valued ambition in a man. In fact, if pressed she would have said the opposite: ambition was a sign of something a little bit wrong, a sign of too much interest in money and status and not enough in the really important things in life, which were – what? Doing good? Making a difference? Having fun? Whatever – it wasn't chasing after money and job titles.

So Brian had been perfect, if a bit passive. Liberal minded; not interested in preparing himself for a life in corporate Britain or in a political think tank, very handsome (and good in bed to boot, much more attentive than the other boyfriends she'd had). His personal and political beliefs had fitted right in with Julia's and her friends'. Unlike them, though, he'd kept them all as he got older. Their friends (and Julia herself) had quietly dropped their professed interest in doing good instead of making money. Their attitudes had hardened (what was the saying? If you weren't a socialist in your twenties, you were heartless, and if you were still a socialist in your thirties you were stupid? Julia and her university cohort were living proof of *that*) and careers had flourished. Not Brian. Ambition had found that Brian was fallow soil and had not taken root in him; he was still the same socialist twenty-something he had always been, with – almost – the same good looks.

Not now, though, not today. His skin was sallow, his face thinned out. The wide-set eyes were dull. Scruffy patches of facial hair sprouted seemingly at random. There was a hint of slackness in the skin on his neck that could have been the start of a double chin. He looked, she thought, old.

'It was a reporter,' she said.

'A reporter? What do they want? They know to go to the police for information.'

'They came here.'

'Why? They know to leave us in peace. It's not like we're the bad guys. We're the victims.'

'Not exactly,' Julia said.

136

She threw the torn paper onto the table. She folded her arms. She didn't want him to see her hands shaking. He picked it up and read it.

'Fuck,' he said, then, with renewed emphasis. '*Fuck.*'

'Can you believe it?' Julia said. 'It's awful.'

He studied it for a long time. 'It's true, though,' he said. 'We can hardly deny it.'

'I know. You don't have to tell me. I *know.*'

'That doesn't bring Anna back.'

'Brian,' she said. 'Why are you doing this? Are you trying to make me feel bad? Because it doesn't work. Nothing you can do or say can make me feel any worse than I already do. Our daughter is missing. Probably *abducted.* If not dead, then maybe in the hands of a paedophile ring, or sold into slavery. I'll think about that – wonder where she is and what's happening to her – for the rest of my life. And it's *my fault.* I'll think about that too. So do you think you can make me feel any worse?'

He didn't reply. Eventually, he looked at her. 'I don't care,' he said. 'I don't care how you feel. You did this. You chose divorce; you failed Anna, and I feel like I've lost everything. And I blame you. I can't help it. And since our daughter disappeared the week after you announced you want a divorce, we don't even have each other to help us get through this.' He looked at her. 'You really screwed up, Julia.' He shook his head, as though scolding her. 'You really screwed up.'

Julia was not an angry person. She got frustrated or upset or irritated, but rarely angry. She could remember

137

only a few occasions on which she had felt real, boiling anger of the kind that diminishes your capacity for self-control, most of which were when she was a teenager and felt that her mother was thwarting a totally reasonable wish of hers to shave her head or go to a nightclub or sleep at her boyfriend's house. Back then, her anger was intensified by the raging hormones of the teen years, but it was nothing compared to what she felt now.

Who the hell did Brian think he was? She didn't need to be told that she had screwed up; she knew. She thought about it every minute. Worse, she got the distinct impression that he enjoyed pointing it out to her. By all means blame her; she expected that, but to take pleasure in it? To gain some advantage in their marital fight from their daughter's disappearance? That was not on, and it added the fuel of self-righteousness to her rage. While Brian was in the right it was hard for her to feel angry at him; if he was in the wrong the dam was breached, and her anger surged through the gap.

'I might have screwed up by not picking Anna up,' she said. 'And I don't need you to tell me that. But there's one thing I didn't screw up. One thing that I got exactly right. And that's getting divorced from you. You're even weaker than I had thought, Brian, and trying to use my daughter to make me feel bad so that you can feel good proves it.'

The shock on his face encouraged her; it was like a target, and her fury zeroed in on it.

'I knew marrying you was a mistake a long time ago. I should have known when I was seeing Chris that if I truly loved you I wouldn't have been with someone else, but I ignored the signs.' She was aware that this was not exactly true; the reasons she had the affair with Chris were complicated and not really to do with Brian, but that didn't matter. What mattered was hurting him, and this was working. 'And I wish I hadn't, because I made the biggest mistake of my life. The only thing which made it right was Anna, and now she's gone.'

He licked his lips, then swallowed. 'Marrying me wasn't the biggest mistake of your life,' he said. 'You made the biggest mistake of your life three days ago when you didn't bother to pick up Anna. That was the biggest mistake of your life, Julia. Losing our daughter. Maybe *killing* our daughter.'

There are arguments that are easy to get over, and arguments that are hard to get over, and arguments that require marriage guidance counselling to get over. And then there are arguments that can never be got over. This was one of those, and they both knew it. Part of the problem was the gravity of what they had said; the more important part was that a lot of it was true. Julia would not be able to say that she hadn't meant it – she'd already declared that she wanted a divorce. In those circumstances, saying that the entire marriage was a mistake was entirely believable. And as for what Brian had said: well, if it turned out that Anna was dead – or as good as – then it might not be literally true that Julia had killed her, but it was true enough as to make no difference.

Julia didn't know what to say. Should she acknowledge the moment, or let it pass? Should she scream that she hated him or just turn and walk away and never speak to him again?

She was saved from making a decision by her phone ringing.

She glanced at the screen. It was DI Wynne.

iv.

'Mrs Crowne,' she said. 'Have you seen the news?'

'Yes,' Julia said, then paused and looked at Brian. She didn't want him to hear this. She didn't want him to hear anything. 'Hang on a minute.' She walked into the dining room and closed the door behind her.

'I was at the petrol station,' Julia said. She lowered her voice. She was pretty sure she had heard a floorboard creak outside the door, and an image of Brian, his ear pressed against the wooden panels, came to her. 'I saw the *Daily World*.'

'I'm sorry to hear it. That's not what you need right now.'

'It's ok.'

'I want to reassure you that none of the team working on the case spoke to the press,' the detective said. 'I've spoken to all of them to confirm it. I also want to reassure you that we don't operate that way.'

Julia realized that the DI had not called to commiserate – how could she, the story was true – but to make sure that there was no hint that she or her team were implicated in the leak of the story. Ironically, Julia hadn't thought they were. She might have, had she wondered how it had come out, but she had not got that far, yet. The shock of finding out and then finding a reporter outside her house still hadn't worn off. She was still coming to terms with the fact that *she* was the story now; the narrative had moved on from a missing, probably abducted, possibly murdered, child to a missing, probably abducted, possibly murdered, child with a neglectful mother. It was a familiar movement in the public mood: from sympathy to head-shaking disapproval: *how could they let that happen to their child?*

Julia didn't begrudge them. Perhaps people needed to think that it was the fault of the parents – or in this case, the mother – so that they could feel that their children were safe, immunized to a similar fate by the fact of their good parenting. After all, if Anna's disappearance was the result of bad parenting – *how could they let it happen?* – then their children were safe, as they would *never* let it happen. Better blame it on a crappy modern parent in the soup of Broken Britain than accept that the world was random and they were not in control of what happened to their children. That was a terrifying prospect, and if people needed to be insulated from it by the belief that they could stop bad things happening to their children then there was nothing wrong with that.

'Have you any ideas where the story came from?' DI Wynne asked.

141

'No,' Julia said. 'But quite a few people knew. The school staff, the parents. One of them could have said something.'

'We'll try and find out, not that it matters too much now.'

'Does this affect the investigation?' Julia said. 'Does it make it harder to find Anna?'

'Not really,' Wynne said. 'It might make it easier. More publicity. But it might make things harder for you. Let me know if there is anything I can do.'

'There was a reporter outside the house,' Julia said. 'He might still be there. Could you get rid of him?'

'I'll send someone along to have a word.'

Julia looked at the sideboard. On one end was a picture frame with two photos in it. One of them was Anna as a baby; the other was of Edna and Jim, just before he disappeared, and next to it was another frame containing a photo of her and Brian on holiday in Turkey, and next to that was one containing a photo of her parents, on their wedding day. With Anna gone, and Brian and her divorcing it seemed as though the whole family was going to come to an end with this generation.

Unless, of course, Anna was alive, and managed to grow to adulthood and have children of her own in some faraway country. Then the family would live on, but in fact only. No one would know, so, to all intents and purposes the family would be finished.

'Have you made any progress?' Julia asked. 'Did you find the janitor?'

Wynne's pause was answer enough. 'No,' she said. 'We haven't found him – his name is Lambert, Julian Lambert – but we are making some progress. He had no car registered in his name, but he does have a driving licence, so right now we're trying to see if he rented one. We're also speaking to anyone who rented a car in the area, but nothing has come up yet.'

'Nothing else?' Julia urged. 'How does someone just disappear like that?'

'It's unusual,' Wynne admitted. 'But we'll find him.'

'I think he has Anna,' Julia said. 'He must. Or why would he vanish? There must be a reason.'

This was it, she thought, *this was the lead that would end with the return of her daughter.*

'It's suspicious,' Wynne agreed. 'But we don't want to jump to conclusions prematurely. We're also concerned about the absence of your husband's father. We haven't been able to locate him.'

'He's been gone a long time,' Julia said. 'I don't think Brian and Edna – his mum – really know anything.'

'I don't suppose they do,' said Wynne. 'But we would expect to find some trace of him, and of Miss Wilkinson—'

'Miss Wilkinson?' Julia said. 'Is that the teacher?'

'Yes,' Wynne said. 'We contacted the school. They have no idea where she's currently living; neither do any of the people we talked to. We can't locate her, either.'

'Do you think they have anything to do with Anna?' Julia said. 'I see why it's odd that you can't find them, but I don't see the connection with Anna.'

'I don't, yet,' Wynne said. 'But anything unusual is of interest in a case like this. We have to explore every channel.'

'They're probably living abroad somewhere,' Julia said.

'Normally we can find people,' said Wynne. 'Tax returns, police records, bank accounts. It's not especially difficult.' She paused. 'Unless, of course, they don't *want* to be found, for some reason.'

'For some reason,' Julia echoed. 'Like—'

'Like anything,' Wynne interrupted. 'And everything. Let's say that Mr Crowne's father was up to something he shouldn't have been – perhaps something involving underage pupils – and let's say Miss Wilkinson was also involved, under the sway of a charismatic older man. Let's also say that they were found out and decided to disappear.'

'But I don't – I mean, I knew Jim. He wasn't that kind of man.' Jim Crowne wasn't a paedophile, Julia was sure of it. But then, you never knew. You never knew.

'We'd still like to talk to him,' Wynne said. 'I was wondering whether you would have any objection to us issuing a statement asking him to come forward?'

Julia hesitated. She had no problem with it, but Brian might, and Edna almost certainly would.

'I – I don't know,' Julia said. 'I'd have to ask Brian.'

'I think it's important for us to do it,' said Wynne. 'I wouldn't want there to be any reason we couldn't. And – if I'm honest – we'll do what we have to, to aid the investigation.'

So it wasn't really a question, Julia thought, in which case she might as well give her assent. And if it helped get Anna back she'd deal with the fallout with Edna.

'Ok,' she said. 'Do it. Is there anything else you need from me?'

'Not right now,' Wynne said. 'But I'll let you know if there is. And I'll send someone down to help shift the press. You might want to lie low today, take it easy. Stay home.'

Wynne's tone suggested that she thought staying at home was a warming, welcoming prospect. A safe place. A place where whatever comfort was available in this godawful situation could be found. Perhaps it was for DI Wynne. It was not for Julia. For Julia home meant memories of Anna and the looming presence of her failed marriage.

But where else was there?

'Ok,' she said. 'I'll do that.'

v.

'Well,' Brian said, 'nice of you to come. Just a shame that this is what it took.'

His brother, Simon, put down his bag and folded his arms. He was taller than Brian, maybe 6' 2", and thinner, and he was going bald. His face was lean, and he had two deep lines running from his cheekbones to his jaw. He looked like an actor who might play a Second World War army officer: distinguished, severe, yet kindly when in the right mood.

'I'm here to help,' he said. His voice was similar to Brian's but a shade deeper, a tone richer, and it had a North American suppleness to it. 'I'm your brother.'

Brian tried to look unimpressed, but it was clear to Julia that he was both desperately happy to see Simon and desperately sad that he did not see him more often. He could not disguise the longing – for approval, companionship, friendship – in his eyes. He was in awe of Simon, perhaps because Simon had not stayed around long enough to lose the aura that a big brother had for his younger sibling.

Julia began to get a glimpse of just how damaged her husband was, just how badly his family had let him down: his father and brother had both deserted him, leaving him with Edna, of all people. It was hardly a recipe for a happy life. To put it in terms that Laura's therapist would have understood: his shelves had been stacked with a whole supermarket's worth of problems for the future.

Simon turned to Julia. 'Good to see you,' he said. 'I'm just sorry it's in these circumstances. What happened is awful.'

'They have a lead, at least,' Julia said. 'That's something.'

Simon tilted his head. 'Oh? Can you share?'

Brian told him about the janitor. As he did the mood lifted slightly.

'Sounds promising,' Simon said. 'Let's keep our fingers crossed.' He caught Brian's eye. 'How's Mum?'

'Good. Fine. You know Mum.'

'I do. Not as well as I used to.'

Brian shrugged. 'She hasn't changed. Same old dear; bossing everyone around.'

Their conversation was an odd mixture of familiarity and distance. They shared so much – they were the only people in the world who knew Edna as a mother, for starters – but there was so much that they did not know about each other. And then there was the fact of Simon's leaving. It hung between them, an unspoken accusation of betrayal on Brian's part and an unspoken reply of self-defence on Simon's. As she listened, Julia wondered exactly what had happened when Simon left, what had made it necessary, and – even more intriguing, this – what had driven Edna to such profound hatred of Laura?

'Will you see her?' Brian said. 'Go out to her house?'

'She hasn't invited me,' Simon said. 'And I don't feel much like turning up unannounced. That might not go down so well.'

'You two have plenty you need to talk about,' Brian said.

'We do. But I'm not sure Mum's the talking type.' Simon smiled. 'Unless she's changed, of course.'

'She hasn't.'

'Then I suspect all she would want to say to me would be to remind me of my folly in marrying Laura and leaving England. I don't imagine we would have a productive conversation about how we both might have made mistakes but it all happened a long time ago and why don't we just forgive and forget and move on.'

'It's up to you,' Brian said. 'But she is your mum, after all.'

'She is,' Simon said. 'But I'm not sure whether that's important anymore. Or whether I want it to be. I've done pretty well without her in my life the last ten years, and it was hard enough getting her out. Bringing her back in ... well, it doesn't exactly appeal. I'm here for you, Brian, here to give you whatever support I can. That's the only reason I came.' He picked up his bag. 'I'm staying at the Apple Tree Hotel. I need to check in, get some rest after the flight. Call me whenever you want and let me know what I can do.'

'Thanks,' Brian said. 'I will.'

Julia stood up. 'I'm going to get a drink,' she said. 'See you soon, Simon.'

In the kitchen, she poured a glass of water. She wasn't thirsty but that wasn't the point; she wanted to leave Brian and Simon alone. She felt as though she was intruding on something she had no right to witness. She'd known there was something ugly in the past, but she hadn't understood how big it was, how it had destroyed the bond between Brian and his brother. It was obvious they loved each other – Brian's devotion was plain to see, and the mere fact of Simon's presence was proof of his – but something had gone badly wrong.

And, as she heard the front door close, Julia wondered whether she would ever find out what it was.

6

The Fourth Day

i.

So the truth about the mother is coming out. About her neglect of her daughter. You can imagine her, sipping wine with her friends or lying back while a white-coated manicurist picks at her nails, chattering about how her daughter is the most important thing in her life, the thing that gives meaning to her pitiful existence.

And yet she did not bother to pick her up on time.

Did not bother to pick her up on time. It sounds so slight, almost like nothing, just a simple error. Hardly a crime, is it, to be a little late? But it is. It is when you are late for something so precious, so perfect. When your lateness puts such a delicate flower at risk.

There is great responsibility in being a parent. Responsibility that the mother failed to fulfil. And this is her punishment. *You* are the instrument of her punishment. You will not fail the girl, as her mother did.

The girl is sleeping. Her eyes fluttered open when you went in this morning, but that was all.

You got it right this time. The drug kept her asleep through the night and another dose this morning meant she has not been awake for twenty-four hours, not since the mistake you made yesterday.

Well done to you. You don't like the memory drug, not for one so young, but the sedative presents no problem. You can keep giving her that for as long as you like. But you won't need to. Because it's nearly time.

You can sense that the time is coming for your plan to bear its final fruit.

Not yet.

But nearly.

ii.

Julia sat in the kitchen at her laptop. She had a headache and her vision was blurred. She had slept for maybe two hours. Two troubled, nightmare-haunted hours. The rest of the night she lay in the darkness, checking her phone for emails, waiting for it to ring, waiting for some news of Anna or of that damn janitor who she knew had taken her daughter and who the police still could not find, who had disappeared so thoroughly that he *must* have taken her daughter, or why would he have gone? So all they had to do was find him and then they'd find Anna, and call her, but the phone didn't ring.

And so, early in the morning she got out of bed and read the news. She was aware that it was the worst possible thing she could do, that she was going to find nothing but heartache and trouble along this path, but she did it anyway. It was, she thought, almost a form of penance.

It was worse than she could have imagined.

NEGLIGENT ANNA MUM PLANNED TO DESERT DAUGHTER

It emerged yesterday that the mother of vanished child Anna Crowne had been planning to leave her family in the coming weeks. This revelation followed earlier reports that she had failed to pick up her daughter and also failed to inform the school that she would be late, a failure that was a key element in her daughter's disappearance.

Mrs Crowne is fast becoming a figure who provokes a mixed response from the public. On the one hand, she is suffering the disappearance of her daughter. On the other, it is hard to avoid concluding that she is in some way at fault for this tragedy, both in the sense that she was not there for her daughter on the day, and in the sense that she was planning to desert her family.

Julia's hands shook. It was bad enough that she was accused of negligence; now the press had got hold of the information that she had been planning to divorce Brian, and they were claiming that she had also been planning to leave her daughter.

Which she hadn't, but who cared about the truth in a case like this?

She carried on reading. The first story, it turned out, was relatively measured. The rest of the press was not so restrained, and hinted that she might be deranged – as one put it, *what kind of mother chooses to leave her husband and five-year-old daughter? The kind who doesn't bother to pick her up from school, the kind who might take extreme and unpredictable action to resolve whatever personal difficulties she was having*, which seemed to be a hint that she had something to do with Anna's disappearance.

And it was a hint that had been picked up by the commentariat, by those brave warriors on the battlefield of Twitter, who had no problem indulging their most salacious fantasies. It was hard to ignore the conclusion that their tweets were what they wanted to have happened, as much as what they thought had happened:

shes fucking mad. she killed the kid #JuliaCrowne #Madmum

This was replied to by someone called @DB2FCT, who opined:

Any woman who would leave their kid could KILL their kid #JuliaCrowne #notfittobeamum

It was this hashtag – *#notfittobeamum* – that was trending. It drew a lot of hits:

people like that should be sterilized. #JuliaCrowne
#notfittobeamum
I can't have kids. It's crime that people like her can
#JuliaCrowne #notfittobeamum
This bitch is everything wrong with Britain today
#JuliaCrowne #notfittobeamum

It seemed the commentariat were particularly incensed that she planned to leave Anna. It was ironic; the crime they were most agitated about was the only one she was innocent of. Added to the grief and guilt, Julia felt a sense of mounting injustice. She had plenty of things to feel bad about, but this wasn't one of them.

It wasn't the only untruth doing the rounds. As she clicked through the stories, another theme began to emerge: reports of an affair she had been having. Most of the newspapers steered clear of it, but one of the bolder – or better equipped with lawyers –tabloids ran the story. It too was an instant hit on Twitter, but with a different hashtag, this one – *#mumslut* – even more charming than the others:

Fucking around while her daughter was taken
#JuliaCrowne #mumslut

It was too much to bear. She closed her laptop. She stared at the painting above the fireplace. It was a large oil of a golden beach under bright blue, cloudless, Cornish skies, one of many thousands sold in the hundreds of art galleries down in the beach communities of Cornwall. The artist had little skill and less imagination, but for all that it captured something of the essence of holidays by the sea. It was the way you remembered them, rather than the way they really were. When you were sitting in a drab midwinter office staring at the walls of your cubicle, listening to people mutter half-heartedly into their phones, or tap on their keyboards, the summer seaside holiday seemed like that painting: golden and bright and flawless and endlessly enticing.

She would like to disappear into it now. To stand on the warm sand then walk into the bracing waters of the sea and keep on going until it swallowed her up. She never wanted to come back, didn't want to face the storm.

Had she done this when other, similar, news stories had broken? Had she watched the news reports and read the articles on the internet? Had she felt a shudder of prurient glee at the sight of someone else's suffering, while also thinking that the press were animals who intruded without a shred of moral decency into people's private lives and exposed them, all in the name of enriching their rapacious owners?

Probably, she had. But she had felt that she was not part of it, because she didn't buy their papers and didn't subscribe to their websites. She felt blameless because she didn't fund them; but she fed them nonetheless. She only read the free content, but her clicks and comments added to the weight of public interest – public rubbernecking, that is – which was the raison d'être of the whole sorry media circus.

And she was now at the centre of it, facing the full force of its scathing, moralistic force, a force that made her – a mother whose daughter had disappeared and was maybe dead – into a villain. It was hideous, a modern version of a public execution, but people wanted stories, and the villainous, neglectful, slutty mother was a good one. What better than a grieving mum? Why, a grieving mum who was also a slut and a home-wrecker.

Except she wasn't.

She hadn't been having an affair, and she hadn't been planning to leave Anna. But that didn't matter now. That was the story, and it had enough truth in it – the fact she wanted a divorce – to give all the allegations the ring of truth. Add in the fact of her negligence, and she was public enemy number one.

But how did they know this? How did they know about her twin failures, both to pick up her daughter and to be a good, dutiful wife? There was only one way they could have found out. There was only one person who would have told them, although why he thought it was a good idea was beyond her.

She slid the laptop onto the pine countertop, and went upstairs to talk to her husband.

iii.

The guest bedroom was fetid. From the rankness in the air and the stillness of the form in the bed she guessed that

Brian was asleep. On one of the occasions she'd heard him up in the night, around dawn, she'd heard the clink of glasses and then the thud of a cabinet door closing. When she'd come downstairs that morning she'd seen the empty glass by the sink, still sticky with cheap bourbon, his lip prints smeared on the rim. It had made her feel sick.

No wonder he was asleep, then, but even though it wouldn't last – sleep was a fragile state for both of them, even when drink-induced – she couldn't wait. He could get his rest later. There'd be plenty of time.

'Brian!' she called. 'Brian! Wake up!'

He didn't move. His leg, pale and thin, dangled over the edge of the guest bed. A wave of regret washed over her, not, this time, for what had happened to Anna – although she regretted that plenty – but for what had happened to her and Brian, to their marriage, to the life they had set out to make together. She couldn't fathom how it had ended up like this, how they had let it get so bad. The only explanation she could think of was that, as they had grown up in the years since they met, they had grown apart instead of together. Whatever had happened, they were different people now, and they were no longer compatible.

'Brian! Wake up!'

Her tone was urgent, and Brian stirred, then mumbled. She couldn't make out what he said; she guessed it was something along the lines of *go away* or *leave me alone*.

'Brian,' she said. 'Wake up. I need to talk to you.'

Suddenly his eyes snapped open and he sat up, fully alert, his face poised in a moment of pure anticipation.

Oh shit, she thought, and, even though she was furious at him, she felt a wave of sympathy for him. What she was about to do was the worst thing she could have done. She could see in his face that he thought she was waking him to give him news of Anna. Good news, too, because she wasn't wailing.

He propped himself up on his elbows.

'Have they found her?' he said. 'Did they find the janitor?'

Shit. Julia shook her head. *Shit, shit, shit.*

'No,' she said. 'But I need to talk to you.'

His expression – the transition from hope to desperate, utter disappointment – was like a mirror to her soul. Her anger dissipated.

'Later,' he said, and lay back in his bed.

'Now,' Julia said; her voice softer. 'I'm sorry.' He ignored her. She stayed in the doorway. 'Brian,' she said. 'It's important.'

He turned and looked at her. 'Was that deliberate?' he said. 'Making me think there was good news?'

'No,' she replied. 'It wasn't.'

'Right,' he said. 'Of course not.'

'It wasn't. I wouldn't do that to my worst enemy. And we may be having some difficulties – serious difficulties – but you're not my worst enemy. Far from it.'

'So what is it?' he said. 'What do we have to talk about?'

'I think you know.'

'I don't know.'

She closed her eyes. 'Why did you do it, Brian?'

'Do what?'

For some reason she thought that giving him a chance to confess might help. It wasn't going to repair the damage, but it might at least allow them to have an adult conversation about it. If he denied it then they would end up having an argument about whether he had done it or not, and that would be a complete waste of time.

'You know.'

'I don't know,' he said. 'What have I done?'

'Brian,' she said, 'now's not the time. Let's just be honest with each other.'

'All right,' he said. 'Let's. Why don't you start by telling me what it is you think I've done, and I'll tell you whether I did it? I'll be totally honest with you, I promise. After all, I haven't got much to lose have I? Not after what you've done.'

'OK,' she said. 'Why did you tell them? Who did you tell?'

'Are you talking about the press?'

She nodded, a sense of triumph glowing at what she took for a confession. It didn't last. There was something not quite right about it. It was too nonchalant, too matter-of-fact, as though it meant nothing. As though his treachery and lies were obvious, expected almost.

'Exactly,' she said. 'Why did you tell them?'

'I didn't,' he said. 'I thought we'd talked about this yesterday. One of the parents must have told them, or one of the school staff. Either way, it wasn't me. Who's saying it was?'

'Not that,' she said, exasperated at his denial. 'The other stuff.'

'What other stuff?' he said.

And then she understood that he didn't know what the press were saying today, that he thought she was talking about yesterday's story. He wasn't a good enough liar, or actor, to pretend so perfectly that he didn't know, which meant that he really hadn't told them about their failed marriage, or made up the lies about her affair or her leaving both him and Anna. He was not one of those people who could lie with a straight face, or keep calm under interrogation. Even if he wanted to lie, Brian would give away his secrets at the first hint of pressure. When they were first together she had been able to guess what he had bought her for her birthdays or at Christmas by simply asking him: *is it jewellery? Is it clothes? Is it a pass to a spa?* Eventually, when she hit on the right category, his denial would take on a different, more sombre tone and she would know she had it, and then she would get more specific. *Is it a ring? A necklace? A bracelet? Diamonds? Silver? Gold?* It was a fun game. A game that was now over for good.

'There's more,' she said. 'In the press. A lot more.'

'A lot more what?'

'A lot more in the press. About me.'

'Like?'

'Like, our marriage was over because I wanted out, and I was planning to leave Anna with you—'

'Were you?' he said. 'It's fine by me.'

'No,' she said. 'Not at all. We would have had – will have – some kind of shared custody. You're a good dad and she needs you. She needs me as well. And I wasn't planning to leave her.'

'Well,' he said. 'It doesn't really matter now.'

'And they said I was having an affair, which was why I was leaving.'

'Were you?'

'No.'

She stopped. She could see that he wasn't really concerned, that he was thinking *sorry to hear it, but it's not really my problem.* And he was right, it wasn't. It was her problem. She would have to face the destruction of her reputation alone, the sideways looks from colleagues and clients, the muttered remarks about her suitability to work as a divorce lawyer when she had made such a spectacular mess of her own life. It didn't matter that it was all a lie. She couldn't prove that it was. How do you prove a negative, that you weren't having an affair? You could prove the *existence* of an affair, with photos and cameras and DNA evidence, but proving the *absence* of one was impossible. All you could do was deny it.

And she could only deny part of it. *I wasn't having an affair and I wasn't planning to leave Anna, but I did want a divorce and I did fail to pick her up on time.*

Hardly a convincing denial. And even if somehow she managed to prove it then the stain would remain. Shit sticks, as Edna had said, and she was right.

Although there was perhaps a way. The politician's way. Deny everything. But for that she needed help. She took a deep breath.

'I want you to say that I wasn't planning to leave Anna and that I wasn't having an affair.' She paused. 'And that I didn't want a divorce.'

'But you do,' Brian said. 'You want a newer, more exciting existence. You told me so. I'm boring. Of no interest. And as for the other allegations – perhaps your new existence excluded Anna and included a boyfriend. I can't say it didn't.'

'Please. Tell them that I wasn't planning to leave you. The stories say that I'd told you a week or so ago. You could deny it.'

'I could,' he said. 'But firstly, that would be a lie, and secondly, it would look a bit odd when you buggered off in a few weeks or months or whenever you plan to finally leave me in peace.' He rolled over to face the window. 'You're on your own in this one, Julia. You brought it on yourself.'

There was a quiet glee in his voice that infuriated her. He may not have told the press, but she could tell that he was glad they knew, and he was enjoying the power of being able to deny her something.

She did the only thing she could think of. She slammed the door when she left. The bang was like a rifle shot. She imagined Brian jumping in his bed, startled.

It was little consolation.

161

The Fifth Day

i.

So she was having an affair. You didn't know but it doesn't surprise you. She's the type, after all. Shows up late for her daughter, doesn't tell anyone. Irresponsible and selfish, the kind who puts herself first, who struggles to see beyond her own needs. Why wouldn't she be having an affair? Someone like that would find it easy enough to justify.

I was unhappy in my marriage.

I just wanted to. I can't help my emotions.

I was unfulfilled. Life should be more than this.

What happened to sticking things out, to putting your own needs after those of the family? Or of society? Of sacrifice? And duty? You often wondered what would happen if the country had to go to war again. We'd lose. People would be too concerned with their own preservation to risk fighting. They'd look for someone else to do it for them. We'd all save ourselves, and in doing so we'd doom the country.

That was the trouble now. People felt sad, so they got a pill. Work was hard, so people resigned. Marriages went through rocky patches and people got divorced. It was selfishness, pure and simple. And it was all justified by emotions. *I'm unhappy. I'm stressed. I need to feel loved.* Just having the emotion was enough justification for whatever people did.

And it was useless. Didn't people see that unhappiness came from within? A person could change jobs, but if they were an unhappy type then they would take their unhappiness with them. People needed to learn to bear things. To be resilient.

Well, she would learn, the mother. She would learn what it meant to be unhappy. When this was over she'd be wishing to be stuck in a loveless marriage. She'd see how bad things could truly be and she'd realize what she had.

More precisely, what she'd lost.

For you had the girl. Sleeping, beautiful, pristine. Unharmed, still.

And the time was coming.

ii.

SEARCH FOR ANNA'S GRANDFATHER
In a further twist to the tragic and thoroughly modern saga of Anna Crowne, it emerged

163

yesterday that the police have been seeking her grandfather, James Crowne, who disappeared over fifteen years ago.

Mr Crowne, now 67, was headmaster at the prestigious Tulcester Grammar School, before leaving his post abruptly during the summer holidays in 1999. Tulcester Grammar refused to comment.

DI Wynne of Cheshire Police, who is leading the investigation, appealed to Mr Crowne to come forward. 'We think he may be able to provide information of use to the investigation,' she said, 'and we are interested in talking to him as soon as possible. We would ask him to contact the police as soon as he can, and, if anyone knows of his whereabouts, we would like to hear from them as well.'

The investigation continues.

There were five journalists outside now. Julia sat at the bedroom window, watching them. One sat in his car, head bent over a smartphone. The other four stood in a huddle, talking and laughing. As she sat there a dark blue Ford Focus pulled up and the *Daily World* reporter climbed out. He was holding a newspaper – Julia recognized the red top heading of his employer – and he brandished it, waving it above his head like a trophy.

The others crowded around him, peering at the paper. One of them, a fat man in jogging pants and a grey exercise shirt with sweat stains under the armpits, slapped his forehead in a gesture of mock failure.

Julia reached for her laptop and went to the homepage of the *Daily World*.

There it was. The title said it all.

DO OUR CHILDREN NOT DESERVE BETTER?

Recent events in Britain beg a question: do our children not deserve better? Babies die under the noses of social workers, twelve-year-olds are admitted to A&E with alcohol poisoning, and toddlers vanish from the school gates, their parents apparently incapable of making adequate arrangements for their pick up. As a society we are forced to ask a question: in the twenty-first century, in a First-World nation, a nation that for centuries was a beacon of progress and liberty for the world, is this the best we can do?

And underneath it was a photo of her, Julia Crowne, the best and most recent example of an entire nation's moral collapse.

Somehow, they had got a picture of her – from Facebook, maybe – at her friend May's wedding. In it, Julia – who was twenty-five when the photo was taken – was leaning towards the camera, her bridesmaid dress exposing a little more cleavage than she would normally have allowed. In one hand she was holding a bottle of champagne, in the other a cigarette. Her eyes were glazed, and she was obviously drunk. There was a caption beneath it.

Julia Crowne in Happier Times

So now they were suggesting that she was a drunk and a smoker. She wasn't sure which was worse in the eyes of the moral majority: many of them liked a tipple themselves, so alcohol itself was ok. It was the abuse of alcohol that was the problem. Drinking too much demonstrated a lack of control – irresponsibility, in fact, which fitted perfectly with the image of Julia they wished to portray – whereas smoking was a crime in itself. Either way, the photo suggested that she was guilty of both.

Never mind that the photo was ten years old and predated Anna's birth by half a decade. Never mind that she had been relatively sober, and had ended up putting one of the other bridesmaids, who was soused in vodka, to bed.

No, none of that mattered to these brave warriors for the truth. All that mattered to them was their so-called story.

She thought about opening the window and screaming at the reporters, about running out and scratching their faces, driving them away from her front door. But she couldn't. It would only make things worse.

She was trapped. This had to end. One way or another, it had to end.

And then her phone rang.

iii.

It was DI Wynne.

Most of the people who called Julia were in her phone as a contact, so their name flashed on the screen when they called. Not so for Detective Inspector Wynne; Julia had not saved her number. It seemed like an admission that this situation would last. Nonetheless, she recognized the number immediately; the digits were imprinted on her memory the first time she saw them, as though the grey matter of her brain had known that they were important and put them in a special place, a separate place; a place where things that had to be remembered at all costs were put.

It reminded her of the compartment Anna claimed she had for puddings, desserts, sweets: anything sugary. She would push aside her knife and fork and declare herself full, too full to eat another bite of broccoli or cauliflower or cabbage or carrot, but then, minutes later, would ask what was for dessert.

I thought you were full, Julia would say, with a smile.

I am. But only for food ('food' being how Anna classified non-sugary comestibles). *Not for ice cream. Ice cream* (or cake or yogurt or Angel Delight) *goes in a different compartment.*

And in a strange way, Anna was right. Many times Julia had been full at a restaurant, stuffed with a creamy starter and bread and a large main course, groaning and unable to contemplate another bite, but then, somehow, when the waiter asked whether she wanted dessert, a little sorbet perhaps, or maybe a crème brûlée, she would find she *did* have room for that. So maybe it was a different compartment. It was as good an explanation as any other.

She answered the phone.

'Mrs Crowne? It's DI Wynne. I have some news.'

Some news. Julia's world shrank to a pinprick focus on those two words and what they could signify. *Good news? Bad news? Big news? Nothing much news?*

'We've found Lambert,' Wynne said. 'The janitor.'

'And Anna?' Julia asked. 'Is she with him?'

'We've not actually physically contacted him yet,' said Wynne, 'but we know where he is, and we have officers on their way to him now.'

'Where is he?'

'In Scotland. He's staying by some place called Loch Maree. It's very remote, which is why it's taken so long. It's easy enough to disappear up there. We put out an appeal for any information on him, and the owner of the cabin passed on his details. He's been there for the last three weeks, and has another three weeks to go.'

'Have they seen Anna?'

'They haven't seen him. He's kept himself to himself. It's the first time he's holidayed up there.'

Julia nodded. It sounded too perfect, too much the kind of place that a child abductor would go. 'So what's next?' she said.

'The local constabulary are on their way up there now. They should be there within the next two hours. I'll call as soon as I hear anything.'

'Thank you,' Julia said, then paused. 'Do you ... do you think this is it, Detective?'

DI Wynne didn't answer for a while. When she did, her voice was uncertain. 'I don't know. It could be. But we don't know what we'll find until we get there. Maybe nothing. It's been a week, after all.'

So all trace of Anna could be gone, Julia thought. *That's what you mean. He could have killed her and dumped her body in the remote fucking loch he's camping by.*

'I have to say,' Wynne continued, 'that it's odd that he used his name to book the place. That doesn't seem right to me. But you never know. I'll be in touch soon, Mrs Crowne.'

Edna and Brian were talking in the living room. Their mutters were indistinguishable in the kitchen, where Julia and Gill were facing the window, looking out at the yard.

'She said two hours,' Julia said. 'It's been two and a half. I don't know what that means. That they found something, surely? I mean, if there was nothing it wouldn't take as long, would it?'

Gill put her hand on Julia's forearm. Her fingers were warm from holding her mug of coffee. 'I don't know,' she said. 'I don't think you can read too much into it.'

She was right, but that didn't stop Julia thinking about it. The mind didn't work like that. It reminded her of being a teenager and going over every possible meaning of every word a boy she was interested in had said.

He said he liked chips with mayonnaise not ketchup after I said I liked them that way was he just saying it to impress me which means he fancies me or maybe he just likes to impress girls or was it true and just a coincidence which means he doesn't fancy me at all but he looked at me in a way which I think means he fancies me and he sort of blushed when I said hello to him or at least there was some redness on his neck but it could have been shaving rash oh I do hope he likes me I like him so much.

And on and on it went, her mind whirring incessantly, and nothing she could do to stop it. It was like that now, only the stakes were much higher. They stakes were the return of her little girl, so that she too could grow into a teenager who worried about whether boys liked her or not.

And then, behind her, a buzzing.

Her phone, ringing. That number, again.

'Mrs Crowne? It's DI Wynne.'

Her voice, flat. Grim. Not a good news voice.

A bad news voice. But what bad news? Anna, dead? Julian Lambert not there? Julian Lambert there but no Anna?

'Yes? What did you find?'

'We found Mr Lambert. He was fishing on the lake. We questioned him about Anna and he said he had no idea she was even missing—'

'He would say that,' Julia said. 'He would say that.'

'He gave us an alibi, Mrs Crowne—'

'Of course he did!' Julia said, her disappointment making her desperate. 'I mean, he's bound to have prepared something!'

'His alibi is watertight: a local farmer he's been helping with some fencing work. There are two other locals who worked with them.'

'Unless they're in on it,' Julia said. 'Did you think of that?'

'His alibi checks out, Mrs Crowne. It wasn't him.'

Brian came into the kitchen. 'What is it?' he asked. 'What did they find?'

Julia let her hand drop to her side. She looked out of the window.

'Nothing,' she said. 'Nothing at all.'

DI Wynne called back ten minutes later.

'Could we talk, Mrs Crowne?' she said.

'Sure,' Julia answered. 'Do you have news?'

'We have a ... well, it's a theory, more than anything.'

Julia wanted to shout down the phone. What use was a theory to her? A theory wouldn't bring Anna back, so why was DI Wynne getting her hopes up? All they had was some bullshit speculation. It was just the cops, useless as always, trying to give the impression they were doing something.

She took a deep breath. 'So,' she said. 'What is it?'

'We're going to change the focus of the investigation,' said Wynne. 'For a little while, anyway. Other than Lambert, we've been working hard on the possibility that

Anna is abroad, but that's getting nowhere. The trail – if there is one – is totally cold, which is unlikely. There's normally *something*.'

'Like what?' Julia said.

'Well, if she is abroad, then it's likely that it was a gang that took her. Only they have the resources and the networks. A lone individual would struggle to take a child out of the country and keep them concealed. And those gangs leave traces. They make noise. We hear stuff through police networks – informers, that kind of thing. It's not always enough for us to find a kidnapped child, but it's there. And there's nothing here. Nothing at all. It's possible it's a gang but it just doesn't feel like that to me. We think she might be closer to home.'

'So she's in the country?'

'She *might* be. She might even be in the area. There's something about this that feels local to me.' DI Wynne paused. 'Which is why we are still so keen to talk to Jim Crowne. We haven't been able to find anything on him. It's very irregular.'

'What did Edna say?'

'Nothing. She gave us a letter he wrote to her before he disappeared, about the affair and how he needed to start a new life. She said she told him not to contact her or Brian again, and he hasn't. She said that he was the kind of person who would do that: put himself first.'

'What about the woman he left with? She must have parents, friends?'

'Both her parents died some years ago,' Wynne said. 'We've spoken to some of the teachers who were around at the time and they didn't hear from her. They assumed that she wanted a clean start. It's odd, but ... it was a long time ago. So anything you know would be very helpful.'

'I don't know anything more,' Julia said. 'I'm not sure I can help.'

'You could ask Mr Crowne. Or Edna.'

Julia could have laughed. There was no way Edna would share anything with her, but she agreed to try.

'And in the meantime?' she said. 'What are you planning?'

'We're just going to focus our resources a little differently for a while.'

'What does that mean?'

'It means we're going to go door to door again. Revisit the people who work at the school. Talk to the parents of Anna's friends, to your relatives. To anyone we can think of who is connected to your daughter.'

'Didn't you do this already?'

'Yes, but we're going to do it again. And this time we're going to ask people if we can have a look around their houses. If we can search their houses. If they say no, then that might be grounds to get a warrant.'

Julia looked out at the reporters. Maybe they'd be gone soon after all. Maybe all this would be over. She didn't want to think it, didn't want to let herself dream it.

'Great,' Julia said. 'That's great.'

8

The Sixth Day

i.

They came yesterday.

The police. They came in the evening, when you had just returned home, when you were at your most vulnerable.

You answered the knock on the door, and there they were. A detective and two constables. Were they constables? Was that what they were called?

The detective gave you her spiel. She had it down pat. The usual thing.

Sincere apologies. Here on routine inquiries. Would like to have a look around. No suggestion you were involved, but have to be thorough. Sure you understand. No stone left unturned in an investigation like this.

You had not seen the girl since lunchtime. What if she awoke and cried out? You considered sending them away, making them get a warrant, but that would have aroused suspicion, given them the impression that you had something to hide. Then they would have been back with their warrant and reason to tear the place apart.

So you had to let them in. Had to take a risk. Had to trust that your plans – for you had planned for this, of course you had – would work.

No problem, come in, you said. *Just got home from work, so I'll be putting the kettle on. Thirsty work, mine. Fancy a cuppa?*

You wanted to stall them. Keep them in the kitchen for a few minutes. Maybe you could make an excuse and leave – go and change, perhaps – so you could listen for signs that the girl was awake. Then you would have to send them away. It would take time for them to get a warrant. Time in which you could get rid of the girl.

Thank God an Englishman's home is his castle, still.

It didn't work. They refused the tea.

Very kind, but no thank you. We'll just get on with it. Other people to visit.

Ok, you said. *But you won't mind if I do?*

You needed something to keep your hands busy. You didn't think your nervousness showed – your iron control was one of the things that set you apart – but it was useful to keep occupied, keep moving. It dispelled the nervous energy.

Not too much, though. That would be a giveaway.

175

They were there a long time. You heard them upstairs, in the attic, in the garage. They trampled across your lawn, into the shed, around the borders of your garden.

There was no evidence. The girl had never been there. She'd been in only two places. One was your neighbour's garage, which they did not search, and the other was her hiding place.

Which was a good hiding place. It had fooled many people over the centuries and you trusted that it would fool many more.

Provided the girl was silent.

It was infuriating. She could wake up at any minute, but there was nothing you could do. Even when they were in the garden you could not act. You could not risk them coming into the house and catching you.

At one point they were in the room she was hidden in, no more than three feet from her.

Three feet. Thirty-six inches between disaster and triumph.

It was the closest you had ever come, and it was the closest you wanted to come.

Then they moved away. Found another room to search.

Eventually they were finished. The detective thanked you.

Neighbours away? she said.

You nodded. *Somewhere abroad, I think. Or maybe Scotland. They might have mentioned the Highlands. I don't see them much.*

Hmm, she said. *Well, thank you. And apologies again for the disruption.*

Not at all, you said. *No disruption at all. Whatever I can do to help. Such a tragic situation.*

Then they were gone, with no idea how close they had been. Twenty minutes later the girl stirred and started to come round, started to mutter to herself.

This is becoming too risky. You have to act. You make up your mind.

Tomorrow is the day. Tomorrow you use the girl. In the morning.

ii.

'Tell him not to bother.'

Julia paused at the bottom of the stairs. The door to the living room was ajar and she could hear her mother-in-law's voice clearly. Edna was using her self-righteous tone, a combination of angry disinterest and long-suffering martyrdom, and Julia guessed she was talking about Simon.

'He only wants to pop in,' Brian said. 'See how things are.'

'Then I'm popping out,' Edna said. 'It's your choice, Brian. I've made my position perfectly clear. I don't want to see him. Not after what he – and his wife – did to me.'

'That was a long time ago, Mum,' Brian said. 'Maybe it's time to move on? He did come all this way, after all.'

In her years in the divorce courts, Julia had seen more or less all the varieties of human weakness and folly that drive families apart: drink, drugs, spousal abuse, gambling, neglect, indifference, infidelity. Often the divorce was at the end of a long period of conflict and unhappiness caused by whichever combination of these was at play, and equally often, this period took its toll on the family members, and in particular, on the kids, who tended to react in one of two ways: to retreat, and try to ignore what was going on, or to play the role of peacemaker.

Simon, it seemed, had taken the former course; Brian the latter. And he was still doing it.

'You don't seem to understand,' Edna said. 'Long time or not, come a long way or not, I don't care. He made his choice, Brian, and he has to live with it. And remember, he left you as well. Just like your father did. It was me who stayed, Brian. So if you feel it is appropriate to prioritize Simon in front of me then go ahead. Have him round to play happy brothers. But I won't be here. And I will remember your choice.'

Julia heard someone place a glass or a mug on the coffee table. It was probably Edna getting ready to leave. She didn't want to be caught eavesdropping, so she crossed the hall into the dining room and waited quietly.

A minute later, Edna left, slamming the front door behind her.

Julia stayed in the dining room. She heard a muffled conversation coming from the living room and went to look through the crack in the door. Brian was standing by the window, his phone to his ear.

'It's better if you don't come,' he said. 'Mum's just gone out but she'll be back soon.'

There was a pause while Simon spoke.

'It's not like that,' Brian said, his voice rising. 'I agree with her. You barely contact me and now you want me to upset my relationship with her just to please you? No way, Simon. No way.'

Another pause.

'She's not manipulating me! She's being perfectly reasonable!'

Julia shook her head. She was manipulating him, and not just into refusing to see Simon. She knew that Simon would accuse him of being weak and under Edna's thumb; she knew that Brian would defend her, and the brothers would argue, further strengthening Brian's reliance on her. What a bitch.

She pushed open the door and walked in. Brian turned to look at her.

'Look,' he said. 'I have to go. Bye, Simon.'

He put the phone down on the windowsill and glared at her.

'What?' he said. 'Why are you looking at me like that?'

Julia smiled. She understood Brian a lot better now, and she felt differently about him as a result. She felt sorry for him, and she wished she'd known what he had been through all along. It might not have changed anything – she would probably still have fallen in love with him, and she would almost definitely still have fallen out of love with him, for these were not things that you could control – but it would have given her the comfort that the failure of their marriage was not her fault. Brian was damaged, and it was that which had forced them apart, not her.

179

'I'm going out,' she said. 'There's something I need to do.'

What she needed to do was visit her brother-in-law. She didn't know him well, could hardly count him as a friend, but she wanted to speak to him. She wanted to understand what had happened with Edna that was so bad.

She called him at his hotel. She was lucky to get him; after his conversation with Brian he was heading to London to see an old friend, but he agreed to meet her at the train station for coffee.

They sat on a bench on Platform Two, styrofoam cups in their hands. Simon unwrapped a Scotch egg. He stuffed the crinkling wrapper into his jacket pocket.

'God, these things are foul,' he said. 'Don't know why I bought it. Childhood memories, I suppose. Dad used to buy them when he took us to London on the train.'

'Did you do that often?'

'From time to time. Took the Intercity 125 to Euston from this very platform.'

Julia caught Simon's eye. 'Where do you think he went?' she said. 'When he left?'

He paused. For a moment he looked like he was a teenager again, angry and lost, then he shrugged.

'Dunno,' he said. 'But if I had to guess, I'd say Italy. He always loved it there. Used to rave on about the quality of life, how they had figured out how to live, how they had their priorities in order. Edna didn't agree, of course. She thought they were lazy and dishonest, and refused to holiday there after I was about thirteen. After that we went to Scotland to swim in freezing seas and get devoured by midges. Bloody miserable, but character-building according to mummy dear. So he's probably on some Tuscan beach living with a false name. You can get away with that kind of thing in Italy.'

'Why do you think he went?'

'Why do *you* think he went?' Simon retorted. 'You've met Mum. I think they were probably happy at one time, but after a while they started to hate each other. And when she wants to Edna can make your life a misery. My guess is that he decided he couldn't take another thirty years of it, so he buggered off.'

'Does it bother you that he didn't get in contact?'

Simon nodded. 'Yes. Since I became a father, even more so. But he did what he had to do.'

'And my guess is that Edna told him she'd let him go in peace if he agreed to stay away from you and Brian,' Julia said. 'Which was probably quite appealing.'

'You know,' Simon said. 'I'd never thought of that. You're probably right. Just another reason to hate Mum, I guess.'

'Is that why you left, because you hated her?'

He gave a rueful chuckle. 'Is that why you came? To ask that?'

'Pretty much,' she said. 'And to say goodbye, but pretty much.'

'So, Mum did not like Laura from the off. She thought she was self-obsessed and brash and thoroughly

American. All the things I liked about her. When it became clear that we were serious, Edna decided that she needed to take control of the situation. She does that, Edna. You may have noticed. You know ... the thing is, her heart is in the right place. She means well. The problem is that she can't see that there is any other opinion than her own that matters, and she won't stop until she gets her own way, which is always justified, because she's always right.'

'It is one of her less endearing traits,' Julia said.

'Anyway, one day when the kids were young – babies, really – we were staying with Mum. Dad had been gone about a year. Laura was out running and Mum collared me in the kitchen and said she needed to have a chat. A chat about Laura. Who, she said, was seeing another man: an American who she had heard Laura talking to on the phone. She wasn't clear on the details, but it was obvious that Laura was making plans to divorce me, take half the money Dad had left when he disappeared, then go back to the US and be with him.'

'What did you do? Did you ask Laura?'

'The thing was that Laura's family was in financial trouble, so the whole thing had the ring of truth about it. Plus, when I met Laura she was engaged to somebody else, and, as Mum pointed out, if she was unreliable then, she was unreliable still.'

Same as she did with my affair with Chris, Julia thought. *Edna liked to make sure people remembered their mistakes.*

'So, did you ask her?'

'I didn't need to. Laura had come back from her run because of a pain in her knee and overheard the whole thing. She was great, actually. She just came in, beamed at Edna, thanked her for giving us a reason to leave, then told me she'd change our train tickets – we were living in London at the time – and start looking for a job stateside immediately. And then we left.'

'Was there a big row? Edna mentioned something like that.'

'Oh, there was, but that came later, when Edna found out that Laura had been telling everyone what had happened. She hit the roof.' He grinned. 'Laura just told her that if she didn't want people to know she shouldn't have done it. I remember it clearly. Laura standing with the phone in her hand and wagging her finger as though Edna was right in front of her. *Don't do things you might be ashamed of, Edna*. She was magnificent.'

'So you went?'

'We did. Up to Seattle. And it was the best decision I ever made. She's my mum, Julia, so it's hard to say this, but life is just better without her around. She just brings tension and aggravation.'

'I know. I just wish Brian had been able to make the leap you made.'

'Maybe he will,' Simon said. 'I hope so. And I'll be waiting with open arms if he does. Tell him that for me, if you get a chance.'

'I'll try.'

183

The station announcer's voice came over the Tannoy and informed them that the delayed 14.05 to Euston was arriving at the station. Simon stood up and held out his hand.

'Good luck,' he said, 'with everything. But especially with Anna.'

As the train pulled away, Julia realized that her cheeks were wet with tears.

iii.

When she got home Brian was waiting for her in the living room.

'We need to talk,' he said. 'About us. About our marriage.'

'Fine,' she said. 'What is it?'

'It's over,' Brian said. He made no attempt to soften the message. Julia, if asked, would have said he took pleasure in his bluntness. 'I'm moving out. I spoke to mum and she suggested that I move in with her.'

It was typical of Brian. Moving back in with his mum at his age. He'd be there until the day she died, when he'd be cast adrift, incapable of taking care of himself. Edna would love it. She'd be back in control. Julia couldn't blame him, though. She thought back to what Simon had told her about Edna's attempt to break up his relationship with Laura, and how close she had come, how it was only the fact that he had witnessed it that had enabled him to see what she was up to. Well, Brian had not seen that for himself, and so he had not been able to break free from the gravitational pull of his mother.

184

'Of course she did,' Julia said. 'But—'

Brian interrupted her. 'What does that mean?'

'What?'

'That snide "of course, she did"?'

'Nothing,' Julia said. She did not want another argument, not now. 'It meant nothing.'

'It must have meant something. So what was it?'

OK then, if she must. 'It meant that I'm not surprised that your mum wants her little boy back where she can keep an eye on him and protect him from the nasty world out there. Simon managed to get away; you didn't. But it's fine with me. You're right; our marriage is over. And I recall being the one to point that out to you. If now is the moment that you want to make it formal, then fine. Go to mummy. I hope you enjoy growing old together.'

'You know something?' Brian said. 'You're a bitch, Julia. A bitch. What has my mum ever done to you, except support and help us? And all you can do it criticize her. She's a good mother. She never left me waiting outside school.'

'She didn't have to. She sent you off to boarding school so that someone else could take care of you.' Julia held her hand up in a gesture of conciliation. There was no point arguing, and she didn't care anymore if Brian went, in the end. But now was not the time.

'You should do whatever you need to,' she said. 'But not now. If Anna comes back we need to be together, at least for a little while. And then there's the press. They'd have a field day.'

'Fuck the press,' Brian said. 'That's your problem. And if Anna comes back I don't care if we're not together. I'll be too busy being happy.' He looked at his knees. 'But you know something else? She's not coming back, Julia. I've been reading about this and talking to experts and if abducted kids are not found in the first twenty-four hours then the chances of them ever being found are not worth talking about. She's gone, Julia. Gone.'

Julia knew he'd spent hours online, reading about abduction or logged into chat rooms talking to so-called experts. It was part of his way of dealing with it; a method to convince himself that he was doing something, that he was finding the answers. It also allowed him to come to terms with Anna's loss: by convincing himself she was gone, he could start to get over it. He was not making the same mistake of hoping that Julia was.

'She might be ok,' Julia said. 'She might. And she needs both of us.'

'You believe that if you want to,' Brian said. 'But I don't.'

'So that's it, then?' Julia said. 'You're moving out?'

Brian nodded. 'I'll go tonight. I'll come for my stuff later. We can figure out what to do about the house and money and all that then.'

Julia decided to make one last appeal. She didn't care about Brian going – she knew as well as anyone that their relationship was over – but she didn't want it to happen right that moment. Apart from anything else, she didn't want to be alone in the house. Even Brian was better than nobody.

'Can we wait?' she asked him. 'Just a week or so?'

'No,' Brian said. 'We can't. And the reason why is simple, Julia. I can't stand the sight of you. Can't stand to be anywhere near you. Can't stand to hear you walking around, to know that I occupy the same house as the woman who ruined my life. I don't care what happens to you now, Julia. I'm just going to take care of myself.'

And then he stood up and walked into the hall. Julia heard him pick up his car keys and open the front door. There was the noise of shutters clicking and shouted questions, and then he was gone.

She sat back in the armchair. The room was silent. It was the same silence she had experienced a thousand times before when alone in her house, but this time it seemed different.

This time it seemed as though it would never end.

9

The Seventh Day

i.

Today is the day.

You take your time getting ready. You have to. There is no way you can allow a mistake now. Not when you are so close. You run a bath, hot and soapy. Wear surgical gloves, disposable clothes – you can burn them later – a mask – Tony Blair, a nice ironic touch – just in case she sees you.

You open the door. The girl sleeps, drugged a little more heavily than usual. You carry her upstairs. She's heavier than she looks, especially when so unresponsive. You strip her and put her in the bath. Her clothes go in a plastic bag to be disposed of. They have traces of you on them.

You wash her carefully; scrubbing her skin until it is pink, working a lather of shampoo into her hair. All through it she sleeps. When you are done you lay her on a towel. Unwrap the brand new clothes. Dress her, making sure your skin does not touch hers.

The towel goes in the plastic bag.

You carry the girl downstairs and into the garage and into the car. Not your car. A new one. Bought for cash seventy miles away, nearly on the other side of the country. No questions asked. You can dump it when the job is done, when the girl is gone. Maybe set fire to it. Maybe leave it with the keys in, in one of the rough parts of town. Let people who have experience in making things disappear get rid of it.

Either way, it will be gone.

Same as the girl.

And once the girl is gone, it is time to turn your attention to the real target.

The mother.

ii.

Julia had not slept. Not even fallen asleep for a minute. Now, at nine in the morning she was sitting on the couch with a mug of coffee and wondering how she would stop herself unravelling. It didn't help that she could not stop reading what the world was saying about her.

'I don't care how busy you are, you don't leave a child alone and unattended in this world full of predatory paedophiles, constantly on the lookout for fresh victims. It is the height of irresponsibility to do so.'

189

Or, another theme, one that reoccurred:

'Mrs Crowne is representative of a certain type of person, the type who cannot do anything other than put themselves first. Never mind the damage to her family, she wants a divorce. Never mind the risk to her child, she has something better to do, so poor Anna can wait until her mother is ready to take her home. If she was having an affair – and who would be surprised to find out she was – never mind who got hurt, never mind if her lover had a wife and a family who would be torn apart. No, none of this matters, as long as Julia Crowne is happy, as long as she gets her sordid moments of fleeting pleasure.'

It was unbearable. Julia didn't think she was perfect, but she was not this person, this amoral, self-interested, irresponsible monster that the press was making her out to be. Yes, she wanted a divorce, but that was hardly news these days, and in any case, most of the journalists condemning her were hardly paragons of virtue. She didn't know the facts, but she would not have been surprised to find out that the number of divorced or adulterous or alcoholic or drug-addicted people working on Fleet Street was well above the national average.

Yes, she had been late for her daughter, and for that she needed no help in feeling guilty. The quiet of the house, the silence between her and Brian, the constant reminders of Anna – the child's cereal at the back of a

190

kitchen cupboard, the Lego piece lodged between the cushions of a sofa, the small step stool by the bathroom sink – made sure that the guilt was a permanent fixture, outbid for a claim on her emotions only by the constant, throbbing pain of missing her daughter.

Worse than missing: it was pure loss. There was nothing else. Just loss. The loss of her daughter, the loss of the future she had imagined for them both.

It was the little things that hurt the most. There was a picture of a whale playing with a dolphin that Anna had drawn on the fridge door; it reminded her of the day Anna had brought it home and Julia had asked her what it was before complimenting it. That in turn reminded her of when Anna had shown her one of her early drawings, a drawing that looked uncannily like a horse, and which made Julia wonder whether her daughter was a gifted artist.

What a lovely horse, she said.

A frown.

Mummy. It's not a horse. It's a turtle.

So now she asked for identification early, and the picture reminded her of that, which reminded her that she may not be the recipient of one of her daughter's unrecognizable drawings ever again, and that was simply too painful to bear.

And it never stopped. All she wanted was for it to stop, for just a few hours, so she could get some kind of a break, have some rest, some sleep.

Julia pushed her coffee away. She needed something stronger, even at nine in the morning. And why not?

What else did she have to do? She stood up and opened the drinks cabinet. There was a bottle of vodka. She stood looking at it. Imagined drinking it all, just so she could pass out. But drink wouldn't do it. She'd just wake up even more paranoid than before, and with a hangover to boot.

She reached for it and took a long swig anyway. What did a hangover matter in the scheme of things? Her marriage was over. Her reputation was in tatters. There was one photo of her doing the rounds in which she had been Photoshopped to look like Myra Hindley. It was everywhere, and it had come to define how she was seen.

Myra Hindley.

Myra-fucking-Hindley.

It didn't get much lower than that. *Lower than a snake's belly*, as her dad, her dear, beloved father, and oh, how she missed him, missed his warmth and strength and love, would have said. If there was a proxy for female evil in the British mind it was Myra Hindley. And Julia Crowne was being put in the same bracket.

And worst of all, Anna was gone. Gone for good, Julia was sure about that. The police were getting nowhere and she could tell from the tone of her conversations with DI Wynne that they were giving up hope. Anna could literally be anywhere. Every year thousands of kids disappeared like this, and few, if any, were found.

God, she wanted a break from these thoughts. *Needed* a break. Needed some sleep, just a few hours of dreamless sleep. Perhaps she could ask her doctor for sleeping pills. Maybe later in the day, though. Better wait until the smell of the vodka was gone.

Or she could take some of Brian's. There were some in the bathroom cabinet, or at least, there had been before he left. She could take one of those. Or two.

She got unsteadily to her feet. She hadn't eaten much in a week and the vodka was burning a hole straight through her stomach to her brain. Upstairs, she opened the bathroom cabinet.

There it was: a small yellow plastic bottle of sleeping pills.

She took the bottle downstairs and emptied the pills onto the coffee table. Nineteen left, nineteen little white pills. How easy to swallow them and end the suffering. How easy to put a stop to all this here and now. It would take a few seconds to consume them. That was all that stood between her and relief. A few painless seconds.

But no. Not while there was a chance Anna would be found. Not while there was a chance Anna was alive. If they told her she was dead, then she would take the pills. But not before. She wanted sleep, not endless oblivion.

She read the dosage on the side of the bottle. *One before bedtime.* One wouldn't do it. She cupped her hand around two of the pills and lifted them to her mouth. She placed them on her tongue. They were bitter. She swallowed them, then washed them down with a large slug of vodka.

Only a few minutes passed before she felt herself losing consciousness. God, these things were strong. For a moment she wondered in alarm whether she had taken too many, then she surrendered to the chemical embrace.

Then her phone rang.

She opened an eye and glanced at the screen.

She recognized – just, through the incoming fog – DI Wynne's number.

She let it ring out. She was sick of speaking to the cop, sick of hearing her reports that nothing had changed.

It rang again. DI Wynne again. She picked up.

'Hello,' she said, her voice slurred.

'Mrs Crowne, I have some news.'

DI Wynne had a strange, high tone to her voice.

'Yes,' she said. 'What is it?' It came out as *wharisit*?

'Mrs Crowne, we've found Anna.'

Julia shook her head. 'What did you say?' *Whadyasay*?

'I said, we've found Anna.'

Through the fog, Julia could not quite grasp the meaning of the words. 'This a joke?' *Shajoke*?

'No,' DI Wynne said. 'It isn't.'

'She ok?' *Shokay*?

'She's fine, Mrs Crowne.' Wynne sounded uncomprehending, as though she couldn't believe what she was saying. 'She's totally unharmed. She just walked into a newsagent and said hello.'

Julia barely understood what she was hearing before she fell asleep, but she understood enough.

As she slumped onto the couch she was smiling for the first time in a week.

PART TWO: AFTERWARDS

10

Back Home

i.

It is done.

You took the girl to a quiet lay-by on a dual carriageway about fifty miles away. You chose it a few days back, attracted by the line of trees that screen it from the road and the fields that stretch out on the far side. It pays to plan ahead. That way you can think things through, examine all the angles. And this was the best place to do it.

The lay-by is on a straight section of the road, so you can see a mile or two in either direction. When you were sure nothing was coming in either direction, you lifted her limp body from the back seat and deposited her in a bus shelter.

You left the girl sleeping in the corner of the bus shelter. She was stirring as you departed, not far from consciousness. That was good; it would not be long before she awoke and wandered into plain sight, where she would soon be found.

You pulled out and drove away, unseen again. You are not surprised by this. You have a talent for this kind of thing, a talent you have used before, when it has been necessary. It is a combination of planning and nerve, both of which you have in abundance.

There is one thing you feared, one thing left out of your control. What if the person who found her was not as honourable as you? What if they saw a lone girl – a girl who was already missing, and therefore could be taken without risk – and did not return her to the authorities? Unlikely, for sure, but possible. There are some disgusting people out there.

Not everyone is like you. Not everyone can be trusted to do things for the right reasons. It might appear to the outside world that you and they are the same; that you are both kidnappers or murderers, but that is not the case. They are crude, base criminals. What you do is different. It is great. It is necessary. It is right. But you can't expect others to understand.

You considered staying in the vicinity so that you could ensure the girl's safety, but that would have been too dangerous. No, you had to let her take her chances. It was a risk, but a calculated one. At that point all you could do was hope.

And hope you did. Because you need her home, safe and unharmed.

Because although this part is done, it is not over yet. You are not finished.

The important part is just beginning.

ii.

Julia was woken by a throbbing in her head. It felt like someone had set up a bass drum inside her skull and was kicking it with a steel-toed boot.

What the hell happened? Julia thought. *Why do I have this foul hangover?*

And then she remembered. The vodka and the sleeping pills. And then another memory, of a phone call. A phone call about Anna. From DI Wynne.

A phone call telling her that Anna was alive, that she'd been found.

She caught the rising excitement and held it in check. She'd been here before, dreaming that Anna was home. This time the memory was very clear, hardly dreamlike at all, but that was perhaps the result of the combination of alcohol and sleeping pills and her frantic wish for her daughter to be with her.

She glanced at the window. It was light outside, maybe late morning. So the pills had knocked her out all night. She closed her eyes against the light and tried to remember what had happened.

She was in bed. She had not been in bed when she had taken the pills, which meant someone had brought her up here. It also meant that there was water nearby, in the en-suite bathroom. It would be nice to have water. Clear, cool, life-giving water.

She'd get it in a minute. As she lay there images came

back to her. Broken memories. The bitter taste of the pills. The burn of the vodka. The phone ringing, then ringing again.

DI Wynne's voice.

Mrs Crowne, we've found Anna.

The dream again. She pushed it away but it was persistent. Fuzzy, clouded by the booze and pills, but persistent. And it felt real. Specific, tangible.

She opened her eyes and stared at the ceiling.

It *was* real. Anna was alive. She knew it somehow. Something in her body felt different.

Anna was alive.

She pushed back the covers and swung her feet onto the carpet. She stood up too quickly for her hangover to handle and the blood rushed from her head. Faint, she sat back down.

Downstairs she heard a laugh. It was man's laugh, a laugh she knew well. It was her husband, Brian. The laugh came again. And again.

Brian was laughing, and there was only one reason for that.

'Anna!' she called. Her voice was high and croaky. She cleared her throat. 'Anna!'

There was a silence, then she heard fast, heavy footsteps on the stairs. She recognized the footsteps; it had always amazed her that someone so light and delicate as her daughter could tread so heavily, as though she was stamping instead of walking.

'Anna,' she said, to herself. 'Oh God, Anna. Is it you?'

She didn't believe it – couldn't believe it – until the bedroom door was flung open and there she was, fresh and smiling and beautiful and Anna, so perfectly Anna, her daughter, her child, the love of her life, there, in the doorway, then running across the carpet towards her and then, finally, in her arms.

Her daughter was in her arms.

It was like nothing she had ever felt before. Everything – the smell of Anna's breath, the heat of her body, the taste of her tears, the sound of her repeated cries of *mummy, mummy* as she ran from the door to the bed – was hyper-real. It was as though Julia's senses did not trust what they were presented with, and so had turned themselves up to a new, more intense level that allowed them to see and smell and taste more deeply so that they could not be deceived. She saw the cracks and valleys in Anna's lips as they quivered, picked out individual hairs on her head, saw the tiny flakes of skin on her ears. And she loved every detail.

The closest she had come to this sensation was on the day Anna was born, when the midwife had placed this tiny, mewling, blood-and-mucus-coated, alien creature onto Julia's newly empty abdomen, and Julia had fallen instantly in love with it. She could bring it back to mind still, as though the memory was minutes and not years old. It was the clearest, most significant, happiest memory of her life.

But it was nothing compared to this.

Back then, she had rejoiced in the gaining of something wonderful; now, she was regaining something wonderful.

She had been as low as it was possible to be; had lost everything, had known the heights of being a parent, and fallen to the depths of having lost a child, a loss made worse by the fact it was her fault. She had been so low she had been in the process of killing herself, and now she had her daughter back. The swing from utter despair to rapturous joy was incredible. She was aware, as she held Anna, that she was one of the very few people to have known such extremes; one of the very few unfortunate enough to have known them.

She tugged her daughter against her chest and pressed her lips to her cheek. Anna was thin, her shoulders sharp and the bones in her face more prominent, but she was smiling as she hugged her mum; she was ok, she was alive and here and that was all that mattered.

'I'll never let you go again, Anna,' she said. 'I promise. I'll never let you go again.'

iii.

'Julia?' Brian's voice came from outside the bedroom. He had not – at least, as far as she knew – crossed the threshold of their former marital inner sanctum since Anna had disappeared.

'Daddy,' Anna said, lifting her head from Julia's chest. 'Come in and cuddle. We can all cuddle together.'

There was a long pause. 'I don't know,' Brian said. 'I—'

'Come *on*, Daddy!'

Brian stepped into the room. His eyes were still sunken and surrounded by dark circles, but there was a lightness in his expression that had not been there since the day Anna disappeared.

'It's ok,' Julia said. She shifted herself to one side of the bed. 'Sit down.'

Brian took a few hesitant steps across the room, then lay on what had been his side of the bed, propped up on his elbow. He reached out and put his hand on Anna's hip; she turned from Julia and flung her arms around his neck.

'I *love* you, Daddy,' she said.

'I love you too,' he murmured. 'So much.'

For a moment Julia wondered whether she had judged him too harshly, whether he was a better, kinder, *fuller*, husband and father than she had given him credit for. Had she expected too much of him? Had she been blinded by the glare of what she wanted him to be, left unable to see the muted light of Brian's qualities, qualities that might have found – might find, still – a fuller expression away from the sunless undergrowth around his mother?

She put her hand on his forearm and smiled at him.

'Brian,' she said. 'She's back.'

He turned his shoulders so that his forearm twisted away from her.

'Yeah,' he said. 'It's amazing. Like a dream.'

'Where was she?'

'They don't know. She woke up in a bus shelter this morning and walked into a newsagent in Tarporley. No one saw her until she was nearly there.'

This morning. While Julia had been drinking on the couch her daughter had been returning to the world. She looked at the alarm clock. Three p.m. So she'd been out six hours.

But it didn't matter. All that mattered was that Anna was here. 'Is she ok?'

'Fine, physically. The police said … ', he paused, and nodded at Anna,. 'can we talk about this later? It's better, I think.'

'Ok.'

'You should come downstairs. DI Wynne is on her way. You need to get dressed.'

Anna rolled away from Brian. 'Can I stay up here with you, Mummy?'

'Of course.' Julia put her hands out and folded them around Anna. She was so warm, so present, so *alive*. Julia had not expected this, had not believed that she would ever see her daughter again. She had accepted that Anna was gone, taking with her the only thing that gave Julia's life meaning and purpose. Julia had faced what that meant, had stared at a life lived without her daughter and with the knowledge that she was to blame for her loss and decided that it was not a life she could live.

She felt goosebumps prickle on her arms. She hugged Anna tighter, grateful for the throbbing in her temples and the pain at the back of her eyes. It meant she was alive; here to welcome her daughter back to her home.

But, despite her joy, a thought nagged at her.

Someone, for some reason, had abducted her daughter. They had taken the risk of whisking her away in broad daylight, had found a way to keep her hidden during a national – an *international* – hunt, only to return her a week later.

It was a huge risk; if they were caught then the implications for them were obvious. If they had had killed her or sold her on then Julia could understand why they had done it – they presumably got whatever pleasure they got from killing, or they got paid, and then they disposed of the body. As long as the police had no leads then they were safe. The motive was also obvious: a random poaching of an unwatched child. It was an old story, well understood.

But that was not what had happened. Whoever had done this had taken all that risk, and then they had taken some more: they had returned Anna. Why? What did they gain? It didn't make sense. There was something missing, something Julia did not understand.

And it worried her. What if it was not random after all? What if they had selected Anna – specifically Anna – for some reason?

Anna wriggled against Julia. Julia squeezed her hard against her chest.

'Mummy,' Anna said. 'You're squashing me.'

'Sorry,' Julia said. 'But I just don't ever want to let you go.'

And she didn't, because if they had selected Anna, if there was some reason for this, then it might not be over.

And whoever had done this was still out there, with whatever reason they had done it for still known only to them.

And they might be watching right now, planning their next move.

iv.

'Mrs Crowne,' DI Wynne said. 'What fabulous news. I'm so pleased for you.'

Wynne's smile was the first truly genuine expression Julia had seen on her face. She was always the same: steady, professional, measured. Bland, almost. So bland that it had to be an act. No one without passion could do her job, but no one who could not control their passion would be able to stick at it. If you let yourself get too involved, it would devour you, Julia could see that.

And the smile: relaxed, relieved, full, was proof that DI Wynne was human after all.

'Thank you,' Julia said. 'For all you did.'

She, Brian, and DI Wynne were sitting in the living room. Julia's hair was wet from the shower; she felt cleaner, but her headache was still sharp, despite taking two doses of ibuprofen. Still, it didn't matter. The world had taken on a soft glow. Anna was sleeping, her head on Julia's lap.

DI Wynne shrugged. 'I wish I could say that we'd done more, but this was really not down to us. She just … well, she just showed up.'

Brian had filled her in on what she had missed. Despite the magnitude of the events, there really wasn't all that much: the police received a call around nine a.m. from a newsagent in the Cheshire village of Tarporley to say that a girl calling herself Anna Crowne had walked into the shop, declared she was hungry, and asked for her mummy. The shopkeeper gave her water and a Crunchie bar, then called the police. By nine fifteen Anna was in the hands of the local police; by ten a.m. she was at the police station with DI Wynne and Brian. Her mum was passed out at home, but nobody needed to know about that.

Anna was fine, Brian said. Lost some weight, but unharmed and quite cheerful. She was very interested in the police station and asked to see the cells; a woman police officer took her down there. When she came back she was eating a choc ice from the canteen. She declared to Brian, DI Wynne, and the doctor who had showed up that she was going to be a policeman when she grew up.

Or a policewoman, DI Wynne said.

No, Anna said. *A policeman.*

I'm afraid it might be my fault, the woman police officer said. *I told her that I didn't eat many choc ices but that the male officers ate them all the time.*

So Anna was fine, except for one thing: she had no memory of what had happened to her. She had no idea who had taken her or where she had been. All she remembered was waking up in the bus shelter and then walking across a field to the buildings she could see, because she was cold and wanted to get warm. DI Wynne pressed gently, asking whether the person was a man or a woman, tall or short, had a nice voice or a nasty voice, but there was nothing. She didn't have any memory of the events at all.

Julia asked how that was possible.

'She was probably given some kind of memory inhibiting drug,' DI Wynne said. 'There are plenty about.'

Julia wondered, briefly, – before she forced the thought from her mind, although she knew it would intrude again, late at night or first thing in the morning – what had been done to Anna that was so bad it needed to be erased from her memory. She could think of a few things, and none of them were anything other than awful.

'A child psychologist will have to see her', DI Wynne told Brian, 'but there don't seem to be any signs of emotional trauma.'

There were also no signs of sexual abuse. It didn't mean there hadn't been something, but if there had it was not violent or invasive and it had left no trace. Julia found this both reassuring, and disturbing. She didn't want there to be signs of sexual abuse, but she also wanted to know for sure that there hadn't been any. The thought that someone might have abused her daughter so cleverly that they left no evidence of having done so was cold comfort.

'So you don't know who took her?' Julia said. 'Was there anything on her clothes? Fibres? DNA?'

DI Wynne shook her head. 'Nothing. Someone did a very thorough job of removing all traces of themselves. Her clothes had been washed. My guess is that whoever did this handled them with gloves from the moment they took them from the washing machine. Then they put them on Anna before leaving her in the bus shelter this morning.'

Julia nodded. 'So you have nothing?'

Wynne sipped her tea. 'Very little.'

'And will you keep the investigation open?' Brian asked.

'We will,' Wynne said. She glanced up at the ceiling; it was an odd, evasive gesture. She looked back at Julia. 'We are still interested in finding the person who did this.'

'In case they do it again?' Julia said.

'That,' Wynne said. 'And also … well, this is a bit of a confusing situation. I've never come across something quite like this. I'd be happier if we had the perpetrator behind bars.'

'Right,' Brian said. 'The child rarely shows up. If they do it's often years later.'

He was an expert now, Julia thought. It was an unpleasant thing to have needed to become an expert in, but at least now it was just knowledge, and not his own experience.

'Exactly,' Wynne said. 'But to just return the child, unharmed, well, it's unheard of.'

'Perhaps they felt sorry for us,' Julia said. 'Maybe they saw our press conference.'

'It's possible,' Wynne said, although it was clear she didn't think that was the case. 'But we don't know for sure. We don't know much. Why they would do this, for example. Why they would take such a risk, when there's nothing in it for them.'

'So you think there is more to this?' she said. 'You think there is more to come? Are we at risk?'

Even if this *was* over, she thought, she would never know. She would have to live for the rest of her life with the fear that it might happen again.

'It can't have been for no reason,' DI Wynne said. 'That's what worries me.'

'But what would the reason be?' Julia said. 'It doesn't make sense. Maybe it's – I dunno – like a game to them. Maybe they want to create the hardest possible conditions in which to kidnap a child – I mean, we'll watch her like a hawk – and then prove they can do it.'

The sense of powerlessness was overwhelming. How could she protect her child against some unknown, unquantified, unguessable threat? If, at that moment, DI Wynne had offered her a new identity in Australia she would have taken it without a moment of hesitation. She just wanted to get away, to be able to raise her daughter in safety. It wasn't too much to ask, was it?

'We'll put a squad car outside your house,' Wynne said. 'At least until we have more certainty about what is going on.'

Julia nodded, partially – for the moment, at least – reassured. 'And the press,' she said. 'Are they still out there?'

'No. We moved them on. You need your privacy at a time like this. I can't say they won't be back eventually, but hopefully all this will have died down a bit by then. There'll be another story for them to sink their teeth into.'

'Some other poor bugger's life to ruin,' Brian said. 'Bunch of bastards, the lot of them.'

On her lap, Anna stirred. Julia looked down at her daughter's face, her mouth slightly parted, her eyeballs twitching as she dreamed.

What are you dreaming about? she thought. *Are you seeing whoever did this? Are they in your mind at this moment, right there in front of me but totally inaccessible?*

She looked up at DI Wynne. 'So what's next?' she said.

'Well,' Wynne replied. 'We'll be carrying on with the investigation. I'd like you to monitor Anna closely, see if she says anything that might give us an indication of where she's been. The memory is a strange animal. It can throw things up at the least likely moment.' She looked at Brian. 'And if you hear from your father, we'd be interested to speak to him. But other than that, try and keep things as normal as possible.'

Brian started to get to his feet. DI Wynne motioned him to stay seated.

'I'll see myself out,' she said. 'You stay there.' She walked towards the door. When she reached it she turned around. 'And Mr and Mrs Crowne? I want to let you know how happy I am for you that your family is back together. Have a good night.'

v.

The front door clicked shut and the house was silent. It seemed to Julia that it was the first time in a week that the house had been truly quiet: yes, there had been plenty of moments when there was no sound, but the lack of sound had almost been a noise; a reminder of Anna's absence. And, in any case, whether there was noise or not had made no difference to the clamour inside Julia's skull. Her mind had whirred, cogs flicking her thoughts from memories of Anna to wretched fears about where she might be to lacerating feelings of guilt.

Now, though, with her daughter's head in her lap, there was peace in the silence.

'Are you going to take her up to bed?' Brian asked.

'I suppose I should,' Julia said. She looked again at Anna's sleeping face and fell in love all over again with her daughter. 'But I can't bring myself to let her go.'

'I know. I can't believe she's back. I didn't think – I mean, I hoped, but I just didn't dare think she'd – you know. Come home.'

'I know,' Julia said, aware of the exact feeling he was trying to describe – a mixture of disbelief and wonder with the feeling you get when you realize that you nearly ran into a car or made some huge mistake but just missed it, the feeling of being simply *lucky* – but equally unable to put it into words.

There was a long pause. It grew heavy and pregnant.

'We need to talk,' Brian said.

'About us?'

'About us. But also about you.'

'What about me?'

'I found you passed out on the couch, Julia, surrounded by sleeping pills and vodka. I'm worried.'

'Don't worry about me. I'm fine.' *A bit embarrassed*, Julia thought, *but fine*.

'You tried to *kill* yourself,' Brian said. 'I'd hardly call that fine.'

Julia shook her head. 'No,' she said. 'No. That's not what happened. It wasn't ... I didn't try to kill myself. I just wanted some sleep. A break.'

Brian did not look convinced. Julia felt indignation swell in her throat.

'Brian! I didn't try to kill myself! I can't believe you think that!'

'If you say so,' he said. 'But it looked a lot like that.'

'If I'd tried to kill myself I would have done it,' Julia said. 'I would have taken more than two sleeping pills. I would have taken them all.' She shook her head. 'This is ridiculous. The worst thing is that I thought about it, but there was no way I could have done it. Not while there was a chance Anna was still alive. And she is, Brian. That's what we should be talking about, not some imagined suicide attempt.'

Brian nodded. 'Ok,' he said. 'It's your business. I have something else I want to say.'

'Go ahead,' Julia said. 'Get it off your chest.'

'We need to make arrangements. For the separation.'

'Do we have to do this now?' Julia said. 'Can't it wait?'

213

'No,' Brian said. 'Now's best.'

'Ok.' Julia kept her eyes on Anna's face. Nothing could bother her while she had her daughter in her arms. 'What are you thinking?'

'That I would leave. Go to Mum's, maybe. We'd sell the house. Split the proceeds. Or you could buy me out with your share of our money and stay here.'

Julia was ready to accept that Brian and her were over. She wanted her and Brian to be over, but this was not the time. They did not need the disruption of a messy divorce hot on the heels of Anna's disappearance and miraculous return.

'Look,' she said. 'I know things aren't great between us, but couldn't we put this off? I think Anna's going to need us both. She's going to need the stability of a familiar home and both her parents.'

'Our relationship is over, Julia. After what ... ' he paused, uncertain about whether to carry on, then gave a little shrug, as though reconciled that whatever he was going to say needed to be said, and carried on, 'what you did, there's no hope of it working between us. You told me you wanted a divorce; that the life I offered wasn't enough for you, and then you didn't bother showing up for Anna. The fact that it turned out ok in the end doesn't justify it, and I don't forgive you. For *either* thing.'

'I get it,' Julia said. 'And I don't expect us to stay together forever. I just think we could hold on before we tear everything apart. We can sleep in separate rooms.

It might be miserable for *us*, but at least Anna will have stability. I mean, it's not perfect, but we'll hardly be the only couple with a shitty relationship who stay together for the sake of their children.'

Brian hesitated. 'How long for?' he said.

'I don't know. Six months. A year, maybe. Whatever it takes until it feels like it's the right time to do it. And don't worry. You can see other people, do whatever you want. I don't care. I just want to protect Anna.'

He reddened. 'That's not what I want,' he said. 'This is not about seeing other people.' He shook his head. 'It's so *typical* of you to think that it is. You always find a way to see me in the worst light. I just thought it was for the best.'

'I'm sorry.' She realized she was about to manipulate him, but didn't care. 'If you want to do what's for the best, then stay, for a while at least. That's all I'm asking. Do it for Anna.'

'Fine, I'll do it. I'll stay.' He sat upright, his shoulders squaring in an attempt to keep his pride. 'But I'm only doing it for her. Not for any other reason. Not for *you*.'

Julia sighed. 'Good,' she said. 'Thank you.' She cinched Anna tighter to her, then levered herself to her feet. 'I think I will put Anna in bed. She can sleep with me tonight. See you in the morning.'

She left him downstairs, the bitterness hanging between them, but she didn't care. As long as she had Anna she didn't care about Brian or her marriage or her career. She didn't care about anything. As long as she had Anna everything was ok.

vi.

The psychologist was not what Julia had expected. He was in his early fifties, had a pot belly, wore black nail varnish on his left hand, and finished every sentence by slightly tilting his head and saying 'y'know?'

He sat next to Anna on a faded, sagging couch. On the table in front of him were some children's books and toys. Julia sat in an armchair, a little off to the side. There had been a suggestion that Anna would go in alone, but Julia had not agreed.

'So,' he said to Anna. 'My name is Robert, but you can call me Rob, Robbie, Mr Robbie, Bob, Monsieur Bob, or, if you really want, Dave.'

Anna giggled. 'Can I call you Thomas,' she said. 'Like the train?'

Robert – Rob, Robbie, Bob – nodded. 'If you wish. 'Do you like trains?'

'A bit.' Anna paused. 'But not a lot. Boys like trains.'

'Girls too,' Robert said. 'Girls like trains too, y'know.'

'I know,' Anna said. 'But mainly boys do.'

Julia stopped herself jumping into the conversation and explaining that she and Brian had tried to avoid gender stereotyping as much as they could, but, despite their best efforts, Anna had still picked up the idea that girls and boys liked and did different things. It was infuriating to Julia – she was sick of pink fairies and princesses – but there seemed to be little she could do about it.

The conversation went on. Robert asked Anna what she liked to do, who her friends were, where she went to school. He asked if she had been anywhere new recently, if there were things she didn't like (spiders and broccoli, apparently), if she ever felt unsafe or worried. She answered his questions freely, and, at the end of the half hour, he clapped his hands gently and smiled at her.

'Well,' he said. 'That was every interesting. I enjoyed meeting you, Anna. Would you like to see me again?'

Anna nodded. 'You're funny.'

'OK. Well, I'll arrange it with your mum. But other than that, we're done for the day.'

In the lobby Robert asked the receptionist to take Anna to choose a sticker from the basket they kept behind the desk. He shook Julia's hand.

'I'll write up a full report,' he said. 'But she seems fine. No signs of trauma. Chatty, confident, relaxed. A very happy little girl. I'll meet with her once a week for a while and see if that changes, but for now it seems things are well.'

'Thank you,' Julia said. 'I can't tell you how happy I am to hear that.'

'I have six of my own,' Robert said. 'From twenty-two down to ten, so I know how you feel. There's no worry like the worry you have for your kids. I find it physically painful.'

'And with six there must always be something to worry about.'

'There is with one,' Robert said. 'And you can only worry so much. With six you just spread the worry around more.'

'I don't even want to think about that,' Julia said. 'I don't know how you manage.'

'Manage?' Robert said. 'Who said I manage? With six kids I just focus on survival.'

The receptionist walked over, holding Anna's hand. 'She wanted two stickers,' she said. 'Normally we only allow one, but I let her have both.'

Anna was going to get that kind of special treatment for a while, Julia realized. It came of being *the little girl who was abducted*.

'Which did you get?' Robert asked her.

'The unicorn and the butterfly,' Anna said.

'Not the train and the racing car?' Robert said.

'No,' Anna said. 'I told you. Trains are for boys. And racing cars. I like animals. And the big doll's house.'

'OK,' Robert said. 'Have it your way.'

Julia paused. She looked at Anna and replayed what her daughter had just said. There was something odd, something out of place.

'What big doll's house?' she asked.

Anna titled her head upwards. She frowned. 'The big one,' she said. 'The one I slept in.'

Julia's heart rate increased. 'When did you sleep in a dolls' house?'

Anna didn't answer for a few seconds. When she did, she looked thoughtful. 'I don't know,' she said. 'I don't remember.'

'What was it like?' Robert's tone was exactly as it had been before: calm, measured, playful, but there was an urgency underneath. 'Tell me about the doll's house. I love doll's houses.'

'No you don't,' Anna said. 'You're a boy.'

'You have an appointment starting,' the receptionist said. 'Mr Newall.'

'Could you let him know I'll be a few minutes late?' Robert said. He addressed himself to Anna. 'I love them,' he said. 'Boys can love them, too. Tell me about yours. The big one.'

'I can't really remember it,' Anna said. 'I just remember that it was big, and I slept in it.'

'How could a doll's house be big enough to sleep in?' asked Robert. 'Surely that would make it a house for people?'

'No,' Anna insisted. 'It was a doll's house. But it was very big.'

'Do you remember where it was?'

Anna shook her head. 'No,' she said. 'Maybe it was a dream.'

'Maybe.' Robert looked at Julia. 'Let's have a chat,' he said.

Julia and Brian occupied the couch in Robert's office. DI Wynne sat in the armchair. Robert stood by the door.

'She said she had slept in a big doll's house,' Julia said. 'That was what was strange to me. She was very specific. She said she had slept there. Not played with it: slept in it. It's not the kind of thing she would make up.'

219

'Take me through what she said,' Wynne urged. 'Try and get it as close as possible to her exact words.'

Robert drummed his fingers on his upper lip. He recounted the conversation. He talked slowly, stopping every few words to make sure that what he was saying was as close as possible to what he remembered.

'So,' Brian said. 'What do you think?'

'Well,' said Wynne. 'It could be nothing. A dream, a figment of her imagination—'

'I don't think it is,' Julia said. 'It's not like Anna to make things up like this.'

Wynne nodded. 'If it's true, then it tells us that Anna was in a place with a big doll's house. Big enough to sleep in. So we need to find places with something that fits the bill.' She got to her feet. 'I need to get started,' she said. 'Find manufacturers of doll's houses, speak to places that sell them, start the team digging on this.'

'It doesn't seem much to go on,' Brian said. 'Just a doll's house.'

'You'd be surprised,' DI Wynne replied, a sharp, hunter's look in her eye. 'If we can get some telling detail then we can start to track it down. Assuming it's real, we already know it's big, big enough to sleep in. So we find places that sell big doll's houses, ask them how many they've sold, who bought them. If the buyer used a credit card, then we can trace them easily; even if not, a sales rep might remember something. A lone man buying a doll's house – might have stood out.'

'Sounds good,' Julia said. 'What can we do to help?'

'Speak to Anna,' DI Wynne said. 'Ask her what else she remembers. Anything at all: smells, voices – a man's voice or a woman's voice – sensations, feelings – was she scared? Happy? Sad? Was it light or dark, day or night? Did anyone touch her? Were they strong? Wearing rings? A watch? Any details on clothes they were wearing? Anything at all.'

'Maybe make it a game,' Robert said. 'Lie down, eyes closed and play make-believe that she is taking you on a trip to the big doll's house with her. Get her to describe it to you. That might help jog her memory.'

Julia was reluctant to do anything that took Anna back, even if it was only in a game, but she nodded.

'OK,' she said. 'We'll try.'

She tried that night, lying beside Anna in bed. Anna was freshly bathed and ready for bed and the smell of her filled the room.

'I was thinking,' she said. 'About getting you a special treat.'

Anna stiffened with excitement. 'What kind of treat? A present kind of treat?'

'Maybe a doll's house,' Julia said. 'If you want one.'

'Mummy,' Anna said. 'Of course, I want one!'

'One like the one you slept in?'

'No!' Anna said. 'I would like one with doors and tables and chairs and lots of dolls. '

'That one didn't have those things?'

'No. It didn't have anything.'

'What did it have?'

Anna shook her head. 'I don't remember, Mummy. It was dark. And I was sleepy.'

'Are you sure?'

'Mummy!' Anna rolled her eyes. 'I don't want to talk about it. I want to talk about the doll's house you are going to buy for me!'

'OK,' Julia said. 'Let's talk about that.'

She lay back and listened while Anna rattled off all the things her doll's house would have. There were a lot of them – it was going to be more like a doll's castle than a house – and Julia was glad that her daughter did not seem traumatized by whatever had happened to her.

She, on the other hand, could hardly bear to hear the words *doll's house*. It reminded her that someone had kidnapped Anna and held her captive, reminded her of the utter anguish she had gone through.

And it reminded her that whoever it was had not been caught. Maybe that didn't matter. Maybe this really was over. But maybe it wasn't. Maybe there was more to come, some sinister plan that Julia could not even guess at.

So she was glad when Anna fell asleep, and she could lie in the silence and hide away from her fears.

vii.

It was late when Julia woke up. Anna was already out of bed, the duvet pulled back, the pillows in disarray. Anna's favourite monkey was lying face down by the headboard. Julia put her hand out; the bed was still warm.

Downstairs, Edna was sitting at the breakfast table, the remains of two boiled eggs in front of her. Anna was in the living room, skimming through photos on her grandmother's iPad.

Edna sipped her coffee.

'I sent Brian for the paper,' she said. 'I don't normally read them, but he needed the fresh air.'

Typical Edna. A robust, common sense solution for every situation, which normally involved exercise, fresh air, pulling yourself together, or all three. She'd have made a good Victorian schoolteacher, although she might have been a bit too harsh and unforgiving for even that environment. Not for the first time, Julia felt sorry for Brian, although it was now mixed with relief that trying to please her mother-in-law was no longer going to be required of her.

'Good,' Julia said. 'He's a lucky man, having you to take care of him.'

'He is. And he's going to need it when he leaves his home.'

'That won't be for a while, at least,' Julia said.

Edna was, as always, sitting totally upright, but she still managed to straighten in her chair. 'What do you mean?' she said.

'Brian's staying here. Until things settle down.'

Edna nodded slowly. 'I see. And how long will that be?'

'I don't know. Six months. A year. However long it takes, I guess.'

'However long what takes?'

'I don't know, Edna,' Julia said. 'It's not one specific thing. It just doesn't feel like now is the right time for him to leave. It might unsettle Anna, for starters.'

'Anna will be fine,' Edna said. 'Children are more robust than we give them credit for.'

'Right. Of course.' This was another of Edna's firmest beliefs: children were tough and were only damaged by mollycoddling. They needed to learn that there was bad as well as good in the world and how to deal with it. Insulating them from it only meant that, when the lesson finally came, it would be harder to learn; far better for them to develop early the skills they needed to cope with disappointments and failure.

Julia happened to disagree. If her daughter could live in a cocoon in which only good things happened then fine. There was plenty of time for misery and upset later. She'd never bothered to argue the point with Edna – it would only have created a problem – but now she had nothing to lose.

'You know,' she said. 'I don't think they are. I think they are fragile and delicate and need our love and support. Divorce is disruptive and confusing for children, and I don't think now is a good time for Anna to suffer through it. There's too much other stuff going on.'

'Nonsense,' Edna said. 'Thousands of—'

'You know,' Julia said. 'I don't really want to discuss it. What Brian and I do is our business, and we'll decide between us what course to take. Whether you agree with it or not is really not of interest to me.'

'It should be,' Edna said. 'I have a *lot* of experience—'

'Of what?' Julia said. She was uncontrollably angry; she wanted nothing to do with Edna, and the more she could insult her the more chance there was she would leave Julia alone. 'Of failed marriages? Of how to drive away your husband? Because that's what happened, isn't it? You were so awful that Jim found comfort in the bed of another woman and left.'

'So,' Edna said. 'That's what you think of me. I'm glad to see your true colours at last. They might not be all that impressive, but at least now you can claim the virtue of honesty. Maybe, anyway. You don't have much of a track record in the honesty department, after all. And you'd know a thing or two about providing comfort to married men. What was the name of the man whose marriage you destroyed again?'

Julia stopped herself replying. She could see Edna wanted an argument, wanted them to end by shouting insults at each other. Then she could use this as evidence of the unsuitability of Brian staying at home. Julia could picture her now, shaking her head at Brian, saying *how can I set foot in that house again, after what she said to me*. She couldn't make the decision herself, so she wanted to create conflict, drive an even deeper wedge into their marriage so that the few remaining bonds were torn apart.

Julia didn't want to let her have that, so she shook her head and walked into the living room. She sat next to Anna and pulled her close to her.

'Want to read a book?' she asked.

Anna looked up at her and smiled. 'Can we read *The BFG*?' she said.

They'd read it twice a few months back and Anna loved it. Julia would not have chosen it again, but she didn't care. She would have her read the ingredients on a toothpaste tube. She was just glad to be reading to her at all.

They were just arriving at the BFG's cave when the front door opened. Brian came into the living room, carrying a newspaper and a purple box of chocolates.

'Oh,' he said. '*The BFG*. My favourite.' He made a puzzled face and put on a deep West Country accent, which, Julia remembered, was his BFG voice. 'Where's my Snozzcumbers? Human beans is very tasty beans.'

Anna giggled. 'Daddy,' she said. 'You're so funny.'

Brian waggled his eyebrows. 'I trys me best,' he said, still in his BFG voice. He held out the box of chocolates. It was about two feet square; Julia wasn't sure she had ever seen such a large box. Anna reached out and took it.

'For you,' Brian said. 'Some choccies.'

Anna pulled the lid off the box. Her eyes widened. 'For me? All of them?'

'All for you.'

'You can have one, Daddy,' she said. 'Or two.'

'Or three?' Brian said.

'Two,' Anna clarified. She looked at Julia. 'And you can have two as well, Mummy.'

Julia took a chocolate. She bit into it; it was a rose cream. She hated rose creams. 'It's delicious,' she said. 'Thank you, darling.'

Brian picked a chocolate from the box. 'I'll take one for grandma,' he said. 'She loves chocolates. Then I'll be right back for mine.'

He went into the kitchen. Julia heard him put the newspapers on the countertop, then tell Edna he had a surprise for her.

'So,' Julia said. 'Were there chocolates in the doll's house?'

Anna paused. 'No,' she said. 'Just dust.'

'Oh?' Julia said. 'Was it an old doll's house?'

'I think so,' Anna said.

'Did it smell new or old?'

'Mummy,' Anna said. 'You can't smell old! It's not a thing, like flowers. It doesn't smell.'

'I know,' Julia said. 'But sometimes things smell stale if they're old. Like dust. You mentioned dust.'

'Oh,' Anna said. 'The dust wasn't in the doll's house. It was on the floor.'

'What floor?'

'The floor of the room the doll's house was in.'

Julia tried to act calmly, despite the adrenaline flooding her body. 'What room was it in?'

Anna pursed her lips. 'I don't know. A dark room. It was a bit cold, as well.'

'Like a cellar?'

'What's a cellar?'

227

Julia thought for a second. 'Was the floor hard? Like stone?'

Anna nodded.

'Were you standing on the floor, looking at the doll's house?'

'Maybe,' Anna said. 'I don't really remember. Mummy, don't ask me any more questions. I don't like it.'

'One more, darling. Can you think what colour the doll's house was?'

'I think red,' Anna said. 'Or blue, maybe.'

'Red,' Edna said. She was standing in the doorway, watching. 'Or blue, maybe. I think you may be wasting your time.'

'Thanks for the words of support, Edna,' Julia said. 'But since it's my time I feel as though I am free to waste it all I want.'

'Very good,' Edna said. 'I have to leave.'

She smiled at Julia. It was a strange smile, although Julia could not work out exactly what it was about it that was odd. It was forced, somehow, almost mocking.

'Bye,' Julia said. 'See you later.'

'Yes,' Edna said. 'You will.'

viii.

Julia let the hot shower course over her body. She understood why religious ceremonies of rebirth often took place in water; the idea of washing away the sins of the past wasn't simply symbolism – there was a definite physical sensation that things were changing,

228

that the old was sluicing off and making space for the new.

And who knew what that would be?

She'd left Anna with Brian and *The BFG*. Anna was folded at the waist with laughter at her dad's funny voices; Julia had been both delighted and puzzled by it. Delighted, because her daughter was home and happy, and puzzled because she couldn't quite work out how she had missed the strength of Anna's love for her father. Maybe her own disillusionment with Brian had clouded her view, and she had assumed that Anna too found him tedious and uninspiring, but that was emphatically not the case. Seeing them together that morning she had realized that Anna *adored* him, that she found him the funniest and kindest and strongest man in the world.

And it changed her view of him, too. Not completely; she still didn't get a thrill at the thought of him, didn't see him as the rock she could lean on through the rest of her life's journey, but enough to make her wonder whether she had misjudged him, whether the root cause of her disenchantment with life was not Brian but something inside her. Maybe she was unfulfilled because of her approach to life, or her job, or the lack of adventure in her character. And if that was the case, then breaking up the family would not solve her problem. Taking up scuba diving or adopting a baby or learning the piano might, but not breaking up the family.

So she was glad to have the chance to keep them all together for a while. It would allow her to figure things out, to see whether her newfound admiration for Brian was just part of the general euphoria at Anna's return or whether it really was a change in her view of him. And if it was the latter, then maybe it signalled a change in their relationship. Maybe they had a future together, after all.

Maybe. Maybe not. But at least she was going to have the opportunity to find out.

She took a bit of time getting dressed. Applied a light perfume. Wore a pair of jeans that hugged her hips and butt, which she knew Brian liked. She wasn't planning to seduce him, but there was no harm in raising her game a little. If their relationship was to have a chance at all then she owed it to them both to fan whatever tiny flame there was.

He was coming upstairs as she crossed the landing, Anna in his arms.

'She crashed out,' he said. 'Fast asleep. Too much BFG and too much sugar. You know how it goes: big high, sudden low. I'm going to put her down. I'll put her with me in my bed. I need a nap too.'

'Right,' Julia said. 'Sounds like a good idea.'

He looked at her. 'Are you going out?'

'No. Just wanted to spruce up a bit. After the last week.'

'Good,' he said. 'Because before I go to sleep I want to discuss something with you.'

There was briskness in his voice, an air of decisiveness, of a mind being made up. She got the impression he had something important, no, *crucial*, to tell her.

Something like the possibility that their marriage may not be over after all. Julia felt her stomach contract with anticipation.

Look, he would say. *I know things have been bad – awful – between us. But perhaps this whole episode with Anna has been good for us, in a strange kind of way. Maybe losing everything made us see what we have.*

Hmm, she'd reply. *I know what you mean. So what should we do?*

He'd get a slightly nervous expression, like a teenager asking a girl out on a date that he thinks will make or break his existence, before continuing. *Well, I know it won't be easy. But perhaps we should give it another chance. See if we can make it work.*

OK, she'd say. *I think you're right. Let's try.*

And then ... what? They'd hug? Kiss? Make love? Take a nap together? Or just separate, her going make a cup of tea and him going to lie down with Anna. Probably the latter, which would be fine. There'd be plenty of time later to work out the details, to decide when and whether to move back into the same room, or to rekindle their sex lives. Maybe they'd go away on holiday for a week, snuggle up as a family. It would be good to get away, use a fresh place to get a fresh perspective. They could put Anna to bed in the evenings and then they could sit down and sort it all out.

'OK,' she said. 'I'll be in the living room.'

*

He came down a few minutes later. Julia was sitting at one end of the couch. She gestured to the other end. He ignored her and remained standing, by the door.

'So,' he said. 'Earlier we talked about staying together, in the house, for Anna's sake.'

'Right,' Julia said. 'Keep the family intact.'

'That's kind of the thing,' Brian said. 'The family is not intact. Pretending it is, is – it's ridiculous, Julia.'

She blinked. 'It's just for a while. So Anna can settle back in.'

'I don't see the point. It's over. We should just accept it and move on.'

'So, what are you saying?'

'I think we should stick to our original plan. I move out and stay with Mum.'

'I don't believe this. We agreed that it was best for Anna if you stay here!'

'Things changed.'

'What changed?' Julia held up her hand, her palm facing Brian. She didn't need to ask. 'Don't answer,' she said. 'I know what changed. Edna. She told you off for not doing what she wants and you jumped into line. I should have known.'

Brian blushed. 'That's not what happened.'

'No? So how come we agreed something last night, then Edna shows up, finds out, has a chat with you, and mysteriously you change your mind? Mummy told you what to do, Brian, and you're doing it.'

He was standing back on his heels. He folded his arms. 'Not at all. It's my decision.'

'Yeah? Then what happened to it being best for Anna if you stay? I thought we were going to do what was best for her, not each other?'

'We are. And it's best for Anna if we go through this now. There's no point in her living in a miserable household for a year, watching us argue, wondering whether it's her fault, and then seeing us separate. It's better just to do it now. It's like removing a plaster. It's better just to rip it off.'

Now she knew he'd been influenced by his mother. The 'rip-off the plaster in one go' philosophy was pure Edna. It might as well have been her speaking.

'This is pathetic, Brian, you know that? We make a decision as parents that we both agree is for the best, and then you change your mind because you don't have the balls to stand up to your mother.'

'That's not true,' he said. 'That's not how it is.'

'You keep telling yourself that,' Julia said. 'Maybe you'll convince yourself one day. Until then we'll both know the truth.'

'So I'm going to go,' he said. 'This Monday. We'll have the weekend and then I'll be gone.'

'Fine. You do whatever makes Mummy happy.'

He shrugged and left the room. Julia rubbed her temples. So that was that, then. Anna was going to have to suffer her parents' divorce on top of everything else. Fucking Edna. She had to win, whatever the cost.

There was no point arguing, either. Edna was always right. If she thought it was best for Anna to do this quickly and immediately, then no amount of argument or evidence to the contrary would work. Once Edna decided something it was decided forever. The problem was she was so convinced of the superiority of her intellect that she could not accept that other people's experience was valid. For example, she didn't believe in depression; she saw it as weakness and so could not imagine herself ever succumbing to it. As a result she dismissed all those that did as malingerers who needed a sharp kick up the backside. No amount of expert opinion could change her mind. If shown – as Julia had once done – a medical opinion that claimed depression to be an illness with a physiological basis, she would simply dismiss it. *Of course, they think that, she'd say. That's exactly the problem. They allow these people to think they have an illness, when what they have is an attitude problem.*

And Brian shared Edna's belief in her infallibility, so he would parrot her opinions. It was one of the things about him that infuriated Julia.

So there would be no appealing to arguments about Anna's welfare, and there would be no convincing Brian his mum was wrong.

Still, at least one good thing had come of this: she no longer harboured any illusions that she and Brian might get back together. The last few minutes had reminded her exactly why she had wanted out in the first place.

So fuck him. He could go. He could limp back broken-winged to the safety of the nest, and good riddance to him. She'd stay here with Anna, and together they'd make the life they deserved. It wouldn't be that bad; tough at first, maybe, but then she'd been ready for that anyway. She'd make it work.

She smiled. Perhaps Edna – the interfering old bitch – had done her a favour. If she hadn't intervened Julia might have tried to keep it going with Brian, might have been fooled into thinking it could work. And who knew where that would have ended up? She might have wasted months, *years*, before she finally started on her new life. Or maybe she would never have done it, and ended up a bitter old woman in an empty house and a loveless marriage.

So yes, maybe this was for the best after all.

11

Not Over Yet

i.

It worked. The girl did what she was supposed to do and now she is back at home. The country rejoices, a miracle! But who took her? And why did they return her? It's a mystery, a puzzle, and this country of crosswords and quiz shows loves nothing more than a puzzle.

Was she raped? Experimented on? Taken by aliens and implanted with a chip? All these theories and more are out there, running the full gamut from the cerebral to the crazy. They look for patterns, these denizens of chat rooms, these speculators in the comments section of newspapers. Was there ever a more public demonstration of the bizarreness of the human species than the comments sections? You can find any opinion you can imagine (and more besides) below the line. People's minds run in all directions and you can see it on the internet.

Like the patterns they discern – the girl was gone a week – seven days from disappearance to return. Is this significant? Does this mean something? Can we infer that the kidnapper likes completeness? That he or she deals only in entire months or weeks or years? Perhaps they are autistic, or religious, or maybe it is a simple coincidence.

No, not that. Not a coincidence. That would never do. That would not fit their need for explanations.

And the day chosen for her return was not random. But it was nothing to do with the fact that a week had passed. No. You chose that day for a real reason, a good reason: because it fitted your design. Because it moved your plan along. Because it was the right thing to do.

But they will keep looking. Keep generating their theories. No doubt they have doctors checking her, but she is unharmed. You could tell them that. You won't, of course. That would give the game away.

And the game is not yet over. There is more to come. And soon.

And the girl is no longer the target.

This time, it is the mother.

ii.

Julia heard them before she saw them.

It was just past six a.m., Saturday morning, and Anna and Brian were still sleeping. When she reached the bottom of the stairs she did not meet the silence she expected: there was a low buzz of voices and of engines running.

She went into the front room and put her eye to a crack in the curtains, careful not to move them.

They were back. Those bastards from the press were back. This time there were camera vans as well as reporters.

What the hell did they want? The story was old news by now, or old enough, anyway. She and Brian had made it clear they wanted to be left alone and any statements would be issued by the police's press department. There was nothing for them to gain by hanging around outside the house. Besides, she thought that DI Wynne had put a stop to it, but evidently it hadn't worked.

So fuck it. She was just going to get on with her day. She'd have a cup of tea, make some breakfast, and then she'd go for a run. She'd been planning a morning run – to get some fresh air, in Edna's words – and she was damned if she was going to change her plans because of those vultures.

As the kettle boiled she reached for her computer, then stopped herself. She wasn't going to read the news. She was going to keep herself isolated from it. She was going to rise above.

When she had finished her cereal she put on her trainers. For a second she considered sneaking out through the back garden, climbing over the wall to the neighbours' garden and vanishing into the grey morning, but she shook her head. She wasn't going to sneak around. She had nothing to hide from.

She opened the front door. There was an instant snap of activity: cameras raised and shutters sounding, bodies pressing forwards.

'Excuse me,' Julia said. 'But I'm going for a run. Please let me past.'

The scrum in front of her didn't react. One man – she recognized his acne-scarred face from the last time – held out a phone, no doubt set to record.

'Mrs Crowne,' he said. 'Is it true that you tried to commit suicide the day Anna was found?'

She froze.

'I'm sorry?' she said.

'Is it true that you suffered a failed suicide attempt the day Anna was found?'

A tall red-headed woman with big eyes leaned forwards. 'Was it before or after you heard that your daughter had showed up?'

Julia stepped back inside. She slammed the door. Her hands shook on the Yale lock as she deadlocked it.

How did they know about the sleeping pills? There was someone in the police leaking this stuff, there had to be. It made sense: cops and journalists were close, but how could they do this? How could they put her through it?

She went into the kitchen and opened her laptop.

She started to read.

iii.

ANNA MUM IN SUICIDE BID

It emerged yesterday that Julia Crowne, mother of Anna, the five-year-old who walked into a newsagent a week after her disappearance had launched a global manhunt, attempted suicide on the morning of Anna's return.

Mrs Crowne took a combination of sleeping pills and alcohol in an attempt to end her life. Her husband, Brian Crowne, found her unconscious on the couch, and, with the aid of his mother, Dr Edna Crowne, managed to revive her.

There has been speculation that Mrs Crowne's suicide attempt may have been triggered by the discovery that her daughter was still alive. On top of Anna's abduction, Mrs Crowne had also endured a difficult time, with suggestions that she may have been at fault for her child's disappearance common in the press.

In the weeks before their daughter vanished Mrs Crowne had informed her husband that she wanted to leave both him and Anna, leading to speculation that she might have been suffering from depression. According to one acquaintance Mrs Crowne also has 'a difficult relationship with alcohol.'

Julia closed her laptop. She could not grasp what she *had* read, could not get a handle on the implications of the contents of the story.

She could think only one thing: it was happening again. Once again they were painting her in the worst possible way. According to this she was an unstable, suicidal alcoholic, suffering from depression, who had already failed to take adequate care of the daughter she was planning to leave.

I know I shouldn't do this, she thought. *I know I shouldn't, but I can't stop myself. I have to know what they're saying.*

She opened Twitter and searched for her name. There was no shortage of hits. She was, it seemed, trending:

OMG *did you see what #JuliaCrowne did? failed suicide – would have been better if it worked.*
#JuliaCrowne failed mum failed suicide #Britain'sBiggestFailure

The hashtag *#notfittobeamum* was still out there:

Doesn't deserve her daughter back. #JuliaCrowne #notfittobeamum

As well as some new ones, freshly-minted by the internetariat, one tweet had managed to invent two further new ones:

#betteroffdead Britain's Biggest Bitch #BBB #JuliaCrowne

Who were these people who felt the need to abuse strangers? Did it make them feel better? Braver? That they were saying something important, which might have an impact on the world? Or were they just lashing out, hoping to hurt someone? Thank God they had Twitter to help them with that. For all the benefits of

interconnectedness that Twitter – and the internet gener-
ally – gave to mankind, there was the ever-present draw-
back that it was an open window to the sewers of the
human mind.

She hear Brian's footsteps on the stairs. Seconds later
the living room door opened.

'What do they want?' he said. 'I heard them shouting
from my bedroom window.'

She handed him her laptop. 'This.'

He scanned the screen. 'Jesus,' he said. 'How did they
find out?'

'The cops,' Julia said. 'They must have a contact on
the inside.'

He carried on reading. 'And it's not even true,' he said.
'According to you, anyway. And Mum said you'd be fine
when you woke up.'

Good for fucking Mum, Julia thought.

'So what now?' she said.

Brian shrugged. 'Ignore them, I guess. They'll go away
in the end.'

'That's easy for you to say. It's not your life that they're
splashing – wrongly – all over the world. I mean, they're
making me out to be this awful, drunken, crazy bitch.
It's just not fair.' She looked away. She didn't want him
to see her cry. He might try to comfort her, put his arms
around her, and that, she feared, would make her vomit.

But it seemed he was not interested in comforting her.

'Yeah,' he said. 'Well. What goes around, comes around.'

Julia looked up him. 'What's that supposed to mean.'

'Just that you started this. You declared that you wanted out of our marriage. If you hadn't done that then we'd be fine now, wouldn't we? Anna would be home and we'd be getting on with our lives.'

Julia stared at him. 'Are you serious?'

'It's true, isn't it? Forget that your mistake meant Anna was taken; she's back now. And if you hadn't decided to end our marriage we'd be ok. The press might have blamed you a bit, but that would have passed. There'd have been no suicide attempt, if that's what it was, because we'd have had each other. Apart from Anna's abduction, this ... ' he made a vague, sweeping gesture, 'all stems from your decision to break this family apart.'

'So I was supposed to stay with you in case this happened? Every woman who wants to leave a relationship should stay, in case this happens to them? Don't you see how ridiculous that is?'

'Maybe. But it's true.'

'No. It isn't. If I hadn't decided to end our marriage, I'd still be unhappily stuck in it.'

'You can't admit it, can you? Even now?'

'Admit what?'

'That it was a mistake.'

'No,' Julia said. 'I can't. Because it wasn't. Not picking up Anna was a mistake, I'll admit that. But ending our marriage wasn't. And you know how I know that? Because if I hadn't done it then, I'd be doing it now.'

She was surprised by the bitterness, by the sheer rage and hatred between them. All she wanted was to wound

243

him. Hurt him. Stab him with her words. Stab him with a knife. Kick him. Bite him.

It was a terrible, awful feeling. She closed her eyes against it, against him, against the world.

Forget Monday. The sooner he was gone, the better.

'I think you should leave,' she said, eyes still closed. 'Go to your mum's, today.'

There was no reply. When she opened her eyes he was gone.

iv.

'Mum says I can come tonight.'

Brian was standing in the kitchen door frame.

'Ok,' Julia said. 'Sounds good.'

'What will we tell Anna?'

'I don't know. What do you think?'

'Mum suggested saying nothing. Just tell her that I'm going to her place for a night.'

'We'll have to tell her the truth soon.'

'I know. But not today.' Brian's gaze met hers for a second, then he looked away, as though he couldn't bear to look at her. 'I'll come back tomorrow afternoon to get some of my belongings.'

'OK. What time?'

'Two p.m. Something like that.'

'Fine.'

And so it was done.

*

Julia woke abruptly, snapping into consciousness, her heart racing, her body flooded with adrenaline.

She was on high alert, and she didn't know why. What had woken her? What had triggered her body's sudden leap into this tense, wired state? A noise? Had she heard something?

Next to her, Anna lay asleep. She glanced at the alarm clock. Three twenty in the morning. She lifted her head off the pillow, straining to listen.

Outside, the sound of the wind in the trees. Inside, silence. Just the normal creaks and groans of a house. Just the noises of the witching hour.

Unless they were the creaks and groans of someone stealthy. Someone who could successfully kidnap a child. Someone who could return the child and not be caught.

Someone who might be in her house right that moment.

Julia sat upright. She got out of bed and pulled on her jeans and a T-shirt. She walked to the bedroom door and stood there, listening.

Nothing.

She crossed the room to the window and looked out. The police car was there, outside the house. Two officers sat in the front seat. Her heart rate fell, the panic subsiding.

And then she saw him. A man, wearing a dark hoodie, standing under a sycamore tree at the far end of the street. He was motionless, staring – at least, Julia thought he was staring – at the house.

Oh my God, Julia thought. *He's here. He's here right now. Watching us. I have to wake Brian up.*

But Brian wasn't there. Brian was with Edna.

Julia picked up Anna, and ran.

'Yes, ma'am,' the officer said. He was in his late twenties, and bleary-eyed. He held the top of a silver flask in his hand. It was filled with coffee. Julia wondered whether his wife or girlfriend or mother had made it for him as he left for night duty. 'We'll have a look.'

Julia held Anna –who was still asleep – against her chest. 'I saw him,' she said. 'I know I did. Right there, at the end of the street.'

She felt foolish. She'd run outside and banged on the window of the police car, babbling about the man watching her, watching and waiting.

But there was no one there, and she could tell that the police officers thought she was seeing things.

She couldn't blame them. Even she thought she might be seeing things.

'I'm sure you did,' the officer said. 'I'll walk up there now and take a look.'

'Look for clues,' Julia said. 'Footprints. Things like that.'

'I will do, ma'am,' he said, and smiled. 'Why don't you go back inside? See if you can get some sleep. You're safe with us here.'

Julia nodded and went back into her house.

It took her a long time to fall back to sleep.

v.

At midday the next day the doorbell rang.

Brian, come to get his stuff. So he rang the doorbell now. How quickly something as fundamental as your home could change. Just like that he no longer had the right to put his key in the door and open it unannounced.

He was with Edna. They stood on the front step, both wearing matching new Ray-Ban sunglasses.

'A lovely day,' Edna said. 'Summer's finally here.'

'Come in,' Julia said.

They stood in the hallway. It suddenly seemed very narrow and awkward. Julia backed away.

'So,' she said. 'What's the plan?'

Brian was saved from answering by Anna's arrival.

'Daddy!' she shouted, as he scooped her into his arms. 'Did you stay at Grandma's last night?'

'I did,' Brian said.

'Why?'

'Because ... ' he glanced at Julia and Edna, 'because I had a—'

'Because I needed help with something,' Edna said. 'Daddy's going to be helping me quite a bit from now on, so he'll be staying with me.' She looked at Julia, her face fixed and hard. 'Your mummy will tell you all about it.'

'That's right, darling,' Julia said. 'We can talk about it later.'

'Do you want to see my painting, Daddy?' Anna said.

'I'd love to,' Brian replied. 'Where is it?'

'In the breakfast room. Come on.'

They followed Anna through the house. When they reached the two easels she turned and flung her hands out like a circus showman.

'Ta-da!' she said.

'Wow,' Brian said, nodding at the morass of paint smeared on the paper. 'That is amazing. Can you tell me what it's called?'

'It's called *Pony Trek*,' Anna said. 'It's ponies. Lots of them.'

'I see that,' Brian said. 'I love it.' He ruffled her hair and bent down to kiss her. 'I just have to go upstairs for a few minutes,' he said. 'I'll see you in a sec'.'

When he was gone Edna beckoned Julia into the kitchen.

'You know,' she said. 'It might be nice for Brian to have a few moments alone with Anna. To say goodbye. He won't make a fuss of it, but this is a big moment for him.'

'What are you saying, Edna?' Julia said.

'I'm saying that you could go for a walk for an hour or so. That would give Brian a chance to pack up and also to spend a bit of time with his daughter.'

Julia folded her arms. 'I don't know,' she said. 'I can go in the other room. Or stay upstairs. I don't feel like going out.'

'There are no press, if that's what you're worried about. They're gone.'

'It's not just that. It's ... you know, seeing people. I don't want them staring at me.'

248

'Wear a cap. No one will recognize you. And if they do they won't say anything.'

'I don't think so, Edna.'

'You're going to have to face it sooner or later,' Edna said. 'Might as well get it over with. It's like removing a plaster. Better just to rip it off.'

Jesus, Julia thought. *She never gives up.* She looked out at the blue skies. She hadn't seen much sun recently, and it was a lovely day.

'Fine,' she said. 'But I might not be an hour.'

'Whatever you can give him will be greatly appreciated,' Edna said. 'Thank you, Julia.'

At the end of the road, Julia took a narrow snicket that led to the canal towpath. The canal was a narrow, lazy band of muddy water that saw little traffic beyond the day cruisers and occasional canal dweller. She had always considered it as inferior to the river in the park, preferring the livelier charms of the moving, rushing water, but on such a warm day the park would be busy, whereas the canal would be populated only by the usual band of dog walkers and solitary fishermen.

It felt good to move. Good to be outside with the sun on her skin. Good to feel the blood rush in her body. Much as she disliked Edna's way of declaiming the benefits of fresh air and exercise, and much as she did not agree that they were a cure for all ills, she had to admit that her mother-in-law had a point. She felt better than she had since Anna's disappearance.

She strode along. On the opposite bank a family of swans, the cygnets fluffy and grey and already the size of ducks, pecked at some weeds. The surface of the water rippled with the movements of invisible insects; bubbles – from fish, maybe – occasionally rose to the light. In what appeared, at first glance, to be a still, barren landscape there was so much going on. There was so much life.

A few miles from home she passed a bench. It was by a bridge that led up to a main road, where she knew there was a petrol garage with a small convenience store. She was thirsty, so she climbed the steps and headed for the garage.

In the store, cap over her eyes, she grabbed a bottle of Buxton spring water and a Twix. She avoided looking at the newspapers.

'Nice day,' the man behind the counter said. He was tall, well over six foot, and in his mid to late fifties. He had a crown of greying hair around a bald spot. His eyes were sharp behind thick glasses. 'You out for a walk on the canal?'

'Yes,' Julia said. 'How did you know?'

'Not many people walk here. Those that do come from the canal path. See many people, did you?'

Julia shook her head and handed him a twenty pound note. She felt suddenly uncomfortable, suddenly very aware that she was alone in a secluded place and that this man knew it. This man with hard eyes and an abrupt manner knew it.

She told herself not to be stupid. There was nothing wrong with the guy. He wasn't a rapist; just bored and a bit blunt. There were plenty of them around. Two weeks ago she wouldn't have thought twice about him.

But this wasn't two weeks ago. Two weeks ago she had been aware in a vague way that there were people out there who abducted children or raped and killed people, but now she knew it in a different way, and she knew something about it that she had never really thought true: she knew it could happen to her.

What if he was a rapist? What if he was the one who had taken Anna? What if he didn't even really work here, but had been following her and had somehow dashed in and killed the person – a young girl, in Julia's visions – who worked here?

He held out her change. She stared at it. She didn't want to take it from him, didn't want to touch his hand.

'You all right?' he asked.

She didn't answer. The connection between her brain and her mouth was frozen.

'Hey,' he said. 'You ok?'

Finally, she managed to get some control of herself.

'Yes,' she said. 'I'm ok. Just a bit hot.'

He frowned. 'You far from home?'

'A bit. No. A few miles.'

'You should get a taxi, love. You don't look all that well. You want me to call you one?'

She opened her mouth to say *yes* but then she stopped herself.

What if he calls a friend? she thought. *What if this is part of his plot?*

But then a taxi did sound like a good idea. The thought of the walk home was not very appealing. She looked at the clock on the wall. She'd been gone forty minutes. She should probably be getting home.

'I'll call one,' she said. 'I've got my phone.'

'All right,' he said. He put her change – a ten pound note and some coins – on the countertop. 'Have it your way.'

She left. There was a bus stop up the road. She went and sat on the bench inside. It was red, the paint chipping off it. She put her head in her hands and massaged her scalp. She felt like she was crazy. The guy was just doing his job, just an ordinary guy selling petrol and newspapers and snacks, and she was thinking he was a murderer or rapist or some kind of predatory paedophile. Was she going to turn into someone who saw bogeymen behind every shadow, who was paralysed by their own fear? She understood why she might but, nonetheless, it was ridiculous. She couldn't go through life in terror. It would have to stop.

There was a knock on the glass window of the bus shelter.

The man from the garage was standing there.

Julia screamed. She jumped to her feet and backed into the corner of the bus shelter.

'Please,' she said, breathless. 'Please, leave me alone.'

The man stared at her for a few seconds, then backed away.

'Whoah,' he said. 'I don't know what you're thinking, but you're wrong. I just came because you left your change at the garage. That's all.' He held out his left hand. It contained a ten pound note and a handful of coins. He bent down. 'I'll put it here,' he said. 'You pick it up when you're ready.' As he stood he paused. 'Hey,' he said. 'Are you … '

Julia nodded.

'I'm glad your daughter came back. You should be getting home. Did you call a cab?'

'Yes,' Julia lied. 'It's on the way.'

The man smiled. 'Good. You take care, now.'

Julia watched as he walked back to the garage. As he went inside, she called for a taxi.

The taxi pulled up at the house. She paid the driver and opened the back door. On the way back she'd made a decision. She didn't think she was ready to be alone. The thought that Anna's abductor was still out there was too unsettling. She couldn't even go for a walk without ending up running home in a panic. She needed company. She needed support. She needed protection.

She was going to ask Brian to stay. She had to. They didn't need to be a couple, they didn't need to even talk, but she could not be alone right now. She didn't need a husband; she needed a protector.

He'd understand, she was sure. Whatever had passed between them he was still a decent man and he'd see that she needed him. Even if he didn't, he'd see that Anna

253

needed him. What if the abductor was out there? She'd be safer with two parents than one.

Once this was over, he could go. But not now.

She turned the key in the top lock and the door swung open.

'Hi,' she said. 'I'm back.'

There was no reply. In fact, there was no noise at all. The house was silent. No television, no footsteps, no murmured voices.

'Anna!' she shouted. 'Brian! Where are you?'

Still no answer.

The garden, she thought. *They're in the garden. Of course.*

She went through the kitchen to the back door. It was locked.

Which meant they were not outside.

Near frantic now, she grabbed the key from the windowsill – not the best place to keep it, she knew that – and turned it in the lock. The door opened.

She heard birds, car engines, the distant shouts of a Sunday football game.

But no Brian. And no Anna.

She grabbed her phone and called her husband's mobile. It rang twice, then he answered.

'Brian,' she said. 'Is Anna with you?'

'Of course,' he said. 'I wouldn't leave her on her own, would I?'

'What are you doing?' Julia said. 'Why aren't you here?'

'I'm taking her to Mum's,' he said. 'It's the best – the safest – place for her.'

'You can't do that!' Julia said. 'You can't just take her without my permission!'

'I knew you wouldn't give it,' Brian said. 'But it's best for her if she's with me.'

'You turn around right now and bring her back!' Julia shouted. 'You do that right fucking now or I'll call the police!'

'I already did. They needed to know to have the police guard outside this house.'

'You can't do this,' Julia said. 'You can't.'

'I can. I did. I had no choice, Julia. I have to do what's best for my daughter.'

'What's best for her is to be with her mum!'

'I don't agree.' He paused, and she heard Edna's voice in the background. Edna. She should have known that Edna was behind this. 'Mum says you should come to the house tomorrow to discuss things.'

'I'm coming today. I'm coming right now!'

'You need to calm down first. It'll just upset Anna. Tomorrow. Nine a.m.'

The line went dead. Julia pressed redial, but it went straight to voicemail.

Fuck tomorrow. Fuck nine a.m. She was going there right that instant.

12

Losing Control

i.

So the mother had lost her daughter. You did not expect it so soon but that is ok.

You will adapt. That is another of your skills: you recognize when things change and you change yourself accordingly. It's like evolution. Adapt, or die. The difference is that evolution is dumb. Animals don't know that they are adapting. They don't see the changes in their environment. They don't sense the world shifting around them. You do. You stand outside events and observe them. You see yourself and your place in the world, understand your role, what your strengths and weaknesses are, where your threats and opportunities lie. When something changes, you see how you need to change. You are not surprised by events.

You are a watcher. A waiter.

But you also act. When necessary, you act swiftly and decisively.

And the time is coming for action. For the final action.

ii.

Julia banged on the front door of Edna's house. There was no doorbell: Edna thought they were vulgar, and vulgar was not what she wanted for her not-so-humble abode. The house was an old carriage house. Years back Edna and Jim had agreed to sell some of the land it sat on to a developer, who had put a large detached house on it. They made a killing from the sale; money which, recognizing even then that Brian was not going to become rich from his own efforts, they intended to use to fund their grandchildren's educations. Now, with only one grandchild to pay for, Edna regretted it bitterly; she didn't need the money and she hated having the new house visible from her garden. It wasn't that it was ugly; far from it, the architect had done a fine job of fitting it sensitively into its surroundings, but that it reminded Edna both that she had made a mistake in selling the land and the reason it was a mistake was that her plans for Brian had failed.

'Brian!' Julia shouted. 'Brian!'

She thumped on the door with the side of her fist.

'Brian! Edna!'

The door opened. Brian was standing in a small vestibule. Behind him the door into the main house was closed.

'Julia,' Brian said. 'Calm down. You were supposed to be coming tomorrow.'

'Fuck you, Brian!' Julia shouted. 'I want Anna. I want my daughter!'

'She's better off here,' Brian said. 'It's quieter. There's no press. And like you said, whoever took her is still running around out there. This is the best place for her.'

'The best place for her is with me.'

'Julia, we have to be grown up about this. We have to do what's best for our daughter. I know you're upset but our feelings don't come into it.'

'You took her. You kidnapped her!'

'Don't be ridiculous. Bringing her to her grandmother's house is hardly kidnapping. And even if it is, I think the fact I told you where she is rather disproves your theory.'

Julia could see what he was saying made sense; she also knew that, whether it made sense or not, it was just a convenient excuse for taking her daughter from her.

And she was not going to allow that. Rage narrowed her world to one thought: get Anna.

'I want to come in. I want to see her.'

'No. She's sleeping. And she doesn't need to see this.'

'See what?'

'Us fighting.'

'Then stop fighting! I'll come in and take her home quiet as a fucking mouse!'

'Julia. You need to calm down. We have guests. Don't make a scene. Mum'll be embarrassed.'

Julia's rage intensified. They had taken her daughter and she was supposed to be nice and polite and genteel because Edna had some fucking guests for Sunday lunch? And what the fuck was that anyway? In the midst of all this, Edna found time to have a nice dinner party? It was fucking typical.

'You think I give a shit about upsetting your guests?' she shouted. 'I want to see Anna, and I want to see her now.'

She tried to dart past Brian to the inner door, but he put his right arm out and caught her around the waist.

'Let me go!' she shouted. 'Get your fucking hands off me!'

She hated him at that moment, would have snapped his neck in two in the beat of a drum had she been able to. As it was, she lashed out with her right hand, her nails clawing at his cheek.

He shrieked, a high-pitched wail that infuriated her even more, and she shoved him as hard as she could. He lost his balance and fell against the tiled wall of the vestibule, his hand clutching his cheeks. She could see the red scratch above his fingers.

'You're a piece of shit,' she said. 'A worthless piece of—'

'What on earth is going on here?' Edna had opened the inner door and was standing there, arms folded. Behind her was a man of her age, dressed in the smart casual attire of the upper middle classes out to Sunday lunch at the home of a distinguished doctor.

'Is everything ok?' he said.

'She scratched my face,' Brian said. 'She's crazy.'

'I think you need to leave,' Edna said. 'Now.'

'I'm not going anywhere without my daughter,' Julia said. 'I'll stand here all day and all night until you let me see her.'

Edna's expression hardened. 'Don't make the mistake of threatening me, young lady,' she said. 'And especially not in my own home.'

She took a smart step forward and took hold of Julia's elbow. Her grip was strong, and as she pushed, Julia pivoted towards the front door.

'Out,' Edna said. 'Out you go.'

Julia twisted in her grip. 'I'm not going,' she said. 'You can't make me.'

'Can't I?' Edna said. 'We'll see about that.'

She grabbed Julia's other elbow and backed her over the threshold of the front door.

'No,' Julia shouted. 'No! Get off me!'

She bucked violently and shoved her shoulder against Edna. Edna stumbled backwards into the door jamb, still holding onto her.

'You let me see my daughter!' Julia shouted. 'Or I'll claw your eyes out, you fucking bitch!'

She felt someone grab her arms and pin them to her sides. She looked up. Brian was on one side of her, the lunch guest on the other.

'Should I call the police?' the man said.

Edna stared at Julia. 'No,' she said. 'I don't think so. I think Julia is about to leave.'

Julia felt the rage drain from her like air from an untied balloon. She didn't reply.

'Julia?' Edna said. 'Should Derek call the police? Or will you go of your own accord.'

Julia let her head fall forwards. 'I'm going,' she mumbled.

'Good,' Edna said. 'Let her go.'

Brian and Derek released their grip on her, and she turned to walk back to her car. As she did so, she heard Edna call out to her.

'I suggest you come by tomorrow. We need to talk.'

It was not a talk that Julia was looking forward to.

iii.

Julia was up early, unable to sleep. Her mind was stuck in a loop in which variations of the previous day's events played out. In the end, she gave in and slumped in front of the television, a mug of tea cradled between her palms, the base balanced on her stomach. It was the way her dad had sat when he watched *Match of the Day* or *Grandstand*, before the evening came and he pulled on his weekend shoes and coat and left the house.

Just off out early doors, love, he'd say, before kissing his wife, always on the lips and often more than once. Julia had grown up thinking that all parents kissed each other hello and goodbye and danced around the kitchen to the radio and cuddled on the couch like teenagers to watch whatever film the Beeb was showing. It was only when she was a little older that she realized that her mum and dad were the exception; that the fruitful, abiding love at the heart of their marriage was an island in an ocean of desiccated, hollow relationships.

I'll be back in a while, he'd say. *You get your dancing clothes on while I'm gone.*

And he'd be back an hour or two later, smelling of cigarette smoke and beer, to take his bride for a meal or to the movies, or, in later years, to the wine bar that had opened in the village. Sometimes he'd sit with Julia while he waited for her mum, and he'd talk to her, share his thoughts about the world, his mood opened by the beer he'd drunk. She remembered these times well, remembered the advice he'd given her:

You can spend a long time listing out all the things you've not got, Julia; so long, that you never find time to enjoy the things you do have.

Most people are all right, at heart, but never forget that there's some buggers in the world who'll do things you'd never dream of to get what they want.

And her favourite, the one that summed up her mum and dad and their marriage:

A man can count his friends on the fingers of one hand, and one of them's his wife.

They would never have divorced. The thought would never have entered their minds. Theirs was a love story, and Julia missed both it and them.

She fell asleep in the armchair. When she woke up it was nearly eight. Brian was expecting her at nine, so she went to shower and dress and see what exactly he had to say.

*

It was overcast as she pulled into Edna's driveway: the dark clouds low and heavy. The air smelled of rain. She knocked on the door, her banging less frantic today, but her heart racing just the same at the thought of seeing Anna. She'd ask her daughter whether she wanted to come with mummy, and she was sure her daughter would say yes.

Brian opened the door. He looked relaxed, clean-shaven, and smartly dressed. Just how Edna liked him. The smart, confident scion of an important family.

There were only faint traces of her nails on his cheek.

'Morning,' he said. 'Come in.'

She stepped into the vestibule and then into the hallway. The dark wooden floorboards were polished to a mirror gleam. She looked around, listening for the sounds of her daughter. She'd been picturing a rapturous reunion.

'Where's Anna?'

'She's gone out for breakfast with Mum.'

Julia felt the anger ball up just below her sternum. 'I want to see her! She's my daughter, for God's sake! Why are you doing this, Brian?'

'It's fine. Relax. She'll be back any moment. I wanted to talk to you alone, before you see her.'

'About what?'

He looked at the ceiling and then at the floor. His gaze remained low. 'About custody,' he said.

Julia folded her arms. 'What about it?'

'I wondered what you were thinking.'

263

'I was thinking that Anna would be with me. You'd have full access. Wednesdays, and every other weekend. Maybe more. Whatever we decide is best for her.'

He looked at her with a thoughtful, slightly patronizing expression. 'I guessed that might be your position.'

He let the words hang between them. Eventually, Julia shrugged.

'What's your position?' she asked.

'The opposite. I think she'd be better off with me. You'd have full access,' he said, using her words. 'Wednesdays, and every other weekend. Maybe more. Whatever we decide is best for her.'

Julia laughed. 'What makes you think I'd agree to that? You forget, Brian, that I am a divorce lawyer. I know the law and I know how it's applied.' She leaned forwards and spoke in a lowered voice as though sharing a secret. 'Between you and me, the mother always gets custody.'

'I'd rather avoid a custody battle,' Brian said. 'It'll just be expensive and difficult.'

'Then don't start one,' Julia said. 'There's no point. You'll lose.'

'I'm not so sure about that,' Brian said.

'Well, I am.'

'OK,' he said. 'Fine. I guess we'll find out. Take a seat. They'll be back any second. Would you like a drink? Tea? Coffee?'

'No,' Julia said. 'And what do you mean, "I guess we'll find out"?'

'Just that. I guess we'll find out how the court rules when we get there.'

'So you're saying you're going to drag us through a custody battle?'

'No. You're going to drag us through a custody battle.'

'I don't think you get it, Brian. This is a fight you can't win. If you start it, knowing that, then the fallout is on you. There's no reason for you to do this.'

'There's every reason. I want custody of my daughter. If that's the only way to get it, then so be it.'

Julia shook her head. 'But you won't get custody, Brian. You'll lose. Don't you see that? There's much less heartache if we just agree it between us. You said it yourself; it'll be expensive and difficult.'

'I think I will get custody.' He shrugged. 'But you disagree. We can put it to the test.'

She found this new, calm, rational version of him infuriating. She could tell that, whatever she said, however insulting, he would not take the bait. He was so confident. The question was why. It gnawed at her.

'Why are you so sure, Brian?' she said, suddenly. 'Why do you think a judge would favour you?'

'Well,' he said. 'The court has to act in the best interest of the child, as I understand it.'

'And that is almost always to stay with the mother.'

The front door opened. It was Edna and Anna, back from breakfast. Brian smiled.

'Fine,' he said. 'Then you should be ok. Enjoy the visit.'

iv.

Anna came into the hallway. Her black shoes – new, patent leather, relics from 1970s fashion and almost certainly selected by Edna – clicked on the hardwood floors. She was smiling, happy, holding her grandmother's veined hand with her left hand, a boiled sweet lollipop in the right.

'Mummy!' she said. 'We had pancakes for breakfast! With honey!'

'We went to the garden centre,' Edna said. 'They have a very good café there. The honey comes from their own bees.'

Julia ignored her. Edna's tone was the same as if she and Julia were ancient bosom pals. It was as though there was nothing out of the ordinary going on, as though Anna's disappearance and the divorce and the volcanic argument of the day before hadn't happened. Well, Julia wasn't going to play the game. She wasn't interested in pleasant conversation with Edna. She'd had enough of this farce.

She bent down and picked up Anna. 'That's great,' she said. 'Did you like it?'

'I loved it!' Anna wrapped her arms around Julia's neck and rested her cheek on her mother's collar bone. 'I missed you, Mummy. Where were you?'

'I was at home. I missed you too.'

She closed her eyes. She was not going to let this happen. She was not going to allow Edna – for it was Edna, not Brian behind this – to take Anna from her,

266

even for however long it took for all this to settle down. Anna was her daughter, and she was going to be with Julia. She was not going to be Edna's protégé, a shiny-shoe wearing, horse-riding, hothouse plant raised in her grandmother's image. Never mind 'Tiger Mums'; they had nothing on Edna.

She could just walk out of here now, right this second. Take Anna home, lock the door, and refuse to let Brian in. Plenty of marriages broke down that way, with the father's face pressed up against the window, looking in at what he had lost. She didn't doubt that she would get custody, in the end, but it would be easier if Anna was living with her, if she could point to the current situation and say *look, it's working just fine*. Precedent was important. The court would err on the side of the minimum disruption to Anna's life, and if she was already with Julia then that would be to let her stay there.

Edna knew that, of course, which was why she had brought Anna to her house. But although Julia might not have measured up to Edna in a majority of ways, she was a match for her when it came to child custody. This was her world. She knew all there was to know about it: the letter of the law, the spirit of the law, and the application of the law.

And she knew the most important thing about all of if: the mother always got custody. She knew Edna and she knew what Edna was thinking: the court will act in the best interests of the child and the best interests of the child are to be with me, Dr Edna Crowne. How could they not be? How could the best interests of any child not be to be brought up by Edna Crowne? It was a rare privilege, a blessing, a near guarantee of lifelong success and happiness. Yes, maternal bonds and familial love were important, and in most cases they would be decisive, but this was not most cases. This child had the opportunity to be raised by Edna Crowne, to attend the best schools, to enter the professions, to become rich.

But this was a perfect example of Edna's blind spot. She was so convinced by the strength of her argument that she could not even imagine that there was the possibility of someone disagreeing with her, especially not a judge. Judges were calm and intelligent and rational, and people like that could not help but be persuaded by the force of Edna Crowne's presentation.

It didn't work like that, though. Mothers got custody. Perhaps it wasn't always the best decision, perhaps it wasn't fair, perhaps those dads with the purple T-shirts demanding *Justice for Fathers* and more rights to see their children had a point. But it didn't matter. Because mothers got custody. They just did. It was the way it was, and even Edna Crowne could not change it.

'OK, Anna,' Julia said. 'Say goodbye to Dad. It's time to go home now.'

'Oh,' Anna said. 'Bye Daddy.'

Brian was standing in front of Julia, a few feet further inside the house. He moved towards the door to the vestibule; Julia backed against it to block him off. She put her hand on the doorknob, ready to open it.

268

'Don't do this,' Brian said. 'It's not a good idea.'

'Do what?' Julia said. 'Take my daughter home? How can that not be a good idea?'

'Trust me,' Edna said. 'It isn't.'

Julia snapped her head around. She stared at Edna, keeping her eyes fixed on those of her mother-in-law in a deliberate challenge. 'You,' she said, 'can keep your mouth' – she glanced at Anna – 'can remain quiet on matters that don't involve you.'

'It does involve me,' Edna said. 'After all, I'm going to have to open my house to my granddaughter when she comes to live here. I think that counts as involvement.'

'It would,' Julia said. 'If it was going to happen. But since it isn't going to happen, you aren't involved. So kindly,' she mimed pulling a zip across her mouth in the kind of modern, disrespectful gesture that she knew would infuriate Edna , 'zip it.'

It had the desired effect. Edna straightened to her full height. 'You are a—'

Julia raised her hand, palm outwards. 'Talk to the hand,' she said, enjoying the look of fury on Edna's face. ''Cos the face ain't listening.'

'Be careful, young—' Edna began.

'Zip it,' Julia said, performing the mime again. This was almost fun. She should have done it years ago. 'Zip it.'

Edna nodded slowly. She shrugged. She turned to Brian. 'Do you want to tell her, or should I?'

'I will,' Brian said. 'If you want.'

'Tell me what?' Julia asked.

'In fact,' Edna said, still looking at Brian, '*I'll* tell her.'

'Tell me what?' Julia asked, again. She did not like the narrow-eyed smirk on Edna's face. It looked suspiciously triumphant.

'Why your confidence in the outcome of any custody battle might be a little misplaced.'

'That old chestnut,' Julia said. 'I don't think it is. But enlighten me, nonetheless.'

'You might prefer it if Anna doesn't hear this,' Edna said. 'It won't be very pleasant for her.'

'Right,' Julia said. 'I'll put her down then you'll throw me out. You must think I fell out of the tree yesterday, Edna. Go ahead. Say your piece.'

Edna shrugged. 'Very well,' she said, 'if that's how you want it.'

Brian was impassive. When Edna began he looked away, almost as though he was ashamed.

'As I understand it,' Edna said, speaking slowly and taking care to enunciate every word, in the same deliberate way that someone might eat a meal they wanted particularly to savour, 'the court's main – if not only – concern is the welfare of the child.'

'Which they normally conclude lies in granting custody to the mother,' Julia said. 'Unfortunate for fathers, but just the way it seems to be.'

'They do,' Edna said. 'Unless the mother is incapable of taking care of the child. Say, for example, if she is unstable. Or depressed, or suicidal. Or has a drinking problem. Or an anger management issue.'

Julia opened her mouth to speak, but she did know what to say. Her tongue was dry and stuck to the roof of her mouth.

'I see that you understand what I am saying,' Edna said.

Julia did, but she couldn't quite believe it, couldn't quite grasp how serious the situation was. Grasping at straws, she shook her head.

'You're wrong,' she said. 'You're wrong.'

'I don't think I am. I have taken counsel on the matter and, if a judge thought that a mother – say you, for example – had some issues to work through, then they might well award custody to the father.'

Julia stared at Edna. 'Are you saying you're going to lie about me in order to get custody?'

'No,' Edna said. 'Not at all. The facts are what they are, Julia. Now, let's think through what a court might see when presented with this case.' She gazed at the ceiling, as though deep in thought. 'First, you don't show up to collect your daughter, who is then abducted. Then, second, it comes out in the press that you were planning to abandon her anyway—'

'I wasn't!" Julia said. 'You know that! I might have wanted to leave Brian, but that did not mean I was going to abandon Anna! The press made all that up!'

Edna held up her hand, palm facing outwards. 'I'm just telling you what might be presented in court. And as far as I know, you were planning to abandon Anna. If asked, I would say it seems precisely the kind of behaviour I might expect from you.'

'I don't believe you're doing this. Even you, Edna. I can't believe you would stoop so low.'

'Who's stooping?' Edna said. 'These are just the facts.' She smiled. 'And there are more. I'll go on, shall I?'

Julia lowered Anna to the floor. She'd changed her mind. She didn't want her to hear whatever was coming next.

'Go and play in the sunroom,' she said. 'I'll just be a minute or so.'

After Anna left, Julia turned to Brian. 'Are you going to let her do this?' she asked. 'Are you going to be part of this? Because if you are, then it's on your conscience.'

'I have to do what's best for Anna,' Brian said, unable to meet her gaze. 'And that means she stays with me.'

'I have some more facts, if you're interested,' Edna said. 'Ready?'

Julia didn't reply; Edna cleared her throat theatrically. It was her turn to enjoy herself.

'Third, you are mentally unstable. A few days ago you attempted suicide, which is not the action of a well person.' She was holding out her fist and extending one finger for every point she made.

'I did not!' Julia said. 'You're lying! You know you are!'

'But would a court know that, Julia?' Edna said. 'That is what you must ask yourself.' She extended a fourth finger. 'Fourth, there are signs that you have a drinking problem, a problem which may have played a part in your failed suicide. Fifth, and finally, you appear to be unable to control your anger, something that may also be a result of your alcohol abuse. The gentleman who was here yesterday happens to be a magistrate, and he was appalled at your behaviour. I am sure he would have no problem describing it in court.'

She held up her hand, all five fingers now extended. 'So,' she said. 'Five reasons, any one of which might be reason enough for a judge not to award custody to you. In the presence of all five' – Edna shrugged – 'a responsible person would have no choice but to award custody to the father. Rare, these days, but not impossible.'

Julia found it hard to think what to say. There was so much wrong with what Edna had said, so much that was either a distortion or an outright untruth – she was not an alcoholic, nor was she suicidal, nor did she have anger management issues – but she knew there was no point denying it. Edna already knew none of it was true, but that was irrelevant. Edna was not asking her to give her opinion; she was showing Julia her hand.

And what a hand it was. A straight flush, or a royal flush, or whatever was the best hand in a poker game. Even before she'd had an opportunity to think it through she could see how strong a position it was, and how weak a position she had. Her neglect and desire to abandon Anna, and attempted suicide, were a matter of public record, at least, as far as the newspapers were concerned – and even though the press were wrong, it was her word against theirs, as she could hardly expect Brian to stand up for her – and as for the drinking and anger issues, well, they might not be provable, but they were also not disprovable, and once the allegations were made then the stink of them would hover over her.

Especially since the good magistrate had seen her screaming at Brian, and would take his place in the witness box to say so. Julia closed her eyes.

'So,' Edna said. 'Any comments?'

Julia could think of nothing to say. All she wanted was to get out of that house as fast as she could. She faced Brian.

'Your mother is going to ruin your life,' she said. 'In the end, she'll ruin it, because she's poison. Pure poison. I hope for your sake you get out before it's too late.'

'You don't understand,' Brian said. 'You already ruined my life. All I have left is Anna, which is why I'm not going to let you take her as well. Remember Julia, this is your doing. You chose this. We could still be together, if it wasn't for you.'

Julia looked from Brian to Edna, and back to Brian again. 'No we couldn't,' she said. 'I couldn't stand another minute with you and that twisted old bitch that gave birth to you. I'd rather be dead.'

'More suicidal wishes,' Edna said. 'Tut tut.'

'Fuck you,' Julia said. 'Fuck you, you inhuman bitch.'

'And anger,' Edna said. 'Gosh. You never learn, do you? You created this situation, Julia. Don't you see that? This all comes from your actions. Your neglect and anger and selfishness. Take those from the picture and there would be no problem here. But there they are, and so how could I leave my granddaughter in your care? God alone knows what might happen to her.'

'I'm taking her with me,' Julia said. 'She's coming home.'

'I don't think that's a good idea,' Brian said. 'Don't make this worse for yourself. At the moment you get access. Alone, with Anna.'

The threat was clear: give in or they would try and deny her any access at all, or limit it to supervised access. They would use what they had to paint a picture of her as wild and crazy and totally unsuitable for any kind of maternal role, especially when Anna had the option of solid, hard-working Brian and his heroic mother.

'So now what?' Julia said, her voice a whisper.

'Now you go home,' Edna said. 'And wait to hear from our lawyers.'

Our lawyers.

That 'our' was as eloquent an expression of who was behind this as a thousand-word essay could have been.

Julia was reeling, her head spinning. She was a lawyer herself; she knew how to fight this. She just needed to think about it, to work through the options. But she couldn't. At that moment she was unable to get any purchase on the situation, unable to fully understand what Brian and Edna were saying, unable to tell whether they were right.

'Can I say goodbye to Anna?' she said. 'Please?'

Edna started to shake her head, but Brian interrupted.

'Of course,' he said. 'I'll go and get her.'

v.

Julia took a long time over the drive home. It was a warm day and the Cheshire countryside was showing its best: the ancient hedgerows buzzed with life, sun dappled the ponds and rivers, the stone cottages gleamed with fresh vigour.

She didn't notice any of it. Julia could understand why Brian was doing this, or at least, why he was letting Edna do it. He would not have had the imagination or ruthlessness to do it on his own. It was simple enough: he wanted his daughter. Unlike many dads he had the chance to get her. If it meant destroying Julia's reputation then that was a price worth paying. And he occupied the moral high ground, at least, as far as he was concerned, because he had not started this. It was she who had demanded that they break up, not him, and so she should pay the price.

But she had not started this. That was what he refused to see. Their marriage had failed. That was simply a fact. Look at how they were treating each other now. There was no love there anymore. All Julia had done was to recognize that, and apply the final mercy to what their relationship had become.

There was no blame in that. None. The opposite, in fact. It took more courage to put an end to something that was dying than it did to let it suffer. When she was a girl – perhaps seven, or eight – she had been eating

276

lunch with her father (he had made his specialty dish: fried eggs, pickled onions, beans and bacon) when there was a thud against the window. Julia jumped up to go and look.

Tottering on one leg on the flagstones was a small brown bird.

Dad, she said, *It's a bird. It's alive.*

Its wing's broken, her dad said. *It's a swallow.*

Can we help it?

No, her dad said. *We can't.*

We can take it to the vet!

There's nothing he can do.

Julia felt a sense of deep injustice at the ways of the universe at that moment. How was it possible that there was nothing they could do to help this tiny, damaged creature? Nothing the vet could do. Nothing her dad – a superman – could do?

Well, she said. *We can't just leave it there.*

No, her dad said. *We can't. I'll sort it out after lunch.*

What do you mean?

I have to put it out of its misery, Julia. It's the only kind thing to do.

It had taken her a few seconds to understand what he meant, and when she did she struggled to believe it, struggled to accept that her dad could even contemplate such a thing.

You're going to kill it? she said, tears both for the fate of the bird and at the cruelty of her father springing to her eyes. *That's horrible.*

It's not, her dad said. *It seems that way, but it's the kindest thing we can do for it. The bird is suffering, Julia, and it will suffer until it dies from hunger or thirst or at the hands of some damn cat. Sometimes you have to be tough. Sometimes that's the only way to help something.*

She'd understood it. She might not have if it had been anyone other than her father telling her – she might have just thought they were making excuses because they wanted to kill the bird – but coming from her dad, she could believe it.

Do it now, she said, and he had. He'd left the house and gone to his shed and come back with a shovel. Gently he pushed the bird onto the metal blade and carried it around the back of his shed, out of his daughter's sight.

It's ok, he said, when he came back, his face grave. *The bird is happy now.*

And that was what she had done to their marriage. It was broken, over. There was no point in letting it limp on. Of course, it was sad that it hadn't worked, and that Anna would have to deal with the separation of her parents, but it wasn't anybody's fault. Some marriages worked, others didn't, everyone knew that, and everyone knew that it was better to make a clean break than keep an unhealthy, unhappy marriage going. The days of living in misery because of the shame of divorce or 'for the kids' were over. Maybe Edna – and therefore Brian – didn't agree, but so what? On this particular issue, Edna was wrong, not that she could ever have accepted that.

278

So Julia had done the right thing. She had told Brian it was over, adult to adult. She had avoided drama and affairs and high emotion, which would have been damaging to Anna, by taking the wounded sparrow out of sight – calmly, like her father – and giving it a dignified end. In doing so, she had prepared the ground for a civil and well-managed divorce, after which, Anna would live with her mum and see her dad as often as made sense. It was a situation that occurred all over the country every day.

And then Anna had been taken. That was at the heart of this. That was what had gone wrong. That was to blame, not Julia. If it hadn't been for the kidnapping, right that moment Julia and Anna would be enjoying ice cream at a Cheshire farm.

But that was not what had happened. Anna had been taken, the press had built a simple story in which Julia was the villain, and now she stood, for the second time in as many weeks, to lose everything, and she wasn't sure there was anything she could do about it.

The case they would make against her was strong. She didn't need to be a lawyer to see that. Did it matter that half of it was embellished, twisted, or just plain wrong? Not really. There were enough facts – her late arrival at the school, her desire for a divorce, the so-called suicide attempt, her scratching Brian – to make the picture of her as an unhinged, alcohol-dependent, non-maternal monster seem plausible.

She couldn't go home. Not yet. It was too empty, too obvious a symbol of what her life had become and what it would remain.

She needed something else, something human.

She needed her mum.

vi.

'Hi Mum,' Julia said.

The woman sitting on the worn upholstery of a large wing chair blinked at her. She had liver spots on the back of her wrinkled hands. She didn't speak.

Julia put her hand on her mum's elbow.

'I missed you,' she said. Normally, she would recount what had happened to her, what Anna was up to, in the hope that some of it went in, that some of it lodged somewhere in her mum's shattered mind and maybe came out in her dreams, maybe gave her some subconscious comfort.

Now, though, she had no comfort to offer.

'I missed you,' she repeated. 'I *miss* you.'

She blinked back tears. 'Oh, Mum,' she said. 'What happened? Where did I go wrong? Should I never have married him? It felt so right at the time.'

She hesitated, unsure of whether she should carry on, but she had no choice. Now she had started, she was unable to stop.

It all spilled out. She told her mum what had happened. About the divorce, about Anna, about Edna. About how it was her fault. About how she had been forced to leave her daughter, after only just getting her back, about how that made her feel like the worst mother, the worst person, in the world.

'I just wish I could go back in time,' she said. 'Go back in time and fix it.'

Her mum frowned. Her jaw clenched, the muscles working. She turned to Julia, and blinked again. Her frown deepened, then, suddenly, there was clarity in her gaze, knowledge in her eyes. She chuckled, and patted Julia's hand.

'Don't worry, love,' she said. 'You'll be fine.'

For a moment Julia believed that her mum had returned, was whole again.

'Mum?' she said. 'Are you ok?'

Her mum looked at her for a few, long seconds. The clarity gave way to a slightly puzzled, faraway expression, as though she was lost deep in thought, then the old lady's eyes clouded over and she spoke again.

'Whoever you are,' she said.

She was gone – if she had even been there – but that fleeting instant was enough for Julia. She smiled, got to her feet, and kissed her mum goodbye.

'Thanks,' she said. 'I love you, Mum.'

13

Legal Questions, Moral Questions

i.

They are so foolish. They – the forlorn parents, the bumbling police, the rabid animals of the press – don't know that they are all simply pieces on your chessboard, being moved around as you see fit, all the while thinking that they are in control, that their destiny is in their hands, that the things they do can make a difference to the final outcome.

They cannot. Their free will is an illusion. Whatever they do will lead them to the same place. Even if they do something you did not expect, you would adapt. Change your plans. Rethink. Make it so they are back on course. All roads lead to the same destination. They do not know that they are headed there, but they are.

Only you know what that destination is. They will find out soon enough.

For your plan is nearly complete.
For the girl, the end is coming.
For them *all,* the end is coming.

ii.

Julia's office was quiet. It was early Monday afternoon and most of the lawyers were out, either in court or meeting clients. She was not ready to do either yet, but she had come into the office anyway. The prospect of staying alone in an empty house was bleak and unappealing. At least in the office she had things to distract her: administrative tasks in whose monotony she could lose herself. At home that morning she had found herself unable to resist the allure of reading the latest developments in her life, as told by organs of the Great British press.

One opinion piece, in particular, had stuck with her. It was written by a well-known crusader for family values, corporal punishment in schools, and prison ships in the Thames. Well, not that last one, but it would not have been too much of a stretch to imagine her calling for their return.

So, it began, *she got what she wanted.*

*This column has learned that Julia Crowne, argu-
ably the worst parent in Britain today and unargu-
ably the most reviled, instructed her long-suffering
husband and recently kidnapped daughter to leave
the family home this weekend. Fortunately, Mr
Crowne and Anna have the sanctuary of his mother,
Dr Edna Crowne, to which they can retreat.*

Hopefully this will be a place where Anna can begin the process of healing after her terrible ordeal.

She will have to do so without the presence of her mother, who has gone ahead with the plans to leave the family, plans which she made before her daughter was abducted, because, sources close to her suggest, she wanted to 'find herself'. Her marriage, it appears, was not what she wanted, not what she deserved. It was stifling her, so, rather than work at it, she simply decided to end it.

Fine. That happens often enough in these benighted times, in this era of devalued wedlock and easy divorce.

But could she not have waited? Could she not have held off for a few months, or even weeks, if only for the sake of her daughter?

I have said it before, and I will say it again: this country, this island of Shakespeare and Milton and Churchill, Elizabeths I and II, is going to the dogs. Whatever canines that phrase refers to are feasting upon the carcass of this once great nation. And the reason for the laying low of this nation? In my mind the answer is simple: selfishness. We have lost the ability to sacrifice our own selfish interests for a greater good.

And there is no better demonstration of this than Julia Crowne. I hope she is happy. And I hope that she thinks her happiness is worth the destruction of her family.

I, I am afraid to say, cannot agree.

So that was Julia. That was what the world thought when it thought about her. She had given up feeling aggrieved at the inaccuracy of it all, at the injustice. It was pointless. All she could do was to deal with it as well as she could.

There was another document she had read that morning which stuck with her. It was from Steve Palmer, a lawyer she knew well who was now acting for Brian.

It laid out the custody terms. They were simple: Wednesday nights and every other weekend. She had seen these terms a thousand times during her career. She had even anticipated them forming part of her private life. She just had not anticipated them being this way around. She had never expected that she would be the one getting Wednesday nights and every other weekend with her daughter.

And her instinct was to fight it, to lay everything before the authorities and to trust in them to see the truth, to recognize her for what she was and not how she was portrayed. But she knew that, even in a courtroom, perception is reality, and Brian and Edna would shape that perception to meet their needs.

The risk was clear. If she fought it, they would use everything they had – the anger, the drinking, the neglect, the suicide attempt – and they would stop her seeing her daughter at all. She was being offered a deal: go quietly and you get something from this. Make a fuss and you get nothing.

The mother in her said: make a fuss. The lawyer said: take the deal.

She needed help. She needed an unbiased legal opinion. She picked up her phone and dialled her partner, Mike Sherry, the man who had hired her.

iii.

Mike sat opposite her. He looked uncomfortable in the office chair, his thighs pressed against the hard edges of the arm rest. He was in his late fifties and fighting a losing battle against obesity. In the ten years Julia had known him he had always had a paunch, but in the last couple of years it had started a slow colonization of the rest of his body, spreading around his middle to his lower back, then up to his shoulders and down his arms, and into his neck and chins. Finally, his face was thickening out, his eyes sinking into the expanding flesh of his head.

The lipid colonization had begun when he got divorced. His wife, Carla, had left him for a tax inspector, an occupation that seemed to make the humiliation even greater. A footballer, a doctor, even a virile young labourer would have made sense. But a taxman? How bad a husband and lover must Mike have been if even a taxman was a preferable alternative?

He was fighting other battles, as well. His clothes were becoming dated through lack of attention – he had plenty of money, but like many men he did not have an eye for the small increments in which the fashions in men's business clothes evolved. His jackets were double-breasted, his trousers pleated. Nothing wrong with that, but they made him look an old fifty-something, and not a young one.

286

Moreover, he left a few too many weeks between haircuts, letting it become a necessity to visit the barber, and not a luxury. It all added up to give the impression of a slight shabbiness.

He lived on his own. His two daughters, Lucie and Gemma, were at university, and Julia got the impression they did not visit often. She had seen them out at a restaurant with him a couple of years back. They had been sullen and dismissive, scowling at him and rolling their eyes. In response, he was craven, simpering, pathetic. This lawyer, this competent, intelligent, tough professional fawned over his daughters like an out-of-favour courtier begging for titbits at the feet of a medieval king. It made her uncomfortable and embarrassed to see him brought so low.

It was made worse because she could see the father he had once been: successful, intelligent, adoring and adored. Now, though, he was a fallen idol to his girls, and they resented him for it.

No doubt, it contributed to the other battle he was engaged in, a battle that kept its scorecard in the broken capillaries that surrounded his reddening nose. A few times recently Julia had been alarmed to see him arrive at work, his eyes watery with a hangover. It was hard for him. Had Carla not left him he would still be who he had always been, would still have the life he had made for himself. But it was all gone now. At least Brian was young enough to start again. Hell, Mike was young enough to start again, but she didn't think he would. She didn't think he knew how. She was worried that it was obvious how this was going to end for Mike: alone, drunk, and bitter.

And he deserved better. He was warm, considerate, calm. As a boss he was supportive and honest. He was generous with his advice and with his money. When Julia had made partner she and Brian had been in the process of buying a house so she had not had enough money to buy in. Mike loaned it to her. It was a personal loan, with his – not the firm's – money.

He was also a good lawyer. Not flashy, not blessed with a lacerating, brilliant mind, but experienced and thorough. Which was why she wanted to speak to him about Anna.

'Hey,' he said. 'Good to have you back.'

'I'm not sure I'm adding much value,' Julia said.

'Do whatever you need to do,' he said. 'There's no pressure. Now, or later.'

'Thanks. I appreciate that, Mike.'

'I must say I wasn't expecting to see you so soon,' he said. 'Although, it is a treat. How are things?'

'Not great. That's kind of why I'm here so soon.'

'Oh?'

'Brian and I split up. He's gone to live with his mum. I'm surprised you haven't read about it in the newspapers.'

'I don't bother. I saw what they said about you last week. I don't need to read any more garbage like that.' He paused. She could sense the wheels of his lawyer's mind turning. 'So where's Anna?'

'That's the problem,' Julia said. 'She's with Brian.'

'What do you mean, "with"?' Mike said.

'I mean, she's with him at his mum's house, and it looks like that's where she's staying.'

'I don't get it,' Mike said. 'Why would she be staying there? Don't you want custody?'

Julia nodded. 'Of course. But I don't think I'll get it.'

'Why not? Why wouldn't you?'

'It's a long story,' Julia said.

Mike shrugged. 'I've got nothing better to be doing. But it sounds like it might go better accompanied by a beer. The Red Lion?'

'Sure,' Julia said. 'Why not?'

They sat in at a table in the corner. It felt odd to Julia to see so many people after the last few weeks of isolation. The pub was filling up with the after-work crowd, young people with no families to go to, thirty-somethings having a quick one before heading back to nappies and bath time, larger groups out on a work do, and solitary drinkers putting off the inevitable return to a dark, quiet, musty home.

'So,' Mike said. 'What's going on?'

Julia took a few seconds, considering how best to tell the story.

'Well,' she said. 'Brian wants custody. And he's offered me a deal. I get Wednesdays and every other weekend; he gets the rest. That way we don't need to go to court.'

'But why would you do that?'

'Because it might be the best deal I get.' Mike frowned. Julia held up her hand. 'Let me explain,' she said, 'if we go to court they're going—'

'Who's "they"?'

'Brian and Edna, his mother. She's behind this. Brian would never have the balls or the brains to come up with it. So, if we go to court they're going to say it's in Anna's best interests to be with Brian.'

'It isn't. And courts never award in favour of the father. I don't see the problem.'

'The problem is they're going to paint a picture of me that means it will be in Anna's best interests to be with her dad. They're going to say I'm irresponsible. I didn't show up at the school, remember—'

'Anyone could have made that mistake. It happens all the time. You were just unlucky. You can't be punished for that.'

'And I was planning to leave them both, anyway—'

'Which isn't true.'

'And I am unstable, as shown by what they will paint as my suicide attempt—'

'Which was not a suicide attempt.'

'And I have a drink problem. And an anger management problem.'

'Which you don't.'

'They'll convince the court I do.'

'How?'

Julia paused. 'There was … an incident. At Edna's house.'

'What kind of incident?'

'I … I lost my temper and hit Brian. Well, I scratched him. It left marks on his cheek. He was bleeding.'

'Just deny it.'

'There was some magistrate there. He saw it.'

'But still. It's lies and exaggerations, Julia.'

'But taken together, in a courtroom. You can see how it would play out. I did try to kill myself, I did hit Brian, I did fail to pick up Anna, leading to her being kidnapped. Why wouldn't the rest of it be true? They can paint a pretty horrific picture of me. You see?'

He massaged his temples. 'Yes,' he said, after a long pause. 'I see.'

'And then they'll refuse me custody other than under supervision. That's the deal. I take what they're offering, or they give me nothing.'

'That won't happen. The judge would at least give you what they're offering now. They must think you're a fit mother.' he paused, the use of the formal *fit mother* awkward, 'I mean, of course, you're a fit mother, and by offering you this deal they recognize that. To change their mind later would be bizarre.'

'Probably. But they would say they'd learned more or re-evaluated the situation. And is that a risk I want to take?'

Mike shook his head slowly, his eyes on hers, his teeth clenched, his face unsmiling. It was an expression that spoke both anger and disbelief. 'What a pair of heartless bastards,' he said. 'I mean, really.'

'Right,' Julia said. 'And I was married to one of them, although sometimes it felt like both.'

291

'Don't they feel ashamed of themselves?'

'Brian just does what Mummy says. And Edna is not very well acquainted with shame, at least, not her own. As far as she's concerned she's doing this for her granddaughter. What better outcome for a child than to be brought up by Edna Crowne? All she's doing is playing the hand she's been dealt. Why be ashamed of that?'

Mike leaned forward. 'Because it's fucking appalling!' he said. 'Truly appalling.'

Julia smiled a wry, resigned smile. 'Is that a legal opinion?'

'No,' Mike said. 'It isn't.'

'So how about giving one?'

'I need to think.' He sipped his pint. 'I'm going to the gents. Back in a minute.'

He disappeared into the growing throng. For the first time since she'd left Edna's house Julia felt a sense of calm. Her mind had stopped whirring, stopped running through all the possibilities, stopped weighing this and that and imagining what a judge might say. All she had to do now was wait and see what Mike said. She might not like the answer – and the whirring might restart – but for now it was not in her hands. It was a blessed, sweet relief.

'Are you Julia Crowne?'

A woman in her late twenties, heavyset and tending towards outright obesity, was glaring at her. She had a fierce, hard-bitten face and an aggressive demeanour, almost too aggressive, as though her tough exterior had been developed over the years in response to the knocks that life had thrown at her. Julia got the impression that, as a teenager, she had been large, not pretty, unloved, and her aggression was a way of telling the world that she didn't give a fuck.

She was unmarried – at least, she was not wearing a wedding ring – and she had the flushed, glassy look of someone who was on the edge of being drunk.

'Yes,' Julia said. 'I am.'

'Yeah,' the woman said. 'Well, I've got something to say to you.'

iv.

Julia could picture the scene: the woman standing at the bar with her friends, one of them spotting Julia and whispering to the others *is that the woman, from the news? You know, the one with the kid who got kidnapped then came back?* Another replying *yeah, it's her, Julia Crowne. She's a right bitch.* And then the woman staring at her now would have said *I'm going to tell her. She needs to know.* The others squealing *you wouldn't,* knowing that she would, that this kind of thing was her speciality, that she prided herself on her fearlessness; that she did not understand the difference between being bold and being rude and if she did, she didn't care.

She didn't give a fuck.

And she would have told them that and then marched over, ready to say her piece, and afterwards she would say *I know it was a bit out of order but I had to say*

293

something. I couldn't just keep quiet. You have to speak out. People can't be allowed to get away with that kind of thing. I mean, how could she think it was ok to just be sitting there, drinking with another man? So soon? What a bitch. I had to tell her.

Julia met her gaze. 'How can I help you?' she said.

Now she was there, the woman seemed less confident, as though she hadn't thought about what she was actually going to say when she reached her quarry. 'You,' she began, 'you are the most, the most selfish fucking person I've ever known.'

'You don't know me,' Julia said.

'I know enough,' the woman said. 'I know enough to know that you don't deserve to be a mother to that little girl.'

Who the hell did this woman think she was? All she knew about Julia, about Anna, about what had happened was what she had read in the press, and that was bullshit. Yet she felt she could approach Julia and tell her she didn't deserve to be a mother?

'Right,' Julia said, looking away from the woman in case the sight of her roused even more fury in her. 'Well thank you for that.'

'There's more,' the woman said. 'I've not finished yet.'

She was of a certain type, this woman; the type of people who were angry and bitter and wanted to make other people as unhappy as them, but who were just smart enough to understand that they could not just go around abusing people, and so they found cover for their wish to

294

abuse people in self-righteous anger. This woman did not care about Anna. She just wanted to cause misery, and Anna was a good excuse to do so.

'What's your name?' Julia asked her.

'Juliet,' the woman said.

'Juliet,' Julia said. 'It's a nice name. A bit like mine.' She leaned forwards, keeping her hands on her knees so that Juliet did not see how much they were shaking with anger. 'Well, Juliet,' she said. 'You know what you can do?' Julia held up a hand. 'Don't answer. I'll tell you. You can take your fat arse back to whatever shithole you call home. Go and read your shit books and watch crap TV and tend to your loneliness. And get used to it, because that's going to be your life. Got that, Juliet?'

The woman stared at her, stunned. She'd been expecting apologetic stammering, or meekness, or a fleeing of the scene. Not this. Not *aggression*. She was the aggressive one.

'Go on,' Julia said. 'Off you go. And on your way out you can think about why you don't have kids, or a husband or a boyfriend. And if you want a clue, here's one: it's because you're a disgusting blubbery whale, although, I have to say that there are probably disgusting blubbery whales out there saying "hang on a minute, don't compare me to that horrible thing, I'm not that bad".'

Juliet's face creased into an expression of pure hatred. 'You fucking bitch,' she said. 'How fucking dare—'

'What's going on here?' Mike pushed his way through the crowd, some of who were tuning into the entertainment on offer. He had two fresh drinks in his hands: a pint of bitter and a glass of white wine.

'That bitch is insulting me,' Juliet said. She was breathless with anger, her chest heaving. 'She, of all people, is—'

'We need to go,' Mike said. He stepped in between the woman and Julia and put the drinks on the table. 'Come on,' he said. 'Now.'

Julia grabbed her coat and bag and stood up and headed for the exit, Mike just behind her. Outside, he took her by the elbow.

'Jesus,' he said, 'that wasn't the smartest thing to do, was it? After what you were just telling me?'

'I know,' Julia said. 'But I couldn't just let her insult me. Why should I?'

'Fine,' Mike said. 'We'll get over it. You want to come to my house? For that legal opinion?'

Mike lived in a detached house in a village on the edge of the Cheshire plain. It was large and dark and felt unlived in. They sat in the living room, Mike with a large whisky in his hand, and Julia, whose car was outside, with a glass of water in hers.

'So,' he said, 'here's what I think.'

Julia nodded. 'Shoot,' she said.

'As you know, the court acts in the interests of the child. Brian will be trying to show that Anna's best interests are to stay with him, but not because he offers something exceptional. He's claiming that you cannot offer a stable and safe environment. Now, even with all of the stuff he's accusing you of, he can't prove it. A courtroom is not a newspaper. If he wants to say that you are an alcoholic, he will have to prove it, which he won't be able to, because you aren't. Likewise with the anger management issues. So you hit him, once, under extreme duress. That is not an anger management problem. It's a human response. And we just deny the accusation of a suicide attempt. My point is that it's pretty hard for him to prove any of the things he's laying at your door.'

Julia felt mounting excitement. Maybe this was not as hopeless as she had thought.

It must have showed on her face, as Mike frowned. 'Don't get carried away,' he said. 'There's more. Like I said, he can't prove the things he's accusing you of, but that doesn't matter, because he doesn't need to. Remember, the court is only concerned with Anna's best interests. Whether you have a drink problem is only relevant as it pertains to Anna's welfare.' He folded one thigh over the other and took a long drink from his whisky glass. 'Now,' he said. 'This is where it gets kind of grey. In my experience, family courts are very risk-averse. What I mean is that they are looking for reasons why an environment might be unsafe for a child. That's what Brian is playing on. He's saying, yes, I can't prove these things, but are you going to take that risk? When there's a risk-free alternative? It's not a bad strategy.'

'So,' Julia said. 'What do you think I should do?' What do you think a court would do?'

'I think,' Mike said, 'there is a good chance the court would award custody to the father. To Brian.'

Julia wanted to scream at him, shout *no, your job is to say that we can do this, that we should fight, not that I should give up! Not that I should hand over my daughter!*

'Right,' she said. 'So what should I do? If I was your client, how would you advise me?'

'I'd say that the best you are likely to get in court is what you already have – Wednesdays and every other weekend – and that there is a risk of losing that if you do go to court. So there's no upside to contesting custody in this case, only a downside.' He looked at her. 'I would advise against.'

She had known it all along but it took hearing it from Mike to make it real, to make it so that she understood that she was going to see her daughter four days in ten, that Anna would grow up in Edna's shadow, maybe calling another woman Mum, if Brian remarried. She, Julia, would be on the outside, face pressed to the glass, increasingly a distraction as Anna's life filled up. Right now they would spend weekends together, but as Anna grew into a teenager and a young woman her weekends would revolve around friends and boyfriends. Parents saw little enough of teenagers when they shared a house full-time. Julia would be living on crumbs.

'I can't,' Julia said. 'I can't just let it happen.'

'I know,' Mike said, 'but you asked me what I would advise a client, so I told you. I gave you my professional opinion. If you want me to advise you as a friend, then that would be different.'

'So let's say I asked you to advise me as a friend,' Julia said. 'What would you say then?'

'I'd tell you to fight the bastard with everything you've got,' Mike said. 'That's what I'd tell you as a friend.'

v.

'You think I should fight? Even though you would advise a client not to?' Julia said. 'I'm not sure I follow the logic.'

Mike smiled. 'That's because it's not about logic. Let me see if I can explain.' He shifted in his seat. 'I remember your dad, Julia. He coached the rugby team I played in – if you can believe I ever managed to shift this lump of a body around a rugby field – when I was a teenager. He'd played some semi-professional stuff and given it up after an injury. It was probably around the time you were born, but you won't remember.'

Julia didn't, but she did remember playing with the trophies her dad kept in a cupboard when she was a child. She also had photos of him with his teammates. She'd always marvelled at them, at the proof that her dad had an existence that preceded her, an existence when he was a fit, muscular athlete with a full head of hair and a wicked glint in his eye.

'He was great with us teenagers. We were a rum lot, a bunch of tearaways and thugs, but he whipped us into shape. Got us fit, taught us the game, gave us some discipline. But the thing I remember most – and others remember it too – was that he insisted we adhere to a higher standard than the one required by the laws of the game. He told us that the laws of the game were one thing, but we needed to stick to the spirit of the game.'

'What did he mean?' Julia asked. She loved hearing about her dad; loved learning what he had been like as a man. 'What kind of things did he make you do?'

'Well, he used to referee our games, and he would penalize us if, say, one of the bigger players on our team tackled a smaller player on the other team unnecessarily hard. It might have been a legal tackle, but he would penalize us for it. He called it unsporting conduct. The thing that annoyed us was that he didn't penalize the other side for it. He couldn't; they didn't know that he had added a rule, so when he refereed us we were at a disadvantage. But you know something? We applied his rules even when other referees had the whistle. So it worked.'

'Sounds like Dad,' Julia said. 'But how does it help with this situation?'

'The lesson I learned from your dad,' Mike said. 'Is that sometimes you just have to do what's right. You can walk away from this, sign the agreement, hand over custody, and if you were a violent, suicidal alcoholic who had a history of negligent parenting, then I would suggest you did. But you aren't, and the fact that Brian and his mother will paint you that way – successfully, maybe – is not enough reason to accept their terms. Plus, if you do, then you will be admitting that you are what they say you are. I just feel that if you – we –walk away from this, then it will rankle forever.'

'But what can I do?' Julia said. 'If I fight them I might lose Wednesdays and every other weekend. They might push for supervised custody only. I couldn't live with that.'

'That's a risk. The question is, whether it's a risk worth taking.'

'Not if I can't win.'

'There's no *can't*,' Mike said. 'It's not obvious how, I'll grant you that, but there's no can't.' He paused. 'The thing is, their case rests, at least partly, on lies. You aren't violent, you don't drink to excess. We need to find a way to pick it apart. Find the thread that will unravel it.'

'How?' Julia said. 'How do I fight back?'

'A couple of ways. I have a couple of ideas.' He stood up. 'So why don't you let Brian know you don't want his deal, and we can get to work?'

'That depends on what your ideas are,' Julia said.

'Then let me fill you in.'

The next morning, Julia sat at her kitchen table, opened her laptop, and started to type.

Brian, I find what you are doing – exploiting the abduction of our daughter to get custody, although we both know it is your mother behind it – to be

301

*appalling, and I hope you feel the shame of it. I do
not accept your proposal for custody, and my lawyer
will be in touch in due course to formalize matters.*
  Yours, Julia

Then she hit send. She hoped that she was doing the
right thing.

His reply came a few minutes later.

*Fine. Send your lawyer's details. My lawyer will be
in touch.*

She didn't deserve a reply to her letter. A defence against
her accusations. She didn't even deserve a signature.

But that was fine. She smiled. From now on Brian –
and Edna – were not going to have it all their own way.

vi.

Julia scanned the tweets hashtagged *#notfittobeamum*.
It seemed as good a place to start as any other; there
was no shortage of vitriol being spilled onto keyboards.
What was it that drove these people to comment so
viciously on someone they didn't know and would never
meet? Did they think they were somehow making the
world a better place? That they were showing other
people how to live, warning them of what awaited them
if they messed up? Or did they just enjoy it? Were they
simply angry, bitter people who could not resist the
impulse to lash out; an impulse they would never have

dared to indulge publicly, but which they could revel in to their heart's content under the anonymous protection of the internet?

Julia thought it was the latter, and if it was they had miscalculated. The internet was rarely as anonymous as people thought it was.

She read @vernaldraft tweets; @vernaldraft had quite a lot to say about her, from the merely insulting:

#JuliaCrowne is the reason why some people should not be allowed kids*#notfittobeamum*

To the off-topic:

Why's slut *#JuliaCrowne* like a washing machine? Because they both drip when they're fucked *#notfittobeamum*

To the frankly chilling:

#JuliaCrowne should not breed again. *#notfittobeamum* *#forcedsterilization*

Well, Julia thought, *let's see what we can find out about* @vernaldraft. She read through the rest of @vernaldraft's tweets:

Been at the beer festival in Cromer. Best real ale in the country – and the world!

So, a lover of real ale. And, it seemed, amphibians:

Evening listening to frogs at local vernal pond.
#Norfolkboy #BestcountyinEngland

So, a real ale lover from Norfolk. She carried on reading.
Here was something from a year ago:

Love being an engineer. New job in pumps.
Awesome.

And a tweet in reply, from @RobParker:

Congrats mate looking forward to seeing you in the
office and celebrating with a few jars. Nice one.

Almost certainly a man, then, and a man who worked
as a pump engineer in Norfolk, with someone called
Rob Parker.

From then on it was easy. On LinkedIn there was a
Rob Parker working at a small sewage pump company
in Norfolk. He only had seventeen connections, one of
whom was a man called Clive Gaskell, who had joined
around a year ago, and who was chairman of his local
real ale society.

A search on Clive Gaskell revealed a Facebook profile
of a man in his late forties, married, two kids. His profile
picture was a pond in the evening.

Bingo.

A few more clicks and she had the name of the owner of the pump company: Jenny Jones. She had a Twitter profile too. Julia typed out a tweet in reply to @vernaldraft's most offensive effort:

@vernaldraft Not sure about *#forcedsterilization*. Seems a bit eugenics to me. Sure you want him working for you @jjpumps?

Then, just for good measure, she replied to the others:

What about this one @vernaldraft @jjpumps?
Or this one @vernaldraft @jjpumps?

That should make Clive Gaskell think twice before abusing someone again.

She closed her laptop. Fun as it was, spiking the guns of her Twitter enemies was nothing more than a way of taking some kind of control of her situation, a way of breaking the habit of seeing herself as power-less in the face of her husband and the press and the courts and Edna.

Which was going to be important, as the real work was just about to get started.

'You know,' Mike said. 'I think it might be better if I go to see Derek alone.'

Julia stiffened. She glanced out of the passenger-side window of Mike's Audi. A woman pushing a pram looked back at her, her face drawn and harried. They were on their way to see Derek Jacobs, the retired magistrate who had witnessed Julia scratching Brian.

'Why? I thought we were going to talk to him together.'

'I don't want him to feel pressured,' Mike said. 'He might clam up.'

'I do want him to feel pressured!' Julia said. 'He has to know what's at stake here! I want him to have to look me in the eye.'

'I know what you mean,' Mike said. 'But he was a magistrate. If he thinks there's going to be a custody case then he may simply refuse to talk. If it's just me then he might be more relaxed. And I've known him for a long time. I can keep it off the record.'

'You know him?'

'I've been a lawyer in this town for three decades, Julia. He was a magistrate. Our paths crossed from time to time.'

'I don't know, Mike. I want to see him.'

The car slowed to a stop at a red light. Mike turned to face her. 'Trust me,' he said. 'It's better this way. Really. I know Derek. He'll talk to me. If you're there ... I don't know.'

'Ok, we'll do it your way.'

'Thanks. Now, talk me through what happened at Edna's house again.'

'There's not much to say,' she said. 'Brian and Edna pushed me and I lost my temper – wrong, I know, but I was tired and they had my daughter – and I scratched his face. And this guy was there to see it all.' She shook her head. 'It's typical Edna. In the middle of all this and she had a lunch guest. She said it was a long-standing appointment. It's exactly the kind of thing she would do: carry on with some social engagement so that she didn't lose face.'

'You have to admire her,' Mike said. 'She's got balls, if you know what I mean.'

'I'm not sure "admire" is the word I'd use.'

They pulled into the car park of a white-walled pub. Mike switched off the engine.

'Wait here,' he said. 'I'll be back in an hour.'

Julia watched Mike shuffle across the damp tarmac of the pub car park. His suede shoes were stained and his trousers were baggy and shapeless. She felt a tug of sympathy for him: he was going to grow old alone. The highlights of his life: boozy lunches with former colleagues and visits from his daughters; highlights that would only serve to show how desperate the rest of his life was. The problem for Mike wasn't that he would be alone – plenty of people put up with, or even enjoyed, that – but that he didn't want to be. She could picture him as a young dad, warm, goofy, fond of telling bad jokes and reading good books to his girls. And as a husband: loyal, considerate, generous, and prepared to play his role; work hard to provide for his family. It was a shame it wasn't enough for his wife: a woman she couldn't help but dislike because of what she had done to Mike.

307

Of course, people could say that she was no better. Julia wasn't happy with Brian – a fundamentally decent man – so she was walking away. If Mike's wife should have stayed with him, why was it different for Julia? She wasn't sure it was.

Anyway, now was not the time to think like this. She took out her phone and scrolled through her emails. She had a request from LinkedIn. It was an old friend – well, an acquaintance, really – from university. She was working in Leeds as Managing Director of a haulage firm, which was not where Julia would have imagined her ending up. They'd met when Julia had acted in her one and only student play. Charlotte was blonde and petite and girly.

She accepted the request, then flicked through her contacts. A guy she had dated during high school was now VP of Marketing for some big corporate. She should have stuck with him, except for the fact that he could only get aroused if she pretended to be a cat. The first time it was almost enjoyable, but after that it became downright weird. She'd been recommended for strategic thinking by a former colleague. Nice to know. And Brian was celebrating a work anniversary. Five years in his current job. She clicked on his name. He didn't have many contacts. One of them, she was surprised to see, was Edna.

Edna had a mere nine contacts. Of course she did: very few people, Julia included, would merit inclusion in her inner circle. Julia glanced over them.

And then she sat up in the car seat, her stomach tight.

Edna was connected to the News Editor at the *Daily World*.

Julia read it again, then typed the man's name into Google. He had a bio on Wikipedia: Oxford alumnus, at the same time as Edna.

Why hadn't Edna mentioned it? She could have leaned on the guy and stopped them from publishing all the rubbish about Julia. It was amazing she had a contact like that and hadn't used it.

Unless, of course, she had.

'No,' Julia said, out loud in the empty car. 'No, she wouldn't.'

Was it possible that Edna had leaked the information to the *Daily World*? Surely she wouldn't have done something like that. But it made sense: it was either the police or someone else who knew what was going on, and there were very few of them. After confronting Brian, Julia had assumed it was someone close to the police, but what if it wasn't? What if it was Edna?

Her head was spinning. It was a struggle to concentrate. But one thing was clear: if Edna had done it, it would blow the custody case wide apart.

Forty minutes later, Mike was back.

He opened the door and sat in the car, the smell of beer settling in with him. The glassy look in his eye suggested he'd had at least a couple of pints in the hour he'd been in there.

Julia didn't care. She was flush with her discovery.

'Mike,' she said. 'I think I found something out. Something important.'

'That's a coincidence,' he said, 'because so did I.'

vii.

'You go first,' Mike said.

Julia handed him her phone. He read it and looked up at her.

'So?' he said. 'It's Edna's LinkedIn profile.'

'Look who she's linked to.'

Mike glanced back at the screen. 'Oh,' he said. 'I see.'

'Yeah,' Julia said. 'So here's what I think, Mike: I think she leaked the details of my so-called suicide attempt and negligent parenting and rumours of an affair to the press.'

'An hour ago,' Mike said. 'I would have said you were crazy. But not now. Not after what Derek told me.'

'Which was?'

'I asked what happened at Edna's house. His story was pretty much the same as yours. He expressed some regret that you were going to lose out, but he couldn't help. It was your own fault for losing your temper.'

'Sympathetic guy.'

'He has a point, Julia. Anyway, I didn't think I was going to get much, but then I mentioned that it must have been strange to be there at such a difficult time, but Edna was the kind of person who held to her engagements, especially those of long standing.' He paused. 'And then it happened. He looked at me funnily – sort

310

of confused – and said that it wasn't a long-standing engagement. Edna had invited him that morning. She said she wanted to keep things as normal as possible and could do with the moral support.'

'What did you say?' Julia said.

'Not much. I just glossed over it. Pretended that it was nothing.' He started the car and put his hand on the gear stick. 'But it's not nothing, Julia. It means she was planning something. It means she set you up. And if she was leaking stuff to the papers as well … ' he looked at Julia and grinned, 'then we have a case.'

They stopped at another pub, a mile down the road. This time it was Julia who needed a drink. She ordered a glass of Sauvignon blanc; Mike had a diet Coke.

'So what do we do with this?' she said. 'Should I confront her?'

Mike shook his head. 'Do nothing for now, and say nothing. She and Brian think they have the upper hand. The last thing we need to do is warn them that we know more than they think. We need to wait until we have everything in place before we do that. So, for now, act as though nothing's changed: pick up Anna when you're supposed to, return her at the appointed time.'

'And in the meantime?'

'In the meantime, we need to prove she leaked the story.'

'How?' asked Julia. 'The paper will hide behind journalistic privilege. Sanctity of the source, that kind of thing.'

'I know,' Mike said. 'Miserable hypocrites that they are. I've been wondering how we could compel them to reveal their source. But it'll be difficult.'

'Unless we do the same thing ourselves,' Julia said.

'What do you mean?'

'Fight fire with fire. If Edna can leak lies, then we can leak the truth. We can tell a rival newspaper what's going on. If they print it, the *Daily World* will have to confirm it or deny it.'

'Or they can do neither,' Mike said. 'But the absence of a denial will be enough. And I doubt they will deny it publicly. The fallout would be too great.' He raised his diet Coke. 'So, it seems we have a plan,' he said. 'Play dumb with Brian and Edna for now, while we arrange our chess pieces.'

Julia lifted her glass and clinked the rim against Mike's.

'Sounds good to me,' she said.

14

Doll's House

i.

You can relax now. The child is where you want her. You are surprised it happened so quickly, but that's ok. You are not so foolish as to look a gift horse in the mouth. Vigilance is required, of course. You never know what will happen, what people will do when they are desperate. After all, you have been desperate yourself, and look what you did.

You still cannot believe you managed it. To take the child, hide her, and return her unhurt, with hardly a moment when you felt that you might be caught; it was something special, even for you, even for someone with your past, with your *capabilities*.

You can admit that luck has been on your side. You have to. Everything went perfectly. You would have succeeded anyway, you're sure of that – good planning and intelligence would have seen to it – but the luck helped. What was it Napoleon said? Give me a lucky general over a good one?

Well, how about one who is both, Monsieur Bonaparte?

You admire Bonaparte. He was a great man, a bold man. He would have admired you too.

So, you've won the opening skirmishes and prevailed in the first battle. But like all good generals that it not enough for you. Not *nearly* enough.

The battle may be over, but the war is only just beginning.

ii.

Julia was going to be in and out of there as quickly as possible. Once they had a routine she would simply pull up outside the front door and Anna would skip out to the car, climb in, and they'd be away. This first time, though, she knew she'd have to get out, ring the doorbell and face Brian and Edna.

She knocked on the door. It could be a while before Edna opened it. It was quite a way from the back of her house to the front, and the layout meant there was not a direct route. That was what happened when houses grew from a sixteenth-century seed.

It was over four-hundred-years-old, that house. It had seen so much. Births, deaths, marriages, funerals, celebrations, devastations, even, probably, murders. And it was still there, adding to its stories, quietly witnessing the antics of the latest occupants. Brian had once said

314

that, when they first moved in, he had felt it was haunted, felt the presence of the ghosts who had played out their earthly existences at Toad Hall, as she had always called it. They'd moved from a 1930s suburban semi after the death of Edna's father, who had left her a substantial inheritance, and the switch to an old house had spooked him. The feeling hadn't lasted. He'd got used to it, he said.

Grew up, I guess, he said. *Stopped believing in ghosts.*

Julia wasn't so sure that was the explanation. She suspected that, if there were ghosts, if there were spectral presences left by prior inhabitants, they had been silenced by the presence of Edna. It was not Brian growing up, but Edna's ferocious remodelling of the house. It had been a bit ramshackle, in need of some repair, and Edna had seen to it that the repairs were done. Walls were shored up, roofs replaced, chimneys repointed. She'd had the place more or less gutted and rebuilt, rewired and re-plumbed. The ancient shell remained; what lay beneath it was brand new.

And that left no place for ghosts, for those denizens of leaky plumbing and draughty attics, to dwell. How were they supposed to make their presence felt when the creaky floorboards and ill-fitted doors had all been refashioned into neat, straight lines?

And so, if they were ever there, they no doubt gave up in the face of Edna's onslaught. They could afford to. After all, she'd be gone soon enough, and they had all eternity to wait. They'd probably packed up and left, gone to haunt somewhere else until such time as Toad Hall was freed from Edna's grip.

And with them had gone the warmth and character of the house. It was cold and echoey and lonely, and Julia hated the thought of Anna growing up there. And she wasn't going to let her. She'd find a way to get custody. Maybe in a year from now when things had settled down.

At least, that was what she told herself. At the back of her mind a little voice laughed at her, sneering that she was a fool if she thought Edna would let it happen. There was no point even trying. But she would try. And she would win. She had to. If the universe was just, then she had to.

It was, she knew, a very big if.

Edna opened the front door. She was dressed in dark trousers and a blue blouse, a Hermes scarf around her neck, and looked down her nose at Julia, unsmiling.

'Good morning,' she said. 'Anna is playing in the back garden.'

'She should be ready,' Julia said. 'Nine a.m. She's mine from nine.'

'I wasn't sure you were coming,' Edna said. 'Brian didn't mention it.'

Of course, he'd mentioned it. Edna was just being difficult. Well, let her. She didn't know what was coming her way.

'Is he here? I'd rather deal with him. He's Anna's father. The custody arrangement is with him, not you.'

Edna shook her head. 'He's gone out. He didn't say as much, but if he thought you were coming, he probably didn't want to see you.'

She was lying, Julia knew. Brian had told her to expect Julia, and told her that he didn't want to be there when she came. But Edna wouldn't admit it. Even now, she wanted to play her little games.

'I'll wait here,' Julia said. 'You can go and fetch Anna.'

They spent the day in the places that single parents took their kids in an attempt to make life fun. They saw the lions and monkeys and lizards at Chester Zoo, then ate comfort food in a pub. Back home, Julia sat on the floor, her back to Anna's bedroom wall. Her daughter slept in the bed she'd slept in since the day she moved out of the Moses basket. They'd bought it from a specialist children's furniture shop; it was a crib but could, when the time came, be reassembled into a starter bed. She remembered the day they had taken off the bars and converted it. Anna had taken advantage of her new freedom and got out of bed about twenty times. Downstairs, Julia or Brian heard her footsteps then one of them went upstairs and carried her back to her bed. It had taken about two weeks until they could put her in bed and have some degree of confidence she might stay there.

She was getting big for the bed now. In the glow of her pig nightlight Julia could see that her feet were nearly at the end. She'd have to buy a full-sized bed soon.

It wouldn't get slept in much. Just Wednesday nights and every other weekend. God, she'd heard that phrase so often, but she'd never thought it would apply to her. It had always seemed like a reasonable allocation of custody but now she realized that it was nothing. It passed so quickly.

It felt like it was minutes since she had picked Anna up from Edna's house. Tomorrow would be just as quick. A quick breakfast, some TV, lunch, then back to Edna's. Julia leaned her head back against the wall and closed her eyes. It was so *unfair*. She should have had custody of Anna. She was her *mother*, for God's sake.

But Brian – backed by his witch of a mother – had played dirty. She didn't blame him – well, she did, she blamed and hated him – but among the blame she recognized that she would more than likely have done the same thing, if it had meant that Anna could stay with her. Custody battles were the closest thing to a fight for survival that Julia had ever witnessed; it was as though people were trapped and the only way to save themselves involved doing things which most people had never imagined they were even capable of. It turned out that a lot of people did whatever it took. Normal morality was suspended. It was kill or be killed.

And Edna was not going to hold back. She had spotted her opportunity and taken it, leaked information to the press, ruined Julia's reputation. She wondered whether it was a good idea to take her on. Perhaps there was another way, perhaps she could carry Anna down to the

318

car, settle her in the back seat, pack a bag, and disappear. It was nine p.m.; no one would know they were gone for fifteen hours. How far could she get in fifteen hours? She didn't have Anna's passport, so she'd have to stay in Britain, but she could get to Cornwall, or the Highlands of Scotland.

She entertained a fantasy of her and Anna, hidden away in a tiny crofter's cottage, living off the land, foraging for mushroom and edible plants, trapping animals and pulling glistening, silver fish from streams and lakes.

Yeah, right. She wouldn't have the first idea how to trap an animal, and they'd probably die from fungus poisoning within the first few days. And they'd be seen. If Anna disappeared again there would be another nation-wide hunt. They'd be caught in no time, and Julia would never get to see her daughter again.

And they might be vulnerable. Whoever had taken Anna was out there. Julia still had no idea who had taken her, and why they had brought her back. It made her uneasy to think about it. Someone had gone to the trouble of abducting a little girl, and then they had returned her, unharmed. Why? What had they got from it? Had they abused her? Taken photos of her and posted them on the internet? Was it some sick game, which wasn't over? Maybe they were out there right now, watching, waiting for another chance to grab Anna. Or maybe they had planned to kill her and lost their nerve and right now were contemplating another little girl, another target.

And what about Jim Crowne and Miss Wilkinson, whose first name she still did not know. Where were they? She doubted she would ever find out. The police were probably not spending too much time looking for them now. She doubted that Jim had anything to do with Anna's abduction, but she couldn't help wondering whether he had, whether it was a way to get back at Edna.

But if that was what he wanted, why wait until now? It didn't make sense. Like so much of this, it didn't make sense.

No, whatever the story was with Jim it was not linked to Anna. There was a story there, she was sure of that, but she was equally sure she would never find out what it was. Edna was hardly going to confide in her.

And Julia had other things to worry about. Brian, the custody battle, and that nagging fear that there was more of this yet to come. God, she hated thinking about it, hated that it forced her to acknowledge how twisted the world could be.

Most of all, she hated thinking that it might not be over.

iii.

They were a few hundred yards from Edna's house. Julia had just explained that Anna was going back to her grandmother's.

'I think I want to stay with you, Mummy.'

'I want you to as well, darling,' Julia said. 'But for the moment you need to stay with Dad.'

'But it isn't my house. It's Grandma's. I like my house.'

Tell them that, Julia thought, but refrained from saying so. It would only lead to accusations that she was trying to unsettle Anna.

'I know,' she said. 'But Grandma's house is fun.' God, it was painful to have to say those words, even if it was best for Anna that she did not sense the conflict. 'And I'll be back on Wednesday to pick you up.'

'When's Wednesday?' asked Anna. 'Is it tomorrow?'

'Two days after tomorrow,' Julia said. 'It'll be here before you know it.'

They turned into the lane that led to the back of Edna's house. The police car was not there, probably gone for the day while Anna was not there. They'd be back later. There was a parking area there that she shared with the neighbours, their garages forming the perimeter of the square of tarmac. When they pulled into the parking area, Brian was waiting by the back gate. Edna was standing behind him.

'Hi,' he said, his arms outstretched. 'How's my little princess?'

'Good,' Anna said. 'We went to the zoo. I saw a rhinocetus.'

'Wow,' Brian said. 'Is that like a rhinoceros?'

'That's what I said. A rhinocetus.'

'Cool,' Brian said. 'Hey – I have to go to the supermarket. We need something for dinner. What would you like? You choose.'

'A hippopotanus,' Anna said.

'For dinner?'

321

'Amus,' Edna said. 'Hippopotamus. Not anus.'

'No,' Julia said. 'I think it was a hippopatanus.'

Anna nodded. 'Yes,' she said. 'We saw a hippopotanus. For dinner could I have fish fingers and ice cream?'

'Fish fingers and ice cream?' Brian said. 'Done.' He took his car key from his pocket. 'I'll be back soon.'

He opened his car and climbed in.

Julia watched him drive away. He hadn't looked at or acknowledged her. She didn't care for herself – the sight of him provoked in her a mixture of disgust and fury, and she would happily never have spoken to or seen him again – but she did not want their relationship to be an open sore of bitterness and recrimination. She had seen plenty of marriages go that way, and she had seen plenty of children suffer as a result. Without even knowing it the children would start trying to smooth things over, to placate their warring parents. That was not part of the childhood she wanted for Anna, and she was determined not to let it happen. She'd tell Brian to stop; apart from anything else, it would make her feel superior.

'Mummy,' Anna said. 'Can I really have fish fingers and ice cream?'

Julia shrugged. 'If Daddy says so. But maybe just today. Not every day.'

'I'd like it every day.'

'We'll see.' She turned to Edna. 'Maybe you could see that she gets something a bit more nutritious as well.'

'She's in good hands,' Edna said. 'Don't worry.'

'I do worry,' Julia said. 'That's what mothers do.'

'Yes,' Edna said. 'I suppose they do.' She smiled a thin, warmth-less smile that Julia had seen her do hundreds of times before. It was, truth be told, barely a smile at all, just a drawing back of the corners of her mouth. It was what Edna did when she wanted to dismiss someone just politely enough not to be rude. She saved it for people she thought were beneath her, who did not deserve the full beam of her attention. It was a throwaway gesture: *Look,* it said, *here's a smile. It's not much of one, but it's all you're getting. Now sod off and don't take up more of my time.*

It had always angered Julia to see her mother-in-law display such casual arrogance. It reminded her that Edna really believed she was superior – by reason of birth or education or class – to whole swathes of the population, including, for that matter, Julia and most of her friends and family. It was so archaic, so *Victorian*, to assume that some people were simply better because they happened to be upper middle class. Never mind their character, never mind what they actually did; they deserved to be thought of and treated in a certain way simply because they were born to a particular family.

Edna's attitude brought out the class warrior in Julia, but she had managed to bite her tongue over the years. Now, however, she was the target of it, and she felt the resentment and anger swell like a winter storm.

'You know,' she said. 'You think you have all the answers, don't you?'

Edna looked at her, blinking, as though she had not been listening and was trying to recall Julia's words from her short-term memory. Then she smiled her thin-lipped smile again.

'To which questions?' she asked.

'To every question,' Julia said, fighting to keep the bitterness from her voice. 'To every damn question there is.'

'Not at all,' Edna said. 'I don't claim any knowledge of particle physics or Chinese history. Nor of who is winning this year's *Pop Idol* and polluting the airwaves with their so-called music. There are plenty of things I know next to nothing about.'

'That's not what I meant,' Julia said. 'And you know it.'

'Well, what did you mean?' Edna said. 'If you meant something else, then why say what you did? You can hardly blame me if you say something and I respond to it, but you meant something else—'

'Oh, for God's sake, shut up!' Julia said. 'You are so far up your own backside, Edna. So far that you can probably see your son's feet. Do you ever worry about that? About what you've done to your son? No doubt you think he's safe and sound under your wing, but the rest of the world can see is that all you've achieved is to stop him growing into a man. You've *ruined* him, Edna. If it wasn't so sad it'd be funny.'

Edna gave a little shrug. 'Whatever you say,' she said. 'Whatever makes you feel better about your life.'

Julia closed her eyes. She took a long, deep breath. There was no point in letting Edna provoke her. It would just give her more reason to argue that she was not a fit mother. She looked at Edna and smiled.

'Forget it,' she said. 'And at least he's not my problem anymore. It's time for me to go.'

Julia turned to say goodbye to Anna. She had been standing to her left, between Julia and the car.

She was not there now.

'Anna?' Julia said. 'Anna!'

She looked at Edna, whose face was frozen, her eyes wide, her mouth slightly open.

'Where is she?' Julia asked.

Edna looked left, then right. The garden around the house was surrounded by a fence, and Edna was standing by the gate. Anna had not passed her, so she could not be in the house or garden. If she was not in the parking area, then she had either gone into the neighbour's garden or back down the driveway.

Which meant, she would be on the road.

It wasn't a main road, but it was busy enough, but that wasn't what bothered Julia the most. What bothered her was why Anna would have left them.

It was him. It was the abductor. She just knew it, deep in her bones. While she and Edna had been arguing he – Julia couldn't shake the feeling it was a 'he' – had taken advantage of their lack of attention, and taken her daughter again.

How had she let this happen? How had she been so stupid as to leave her daughter vulnerable again? She didn't deserve to be a mother, not if this was how she behaved. God, it wouldn't even have been hard. While she and Edna were wrapped up in their stupid little quarrel, the person who had taken Anna and then brought her back had taken her again, the latest act in whatever crazy, twisted game they were playing.

They must have been there all along, watching, waiting for their chance. Waiting for the moment when the cops were gone and Julia's guard was down.

'I don't know,' Edna said, her face pale. 'I don't know where she is. But we should check the road.'

'God,' Julia said, setting off at a run. 'God. I don't believe this!'

When she reached the end of the drive she stopped and looked up and down the road. It was deserted. To the left, the road narrowed under a canopy of over-hanging trees; to the right, it was more open, hedges lining fallow fields.

Left or right. That choice again.

Edna appeared at her shoulder. 'You go that way,' she said, pointing towards the canopy covered road. 'I'll go right.'

They were allies, suddenly. Seconds ago they were enemies, bitterly pitted against each other in a struggle for the right to Anna; now they were on the same side, searching for the prize they both wanted, and without which their struggle would be meaningless.

'Anna!' Julia screamed, her throat humming with pain at the effort she put into the word. 'Anna!'

Then, in the silence before she set off, she heard a reply.

'Mummy?'

It was faint, very faint, obviously not that close. But close enough. Close enough to hear.

'Anna?' Julia shouted. 'Where are you?'

'Here, Mummy. I'm here.'

The voice was coming from behind them, from where they had just come from. Julia turned and ran back up the drive.

Anna was there. She was standing by the side door of the neighbour's garage, the wall of which formed the far boundary of the parking area. There was a gate next to it that led to a path to the modern, new built house that Edna so detested. It was closed; the family were away on holiday at their place in Spain.

'Anna!' Julia said, picking up her daughter and hugging her tightly to her chest. 'My God. I'm so glad you're safe.'

'Anna,' Edna said, out of breath. 'Where were you? You mustn't disappear like that!'

'I don't care,' Julia said. 'I don't care. I'm just happy you're here.'

'I need to know,' Edna said. 'So I can make sure it doesn't happen again.'

'I went to see the doll's house,' Anna said.

Julia looked at her. 'What do you mean?' she said. 'What doll's house?'

Anna twisted out of Julia's arms and wriggled to the ground. She pointed to the side door of the neighbour's garage. It was ajar. 'The one in there.'

'What?' Julia said. 'What did you say?'

'I told you,' Anna said. 'I went to see the doll's house. The big one.'

'That's enough, Anna,' Edna said, her voice sharp. 'You go inside and wait for me.'

'Hold on,' Julia said. 'Anna. Is it the dolls' house you slept in?'

'Yes,' Anna said. 'It's in there.'

Julia looked at the neighbour's garage. Was it them? Had they taken Anna? It made sense; they would know about her, would have seen her over the years at Edna's house.

'Edna,' Julia said. 'The neighbours are in Spain, correct?'

'Yes,' Edna said. 'Spain.'

'I think ... I think it was them.'

Edna snorted. 'Don't be ridiculous. I would have seen something.'

'Then what's Anna talking about?'

'I don't know. She has a very active imagination. There's probably not even a doll's house in there. Go and have a look.' She took Anna's hand. 'I'm going to give her some dinner. When you've finished your wild goose chase you can come inside and say goodbye.'

Julia pushed open the door and walked into the garage. It was empty, the family car presumably at the airport. At the back was a tool bench, and, to the right, a large doll's house. She stared at it. Was this where Anna had been? It looked home-made, three storeys high, and was the size of a single bed. The ground floor was more or less empty, apart from a bag of sand.

How had Anna known it was in here? Maybe she'd been in here before when she'd been visiting Edna and seen it then, and it had lodged in her mind. Either way, it was unlikely she'd been kept in here during the abduction. As Edna said, she would have noticed something, especially as the neighbours were supposed to be away in Spain.

Unless.

The answer began as a cold feeling, a vague idea emerging, lizard-like from the folds and creases of Julia's mind.

There was an explanation, but it couldn't be true. It was impossible.

Unless it wasn't.

There was the crunch of a footstep on the gravel outside. Edna blocked the light coming through the door.

'So,' she said. 'Is there anything in here?'

Julia started to shake.

'No,' she said. 'No. Please God, no.'

15

Home Time

i.

You watch her stare at the doll's house. Watch her brow furrow and her eyes narrow. Watch her recoil from what she is starting to understand.

She says something. You can see her lips move but you cannot hear the words. It doesn't matter. It makes no difference what she is saying. There is only one thing that matters now.

She knows.

Not everything, but enough. Not the how, and maybe not the why, although that will become obvious to her soon enough, but the who. And the who is the important bit. All the rest is just the story. Just what happened.

Yes, the rest of it is just events. What matters is who did it, and if she knows that, she knows enough.

More than enough. She knows too much.

You almost sigh. It has gone so well, and now this. The girl has some memory after all. Vague and shapeless, no doubt, but there nonetheless. It was probably from some fleeting moment of consciousness when you moved her. But who knew? Who knew how memory worked? What went in and what came out? What stuck and what slid away? What a drug could erase and what it could not? After all, people with Alzheimer's whose minds were nearly destroyed could remember a sunny childhood day by a river in the company of their long-dead grandmother so clearly that they thought they were there. You'd seen it with your own mother, how she would snap from the cruel fog of her dementia into another place entirely, into conversations with people from her past, before lapsing back into her confused, anxious present. It had been a mercy for both of you when you killed her.

That was another act that had to be done, that was hard but right. Another necessary evil. Like the others. They were all necessary, all right. But people would not have understood, which was why you were forced to hide it from the world.

So is it a surprise that the girl had remembered something? No, you suppose it isn't. Especially something like a doll's house. That is exactly the kind of thing that the mind might cling onto: something large and unusual and very, very interesting.

Damn. You should have thought of that. You feel a surge of frustration. It had gone so well. So *perfectly*. *Too* perfectly.

331

But no matter. *Into every life a little rain must fall*, as your mother used to say, before her mind failed her and you had to put her out of her misery. You had to act, make a tough decision. Just like now. You must act, and what you have to do is simple enough. You have to deal with the situation. Yes, things have gone well, but you have been ready all along in case they didn't, ready to do whatever it took.

And now the time has come.

Now you have to act.

Your daughter-in-law turns to look at you, her cow-like face plastered with shock.

'Come inside,' you say. 'Come and say goodbye to Anna.'

ii.

'Come inside,' Edna said. 'Come and say goodbye to Anna.'

She was smiling now, Edna, and there was real warmth to her smile. She had relaxed, and had adopted an open, friendly manner. A bedside manner. Julia had seen it before, seen Edna turn on her charm – and she had considerable charm, when she wanted to use it, when she felt that her interlocutor *deserved* it – but this time Julia did not feel the familiar wistful regret that Edna did not treat her in that way; this time, Edna's sudden warmth was utterly chilling, because she saw it for what it was: the practised facade of someone with no real feelings at all.

332

The facade of someone who would kidnap her own granddaughter. That was what this meant. She had not merely taken advantage of the situation to blacken Julia's name and get custody of Anna for her son, she had created the situation. She had kidnapped Anna with the intent of showing the world what an unfit mother Julia was. She had put her son through all the pain and anguish of thinking his only child had been murdered or sold into slavery or become the victim of a paedophile gang. It was almost unbelievable, but then Edna had form: she had tried to paint Laura as an adulteress so that Simon would leave her.

But this was a hundred times worse. This was the act of someone who was totally insane.

Julia knew what she had to do. She was going into the house to rescue her daughter, and then she was going to the police and from there to a hotel where Edna could not find her. She had no idea how the police would prove that it was Edna who had taken Anna, no idea whether they even could, but it didn't matter. Anna was not staying here a minute longer, and she was never being left alone with Edna again.

'It was you,' she said. 'It was you all along.'

'What are you talking about?' Edna said. 'What was me?'

'You know,' Julia said. 'You know exactly what I'm talking about.'

Edna raised her eyebrows, her lips curling upwards in a bemused smile.

'I dare say I don't,' she said. 'Why don't you enlighten me?'

'Fuck you, Edna,' Julia said. 'Fuck you.'

She started walking towards the gate. Edna moved aside. Julia had feared that she would try to stop her and it was a relief when she didn't, but then what would Edna have done? She was in her late sixties, a good thirty years older than Julia, so if it came to a physical contest she would have no chance.

As she passed her, Edna spoke. This time there was no warmth in her voice at all.

'This makes no difference, Julia. You know that, don't you?'

Julia spun around. 'It makes all the difference. But you can try explaining to the police why it doesn't.'

'What will the police do? Look for Anna's DNA in my house? In the garage? They'll find it, and plenty of it. She lives here. There'll be no way to prove that I took her. You think some vague statement from Anna, some half-remembered dream, is enough?'

'It's enough for me,' Julia said.

'I don't doubt it. But you are not a court of law. Anna's testimony will count for nothing. She's five, and she's been under enormous strain.'

'What if she remembers more? This changes it, Edna. You need to face facts. At the very least the police will be crawling all over your house. Do you really want that, Edna? Do you really think you hid your tracks that well? I don't know what you did or how you did it, but there's always evidence. Always. Maybe someone saw you near the school that day, maybe there's CCTV footage of you in the vicinity, when you were supposed to be at home with burst pipes. Whatever. The police will take every bit of your story and unravel it, strand by strand, and all it will take is one lie, Edna, one little lie, and this will be over. You think you're bulletproof, but you're not.'

'I'm not so sure of that,' Edna said.

'No? You don't think the facts apply to you? You don't think you have to play by the same rules as the rest of us?'

Edna shook her head. There was a hint of sadness in her expression. 'No,' she said. 'I don't.'

'Yeah? Well, I guess we'll find out,' Julia said. 'I'm going to get my daughter.'

iii.

Julia pushed open the back door and stepped into the kitchen. The kitchen door was ajar. She heard Anna talking to herself in the hallway, playing some lonely game in Edna's draughty, cold house. Well, she wouldn't have to do that anymore. Those days were over.

She pictured herself driving away, Anna in her car seat in the back, asking, *what's happening Mummy? Why am I not staying at Grandma's house?*

You don't live there anymore, darling. You live with Mummy now.

A thrill ran from her stomach to her neck at the thought of it.

And how would Brian take the news that his mother had kidnapped Anna? Or had he known all along? Had he been in on it? Julia didn't think so. For all his faults, Brian would not have done something like that to put Anna at risk. And why would he? Why, for that matter, would Edna? What was the point? Was she just crazy?

No doubt, it would all come out in the wash. Right now, she didn't care. Right now she had a daughter to take home.

16

A Necessary Evil

i.

Silly little girl.

Silly. Little. Girl.

Does she really think she can get away with this? Does she not know her mother-in-law? Does she not know Edna?

You are not surprised she found out, truth be told. She has some spark, some inner steel. In fact, in a way you quite like her. Had you met her in other circumstances – at work, perhaps – you would have seen her as someone you could work with, maybe even be friends with, if it weren't for the age gap. She is smart and tenacious and hard-working. All things you admire.

But she isn't a colleague. She isn't an acquaintance. She is married to your son.

You'd known it wouldn't work from the day you'd met her, known that she had been blinded by Brian's looks – he was a handsome young man – and the fact he came from a family with some social status and a fair bit of money.

She is that type of lower middle-class girl, is Julia. She didn't realize she was marrying for money, but she was. She would never have admitted it, not even to herself in the quiet of the night. Marrying for money is the kind of thing posh people do; it goes against everything she stands for. She is modern, blind to archaic notions, such as class or breeding. She follows her own path, is a breath of fresh, meritocratic air blowing away the cobwebs of the hidebound old order. The times are a-changing; no longer will birth determine people's success. It will be determined by hard work and talent, and when people like Julia reach the top they will make sure that opportunity is extended to all.

Fool. Has she not looked around at who has money and power in the country? Has she not bothered to look at how many of the cabinet – we're all in this together, of course, we are – attended the same public school? Not public schools. The *same* public school. Is she blind to the statistics showing how wealth is pooling at the top, being concentrated in the hands of ever fewer people? Has she not noticed that the government has pulled off the greatest redistribution of wealth in history, not from the rich to the poor, but rather the other way around? The country is not getting more open, more meritocratic, fairer. It is reverting to the way it had been when Victoria squatted on the throne.

338

And anyway, Julia is no class warrior. The lower middle class are the most class conscious of all, because they are only one step up from being working class, and they are terrified of being dragged back down. They flaunt their middle class-ness to make sure that everyone notices it: drive their leased, Sunday-polished BMWs and Audis, pull on their shiny Hugo Boss suits for their jobs in insurance or IT.

Oddly, you and Julia are alike in that way. You are class conscious too, you know that. Just like Julia is one rung *above* working class, you are one *below* upper class. Nearly there. Nearly.

You'd hoped Brian might get you there. Might get a degree from Oxford and make millions in the city, or enter government and end up with a 'Sir' before his name. Failing that he might marry some impoverished posh girl with a titled father.

But no. He had scraped into a provincial university and become a junior school teacher. God, it was embarrassing. Not even a high school teacher, which would have at least had him teaching A levels and preparing young minds for university, but a junior school teacher. He reads stories to eight-year-olds. Any fool could do it. You hated it. Hated it. Woke up at night enraged about it. And it wasn't even an act of rebellion against you. It was his level.

His father, Jim, hadn't done much to stop it. He had smiled and said it was a fine job, that those early years were the most important in a child's development, that some people had a gift for educating eight-year-olds and that it was cruelly undervalued in society. Any fool could *not* do it, and those who thought otherwise were fools themselves.

You're glad to be a fool, in that case. And anyway, as far as Jim was concerned you were not too much of a fool to sort out him and his girlfriend, Lindsey Wilkinson, that fucking star-struck floozy Lindsey Wilkinson. When he told you about his affair you pretended to be unconcerned.

I'm leaving Edna. I can't stand our marriage anymore. And I'll be honest, I wish I'd done it sooner but I didn't have the courage. Now I do. And Lindsey gave it to me.

Just like Julia. Leaving a marriage just because they were unhappy. It was not acceptable.

You knew Lindsey, of course, you did. You'd seen her at school functions, fawning over your husband.

Well, you said. *I understand. I won't make trouble.*

Thank you, Edna he said. *I appreciate it.*

You didn't mean it, of course. You were not about to suffer that humiliation. Edna Crowne did not let that kind of thing happen to her, and Jim should have known.

Yet he was surprised when she killed him, after making him watch his girlfriend die.

And you had no regrets. He deserved it, and a divorce was out of the question. So what choice did you have? You had to act; had to take charge of the situation. It was a necessary evil. The strong asserting itself over the weak.

340

A necessary evil. That is what separates you from the common run. You are prepared to do what has to be done.

And now you have to do it again.

It will not be an elegant solution, like your mother's or Jim's.

Circumstances dictate that this will be crude.

You push open the kitchen door.

You heft the hammer in your hand.

Yes, it will be crude.

But crude can be effective.

ii.

Julia heard the kitchen door close behind her. It was probably Edna, come to try and persuade her of her innocence.

No chance. She knew what had happened and she would not be deflected. Edna was going to pay for what she had done, Julia would see to that.

She turned around. Edna was moving rapidly towards her. Her eyes were wide open and staring, her face pale, her lips drawn back over her teeth. She looked, Julia thought, like a drawing of a psychopath.

And she was holding a hammer in her right hand. She lifted it, and swung.

Julia put up her hands to defend herself.

And then, nothing.

iii.

Julia felt the first stirrings of consciousness as she began to wake up. She did not want to. She was not even sure she could; it felt as though some great tidal weight was pulling her down, down into dark oblivion. And she would have let it. She had nowhere near the strength to resist the urge for unconsciousness, an urge which had the force of necessity, a necessity she dimly recognized from her student days, when she foolishly and occasionally drank herself into a blackout. The weight dragging her down was chemical in origin, and it was near irresistible.

But not quite. Something equally powerful was forcing its way into her consciousness and waking her up.

Pain.

She was in a lot of pain.

Her back ached, her shoulders felt as though someone was pulling them from her body, and her hands throbbed in time with her heartbeat. No need to take her pulse: she could just count the bursts of pain in her hands.

The pain, though, was worst in her head, which felt like it had been hit with a hammer. She tried to move it, but her neck was stiff, and the muscles protested loudly. She felt something on her temple crack and flake and fall down her shirt: dried blood, she realized.

She *had* been hit with a hammer. By Edna.

She opened her eyes. She was in pitch-black silence. Perhaps it was the middle of the night; she had no way of telling. She was lying on her side on a hard, cold stone floor. She was in the foetal position, her knees drawn up to her chest. There was a wall against her back and another against her forehead. Wherever she was it was a very small space. She tried to move her legs, but they were tied together. The same for her hands, which were tied behind her back.

She didn't know what was going on, but she knew one thing. She was in trouble. She was in a lot of trouble.

She heard voices. Faint, unclear. It was Brian, saying something. Edna's cut glass tones in reply. A pause.

So she was in the house, somewhere.

Then laughter. Anna's laughter.

She opened her mouth to speak, and there was more pain. There was some kind of gag, a hard, thin metal band, which pressed against the corners of her mouth when she opened it. She tried to make a noise with her mouth closed, but there was something else in there, something holding down her tongue, and all that came out was a low moan.

The pain. God, the pain. It was unbearable. Her shoulders were *screaming*. It felt as if the muscles were being taken apart, fibre by fibre. It reminded her of childbirth, of the excruciating feeling of the body working as hard as it could to push the baby out, working as hard as it could to destroy itself, to tear itself apart. At least, that was how it felt, and it felt endless and impossible, but always, always you had a place you could go to, a place that offered reassurance and comfort; a thought you could cling to.

It's worth it. I'm going to meet my baby. At the end of this I'll meet my baby. I'll see their face, hear their cries, give them a name, a home, a place in this world. At the end of this there will be a new person, a new life.

And that got you through. That gave you the strength to fight the pain.

But this. There was nowhere for her to go. Just the thought that this might be it. That her crazy mother-in-law – and God, Edna was crazy, crazier than Julia had ever thought possible – was going to kill her, and then bring her daughter up, and God alone knew what damage that would do to Anna.

She almost felt sorry for Brian. No wonder he had mummy issues. It was surprising he was as normal as he was. What must it have been like to have Edna hovering around you, getting herself in your business, in your head, all your life? Julia saw it now; saw why Brian was so obedient, why he never argued with his mother. She'd always thought it was devotion, but it wasn't. It was terror. He was scared of her, but being a grown-up he had learned to hide it.

It must have been awful, growing up in this empty house, with a distant father and Medusa for a mother. She pictured him, a little boy, a puppyish longing for affection driving him to try and please Edna, to seek her approval, an approval which was not forthcoming, leaving him scared and lonely and damaged.

And this was the life Anna had in front of her. A tyrant for a grandmother and a craven father, unable to protect her.

She closed her eyes. Her cheeks were wet with tears. She shifted onto her back and pressed her feet against the wall. She pushed against it and levered herself into a more upright position, the back of her neck off the ground. The position was uncomfortable but it eased the pressure on her shoulders and the pain subsided slightly.

It was enough. Slowly, she slipped back into darkness.

17

War of the Roses

i.

You are ready now.

The risky part is over. The risky part was yesterday, knocking Julia out with the hammer and then dragging her to her hiding place without Anna seeing you. It was quite a commotion and could easily have attracted the attention of a curious young girl, and you did not need that. You did not need Anna to see what was going on, or you would be forced to kill her as well, and then – probably – Brian.

You chuckle. Imagine if it came to that! How ridiculous.

So you switched on the television in the living room, put on a DVD of some infantile talking train show that Anna's mother let her rot her brain with – there'd be no more of that, soon enough – and closed the door.

Then you pulled Julia into the dining room, sedated her: a good, heavy dose. It didn't matter if it harmed her. Then you bound and gagged her and stuffed her away in the secret place.

You chuckle again. It was ironic that she was in the same place Anna had been. She had spent all that time wondering what Anna had experienced, what she had been through, and now she knew. She knew everything there was to know about where her daughter had been kept.

Of course, it was more pleasant for Anna. It was perfectly big enough for a five-year-old. She could stretch out. You had made sure you moved her around when she was in there, manipulated her joints, made sure she did not stiffen. No hope of that for Julia. It was a tight fit for an adult, but then it was not designed for someone to spend prolonged periods there.

Not that she would be spending a prolonged period in there.

Her time in there was about to come to a sudden end.

You hadn't done it yet, as you had to get rid of Brian and Anna before you could get rid of Julia. In their case, temporarily, to a surprise night away in Blackpool.

An awful place, but irresistible to kids.

So when Brian dutifully returned with fish fingers and ice cream she told him what she had planned.

You need to get away. Spend some time with Anna, you told Brian.

I don't know, Mum. She seems happy here.

Nonsense. Some father—daughter time will help put all this behind her. And you're still off work. Might as well make use of the time.

You think?

I do. I've booked you into a hotel in Blackpool. Tomorrow night. It's close to the Pleasure Beach. She'll love it.

And now they were gone. Headed out this morning, waving goodbye as they drove away, all the while completely unaware that Julia's car was in the neighbour's garage – who could have thought that it would be so useful – that garage? You'd always regretted selling that land, but it had turned out to be a blessing in disguise – and Julia was inside the house.

Alone. The police – such fools, so easily manipulated – were gone, too. *Have a day off*, you told them, *Anna's going away with her dad and you hardly need to guard me!*

So now for Julia.

It was a simple plan, really. It is one of your strengths, simplicity. You know that simple is always better. There is less to go wrong.

So you will wait until evening, then give her a lethal dose of sedative. It is important not to wait too long before you dispose of the body after killing her, or lividity will set in, and, in the unlikely event that the body is found, it will be obvious she was murdered.

It needs to look like she drowned after taking a combination of sedatives and whisky.

348

Perfectly understandable, given her history. No one would question it at all. An unstable woman who had recently attempted suicide takes her own life while under immense strain.

That is, if she is found at all, which you doubt. What will be found is her car, parked in a remote location near the mouth of the Mersey Estuary, with an empty bottle of whisky and a syringe emptied of the sedative you plan to give her. She will be gone. Disappeared as the tide was flowing out to the Irish Sea. Fish food.

Just like Jim and his floozy. You'll take her to the same place. Jim, Julia. It's neat. You like neat.

You know it is all about narrative. Humans like their stories to be neat, to make sense. It gives them the impression the world makes sense, that it is safe and predictable, when the reality is that the opposite is true. *You* know that. *You* know that the world is a brutal, vengeful place and the only way to survive is to take control, which is what you do.

But you are not normal. Which is why you are so successful.

So Julia will disappear, neatly.

And, just like after Jim and Miss-fucking-Wilkinson disappeared, the world will go on as before.

ii.

Julia had figured out quite a lot of things. Amidst the agony, she'd had quite a lot of time to think about them.

349

She'd figured out that, if she twisted her torso so that her weight was on one shoulder, then moved her hands towards the opposite shoulder, that side of her body would get some relief from the pain caused by the position she had been forced into. After a while she could reverse the movement, relieving the other side. She had no way of gauging time, but she thought that, initially, she had moved every ten minutes or so; now the intervals were much shorter.

She'd figured where she was. She was in a priest's hole behind the fireplace in the living room. That would explain why she had heard Edna, Brian, and Anna's voices.

She remembered Edna showing her the priest's hole some years ago. It was a rectangular box, about four and a half feet in length and four feet in height, and about two feet deep. Just big enough for an adult male priest to squeeze into during the sixteenth century, when Queen Elizabeth outlawed Catholicism and sent her pursuivants up and down the country, searching for priests to torture and kill. The pursuivants were skilled searchers and measured the external dimensions of houses and the internal dimensions of rooms so as to determine whether there were any secret compartments; the priest's holes had to be built so cleverly that they could not locate them, and they also had to be small.

Edna's priest's hole was in the side of a large inglenook fireplace. The fireplace itself was the correct dimensions; the priest's hole had been built into an area above the fire where the chimney would normally have been, so it was undetectable by measurement.

And undetectable by police searching the house.

Julia could not shake the image of the police here, in the house, mere feet from Anna, with a calm, smiling, helpful Edna standing in the doorway of the living room, watching them fail to find her granddaughter, and congratulating herself on her ingenuity in selecting such an effective hiding place.

It was so *Edna*. If she had only thought it through when Anna was missing, she would have seen it. Where else would Edna hide someone, but in a sixteenth-century priest's hole? It would have appealed to Edna's sense that modernity was not all it was cracked up to be, not to mention the air of Gothic that she carried with her. She could almost hear Edna thinking about it.

It's been hiding people for a long time, no reason why it should stop now. Might as well use what you have in front of you. No point in reinventing the wheel. Keep it simple.

And it had worked. The police had been to Edna's house twice and found nothing. She might be batshit crazy but she wasn't stupid.

She'd figured out that her earlier suspicions that Edna had leaked stories to the press in order to discredit her and get custody of Anna were almost certainly correct. Then, she'd thought that Edna was simply taking advantage of Anna's abduction but now she couldn't help wondering whether Edna had planned all this from the start.

351

It was obvious, really; what better way to get custody than to utterly discredit the mother in the public eye? It was an amazing, twisted plan: take Anna, make Julia look bad, and, when she was public enemy number one, return Anna, ready for a custody battle Edna couldn't lose. If Julia hadn't been in so much pain she might almost have admired her mother-in-law's crazy ingenuity.

Although, if that was what it would have taken to keep Anna, she might have done the same herself.

She thought back to the day itself. When Anna was taken, Edna had supposedly been at home, fixing the plumbing. Instead, she had gone to the school and picked up Anna. Julia went over the day in her mind, replayed the phone call when she had asked Edna for help that afternoon, told her that she might be late. Had Edna seen an opportunity and simply acted, or had she formed the plan ahead of time and been looking for a chance to put it into action? Either way, she had done it, had turned up at the school, and, unseen, taken Anna. Maybe she'd beckoned to her from a distance, and Anna, recognizing her grandmother, had gone willingly. Maybe Anna had wandered off and Edna had picked her up. It didn't matter, and Julia doubted she'd ever find out, because she'd figured out one other thing.

She'd figured out that Edna was going to kill her.

But she could not, for the life of her, figure out what she could do about it.

She switched her weight to her left shoulder. The right side of her body relaxed a little, the relief immense. It wouldn't last long.

And then she heard footsteps. Quick, decisive footsteps, approaching the priest's hole.

They stopped. There was the sound of metal moving on metal – bolts, maybe – then the wall in front of her slid back.

It took her eyes some time to adjust to the light. When they did they were not pleased to see what they saw.

It was Edna.

iii.

Edna did not look the same as she usually did. Her hair, normally frozen in an elegant, chin-length arrangement that she modelled on Helen Mirren, was scraped back from her forehead. She was wearing an old, blue wool sweater Julia thought had maybe once belonged to Brian. That was all she could see of her mother-in-law; the priest's hole was about five feet above the floor, so all that was in the frame of her vision was Edna's head, neck, and shoulders.

'You're awake,' Edna said. 'Good.'

Julia shook her head. She tried to speak, but the gag meant that the only noise she could make was a stifled moan. She stared at Edna, opening her eyes wide in supplication.

'Well,' Edna said. 'I have to say it's a shame it had to come to this.' She lifted a syringe to eye level. It was gripped between her forefingers, her thumb on the plunger. 'It needn't have happened. If only Anna hadn't remembered the doll's house.' She shook her head slowly, regretfully. 'I didn't think she would, but even I make mistakes.'

So it *was* her. Even though Julia had held no further doubts about who had taken Anna, it was still a shock to hear her say it.

'So here we are,' Edna said, then smiled. 'The end of the road. It's probably a mercy for you, in the long run. Your life was shaping up to be pretty miserable, after all.'

Julia shook her head as hard as she could, trying to get a message to Edna. *It doesn't have to end like this. It doesn't.*

Edna sighed.

'Oh,' she said. 'I understand your regret. But you can't change this, Julia. It's too far gone now. How could I let you go? I have too much to lose. You'd tell the police.'

Julia shook her head again. *I won't, I promise.*

'You say that now, but when you get out you'll fill up with thoughts of revenge and bitterness and the next thing I know the constabulary will be here and I'll be hauled off to the dock. I don't blame you. I'd do the same thing. And knowing that, I can hardly let you walk away from here, can I? You see that, don't you Julia? This has to happen. I didn't intend it, but now it's inevitable.'

Julia shook her head. It was all she could do, her only hope. And it was patently not working.

354

Edna's face took on a thoughtful expression. 'It was so nearly perfect, wasn't it? Anna went missing for a while – but she was safe, here with me – then – *pop* – she was home again. Brian and I got custody, Anna's welfare was assured, and you went off to do whatever you would have done.'

Julia shook her head again. This time it was not assent: she meant *no, Anna's welfare was not assured. Anna's welfare was* ruined.

'So I suppose I ought to tell you the plan,' Edna said. 'It's a good one.' She smiled. 'I'm going to knock you out with this—' she held up the syringe, 'and then we'll drive your car to a place I know, a place Jim used to take me, where the Mersey empties into Liverpool Bay. It's a fast tide out there, and anything caught in it will go miles out into the Irish Sea. All they'll ever find of you is your car, an empty whisky bottle with your saliva and fingerprints on it, and an empty jar of sleeping pills. And if your body does show up, it'll be so damaged by the fish that will have been treating it as a welcome free meal; no one will ever know the difference. A suicide. Open and shut.'

Edna smiled.

'But your body won't show up,' she said. 'It's a tried and tested method. Jim and his girlfriend went that way and they were never found.'

Julia's eyes widened. She'd killed Jim? Any hope that remained ebbed away. Edna was a *serial* killer, and she'd murdered her *husband*. If she would do that, then there was no way she would baulk at doing the same to her.

'You look surprised,' Edna said. 'I wonder that you never guessed. I always thought someone might. It was obvious, really, but then people don't guess. Same as my mother. Of course, Mum was nearly gone anyway. That was a mercy killing. Euthanasia. Jim, though – he had years left in him – but I let him humiliate me like that. It was a good excuse to get rid of him, as well. He drove me mad, did you know that? He drove me absolutely fucking insane. No ambition. Happy to be a headmaster. He had so much ability; so much charisma and wisdom. He could have gone into politics; become an MP, a minister. Prime Minister, even, but all he wanted to do was run that school. It was his life. I wondered for a while whether he was a pederast, unnaturally attracted to children, that kind of thing, but I don't think he was. I think he was happy to waste his life on them.' She shook her head. 'I couldn't bear to see it.'

She was, Julia saw, even more insane than she had thought. She killed her husband for *not* becoming Prime Minister? If that was normal then there wouldn't be too many men left in Britain. There'd be John Major, Tony Blair, Gordon Brown, and David Cameron. Jesus. Not much of a selection. She'd almost prefer to stay with Brian.

'I mean, he just needed to show a bit more damned backbone, a bit more spine. See the opportunity and grab it. A bit like I'm doing now. Unfortunately, he passed his lethargy onto Brian. It won't happen to Anna, though. She's going to go far, that girl.'

356

The problem with Edna was that she was utterly convinced of the rightness of her cause, a conviction that put her above the law. That was the root of her madness: she did not think she was a normal person, did not believe the normal rules applied to her. It made her look down on everybody else, made her believe they were worthless, disposable.

As far as Edna was concerned it was ok to euthanize her mother because Edna thought it was ok. Never mind that, if everybody flouted the rules, there would be chaos – Edna would happily admit it. But she'd also claim the problem was that not everyone could be trusted to make good decisions, but she could, and so she would.

As for Julia? No problem. Anna had to be with Edna; Julia was an obstacle; Julia had to be removed. Simple.

And there was nothing Julia could do to stop it. Edna was going to slip the needle under her skin and then darkness would come, and it would all be over.

Not for Anna, though. For her the nightmare would just be getting started.

'Right,' Edna said. 'Let's get this over with.' She smiled a lopsided, crazy smile. 'Although aren't you going to ask how I did it? Why I did it? You can't, of course, because of the gag, but I know you're dying to find out.' The smile widened. 'Get that little pun? *Dying* to find out? You will be soon, Julia.'

Edna looked reflectively at the ceiling, then back at her daughter-in-law. 'I have to say it was a brilliant plan,' she said. 'I thought of it on the spur of the moment. It came to me, just like that. I'd been wondering what to do about the divorce since Brian told me what you planned; wondering how to stop you taking my grand-daughter from me. I couldn't let that happen, Julia. Anna has great potential. I couldn't let you ruin it by allowing her to go to some dismal comprehensive school where second-rate teachers would turn her into a hairdresser or beautician, or, at best, a small-town lawyer like her mother. She can be like *me*, Julia. She can be *great*. But you would not allow that, and I could not stand by while you turned her into a mediocrity. You must see that, even if it is hard to take.'

Julia shook her head violently. She did not see, not at all. Edna just sighed.

'This is exactly the problem,' she said. 'You just don't *get* it. Anyway, I knew I had to do something, but I had no idea what. And then you called.' She put on a high-pitched, whining voice. 'Edna, I'm so busy at work, I can't pick up my daughter. Can you do it? Can you help me?' Edna shook her head. 'And in that moment I had it. The solution. I'd take Anna, then watch, as you took the blame for being a negligent mother; a blame that I would make sure fell squarely on you. You didn't realize I knew about Twitter, did you? Most of the early tweets about you were from accounts I set up so that I could get the ball rolling. Once it started it had a life of its own, but I gave it the initial push.'

Edna was glowing with pride, and Julia could see she had no idea that what she had done was in any way wrong or crazy or weird. All she could see was how smart she'd been.

'You're probably wondering how I took Anna,' Edna went on. 'How I took her from under the noses of all those people? It was quite easy, actually. I arrived a few minutes early and sat on a bench – you may have seen it? – about sixty yards up the road from the school. When Anna came out, I stood up and caught her eye and beckoned to her, and she just trotted over to me. The best part of the plan was that, if someone had seen me, I could simply say I had come to pick up Anna; after all, you had called earlier in the day asking for help. They all knew me, so there was no risk. It's not like I would be caught with someone else's kid. I would be with my own granddaughter, and what could be wrong with that? All I needed was a bit of luck to ensure Anna was not seen, and then she was mine. Beautiful, no?'

'Of course, I didn't know that you would attack Brian, or take the sleeping pills, but even without those incidents –which were *perfect*, by the way, the exact things I needed – I would have found a way to get what I wanted.' She shook her head. 'It was all done, Julia, but then, at the last minute, you had to ruin it. Anyway, that's enough chit-chat. It's time to close this chapter once and for all.'

She put her thumb and index finger on Julia's neck and smoothed out her skin. She was wearing surgical gloves, Julia realized, careful to the last. Then Edna leaned forward and looked carefully at the target area, the syringe raised to the level of her cheek. Her face was dispassionate, professional, *medical*.

Julia tried to move away, tried to lift herself into the foot and a half of space above her head, the only place she could go, but Edna pushed her down onto the hard floor of the priest's hole.

'Shhh,' she said, the habits of her bedside manner incongruously surfacing. 'Relax.'

And then there was a knock on the door.

Edna paused.

The knock came again, louder, the metal door knocker banging on the plate.

Edna flushed with anger. She lowered the syringe. Julia heard the snap of plastic as she pulled off the surgical gloves.

'Damn,' she said, then slammed the door shut. 'Back soon.'

iv.

There are not many moments in life when there is absolute clarity. *Go left, go right? Leave your husband, try to make it work? Sleep / don't sleep with a married man?* Not clear at all. Even things that *might* be obvious – especially in hindsight – like *don't be late to pick up your daughter* are not totally clear cut. Events intercede, meetings run over, phones die. The thing is that you never really know what the consequences of your actions or inactions will be. Unless you act on gut instinct – which many of us do, much of the time – you have to

360

weigh things in the balance, try and think your way through the maze of possible outcomes.

Not now.

Now, Julia knew exactly what she had to do.

She had to get out of here or she was going to die.

This was her chance, the only one she would get, and if she didn't take it, Edna would come back with her needle and Julia would end up at the bottom of the Irish Sea.

She heard a loud, low creak, which she recognized as the front door opening. The top hinge needed oil. It had been like that for a while. Julia thought Edna hadn't fixed it because she liked the impression it gave; it sounded like the door in a Transylvanian Castle, opened by a humpbacked butler called Igor.

Then Edna's voice: *Hello. To what do I owe this pleasure? Is everything ok?*

Another voice, indistinct, but familiar. A woman's voice.

Julia had to do something, which meant she had to get her hands free. She arched her back, then pushed one hand under her buttocks. She sat down to trap it, then tried to pull her other hand free.

The rope bit into the flesh of her hand. She pulled harder. The pain worsened and she felt a warm liquid run over her knuckles. Blood. She relaxed, then yanked as hard as she could. The pain was immense; it felt like someone was sawing a knife into her hand, yet her hand had barely moved. The rope was still tied tight around her wrists.

She paused, and listened. The voice came again. Julia recognized it, recognized the Liverpool accent.

It was Gill. Somehow, Gill was here. Julia tried to call out, but the bit in her mouth choked her.

Edna: *She's not here. She came yesterday, but I haven't heard from her since.*

Then a man's voice. Deep, steady: Mike Sherry. They had come looking for her. Of course; she'd invited Julia to meet her on Sunday night – last night – for Thai food and a glass of wine. Gill had three-month-old twins, Wilfie and Teddie, and leaving her sons was a bit of an operation, so Julia had declined. She didn't want to be a burden, and she knew Gill was only doing it because she knew Julia would not want to be alone. But Gill insisted, and Julia, if she was honest, was glad to let her. She was grateful that her friend was looking out for her. She knew she would need it.

And now they were here, looking for her. Gill would have known Julia would not miss their meal unless something was wrong; she would have called, and got no answer. On Monday morning she would have tried the office, and found that Julia was not there either, maybe spoken to Mike, who would have told her Julia went to Edna's on Sunday. And then she would have become really worried, fearful that Julia had maybe done something stupid, alone and depressed after dropping off her daughter. She would have decided to look for her friend, and the first place you always looked was in the last place you knew something or someone had been.

Which was Edna's house.

Edna: *Oh. That's a worry. Did you try her house?*

Gill's reply, muffled.

Would you like to come in? Have a drink? Talk through where she might be?

Edna sounded perfectly composed. She was even managing to sound *concerned*. It was amazing. She had her daughter-in-law trussed up in a priest's hole in her living room, and was planning to sedate her then dump her body in the mouth of the Mersey River, a place from which she'd have to get home without a car, although she'd have a plan for that. A bus to a place with a station. Change of clothes into something smart. Train, then taxi home.

She had all that going on, yet she could chat calmly, as though it was just another day. Wasn't that what characterized a psychopath, that kind of chilling, emotionless distance from the world around them?

So Edna was a psychopath. Or a sociopath. Or a something or other. Whatever – it just made it all the more imperative she get out of here. She yanked her hand again. No change from last time: agony, and no progress. She could feel that the rope had dug into her hand, tearing the flesh apart, but it could not get over the bones at the widest part. It was stuck. Those tiny, thin bones in her hand were going to be the difference between life and death.

Edna: *Well, if anything comes up, I'll call you.*

A pause.

Let me write it down. I'll put it by the phone.

Gill talking, staccato. A string of numbers. Her phone number, for Edna to call if she saw Julia. Fat chance of that phone call ever happening.

Then the Transylvanian creak of the door hinge as the front door swung shut. Igor was coming back, syringe at the ready.

Julia pulled her hand back, twisting it from side to side, trying to saw through it with the rope. The blood was all over her hand now, but none of it made any difference. Her hand was stuck, and she was as good as dead. The rope was never going over the damned bone. Who'd have thought that those bones where your wrist thickens out into your hand would be the difference between life and death? She didn't even know what they were called and they were going to kill her.

Unless.

There was one thing she could try, but it was almost unthinkable. She wasn't sure she could do it.

And perhaps she wouldn't have been able to do it, if it was only to save herself.

But she had to save Anna as well, and that made *everything* possible.

V.

Julia arched her back again. She rotated her torso so that the hand she was trying to free was under the hard bone of her hip.

Then she lifted her hip off the ground and slammed herself down onto the hand as hard as she could.

She had once watched a documentary with Brian about a commercial fisherman out alone on his boat who'd got his hand stuck in the winch that hauled in the long lines. It was a slow moving winch, and it gradually sucked in his hand. The man took his knife from his belt and sawed off his own hand. It was that, or die. Afterwards, he said he got the idea from the glue traps used to catch mice. The mice become stuck to the glue and slowly dehydrate. Sometimes, they are so desperate to escape that they gnaw off their own foot and limp away, easy prey for the cruel world they inhabit. Obviously, mice have no concept of death; they operate on pure instinct, and it was like that, he said. He felt like the mice. If you'd asked him beforehand whether he would cut off his own hand to save his life, he would have answered with reference to weighing up the value of his hand versus his life, but in the moment he had not thought that. He had just done it, like an animal would. Like mice do.

He hadn't thought it would be possible to do if you thought about it too much.

And Julia agreed.

She was no longer acting rationally, or, at least, not only rationally. Yes, the rational part of her was there, observing, but it was not in the driver's seat. That was occupied by instinct. By the animal part of her, and it lifted her up again, then slammed her down again.

365

Her hand was perpendicular to her hip, so the force was concentrated on the bone she wanted to break, and break it did, with a loud crack like a twig being snapped underfoot. She slammed herself on it again, and then again. Each time she felt the bones crumble further.

Finally, she positioned her hand under her hip and squeezed it against the floor. She felt the shape of it change, felt it deform, flatten into something new, and not like a hand.

She put the thought from her mind and pulled.

Her hand and the rope were slick with blood. She felt the bones give and move under the compression of the rope. She gasped in pain then she pulled some more and then some more and then her hand was free and limp and dangling and hurting so goddam much.

She was glad it was dark. She did not want to see the mess she had made of her right hand. With her left she reached down and tugged at the rope around her ankles. It was tight, but, typically for Edna, it was a neat knot and when she found the end it came undone easily.

That'll teach you to be so fucking perfect, she thought. *Soon you'll wish you hadn't got the knot-tying badge in the Girl Guides.*

She hunched her shoulders, her hands in her lap. God, they hurt, but the relief was enormous. She could feel the blood flowing back into them, bringing with it the tingling of pins and needles, although pins and needles didn't really cut it. Knives and daggers, more like.

She heard footsteps approaching the priest's hole. They stopped, then she heard the snap of surgical gloves being put on. It sounded just like it did on the television.

Julia readied herself. She took deep breaths, tensed her muscles, willed them to work, and readied herself for whatever pain was waiting for her.

She pictured Anna at fourteen, Edna looming over her, telling her she had to make something of herself, that she had to work hard, that movies and boyfriends were for other, lesser girls. That she would be punished if she did not do as her grandmother wanted, that she knew the form the punishment would take and she didn't want that, did she?

Anna, fifteen, throwing up in the bathroom, thin red lines on the insides of her arm, where no one could see them. Anna, twenty, neurotic, terrified of failure.

No. Anna was going to have fun. She was going to enjoy her childhood, mess around, laugh, take time to explore art and music and watch television and eat junk food. Anna would understand that balance and cheerfulness and kindness were what mattered, not grades and titles and money.

Julia's way, not Edna's.

The door to the priest's hole scraped open. A gap an inch wide appeared to Julia's left.

She braced herself. She felt good. Strong. Like she could do this, whatever this was.

And then it began.

vi.

You watch her friends – was she fucking that fat man? probably, knowing Julia – get in the car and drive away. You wanted to be sure they were gone. You don't think they suspected anything. It would be too much of a leap for them to suspect you have their friend locked in a priest's hole in your living room. They lack the intelligence, the imagination. They think like every other sheep does. To them it is unimaginable you would be planning to murder your daughter-in-law, and so they do not imagine it. You are glad; the inability of the common run to think beyond themselves is part of what keeps you safe.

And it is most of what sets you apart. You would be a superb detective. You would see beyond the evidence. You would not make assumptions about what had happened. You enjoy reading Sherlock Holmes for that very reason, in fact, he reminds you of yourself. The same penetrating intelligence, the same willingness to do whatever is necessary to get what is desired. Was Holmes a pleasant man? Quite the opposite, but he is admired because he brought bad people to justice. This, you think, misses the point. It is not what he did that is admirable, but how he did it. You would admire him equally if his purposes had been nefarious. More, perhaps, for it would have taken even greater strength of character to follow that path, to break the bonds that society puts on us: something you have experienced first-hand.

To choose matricide was not easy. You had to summon all your reserves of character in order to convince yourself that it was the right thing to do; that your mother needed to be released. And as for Jim, well, that took strength of a different kind, for there was a chance you would be caught.

Just like now. But you will not let that deter you. You cannot. You have no choice in this. You have to do what is right for Anna.

You close the front door. The familiar creak. You could fix it, but you like how it alerts you to arrivals or departures. You hear noises from the priest's hole. She is struggling. She has probably realized that she is about to die, and there is nothing she can do about it. It must be an awful thing to know: all the more reason to put her out of her misery.

It is a wonderful thing, that priest's hole. A marvel of design. Centuries ago it saved the lives of men; housed them, hid them from teams of people whose only purpose was to find them and kill them. They were skilled searchers, these people, and they often knew that a priest was being sheltered in a particular house, yet they still failed to find them. Your priest's hole was typical: a false wall inside a chimney flue. You had been told that the occupants would set a fire in the fireplace to show that there was no one hidden anywhere near the chimney. The priest's hole was so well designed that the priest would survive the heat and smoke.

Most of the time, anyway.

369

But if a few dead priests was the price for a lot of living priests then so be it. They understood that kind of thing in those days. They understood how to make tough decisions. Now the health and safety brigade would put a stop to it. *No one must be hurt. Risks must be mitigated.*

There was always risk, always. Accepting it and acting anyway was what set apart those with greatness from those who would never amount to anything. There were big people, and there were small people. Big people did big things, and took big risks in doing so. Small people did not.

You were one of the big people, obviously. One of the few. Sadly, your son was not. But your granddaughter would be. You knew your interest in her bordered on obsession, but you didn't care.

It is in her best interest, and that is all that matters.

You cross the room. Take your gloves from under the newspaper. Snap them on. It feels good, like being in theatre again, readying yourself to operate.

Could a small person operate? Cut a living human open and remove part of their brain, the *right* part of their brain, then close them up and walk away? Could a small person hold another person's life in their hands and remain calm, detached, able to make good, balanced decisions? Could they accept that, sometimes, they would make mistakes and wives would become widows, husbands widowers, children father-or-motherless? Could they live with these mistakes, understand that, over a career, they would happen, accept it emotionally as well as intellectually? No. You don't think so. Small people cannot do that. They do not have the detachment, the control.

You do, however. You have all the control you need.

You put your gloved hand on the sliding door of the priest's hole and unclick the latch. You added that feature yourself. In the sixteenth century the priest would have wanted the ability to let himself out, but that was not an ability you wanted the present inhabitant to share.

You steady yourself. Focus on the job ahead. You are confident that your plan is good, but even the best plans need to be well executed. There's a saying – of Sun Tsu, or someone like that – that you have always liked:

A bad strategy well executed is better than a perfect strategy badly executed.

You like that. You like how it puts the focus on the individual. Success is down to how you act. How you execute.

How you execute. An ironic thought, given what is about to happen to Julia. This situation really *is* about executing.

And not just executing the plan.

Executing your daughter-in-law. Executing an obstacle.

You take a deep breath, and slide back the door.

vii.

The door slid open and Julia launched herself out of the priest's hole.

371

At least, she intended to. What she actually did turned out to be some distance from her intention. She had pictured herself – visualized, in the terminology of sport – springing out of the priest's hole, her weight transferring squarely into Edna's face and chest, and knocking the older woman to the ground, and rendering her senseless for just long enough so that she could sprint out of the house and into the main road, where a passing vehicle – a white van, perhaps, piloted by a solid, honest working man – would pick her up and transport her to the nearest police station.

But Julia's legs had not been straight for twenty-four hours, and the muscles and joints were stiffer than she had ever imagined possible. She also had two shoulders that, although looser, were hardly in their best condition, a back that screamed in pain as it uncoiled from its foetal curl, and a hand that was little more than a bloody pulp.

So when Julia pushed against the wall with her feet she did not generate enough force to spring anywhere; instead, she performed a kind of slow, barely controlled flop onto the floor.

On the way down she managed to thrust her good hand into Edna's chest, which knocked her mother-in-law into a backwards stagger, giving Julia just enough time to roll onto her back.

Edna stared at her. Her eyes, which had been dilated with surprise, narrowed. She studied Julia, her gaze landing on her bloodied hand.

'So,' she said. 'You got out. Did you crush your own hand? I'm impressed.'

372

From the tone of her voice Julia could tell she meant it. So, finally, she'd managed to impress Edna. So that was all it took, then. She wished she'd known earlier. She would have crushed one of her body parts before.

Julia backed away, propped up on her elbows. She would have replied, but the bit was still in her mouth.

'Shame it won't make any difference,' Edna said. 'I have no choice. Not now you know about Mum and Jim and the floozy. And I haven't even mentioned the others.'

Julia continued to move away. She wanted as much distance between her and Edna as she could get, but more importantly, it felt good to move. Her legs throbbed with the new blood pulsing through them. She flexed them, tensing the muscles, feeling the strength return.

Her elbow hit something hard. The edge of the hearth. She stopped.

'Right,' Edna said. 'Let's get this over with.'

She moved forward, the syringe in her hand. She was cautious, her eyes fixed on Julia, watching for a kick or a sudden motion. Julia waited. She thought she would be able to grab the syringe, maybe keep it away from her body, press the plunger, and empty it.

Then Edna stopped.

'Too risky,' she said. She reached down onto the hearth and picked up a large brass poker. 'It'll be a bit messy, but this will have to do.'

Julia rolled onto her front and dived at Edna. It was not a conscious decision, but something in her understood that this was her chance, that now, while Edna was leaning down, her hand on the poker, her balance not perfect, was a chance – maybe the only one she would get – to act.

This time, her legs worked a bit better. Not perfectly, by any means – she did not so much fly as flutter towards her mother-in-law – but better, much, much, better than before, and well enough so that, when she hit Edna, her shoulder colliding with her target's wrist – which, she thought, she heard snap – Edna collapsed.

There was a loud bang when Edna's head hit the floor, and then she was still.

Oh shit, Julia thought. *Did I kill her?* Then, *that's a good thing, though isn't it?*

But Edna was not dead. Her chest rose and fell, her eyelids flickered. She was unconscious, yes, but not dead.

Thank God, Julia thought. *Evil as she is, I don't want her death on my conscience. I'm not a killer.*

The poker had fallen from Edna's hand and rolled up against the wall. Julia got to her feet and picked it up. She went into the hall. The phone was on an old roll-top desk. She was about to call 999 when she noticed something. Next to the phone was a pad of yellow paper. There was a number on it.

Gill's mobile phone. She'd given it to Edna when she came looking for Julia, not that Edna had any intention of using it. She'd taken it just to keep up appearances.

And now it was going to save Julia. Gill and Mike would be here quicker than the police; she'd left only minutes ago, so would be back equally quickly. She'd know what to do: call an ambulance, call the cops, truss Edna up.

She reached behind her head. The metal gag was held together by a screw at the back. Julia undid it and took the gag carefully from her mouth. Her jaw ached and her swollen tongue was pressed against the roof of her mouth, but the relief was indescribable. She massaged her jaw then picked up the phone and dialled the number.

'Hello,' Gill said. 'This is Gill.'

'It's me,' Julia said, her voice still thick. 'I need help. I'm at Edna's house.'

There was no reply. Not even the hum of a live telephone line. The phone was dead.

'Gill?' Julia said. 'Are you there?'

'You little fucking bitch.'

Julia turned around. It was Edna. She was standing by the wall, the phone cable in her hand. She let it drop to the floor.

'Well, well,' she said. 'If it isn't Little Miss Plucky.' She raised her other hand. It was holding a hammer, her knuckles white. There was a trickle of blood coming from her left ear and her eyes were dark, empty pools. All pretence of humanity was gone, stripped away by Edna's rage, and all that was left was insanity.

She touched her forefinger to the blood on her temple and looked at it. She showed the red smudge to Julia.

'You are going to pay for this,' she said. 'You're going to die in agony. You could have slipped painlessly away, but not anymore. Not now. Now you will know what pain means.'

Without warning, she swung the hammer, low, against Julia's hip. There was a dull thud, then Julia's side lit up in pain and she crumpled to her knees.

'Edna,' she said. 'No. Please. We can stop this. Pretend it never happened.'

Edna laughed; a high, braying, unearthly laugh.

'Yes,' she said. 'Of course, we can. Why didn't I think of that? Off you go, then, Julia. Pop off home and we'll be friends for evermore. Perfect. Happy families again.' She shook her head. 'That, my dear daughter-in-law, is as far from what is going to happen as it possibly could be.'

'What if Brian comes back?' Julia asked her. 'What if he sees this?'

'He won't. He's having some father—daughter time, in Blackpool. I booked them a hotel. I suggested he take her there and he did. Of course he did. He does what I tell him. Such a good boy. He always was. Shame he's also such a pathetic specimen, but then that's genetics for you. You never know what you're getting. Good job I have Anna to make up for him.'

'Thank God, he's not like you,' Julia said. 'We're all safer for it.'

'Yes. But not you. Not for much longer, anyway.'

'He'll stop you, you know,' Julia said. 'Eventually, he'll see that you're crazy and you're hurting Anna, and he'll stop you. He's a father more than he's a son.'

'Do you really think that? Do you really think he could stand up to me? And besides, you assume he'll disagree with me. He won't. He'll go along with everything I tell him.'

Julia knew she was right; knew Brian would toe the line. He always had before, and he would continue to do so.

Edna hefted the hammer in her hand.

'So,' she said. 'Shall we begin?'

viii.

The thing in sport, Julia's dad used to say, *is to do the opposite of what the opposition are expecting.* He usually went on to point out that, if he knew that, and he was merely a punter, albeit a particularly experienced and wise punter, then how in God's name did professional coaches fail to understand it? Why, specifically, did the coach of Warrington Rugby League Football Club, aka the Wire, to whom he had dedicated a large proportion of the Sundays of both his childhood and adulthood, fail to understand it, even in matters as simple as team selection?

There are certain players that the opposition don't like to play against, he would say, often on such a Sunday, when the Wire had lost and he and his friends had discussed the game over one or two or five or six pints of Greenall's Bitter. *And they don't like to play against them because they run straight and hard and with purpose. And the purpose usually isn't to pass on a*

377

friendly greeting. So what do you do if you're a coach? You stick 'em on the field. And you tell 'em to run straight and hard.

At that point he would kiss her on the forehead and grin at her, his breath warm and beery, his teeth stained yellow with pipe smoke.

And those are words to live your life by, petal. If in doubt, run straight and hard. They won't expect that.

And Edna didn't. Julia could tell from the slight furrowing of her brow as she watched her jump to her feet and run – well, lurch, there was a pain in her hip to go with the one in her hand – straight at her. She swung the hammer, but it was a fraction of a second too late, and, for the second time that evening, Julia crashed into her mother-in-law and sent her sprawling to the floor.

This time, Julia did not stop to look at Edna. She bear-crawled – her hip was seizing up badly – to the living room door and, rising to her feet, staggered into the kitchen. Edna kept the key to the back door in the cutlery drawer. Julia grabbed it, opened the back door, and then locked it behind her.

Through the window she saw Edna loom into the kitchen.

Julia set off to the front of the house and the safety of the main road, moving as fast as she could in a kind of half hop, half run. With her good hand she held her crushed arm against her chest to stop it bouncing around; it was agony when it was still, never mind when it was being shaken from side to side.

She glanced back at the door. It was still closed. She didn't think Edna had another key, or if she did, it was not in an easily accessible place. Of course, her crazy mother-in-law would know where she was headed, and could try and cut her off, but Julia thought she should be ok. She was moving more slowly, but her path around the side of the house was more direct and, moreover, she had a head start. She pictured Edna trying the back door, pausing while she realized what Julia had done, and then turning to head for the front of the house.

Julia increased her speed. The pain in her hip flared, and she had a sick feeling that she was doing it some serious harm, but she forced the pain from her mind. She could deal with whatever damage was done later. For now she had to get away. That was all that mattered. She had to get away from this crazy old woman, find her daughter, and regroup. Everything else was just a detail.

She reached the corner of the house. This was it: fifty yards of driveway and there it was. She could see it: the main road. Salvation. She ran into the driveway. She'd made it.

Or maybe not.

To her left she heard the bang of a door slamming open. Edna shot out of the front door like a ball from a cannon. She paused, legs wide, fists raised in a boxer's stance, and looked down the drive. Realizing that Julia had not made it that far, she slowly turned to her right.

'You,' she said. 'You have to stop this. This is not acceptable, Julia.'

'Who are you?' Julia asked. 'The fucking governess?'

Edna smiled. 'I like that. The governess. It's nice. But no. I'm not the governess. I'm the executioner.' She held up her right hand. She was holding an eight inch carving knife.

Julia knew it well. It was Japanese, very expensive, very heavy, and very, very sharp. She remembered Edna demonstrating just how sharp the day she had bought it. She took a tomato, placed it on the chopping board, and rested the knife on it:

No pressure, she said. I just keep the blade upright, and watch.

The knife sank through the flesh of the tomato, slicing it in two with just the weight of the blade. It was sharp, all right.

'No hammer,' Edna said. 'Too hit and miss. But this … '; she glanced at the blade 'one slash with this and you'll bleed to death in no time.'

Julia knew she could not outrun Edna, not with the way her hip was damaged. She hadn't even managed to get to the front of the house before her. She had no chance in a straight race. Perhaps – and she knew it was a long shot – she could talk Edna out of it.

'You'll leave blood everywhere. The police will find it.'

'I'll clean up,' Edna said. She looked up at the sky. 'And anyway, I think it's going to rain. I love British weather.'

Straight and hard, Julia thought. Run straight and hard. She won't expect that.

She looked at the knife in Edna's hand.

Except, I have to keep away from that thing. I can't get anywhere near it. I can't get anywhere near her.

So she took the only option that remained. She ran – limped, hobbled – towards the main road. Each step was a torment, but worse, on her right side, the side of her crushed hip, each step was about half the length and a quarter of the speed she wanted, and, in honesty, she needed.

Because behind her she could hear Edna's footsteps crunching on the gravel driveway.

And they were getting closer.

ix.

Julia glanced over her shoulder. Edna was no more than five or six yards behind her. She was the product of a generation that had played netball and tennis in their youth and taken vigorous walks throughout their lives. So, although she was in her late sixties, she was still able to run faster than a wounded thirty-something. Not much faster, but enough.

Plus, she was crazy. If she hadn't fully realized the extent of her mother-in-law's craziness before, Julia understood it now. She was prepared to hack Julia to death in her driveway. Maybe, she had no other choice, maybe she could not let her daughter-in-law escape with the knowledge of what she had done, but for fuck's sake, couldn't she just give up?

The grim set of her jaw and the focus in her eyes suggested that giving up was not in her plan.

Julia glanced at her hand. It was a raw, bloody mess. It was hard to believe this was happening, here, in England, in middle class rural Cheshire, to her, Julia Crowne, a lawyer and an honest citizen, the extent of whose wrong-doing was limited to six points for speeding and a couple of parking tickets. This kind of thing just didn't happen.

Except, of course, it did. You only had to open the newspapers, or click onto a news website, to see that. Some husband had stabbed his wife to death and then killed the kids. A woman had murdered her married lover. Two teenagers had gang-raped a twelve year-old girl then uploaded the footage to the internet. There was craziness everywhere, and it could turn up anywhere.

It was like talent. Unpredictable. You could train your kid from the age of two on the violin, just to see some prodigy, aged nine, from a broken home, who had been handed a violin by a social worker, take their place at a music academy and turn out to be a virtuoso. Why did some kids emerge at fifteen, fully fledged Premiership footballers, the ball seemingly attached to their feet by a string? Or some sing opera with effortless, perfect pitch, without having had a notes-worth of musical training? You could do your ten thousand hours, or whatever it was, but some people were just born with it, born with ability to do whatever it was you had slavishly trained yourself for. They had talent, they could kick a ball or hit a note or paint a picture.

And some people were crazy. Some people, like Edna, were batshit crazy, and somehow they learned to hide it, found a way to express it in a manner which was socially acceptable. Edna was known to be 'formidable': perhaps that was just the way she managed to hide her craziness.

'You stupid bitch,' Edna said, her voice close now. 'You stupid fucking bitch. Why are you running? What good will it do? You're just making it harder for me, and that means I'll make it harder for you.'

As if to make her point for her, as Julia planted her right foot, her hip betrayed her, and she stumbled. Only slightly, but enough to cost her a precious few feet, and the next thing she knew there was a searing pain from her right shoulder blade to the bottom of the ribcage on her left side.

Edna had slashed her. The Japanese knife had sliced through her clothes and skin as though they weren't there. She felt the warmth of her blood leaking down her back.

She dived to her right and rolled onto her back. Perhaps she could fend off Edna with her legs, maybe kick her hard enough to dislodge the knife or knock her over or something. *Anything.*

She realized it was a mistake immediately. Her right leg was useless, the hip totally frozen in place, and, if she raised her left it would be easy enough for Edna to grab it and use it to lever her onto her front, so that she could apply the executioner's stroke.

The gravel dug into the wound on her back. Her hand throbbed. She'd tried, she really had, but it hadn't been enough.

Edna loomed over her. Her knuckles whitened as she gripped the handle of the knife even harder.

And then there was the sound of tyres on gravel. Edna's eyes widened and she looked towards the main road.

A blue Ford Fiesta, old, 1998, 1.3 litre engine, 117,000 miles on the clock and recently valued at five hundred pounds, which made it not worth selling until it gave up the ghost and died once and for all, at which point its owner would treat themselves to the new (well, maybe one or two-years-old) Volkswagen Polo that they had long coveted.

Julia knew all this because she had been with the owner when the decision was made. She had visited the Volkswagen dealership and listened to the sales rep shrug and say the Fiesta was worthless, more or less, and there wasn't anything he could do about it, but do come back when it dies, and here's my card.

He was a pleasant guy. Half Chinese, early twenties. Handsome. Julia had thought she might pay him a visit when she needed a new car, which would be sometime in the future, sometime after she and Brian had divorced. And who knew? Maybe he had a thing for (slightly) older women. On the way out she'd mentioned it to her friend, who had laughed, and said she couldn't believe Julia was saying that.

I know what you mean, though, she'd added. *He was kind of cute.*

And then they'd gone, her and Gill, for a quick coffee, before Gill had to get home to the kids and make dinner for Trevor and then sort out the laundry and get the house in order for the week ahead.

'Gill!' Julia shouted. 'Oh my God, Gill!'

The blue Fiesta pulled into the driveway, and stopped. Gill opened the door and stepped out, pale and shaking but with her phone in her hand, lifted so that the camera pointed at Edna.

'I'm filming,' she said. 'Don't do anything stupid.'

The passenger side door opened and Mike got out of the car.

Julia didn't wait to see if Edna was listening. She scrabbled backwards across the gravel, leaving a trail of vivid red blood on the grey stones.

Gill walked towards her and stood between her and Edna.

'Jesus,' she said, glancing at the trail Julia had left, then fixing her eyes back on Edna. 'Are you ok?'

'For now,' Julia said. 'I think so.'

Edna started backing towards the house. Mike grabbed his mobile phone and jabbed it three times.

'Police,' he said. 'Emergency. And an ambulance.'

He moved towards Edna, who was nearing the house, the knife held out in front of her.

'Leave her,' Julia said. 'It's not worth it. She's crazy. She'll use that knife.'

'She'll get away,' he said.

'She won't,' said Julia. 'Not any more she won't.'

x.

Julia had never been in an ambulance. It was the kind of experience that, if you were lucky, you never had, although, like funerals and divorces, the frequency and likelihood of it occurring increased as you got older. Oddly, although it was her first time, she found it very familiar, and very reassuring.

Which was a good and necessary thing, as Julia was in need of reassurance. After Edna disappeared, the chemical tide of adrenaline flooding her body had receded, and with its disappearance had come both the realization of how fucked-up this situation was and the pain she was in. She didn't dare look at her hand, her hip was locked, and when she felt it with her good fingers it seemed to be at least three times the size she expected, and her back was a stinging, blazing fire.

She'd lain on the gravel, not moving until the paramedics scooped her onto a stretcher, lifted her into their marvellous vehicle, and filled her with morphine.

Gill – blessed, heroic Gill – followed with Mike in her blue Ford Fiesta, 1998, 1.3 litre engine, 117,000 miles on the clock and recently valued at five hundred pounds. As she'd lain on the gravel Gill had held her hand and told her how she had picked up the call she'd made, only to lose it before she heard anything – *that was Edna cutting the line*, Julia said, *just before she attacked me with a hammer* – and how she had wondered why Edna was calling, as it was Edna's number that had showed up on her phone. She nearly ignored it, but with all that had been going on – with Anna's disappearance and the separation and the Julia vanishing – with all that, it didn't feel right, somehow, so she had turned her car around and headed back to Edna's house.

I couldn't believe it, she said, *when I turned into the driveway. I mean, I knew Edna was intense, and intimidating, but when I saw her standing there with a knife and you lying on the ground, I just couldn't understand it.*

So Julia had filled her in, her words coming with difficulty through the pain, the memories bleeding into one another as she struggled to concentrate.

She took Anna. She wanted to discredit me, so she could get custody.

That's crazy, Gill said. *No one does that.*

She's crazy. Totally insane.

Do you think Brian knows what she did?

Julia didn't think he did. She didn't think that Edna would have told him, didn't think Edna considered him strong enough to live with the secret. He would not have gone to the cops – Brian did not have the guts to do *that* to his mother – but it was likely he would have done something. Started drinking. Taken Anna away from Edna; moved to his own place, stopped her seeing her granddaughter. He would have been unable to live with it, but unable to resolve it, and it would have torn him to pieces. Edna would have known all that, and as a result she would not have shared the secret with him. He was not worthy. That was the whole problem, the reason why she had wanted to take Anna. If Brian had been up to her standards none of this would have been necessary.

So she doubted Brian knew. Which meant someone

would have to tell him, and it wasn't going to be her. She didn't feel strong enough.

Because he wasn't going to take it well.

The paramedics waltzed her through a set of green double doors. She thought she was in the Princess Hospital in Chester – it was the only one she knew of that was within striking distance of Edna's house – but as far as she knew she could be anywhere. The journey had passed in a morphine-induced blur and she could not have said with any confidence whether it had lasted thirty minutes or three hours. She was pretty sure that it was not three *days*, but beyond that she would not have ventured an opinion with any certainty. And, if she was totally honest, she didn't care. She didn't care because all she wanted was to be in the hands of the doctors – funny how you assumed they would make things better – and she didn't care because the morphine made everything seem ok. She could see why people became so addicted to it. It wasn't that it produced a sensation of bliss – although she had no doubt enough of it would do exactly that – but it just made everything ok. Nothing really mattered. Pain, concerns, worries; they all melted away. The world became benign and welcoming; a warm, friendly place that you wanted to hang around in, like a nice hot tub on the edge of a white sandy beach.

'Mrs Crowne,' a voice said. 'I'm glad you're safe.'

Julia turned her head. 'DI Wynne,' she said. 'Good to see you.'

Wynne smiled. 'I wish it was in better circumstances. I hear you've had quite the time of it.'

'Well,' Julia said. 'You know how it is. Good days, bad days. This one wasn't that great, but here I am. Safe and sound.'

She was aware she was babbling and it was the drug that was really talking, but she didn't care. She didn't care about anything, except maybe Anna, and she'd be ok. *Everything* would be ok.

'Yes,' Wynne said. 'Safe and sound. Anyway, Mrs Crowne, I think the doctors are ready to take you. They have some work to do, I understand. As do I, but we can talk later, when you're more – more relaxed. I just wanted to let you know that I'm here.'

'Ok,' Julia said. 'We'll talk later.'

Then the trolley began to move again and she was in a large, clean room. A nurse adjusted the needle in her arm, then she was moved onto a table, for some X-rays, then back to her trolley and into another large, clean room. And then a smiling, mid-fifties woman (*she looks a bit like Edna*, Julia thought) told her she would be ok and they were going to take a look at her hand and her hip, and then another face appeared above her and a voice somewhere else said *this is the anaesthetist* and then she was slipping away, slipping away, slipping away …

xi.

When she woke the first thing she thought was that her mouth was dry and she would love a tall, cold glass of chocolate milk, which was an odd thing to want since she hadn't had chocolate milk since she was a child, if she had even had it then.

But that was what she wanted, and she wanted it a *lot*.

The next thing she thought was *what the hell happened to my body?* She throbbed from a point somewhere at the top of her back all the way down to her right leg and her hand felt like someone was digging knives into it from all sides. And then she remembered how she had smashed her own hand to get out of the priest's hole and how Edna – Edna, that evil, evil bitch – had hit her with a hammer and slashed her with a knife, a Japanese kitchen knife that was very sharp, before Gill had come and saved her and Edna had disappeared.

She heard the door open and then there were rapid footsteps and a girl's voice.

'Mummy!' Anna said. 'I brought you these flowers!'

She thrust a handful of carnations at Julia, then started to climb onto the bed.

'Careful,' Brian warned. 'Mummy's a little delicate at the moment.' He picked her up and settled her on his knee. 'Hi,' he said. 'The nurses said you were awake.' He was grey, his skin slack and pallid, and his eyes were nervous with shock. 'I heard about … ' he paused and Julia realized he was about to say Mum but couldn't bring himself to pronounce the word, 'Edna.' He looked at the floor. His shoulders were slumped, his back bent, his stomach pressed against his shirt. He was broken, Julia saw, badly broken. 'I'm sorry.'

'It's not your fault,' Julia said. 'Could I have a kiss from my little girl?'

Anna hopped off Brian's lap and leaned over the bed. The sensation of her warm, soft lips on Julia's cheek was the most intense, most restoring thing she had ever felt.

'Give me a minute with her,' she asked him.

'Of course.' Brian stood up. His tone was wheedling and high, begging forgiveness. 'Is there anything I can get you?'

Julia was about to say no, there wasn't, when she realized there was something he could get for her.

'If you could find some chocolate milk,' she said. 'That would be great.'

He was back half an hour later with Gill and a Tesco carrier bag. He took out a gallon of chocolate milk.

'Here,' he said. 'I'll pour you a glass. Then we need to talk. Anna can go with Gill, if that's ok.'

'It's fine.' Julia kissed Anna then took a long drink from the glass of chocolate milk. It was everything she had hoped it would be.

'So,' she said, when Anna and Gill had left the room. 'It's been a busy few days.'

'I'm so sorry,' Brian said. 'I want you to know that I'll never forgive myself for this.'

'You didn't do it.'

'I was there, Julia, in the house while she had you locked up in the same place she'd kept Anna ... ' he held his head in his hands, shaking it from side to side, 'my own mother. She kidnapped Anna. I ... I just can't believe it.'

Was this the moment to tell him she had also killed her mother and her husband? Julia decided not to. It would come out eventually, but she didn't think now was the right time for Brian to find out that his mother had murdered his father.

'Brian,' Julia said. 'I can't imagine how difficult this is for you. But I want you to know that I don't blame you. You couldn't have done anything to stop it, no one could. Edna's ... she's insane, Brian.'

'I know. I know.' He had tears in his eyes and Julia saw how hard this was going to be for him. Brian had his flaws, but he also had some qualities; sadly, resilience was not among them. He was going to be meeting with therapists for a long time to come. Even then, she wasn't sure he would ever get over it.

'Listen,' she said. 'I'll do whatever I can to help you with this, I promise. But right now I can't be your best friend. I'm in too much pain. But I'll be there for you. Anna, too. We'll get through this.'

The look he gave her said *I hope so but I don't believe it for a second.*

'Ok,' he said. 'Ok.'

'Would you mind getting the doctor?' Julia said. 'I need some more pain relief.'

'Sure,' he said, and got to his feet. His movements were slow and cramped, Julia saw, like the movements of an old man. 'I'll go and find someone.'

When she had been given more morphine – the nurse informed her that she had a button she could press, but only a certain number of times a day – the doctor, a bearded man called Dr Scala, but who insisted she call him Rick – gave his report.

'It's quite a long list, I'm afraid,' he said. 'It looks like your back will heal quite well. The cut was not too deep, apart from in one or two places. We'll see how it does, but you may get away with minimal scarring, and there's always the possibility of some cosmetic surgery if it becomes a problem. As for the hip, there's a chipped bone, which the surgeon removed, but other than that the damage was fairly limited. It should recover pretty well, especially with some physio. The real concern is your hand, which is going to require a lot of care.'

Ironic, she thought. *That was the one I did to myself. What Edna did turns out to be pretty minor. But then that's life, isn't it? The worst injuries are always self-inflicted, even if you do them for the best of reasons.*

'There are a lot of bones in the hand,' Dr Scala – Rick – said. 'And they work together in quite a delicate balance. If one is broken then it will cause pain in the others, so we have to make sure that it heals before we allow the hand too much motion. In your case, there are multiple bones broken in multiple ways. It's quite a mess in there.'

'I had no choice,' Julia explained. 'It was the only thing—'

He put a hand on her bicep. 'You have no need to apologize,' he said. 'You did the right thing. Frankly, I'm amazed you could do it. It must have been painful beyond belief.'

'So what happens?' Julia asked. 'Will my hand be ok?'

Dr Scala stuck out his bottom lip and bobbed his head from side to side.

'OK is probably the right description,' he said. 'If you had plans to try out as a concert pianist they might be over. But your hand will work, more or less. We'll set the bones and do some physio and keep a close eye on how it develops, and hopefully, in time, you'll be able to do most of the things that you would normally have done.' He gave her a wry grin. 'I'm guessing you'll have really bad arthritis when you're older, though.'

Before she could answer there was a knock on the door. It opened part way and DI Wynne stuck her head into the room.

'Hello,' she said. She was holding a box of chocolates. 'Not the best quality, I'm afraid, but it's all they had at the petrol station.'

'Come in,' Julia said. 'We were nearly finished.'

Dr Scala told her about the medication and the schedule for physiotherapy and about how she had to take responsibility for her recovery and then he waved a little goodbye and left them. DI Wynne took his place next to the bed.

'So,' Wynne said. She raised one eyebrow, as though to say *well, well, you lead quite the life*. 'There's a lot we need to talk about.'

'Did you talk to Brian?'

'I did. And I don't think he had anything to do with this.'

'Neither do I. He looked terrible.' Julia shook her head. 'I feel bad for him.'

Wynne folded her arms. 'I also interviewed Mrs Crowther. She shared some of what you had told her.'

'Oh?' Julia wasn't exactly sure what she had told Gill – Mrs Crowther – as the time she spent waiting for the ambulance had passed in something of a blur.

'She said you mentioned something about Edna Crowne being responsible for more deaths? Specifically, those of her mother and husband?'

'That's what Edna said,' Julia replied. 'But that was it. She didn't give many details. She could have been lying. To scare me, maybe. I wouldn't put anything beyond her.'

'We'll have to look into it, but given what she did to you it seems perfectly possible. We'll have to try and find out more. Perhaps Mr Crowne remembers something from that time which could help.'

'Brian doesn't know yet,' Julia said. 'I don't think now is a good time to tell him.'

Wynne nodded slowly. 'He's going to find out sooner or later,' she said. 'And we really will need to talk to him. But leave it in our hands. We have some experience of these situations, believe it or not. It's not the first time a relative has had to deal with learning their son or daughter or parent is a murderer.' For a second her gaze was unfocused, lost somewhere in the middle distance, and Julia wondered how she did what she did, how she coped with being brought face to face with the worst the world had to offer.

'How about Edna?' Julia said. 'Can't you ask her?'

'We will,' Wynne said. She hesitated and glanced at the ceiling. Julia recognized the gesture; it was what she did when she had bad news. 'We haven't found her yet. When we got to the house her car was gone. She'll show up, though. She can't have gone far.'

'I hope so,' Julia said. 'I damn well hope so. I don't like the thought of her out there.'

'No,' Wynne agreed. 'Neither do I.' She stood up. 'Anyway. You get some rest. It's going to be a busy few days. I suspect the press will be interested in you again.' She smiled. 'Although the coverage may be a little more favourable this time.'

'You know what?' Julia said. 'I can't bring myself to care.'

'I don't blame you,' Wynne said. 'We'll be in touch. Take care, Mrs Crowne.'

18

A Month Later

Julia closed the front door and followed Anna into the living room.

Anna had spent the day with Brian. It was the first time since Edna's disappearance – now a full month ago and still no sign of her – that Anna had been alone with her father. He had seen her with Julia present most weekends, but up to that point he had not felt able to take care of her on his own. As a result, Julia had full custody; Brian had willingly agreed.

Julia was not surprised.

He had taken the news about Edna's murderous past badly. He had lost weight – she wasn't sure how much, but enough that his clothes now hung on him like drapes – his hair had thinned and was greying, and his eyes were flat and lifeless. It was as though he had done a decade's ageing in a few weeks. She knew he was seeing at least one therapist, and suspected there were others, but it wasn't something she discussed with him. Simon did: his brother had been over twice and they spoke on Skype daily. At least some good had come of this, which was small comfort when Julia tallied up the problems it had caused.

Like sleep. She could fall asleep; she managed that quite easily, lying next to Anna in what had once been her and Brian's marital bed, but she could not stay asleep. At some point during the night she would awaken and lie there, her heart racing, listening to the creaks and groans of the house and wondering whether there was someone there, someone in the house coming for them, Edna maybe, a vengeful, monstrous Edna, her eyes blazing fire, her hands hooked around a hammer.

She tried to keep calm, but when she could no longer bear it, she would grab the tyre lever she kept by the bed, switch on the lights and search the house, but there was never anyone there.

Until there is someone, she would think, *until Edna comes back.*

And then she would lie there until dawn, nearly falling asleep ten, twenty times, but being woken every time by a squall of rain on the window or the sound of a car in the street outside.

Then there were the panic attacks. Suddenly, without warning, maybe when driving or shopping or watching television with Anna, she would feel her senses become more alert and her heart would speed up and her head would start to whirl with thoughts she had no control over; thoughts which were not specific concerns or worries but just the awful, terrible knowledge that everything was wrong and there was no way she could cope with it, with life, with anything.

It was all-encompassing; a sense of total mental breakdown and it was accompanied by a feeling of dizziness so intense that she would come close to blacking out. She would have to stop whatever she was doing and find something to hold onto; if she was driving she would have to pull over and wait for it to pass.

The doctor told her it was the body's flight or fight response malfunctioning, a massive and inappropriately timed release of adrenaline, which, given her recent history was understandable. It would pass, he reassured her.

She hoped so.

Physically, she was doing ok. Her hip and back were still painful, but healing well. Her hand was a problem. She'd had three operations to repair it and, from what she could tell, it was now more metal than bone. It throbbed at night, but she could live with the pain, and it wasn't as though it kept her awake.

She was awake anyway.

'How was Dad?' Julia asked Anna. 'Did you have a good time?'

Anna slumped onto the couch. 'Good,' she said. 'We watched *Balamory*.'

'Are you hungry?'

'No. We had biscuits.'

'Right. Biscuits.'

Of all of them, Anna was the only one who seemed unaffected. She'd asked a few times where Grandma was, but seemed happy enough with the explanation that she was on a long holiday and wouldn't be back for a while. She was interested in Julia's injuries, but not in how they had occurred. She would have to deal with all this at some point, when she was older and Julia told her what had happened, but that was a long way off.

'Ok,' Julia said. 'I'm going to make some tea. I'll be back in a tick.'

In the kitchen she switched on the kettle. There was a Sunday paper on the counter, folded open. She'd been about to read it when Brian brought Anna home.

EDNA CROWNE STILL AT LARGE

In what is fast becoming a Lord Lucan-like story for our age, missing killer and abductress Edna Crowne remains at large. In the month since her disappearance the police have found no useful leads.

It is unclear how, with the resources at their disposal, the police have been unable to find any trace of Dr Crowne, who abducted her own grand-daughter before holding her daughter-in-law, Julia Crowne, in captivity. It is almost inconceivable that someone could simply vanish, given modern border controls and the free exchange of information between international police agencies.

There has been speculation that after her daughter-in-law's escape, Dr Crowne, unwilling to face the consequences of her actions, took her own life. Increasingly, this looks like the most likely option.

Julia put down the paper. She wished Edna had been found, wished she could say for certain that she was not out there, watching Julia and Anna. *Then* she would sleep at night. But until then ... well, it was going to be hard.

It was the one thing she wanted: Edna to be found, dead or alive.

She looked at Anna, cross-legged on the sofa, flicking through a book about gnomes.

Preferably dead, she thought. *Preferably dead. And then all this would be over.*

19

Two Months Later

You stand on the beach, your bare feet on the warm sand. The sun sets in front of you, and you stare out across the ocean.

You got away. You had a plan – of course, you did – for just such an eventuality. A bag, with cash – dollars, used notes – and two passports in two different names, one American, one Canadian.

The American is a certain Dr Beth Powers. The Canadian a venerable lady who goes by the name of Dr Nancy Ouelette. Both passports have been used over the years. Beth is a fan of Patagonia, where some of the locals in a small town know her as a doctor who occasionally comes to visit. Nancy is a fan of Southern Thailand, where she has helped out at a local clinic in the past.

And which is where she has been for the past three months. She keeps herself to herself. She has short hair and is totally grey. Green eyes behind her thick glasses. She looks nothing like Edna Crowne. It is amazing what changing a few details can do for your ability to hide.

They are delighted. She is a good doctor, and she works for minimal pay; just enough Thai baht that she is not patronizing the people of this small town.

Although you are glad you invented and documented Beth and Nancy when you did, well before 9/11, when such things were easier. Now it would be much more difficult to get passports and birth certificates and medical qualifications. You would have done it, though. There is always a way.

You see, what most people don't understand is that hard work and intelligence and ability are never enough. What is needed to make those things bear fruit is persistence. Doggedness. You are simply prepared to do more for what you want than other people, and in the end that makes you the winner. Eventually your adversaries will simply give up, and even if they don't they will certainly make a mistake, and when they do you will be there, ready to take advantage of it.

And you will do whatever it takes. That is the other thing most people don't understand. They think they are safe because they assume that other people share some of their values. They don't – can't – understand that some people – very few, but some – will kill them or steal from them or hurt them and cast them aside in order to get what they want. An executive wants a promotion to CEO, and in order to get it he or she has to cut a thousand jobs, destroy the livelihoods of a thousand families, push a city like Detroit into ruins.

Is it justified? Is it fair that, on the back of that misery, one person gets a bigger pay packet? Gets even richer than they already are? Is it fair that bankers who produce nothing of value, who leech wealth from the rest of society, get to pay themselves tens of millions of pounds for doing so? Of course, it isn't. But does anyone think they care about what is fair? You cannot deposit fairness in the bank. What they want is money, and they will do whatever they can, at whatever cost to other people, to get what they want.

Nancy faces just such a situation. She likes it here. She feels at home. She finds the people pleasant and welcoming and, most importantly, respectful. But there is one exception. One of the nurses is sullen and bossy. She annoys Nancy. She talks too much. Asks too many questions.

She will have to go.

There is a double benefit to killing her. Nancy will remove her from her life, and you will have the opportunity to keep your skills up. Murder is not easy. It is a skill like anything else, and it rewards constant practice.

And you need to keep your hand in, because you have unfinished business.

You have to deal with that bitch Julia.

You – in Nancy's name – have booked a flight to Munich in a fortnight's time. Train to Paris, ferry to Dover.

You plan to do it on a Friday night. Kill her in her home. Julia will not be found for a day or two, at least. Who will be surprised if they don't see her or Anna until Monday?

By which time you'll have found your way back to Munich. You have a return ticket booked for the Saturday evening.

Two tickets, to be precise. One adult, one child.

Because you don't plan to return alone. When you get back you'll have company. You picture the introductions.

Hello. This is my granddaughter, Rose. She's come to live with me. Her mother recently passed away.

And at least that last sentence will be true.

You look out at the setting sun and smile. It feels good to have a plan again. Good to know what will happen.

Rose. Your mother's name. It's a good name. You suggested it when Anna was born. Brian was in favour, you knew that, but his wife didn't like it. She preferred Anna. Not for any reason; not because there was an Anna in the family. Just because she liked it. And to spite you.

Well, in the end Rose it would be. Rose would come after Anna.

You smile and walk along the beach, your feet sinking in the warm sand. You turn onto the path that leads to the small hut you have made your home, your refuge.

There is someone standing on your porch.

It is that damn nurse. You smile again. The smile is genuine. This is an opportunity. You will find out if anyone knows she is here. If not, she will be erased.

'Hello there,' you say. 'To what do I owe this pleasure?'

She bows in that way the Thai people have. She raises her hand and waves to her left. There is the noise of an engine, then a car pulls up behind you.

It is a police car.

Three Thai policemen climb out. Two are holding guns. They look nervous, which is not a good sign. The other is the boss. He approaches you and says something in Thai.

You do not understand. He repeats it.

Then he pauses.

Edna Crowne, he snaps. *Edna Crowne.*

You nod.

He scowls and motions for you to put out your hands.

You do so. He produces a pair of handcuffs and snaps them shut.

You smile. They have you, for now. You will be taken home and tried. The papers will rejoice in your capture.

But they are wrong to do so. This is not over yet.

It is not over yet.

20

An Hour Later

An hour later Julia Crowne's phone rang. It was DI Wynne. She had good news.

Acknowledgements

Warmest thanks to:

Sheila Crowley and Rebecca Ritchie, for believing and for getting the book off the ground.

Jessie Chalmers, for her early insight and editorial advice.

Kate Stephenson, and the Killer Reads team: I couldn't imagine a better home for *After Anna*.